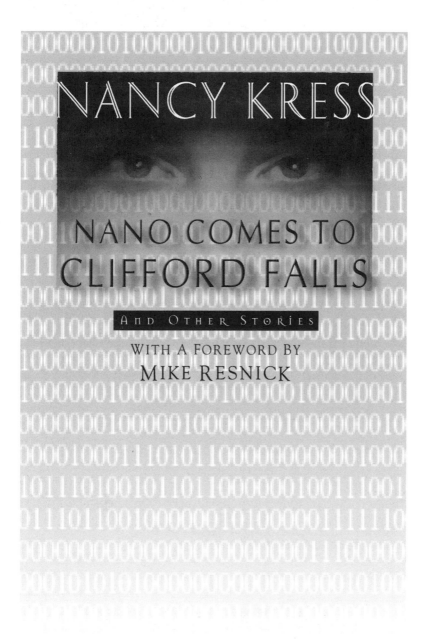

NANCY KRESS

NANO COMES TO
CLIFFORD FALLS

And Other Stories

WITH A FOREWORD BY
MIKE RESNICK

GOLDEN GRYPHON PRESS • 2008

"Foreword," Copyright © 2008 by Mike Resnick.

"Nano Comes to Clifford Falls," first published in *Asimov's Science Fiction*, July 2006.

"Patent Infringement," first published in *Asimov's Science Fiction*, May 2002.

"Computer Virus," first published in *Asimov's Science Fiction*, April 2001.

"Product Development," first published in *Nature*, March 2006.

"The Most Famous Little Girl in the World," first published in SCI-FICTION, May 2002.

"Savior," first published in *Asimov's Science Fiction*, June 2000.

"Ej-Es," first published in *Stars*, ed. Janis Ian and Mike Resnick, DAW 2003.

"Shiva in Shadow," first published in *Between Worlds*, ed. Robert Silverberg, SFBC 2004.

"First Flight," first published in *Space Cadets*, ed. Mike Resnick, 2006, L.A.Con special publication.

"To Cuddle Amy," first published in *Asimov's Science Fiction*, August 2000.

"Wetlands Preserve," first published in SCIFICTION, September 2000.

"Mirror Image," first published in *One Million A.D.*, Ed. Gardner Dozois, June 2005.

"My Mother, Dancing," first (English) published in *Asimov's Science Fiction*, June 2004.

LIBRARY OF CONGRESS CATALOGING–IN–PUBLICATION DATA

Kress, Nancy.
  Nano comes to Clifford Falls and other stories / Nancy Kress. — 1st ed.
      p.   cm.
  ISBN-13: 978-1-930846-50-0 (alk. paper)
  ISBN-10: 1-930846-50-9 (alk. paper)
  1. Science fiction, American.   I. Title.
PS3561.R46   N36   2008
813'.54—dc22   2007038575

First Edition.

Contents

For Jack

Foreword

H ER NAME IS NANCY KRESS, AND I FALL A LITTLE MORE in love with her every year.

She writes a little more every year. There is a connection.

As you're about to find out, Nancy Kress is what we in the trade call a writer's writer, which is to say, she is a writer that other writers read, and admire, and study, and try to learn from. And sometimes fall a little bit in love with.

As an editor, I have been buying stories from Nancy for a couple of decades now. She's never turned in a bad one, or a mediocre one; she's never sleepwalked through one; she always turns in her best effort, and her best effort, as you doubtless know, has been good enough to give her a shelf full of Nebulas, Hugos, and the like.

(I should add that as an editor, I have also been buying from her protégées for almost as long, and it's always easy to spot a newcomer who's been through Nancy's workshops, because they are better-trained in the basics than any other set of beginners I have ever encountered.)

As a writer I have sold to Nancy (well, okay, it was a reprint, but what the hell, it was a reprint anthology), and I have collaborated with Nancy.

And as a reader I have been enjoying Nancy's work for as long as she's been producing it. I have said on a number of occasions that the late Jack Williamson was the only writer I knew who demonstrably improved with every passing decade. Nancy's got a few decades to go to catch Jack (his work appeared in *nine* of them), but she improves by the decade, by the year, almost by the story. Like I say, a writer's writer.

So what does it mean, being a writer's writer?

For one thing, it means you let the story dictate your approach to it. For example, Nancy knows that horror tends to dissipate the longer it runs, so she held "To Cuddle Amy" to under a thousand words. She knows that humor works best in short, strung-together sequences, so she wrote "Patent Infringement" as a series of letters. She knows that some stories, even if you can summarize the basic plot in three or four sentences, have to be novella length to include all the details that are needed to make them work, so she wrote "Shiva in Shadow" (and put twice as much material into her 20,000 words as I put into *my* 20,000 words in the same anthology). She knows when to tell a story in the first person, when to use humor, how to give the reader necessary information without boring him with interminable info dumps. She's no scientist, but I'm not aware that anyone's ever caught her in a scientific error.

And while she writes science fiction, she understands, as all the very best writers do, that eventually every story is about *people*. Ideas are wonderful, and Nancy's stories abound in them; science is fascinating, and Nancy's stories have their share of it; extrapolations can be shocking and mind-boggling, and Nancy can shock and boggle your mind with the best of them; but when all is said and done, Nancy's stories stick in the mind because she—and you—care about her characters.

And oh, the things she can do with the tropes of science fiction! Take, for example, "Ej-Es." Right now that title will make no sense to you. And (I'm not encouraging this, mind you) if you read the last line first, it seems like gibberish. But read the story, let her work her magic on you, and suddenly the title makes sense and the last line is not only comprehensible but is, in retrospect, the very best last line the story could have (and upon even further consideration, possibly the *only* last line it could have.)

Or try "My Mother, Dancing." A perfect title for a near-perfect story. (She spends a lot of time on her titles. It shows.) I dare you to read it without an emotional response. Maybe two. Yeah, that's something else: her stories are only *deceptively* simple. There's the complexity of a brilliant mind at work behind and beneath each of them.

And never confuse complexity with inaccessibility. It is very easy to read a Nancy Kress story; the only hard thing is putting it down before you're finished. And then, like a fine meal, it stays with you a bit while you digest it.

A bit? Hell, I'm *still* digesting *Beggars in Spain,* her acknowledged classic. I've only read it three times; maybe another four or five and I'll have gotten everything out of it that she put in it.

Okay, reader, you're primed and ready to plunge into this collection, and I guarantee that what lies ahead is more interesting and enriching than anything I have to say about it. (And Nancy, if you're reading this, I hope you understand that the next time I pinch you in the elevator at a convention, at least part of that emotion is directed toward your stories.)

—Mike Resnick
Cincinnati, Ohio
June 2007

NANO COMES TO CLIFFORD FALLS

And Other Stories

Nano Comes to Clifford Falls

I WAS WEEDING THE GARDEN WHEN NANOTECH came to my town. The city got it a month earlier, but I haven't been to the city since last year. Some of my neighbors went—Angie Myers and Emma Karlson and that widow, Mrs. Blanston, from church. They brought back souvenirs, things made in the nanomachine, and the scarf Angie showed me was really cute. But with three little kids, I don't get out much.

That day was hot, with the July sun hanging overhead like it wasn't ever going to move. Bob McPhee from next door stuck his head over the fence. His Rottweiler snarled through the chain links. I don't like that dog, and Kimee, my middle one, is afraid of it.

"Hey, Carol, don't you know you don't have to do that no more?" Bob said. "The nanomachinery will make you all the tomatoes and peas you want."

"Hey, Bob," I said. I went on weeding, swiping at the sweat on my forehead with the back of my hand. Jackie watched me from the shade of the garage. I'd laid him on a blanket dressed in just his diaper and he was having a fine time kicking away and then stopping to eat his toes.

"They're giving Clifford Falls four of 'em," Bob said. Since he retired from the fire department, he don't have enough to do all day. "I saw it on TV. The mayor's getting 'em installed in the town hall."

"That's good," I said, to say something. I could hear Will and Kimee inside the kitchen, fighting over some toy.

"Mayor'll run the machinery. One for food, one for clothing, the other two he's taking requests. I already put in mine, for a sports car."

That got my attention. "A car? A whole car?"

"Sure, why not? Nano can make anything. The town is starting with one request from each person, first come first served. Then after that . . . I dunno. I guess Mayor Johnson'll work it out. Hey, gorgeous, stop that weeding and come have a beer with me. Pretty gal like you shouldn't be getting all hot and sweaty at *weeding*."

He leered at me, but he don't mean anything by it. At least, I don't think he does. Bob's over fifty but still looks pretty good, and he knows it, but he also knows I'm not that kind. Jack might've took off two months ago, but I don't need anyone like Bob, a married man, for temporary fun and games.

"I like the taste of home-grown tomatoes," I tell him. "Ones at the Safeway taste like wallpaper."

"But nano won't make tomatoes that taste *processed*," he says in that way that men like to correct women. "That machinery will make the best tomatoes this town ever tasted."

"Well, I hope you're right." Then Will and Kimee spilled their fight out through the screen door into the back yard, and Jackie started whimpering on his blanket, and I didn't have no time for any nanomachinery.

Still, I was curious, so in the late afternoon, when it wasn't quite so hot, I packed up the stroller and the kids and I went downtown.

Clifford Falls isn't much of a town. We're so far out on the plains that all we got is a single square ringed with dusty pick-ups and the teenagers' scooters. There's about two dozen stores, the little brick town hall with traffic court and Barry Anderson's police room and such, the elementary school, Baptist and Methodist churches, Kate's Lunchroom, and the Crow Bar. Down by the tracks is the grain elevator and warehouses. That's about it. Once a movie was filmed here because the movie people wanted some place that looked like it might be fifty or sixty years ago.

Soon as I turned the corner I could see where the nanomachinery must be. People milled around the patch of faded grass in front of the town hall, people who probably should have still been to work on a Wednesday afternoon. A big awning stretched across the front of the building with a huge metal box under it, nearly big as my

bedroom. To one side the mayor, who retired two years ago from the
factory in Minneonta, stood on a crate right there in the broiling
sun without so much as a hat on his bald head, making a speech.

"—greatest innovation since super-cheap energy to raise our way
of life to—"

"What's getting made in that box?" I asked Emma Karlson. She
had her twins in a fancy new stroller. Just after Jack left me, her Ted
got taken on at the factory.

"A dais," she said.

"A what?"

"A thing for the mayor to stand on instead of that apple crate. It's
supposed to be done in a few minutes."

What a dumb thing to make—Mr. Johnson could just as well
have gotten a good stepladder from Bickel's Hardware. But I suppose the dais was by way of demonstration.

And I have to admit it was impressive when it come out of the
box. Four men had to move it, a big, fancy platform with a top like a
gazebo and steps carved on their sides in fancy shapes. After the
men set it down there was this moment of electric silence, like a
downed power line run through the crowd, and then everybody
started shouting.

"Make me a rocking chair!"

"Tell it to grow a table!"

"I need a new rug for the dining room!"

"Make a good bottle of booze!"

Emma turned to me. Her eyes were big and shining. "Some
people are so ignorant. That big nanomachine don't make anything
to eat or drink—the ones inside do that. Three little ones, for food
and clothes and small, quick stuff. Mayor Johnson already explained
all that, but some people just can't listen."

The crowd was pressing closer to the new dais, and a few men
started to climb the fancy steps. Kimee was getting restless, pulling
on my hand, but Will said suddenly, "Mommy, tell the machine to
make me a dog!"

Emma laughed. "It can't do that, Will. Nobody but God can
make a living thing."

I said, "Then how can it make a tomato? A tomato's living."

Emma said, "No, it's not. It's dead after you pick it."

"But it *was* living."

Emma got that look in her eyes that I seen there ever since the
third grade: *Don't argue with me because you'll regret it.* Will
jumped up and down screaming, "A dog! A dog! I want a dog!" The

people around the dais were pushed back by Barry Anderson and his deputy, but they didn't stop shouting at Mayor Johnson. I grabbed Will, smiled hard at Emma, and started home.

Nanotech wasn't going to put Kimee down for a nap or breast-feed Jackie. And it sure as hell wasn't going to get my bastard husband back to help me do those things.

Not that I wanted him.

I waited for nano to make Clifford Falls look like the places in the TV shows. What surprised me was that it did.

I didn't see anything for a few weeks because both Kimee and Will came down with some sort of bug. Diarrhea and cramps. The doctor I got on the computer told me which chemicals to squirt over samples of their shit and when I told him what colors the shit turned, he said it wasn't serious but I should keep the kids in, make them drink a lot of water, and keep them away from the baby. In a two-bedroom rented house, that alone took a lot of my time. But we managed. Emma bought the medicine I needed at Merkelson's and left it on the doorstep. She left three casseroles, too, and some chocolate-chip cookies.

Ten days later, when they were better, I baked Emma a sponge cake to thank her. After the kids were dressed and the stroller packed up, we went outside and I had to blink hard.

"Wow!" Will said. "Mommy, look at that!"

Parked in Bob McPhee's driveway was the reddest car I ever seen, low and smooth and shiny. It looked *fast*. Will ran over to it and I called, "Don't touch, Will!"

"Oh, he can't hurt it," Bob said with a sort of fake casualness. He was bursting with pride. "And if he did hurt it, I'll just wait until my turn comes up on the Big Gray and order me another one."

The Big Gray—that must be what they were calling the largest nanomachine. Stupid name. It sounded like a sway-backed horse.

Bob leered at me. "Wanna go for a ride, baby?"

"Why don't you take your wife?" I said, but I smiled when I said it because I'm a wuss who likes to stay on good terms with my neighbors.

"Oh, I did," Bob said, waving his hand airily, "but there's always room for one more, if you know what I mean."

"A ride! A ride!" Will shouted.

"Not today, Will, we're going to see Jon and Don." That distracted him; Emma's twins are his best friends.

Emma met me at the door dressed in a gorgeous yellow sundress with a low neck and full skirt. Emma was always pretty, even when we were thirteen, but I'd never seen her look like this. She'd done things to live up to the dress, fixed her hair and put on make-up and even had on rhinestone earrings.

"God, you look amazing!" I said, in my old jeans with baby puke on my T-shirt. Emma touched her earrings.

"Real diamonds, Carol! Ted used his second pick at the nanomachine to choose these!"

I gaped at her. The nanomachine could make real diamonds? Will barreled past me toward Don and Jon and I saw that all three of them jumped onto a new blue sofa covered with the nicest material I'd ever seen.

All I could think of to say was, "I brought you a sponge cake. A thank-you for all you done when the kids were sick."

"Well, aren't you the sweetest thing. Thank you. I'd offer you a piece now but, well, Kitty'll be here in a few minutes to take the twins."

Kitty Svenson was the teenager who babysat for everybody. She was saving up for secretarial school. Ted came out from the bedroom dressed in a bathrobe.

"Oh, God, Ted, have you got this diarrhea-thing, too? I'm sorry, it's a bitch. Come on, Will, let's go. Em, I can take the twins while Ted's sick."

"I'm not sick, Carol," Ted said. Emma blushed. I was really confused. This was a Tuesday morning.

"I quit the factory," Ted said. "No need to kill myself working now."

"But . . . the mortgage . . ."

"The nano's making us a house," Emma said proudly.

"A house? A whole house?"

"One part of a room at a time," Ted said. "Em and I are both using all our picks for it. We'll put it on that piece of land my daddy left me by the lake, and the whole house'll finish just before the bank forecloses on this one. I got it all figured out."

"But . . ." My brain wasn't working right. I just couldn't take it in, somehow.

"The food nano is making all our meals now," Emma said. "Just churning 'em out like sausages. Here, Carol, taste this." She darted into the kitchen, earrings swinging, and came back with a bowl of small, round things like smooth nuts.

"What is it?"

"I don't know. But it tastes good. The food nano can't make like, you know, real meats or anything, but it does pretty good delivering things that look and taste like fruits and veggies and bread, and this stuff is the protein."

I picked up one of the round things and nibbled. It did taste good, sort of like cold spicy chicken. But something in me recoiled anyway. Maybe it was the texture, sort of bland and mushy. I palmed the rest of the ball. "Mmmmmmmmmm."

"Told you so," Emma said triumphantly, like the round balls were things she'd baked herself. "Oh, here's Kitty."

Kitty Svenson hauled herself up the steps. Fat and acne-covered and dirt poor, she was the sweetest girl in town, and every time I saw her my heart ached. She liked Tom DeCarno, who lived down the street from me and was the starting quarterback on the football team at the consolidated high school in Remington. He'd notice Kitty on the day that Hell got a hockey franchise.

It was obvious what Emma in her sexy, new dress and Tom in his bathrobe were going to be doing, so I dragged the protesting Will and we went home. I saw things I hadn't noticed on the way to Em's: a new playhouse in the backyard of the big house on the corner. Fresh chain-link fence around the Alghren place. The Connors' pick-up in their driveway, which meant that Eddie hadn't gone to work at the factory, either. Across the street, a woman I thought I didn't know, dressed up like a city girl in a ruffled suit and high heels, until I realized it was Sue Merkelson, the pharmacist's wife.

At home I took the kids into the backyard and weeded the tomatoes, which were nearly strangled with ten days' worth of weeds. Jack used to do at least some of the weeding. But that was before, and this was now, and I kept at it until the job was done.

By late August the factory in Minneonta had closed. Most of the men in town who didn't farm were out of work, but nobody seemed to mind much. The Crow Bar was full all the time, groups playing cards and laughing at TV. I saw them spilling out onto the street the one time I went to the supermarket to buy Pampers and milk.

Emma told me on the phone that Mayor Johnson, Barry Anderson, and Anderson's deputy had the nanomachines on a regular schedule. Every morning people lined up to pick up whatever their food order'd been from the previous day, enough food for all that day's meals plus a little over to store. Another machine made whatever clothes you picked out of a catalogue, in whatever size matched after you give in your measurements. It made blankets and curtains and tablecloths, too, anything out of cloth. The last two machines, including the big one, turned out everything else, picked from a different catalogue, turn by turn.

The county's corn, ready to harvest, sat in the fields. Nobody wanted to buy it, and except for the farm owners, nobody hired on to harvest it.

Nearly every family in town drove a new car, from six different models that our nanos were programmed to make. There was a lot of red and gold vehicles in our streets.

"I want a playhouse, Mommy," Will whined. "Caddie Alghren gots a new playhouse! I want one, too!"

I looked at him, standing there in his rumpled little pajamas with trains on them, looking like his best friend just died. His hair fell over his forehead just like Jack's used to do.

"How do you know Caddie's got a new playhouse?"

"I saw it! From my window!"

"You can't see into Caddie's yard from your window. Did you climb out up onto the roof again, Will?"

He hung his head and twisted the sleeves of his pajamas into crumpled balls.

"I told you that going up on that roof is dangerous! You could fall and break your neck!"

"I'm sorry," he said, raising his little face up to me, and I melted even though I knew he wasn't sorry at all and he would do it again. "I'm sorry, Mommy. Can't we get a playhouse? We been inside all summer, feels like!"

He was right. I'd only taken the kids outside our yard a few times. I'd hardly been out myself. I told myself that it was because I didn't want to see everybody's pitying looks (*"Jack run off with that sexy girl from the hardware store, Chrissie Somebody, just left Carol and those kids without so much as a backward glance."*) But it wasn't just that.

The big freezer downstairs was almost empty. I'd used up everything I could. I run out of Tide last Thursday and the laundry was piling up. Worse, the Pampers were nearly gone. I had to keep the checking account, the half of it that Jack left, to pay the rent and the phone as long as I could. After that . . . I didn't know yet. Not yet.

So I guessed it was time. I didn't understand why I didn't want to go before, didn't understand why I didn't want to go now. But it was time.

"Okay, honey, we'll get you a playhouse," I said. "Find your sneakers."

When I had Jackie changed and fed, Will and Kimee dressed, the stroller packed with diapers and water, we set off outside. Will was good, holding onto the side of the stroller and not running ahead. Kimee stood on the back bar and whimpered a little; she gets prickly heat in the summer. But when we turned the corner toward the town square, she stopped fussing and stared, just like me and Will. The whole place was full of garbage cans. Clean, blue plastic garbage cans, hundreds of them, stacked and thrown and lying on their sides, not a single one of them holding any garbage. People milled around, talking angrily. I saw my neighbor.

"Bob, what on Earth—"

He was too angry even to leer at me. "That Beasor kid! The one that won the state technology contest a few years ago—that kid's too smart-ass for his own good, I said so then! He hacked into the Big Gray somehow and now all it'll make is garbage cans, no matter what you tell it!"

I craned my neck to see the big metal box under its awning. Sure enough, another garbage can popped out. A bubble of something started in my belly and started to rise up in me. "Is . . . is . . ."

"The kid left town! Anderson's got an APB out on him. You haven't seen Danny Beasor, have you, Carol?"

"I haven't seen anybody," I said. The bubble rose higher and now I knew what it was: laughter. I turned my face away from Bob.

"If that kid knows what's good for him, he'll keep on running," Bob said. He was really upset. "Now the mayor's shut down the other nanomachines, except the food one, until the repair guys get out here from the city. You get your food today, Carol?"

"No, but I'll come back later," I managed to say, without laughing in Bob's face. "K-Kimee's not feeling well."

"Okay," he said, not really interested. "Hey, Earl! Wait!" He pushed through the garbage cans toward Earl Bickel across the square.

Will somehow understood that there would be no playhouse today. He screwed up his face, but before he could start to howl, I said, "Will! Look at all these great cans! We can make the best playhouse ever out of them!"

His face cleared. "Cool!"

So we nested and dragged home four garbage cans, with a little help from the teenage Parker boys, who are nice kids and who seemed glad to have something to do. They found some boards in the basement, plus a hammer and nails, and spent all afternoon making a playhouse with four garbage-can rooms. Will was in seventh heaven. I couldn't pay them, but I unfroze and toasted the last of my home-made banana bread, and they gobbled it down happily. Will and Kimee, her itching forgotten, played in the garbage cans until dark.

The next day all the nanomachines were working again, and I put in a daily food order. But I left the kids at home with Kitty Svenson when I picked up my order, and I started canning all the squash, beans, peppers, corn, and melons in the garden.

School opened. Will was in first grade. I walked him there the first day and he seemed to like his teacher.

By the third week of school, she'd quit.

By the fifth week, so had the teacher who replaced her, along with a few other faculty.

"They just don't want to work when they don't have to, and why should they?" Emma said. She sat in my kitchen, drinking a cup of coffee and wearing a strange hat that sloped down to cover half her face. I suppose she picked it out of the nano-catalogues—it must be what they were wearing in the city. The color was pretty, though, a warm peach. It was practically the first morning she'd made time for me in weeks. "With nano, nobody has to work if they don't want to."

"Did the twins' teacher quit, too?"

"No. It's old Mrs. Cameron. She's been teaching so long she probably can't even imagine doing anything else after she gets up in the morning. Carol, look at this place. How come you let it get so shabby?"

I said mildly, "There isn't too much money since Jack left. Just enough for the rent."

"That asshole . . . but that's not what I meant and you know it. Why haven't you replaced those old curtains and sofa with nano ones? And that TV! You could get a real big one, with an unbelievable picture."

I put my elbows on the table and leaned toward her. "I'll tell you the truth, Em: I don't know. I get nano food and diapers, and I got some school clothes for Will, but anything else . . . I don't know."

"You're just being an idiot!" she said. She almost shouted it— way too angry for just my saggy sofa. I reached out and pulled off the sloping hat. Emma's eye was swollen nearly shut, and every color of squash in my garden.

All at once she started sobbing. "Ted . . . he never done anything like that before . . . it's terrible on men, being laid off! They get so bored and mad—"

"He wasn't laid off, he quit," I said, but gently.

"Same thing! He just scowls himself around the house, yells at the kids—they're glad to be back in school, let me tell you!—and criticizes everything I do, or he orders scotch from the nano—did order it until Mayor Johnson outlawed any nano liquor and—"

"He did? The mayor did?" I said, startled.

"Yeah. And so last Thursday, Ted and I had this big fight, and . . . and . . ." Suddenly she changed tone. "You don't know anything, Carol! You sit here safe and alone, thinking you're so superior to nano, just like you always acted so superior to poor Jack—oh, I'm sorry, I didn't mean that!"

"Probably you did," I said evenly, "but it's all right. Really it is, Em."

All at once she got defiant. "You're thinking I'm just dumping on you because Ted hit me. Well, I'm not. It was only that once, most of the time he's a good husband. Our new house by the lake will be done in a few more weeks and then everything'll be better!"

I didn't see how, but all I said was, "I'll bet the house is pretty."

"It's gorgeous! It's got a blue-brick fireplace in the living room —*blue* bricks! And it's equipped with just everything, all those robo-appliances like you see on TV—I won't have to do hardly anything!"

"I can't wait to see it," I said.

"You'll love it," she said, put her hat back on so it covered her eye, and stared at me with triumph and fear.

I pulled Will out of school to home-school him. He didn't mind once I got the Bellingham grand-kids to school at my place, and then Caddie Alghren. The Bellinghams were farmers going bust. Mr. Bellingham was still doing dairy, though, even while his crops rotted in the fields. Mrs. Bellingham's always been sickly and she never struck me as real smart. But Hal Bellingham is smart, and he looked at me real sharp when I said I would home-school his grand-kids because the teachers were all quitting.

"Not all, Carol."

"No, not yet. And some won't quit. But the government's not getting much tax money because nobody's earning and the TV says that the government is taking itself apart bit by bit." I didn't understand that, but Mr. Bellingham looked like he might. "How many teachers'll stay when they can't get paid at all?"

"That time's a ways off."

"Maybe."

"What makes you think you can teach my grandkids? Begging your pardon, but you don't look or sound like a college graduate."

"I'm not. But I did good in high school, and I guess I can teach first- and second-graders. At any rate, in my living room they'll be safe from the kinds of vandalism you see all around town now."

"What'll you use for books?"

"We have some kids' books, I'll get more out of the library as long as it lasts, and we'll make books, the kids and me. It's fun to write your own stories, and they can read each other's."

"You aren't going to get books from the nanomachinery?"

"No." I said it flat out, and we looked at each other, sitting there in the Bellingham's big farm kitchen with its old-fashioned microwave.

He said, "Who's going to watch your two little ones while you teach?"

"Kitty Svenson."

"What's she get out of it?"

"That's between me and her."

"And what do you want in return?"

"Milk, and a share of the spring calves you might have sent to market, slaughtered and with the meat dressed. You aren't going to be able to get in enough hay to feed them anyway."

He got up, walked in his farm boots around his kitchen, and looked at me again. "Do you watch the news, Carol?"

"Not much. Little kids take a lot out of you."

"You should watch. Vandalism isn't limited to what we got in Clifford Falls."

I didn't say anything.

"All right, the kids will be home-schooled by you. But here, not at your place. I'll clear out the big back bedroom for you, and Kitty can use the kitchen. Mattie'll like the company. But before you agree, there's somebody I want you to meet."

"Who?"

"Suspicious little thing, aren't you? Come with me."

We went out to the barn. The cows were in pasture, and the hayloft half empty. In an old tack room that the Bellinghams had turned into an apartment for a long-ago cattle manager, a pretty young woman sat in front of a metal table. I blinked.

The whole room was full of strange equipment, along with freezers and other stuff I recognized. The woman wore a white lab coat, like doctors on TV. She stood and smiled at us.

"This is Amelia Parsons," Bellingham said. "She used to work for

Camry Biotech, which just went out of business. She's a crop geneticist."

"Hello," she said, holding out her hand. Women like her make me nervous. Too polished, too educated. They all had it too easy. But I shook her hand; I'm not rude.

"Amelia's working on creating an apomictic corn plant. That's corn that doesn't need pollination, that can produce its own seeds asexually, like non-hybrid varieties once did, and like blackberries and mangos and some roses do now. Apomictic corn would keep all the good traits of hybrid corn, maybe even with added benefits, but farmers wouldn't have to buy seed every year."

"I couldn't work on this very much at Camry," Amelia said to me. Her pretty face glowed. Her red hair was cut in one of those complicated city cuts. "Even though apomixis was my doctoral thesis. The biotech company wanted us to work on things that were more immediately profitable. But now that I don't need to earn a salary, that oversight agencies are pretty much dismantling, and that I can get the equipment I need from nano . . . well, nano makes it possible for me to do some real work!"

I smiled at her again, because I didn't have anything to say. There was a baby-food stain on my jeans and I moved my hand to cover it.

"Thanks, Amelia," Hal Bellingham said. "See you later."

On the way back to the house, he said quietly, "I just wanted you to see the other side, Carol."

I didn't answer.

My little school started on Monday. Caddie Alghren, whose mother had been killed by a drunk driver last spring, clung to me at first, but Will and she were friends and as long as she could sit next to him, she was all right. The three Bellingham kids were well-behaved and smart. Kitty watched Kimee and Jackie in the kitchen and helped Mattie Bellingham. At night Kitty went home with me, because her stepfather had started to come into her room at night. Nothing real bad had happened yet, but she hated him and was glad to baby-sit for her keep.

After the kids finally got to sleep each night, Kitty and I watched the TV, like Hal said, and saw what was happening in the cities. A lot of people won't work if they don't have to. But a lot of people not working means a lot of broken things don't get fixed. Nano can make water pipes and schoolbooks and buses and toilets. It can't install them or teach them or drive them. The cities were getting to be pretty scary places.

Clifford Falls wasn't that bad. But it wasn't all that far out from the city, either. Kitty and I were watching TV one night, the kids in bed, when the door burst open and two men rushed in.

"Look at this—not just the one, *two* of them," one man said, while I was already reaching for the phone. He got there first and knocked it out of my hand. "Not that it would help you, lady. Not a lot of police left. Kenny, I'll take this one and you take the fat girl."

Kitty had shrunk back against the sofa. I tried to think fast. The kids—if I could just keep any noise from waking the kids, the men might not even know they were there. Then no matter what happened to us, the kids would be safe. But if Will saw either of their faces, if he could identify them . . . and Kitty, Kitty was only fifteen . . .

I said quickly, "Leave her alone. She doesn't know how to do anything, she won't be any fun for you. If you leave her alone, I'll let you both do me. I won't even fight. I'd be a lot more fun for you." My gorge rose and I tasted vomit.

The two men looked at each other. Finally "Kenny" shrugged and said, "The fat one's ugly, anyway."

The other one nodded and his piggy eyes gleamed. Noise—the important thing was no noise. I got down on the floor and unzipped my jeans. Oh, God—but no noise, no noise to wake the kids, and I had to protect Kitty, God, *fifteen* . . .

My head exploded.

No, not my head, the head leering above me. Blood and brains splattered over me. Then there was a second shot and the other man went down. I staggered up, puked, and heard Will and Kimee screaming. When I could see again, the kids stood in the doorway, clinging together, and Kitty still sat on the sofa, the gun in her hand.

She was the calmest one there, at least on the outside. "I stole it to use on my stepfather if I had to, just before you said I could live here. Carol—" Then she started shaking.

"It's okay," I said stupidly and, my own hand trembling, picked up the phone to call the cops.

I got a *recording* at 911. "I'm sorry, but due to reduced manpower, your call may have to wait. Please stay on the line until—" I hung up and called Barry Anderson's cell.

It was turned off. When he finally got there, three hours later, he said it was the only sleep he'd had in two days. His deputy quit last week and left for Florida. By that time I'd gotten the kids back to sleep, the room and myself cleaned up, and Kitty to stop shaking.

The next day, Hal Bellingham moved us all out to the farm.

*   *   *

By spring, there were fifty-four of us on the farm, plus ten kids. And in the spring, Jack came back.

I was coming out of the lamb barn with Will, who saw Jack first. He cried, "Daddy!" and my heart froze. Then Will was running across the muddy yard and throwing himself into Jack's arms. I trailed slowly behind.

"How'd you get past the guards?" I said.

"Bellingham let me in. What kind of set-up you got going here, anyway?"

I didn't answer, just stared at him. He looked good. Well-fed, well-dressed, maybe a little heavier but still the handsomest man ever to come out of Clifford Falls. This was how Will, beaming in his daddy's arms, would look in twenty years.

Jack reddened slightly. "Why are you living here, Carol? Don't tell me you and old Bellingham . . ."

"That would be what you'd think. The answer is no."

Did he look relieved? "Then why—"

"Mommy's my teacher!" Will shouted. "And I can write whole sentences!"

"Good for you," Jack said. To me he suddenly blurted, "Carol, I don't know how to say this, but I'm so sorry, I—"

"Where's Chrissie? You get tired of her the way you did of me?"

"No, she . . . who the hell is *that?*"

His eyes almost bugged out of his head, and well they might. Denny Bonohan strolled out of the house, dressed in one of his costumes. Denny's gay, which was hard enough for me to take, but he's also an actor, which is even worse because he strolls out to do his share of guard duty dressed in outlandish things he and the other two actors brought with him. Now he wore tights with a bright tunic almost as long as a dress, all in shades of gold. Hal is amused by him but I think Denny's loony and I won't let the kids be alone with him. My right, Hal says in his quiet way, and what Hal says goes.

I said, "That's my new boyfriend." I said it to make Jack mad but instead he threw back his head and laughed, his white teeth gleaming in the sunshine.

"Not you, Carol. Never. I know you that much, anyways."

"What are you doing here, Jack?"

"I want to see my kids. And I want . . . I want you, Carol. I miss you. I was wrong, as wrong as a man can be. Please take me back."

Jack apologizing was always hard to resist, although it's not like he ever did all that much of it. Will clung hard to his father's neck.

Also, an old sweet feeling was slipping into me, along with the anger. I wanted to hit him, I wanted to hug him. I wanted to curl up inside him again.

"It's up to the Council if you can stay here."

"*Here?*"

"We aren't leaving, the kids and me."

He took a deep breath. "What's the Council? What do I have to do?"

"You have to start by talking to Hal. If Denny's on guard duty, Hal's probably coming off."

"Guard duty?" Jack said, bewildered.

"Yeah, Jack. You're back in the army now. Only this time, we all enlisted."

"I don't . . ."

"Come on," I said roughly. "It's up to a vote of the Council. For my part, I don't give a damn what you do."

"You're lying," he said softly, in that special voice we used between us, and I damned him all over again because it was true.

July again, and we are eighty-seven people now. Word spreads. About half are people who fled nano, like me. The other half embraced it because it lets them do whatever they'd wanted to do before. Some of those ones have their own nanomachines, little ones, made of course by other nanomachines. Hal allows them to use nano to produce things for their jobs, but not to make food or clothing or shelter or anything else we all need to survive, except for some medicines, and we're working on that.

The two kinds of people here don't always get along very well. We have five actors, Amelia the geneticist, and two other scientists, one of them studying something about the stars. We have a man writing fiction, an inventor, and, finally, a real teacher. Also two organic farmers, a sculptor, a man who carves and puts together furniture all without nails, and, of all things, the United States chess champion, who can't find anyone good enough to play with and so plays against our old computer.

He also farms and does guard duty and lays pipe and cleans and cans and cooks, of course. Like all the rest of us. The things that the chess player didn't know how to do, which was everything, we taught him. Just like Hal, who was a Marine once, taught us all to shoot.

It's pretty bad out there now, although the TV says it's getting better as "society adjusts to this most cataclysmic of social changes."

I don't know if that's true or not. I guess it varies. There was a lot of rioting and disease and fires. Some places have some government left, some places don't, some are like us now, mostly our own government, although Hal and two educated women keep our taxes filed and all that. One of the women told me that we don't have to actually pay taxes because the farm shows a consistent loss. She was a lawyer, but a religious lawyer. She says nano is Satan's work.

Amelia Parsons says nano is a gift from God.

Me, I think something different. I think nano is a sorter. The old sorting used to put the people with money and education and nice things in one pile and the rest of us in another. But nano sorts out two different piles: the ones who like to work because work is what you do, and the ones who don't.

It was kind of like everybody won the lottery all at once. Once I saw a TV show about lottery winners, a show that followed them around for a year or two after they won real big money. By that time, most of them were worse off than before they won that money: miserable and broke again and with all their relatives mad at them. But some used the money to make nicer lives. And some just gave nearly all of it away to charity and went back to taking care of themselves.

Jack lasted two months on the farm. Then he was gone again.

I get email from him every once in a while. Mostly he asks after the kids. He never says where he is or what he's doing instead of working. He never says who he's with, or if he's happy. I guess he is, or he'd come back here. People usually end up doing what makes them happiest, if they can.

A month ago I went with Hal and some others down to the lake to catch fish. A house stood there, burned to the ground, weeds already growing over the blue brick fireplace. In the ashes I found one diamond earring. Which I left there.

Now Kimee is in the garden, waiting for me to pick peas. I'm going to show her how to shell them, too, and how to separate the good pods from the bad ones. She's only five, but it's never too early to learn.

Afterword to "Nano Comes to Clifford Falls"

I like to write stories about people who are outside of the main surge of history. These are not the people who invent, refine, market, or early-adopt technology, but rather the stragglers who eventually have it forced on them. As something of a straggler myself (though not as far behind as Carol), I can identify.

So could some readers, although not all. "Nano Comes to Clifford Falls" was the first-ever story of mine to be disseminated by that new medium, the podcast. Escape Pod hosts a website on which listeners can post reactions to stories, and I was directed there (I never find anything without direction, and not always then). I was astounded at the various ways that people interpreted my story. It was seen as anti-nano, pro-nano, anti-male, pro-green, Luddite, overly glorifying of "heroic single mothers," unrealistic, very realistic, too short, and too long.

I tell my writing students that the main task of writing is to transfer the vision in one's head onto paper in order that it may be re-created in the reader's head. My experience with this story showed me, all over again, how impossible that goal really is. The author can narrow the head-to-paper gap, but the story will always take on a different cast as it traverses the mysterious abyss between people.

Patent Infringement

PRESS RELEASE

KEGELMAN-BALLSTON CORPORATION IS PROUD TO announce the first public release of its new drug, Halitex, which cures Ulbarton's Flu completely after one ten-pill course of treatment. Ulbarton's Flu, as the public knows all too well, now afflicts upward of thirty million Americans, with the number growing daily as the highly contagious flu spreads. Halitex "flu-proofs" the body by inserting genes tailored to confer immunity to this persistent and debilitating scourge, whose symptoms include coughing, muscle aches, and fatigue. Because the virus remains in the body even after symptoms disappear, Ulbarton's Flu can recur in a given patient at any time. Halitex renders each recurrence ineffectual.

The General Accounting Office estimates that Ulbarton's Flu, the virus of which was first identified by Dr. Timothy Ulbarton, has already cost four billion dollars this calendar year in medical costs and lost work time. Halitex, two years in development by Kegelman-Ballston, is expected to be in high demand throughout the nation.

NEW YORK POST
K-B ZAPS ULBARTON'S FLU
NEW DRUG DOES U'S FLU 4 U

Jonathan Meese
538 Pleasant Lane
Aspen Hill, MD 20906

Dear Mr. Kegelman and Mr. Ballston,

I read in the newspaper that your company, Kegelman-Ballston, has recently released a drug, Halitex, which provides immunity against Ulbarton's Flu by gene therapy. I believe that the genes used in developing this drug are mine. Two years ago, on May 5, I visited my GP to explain that I had been exposed to Ulbarton's Flu a lot (the entire accounting department of the Pet Supply Catalogue Store, where I work, developed the flu. Also my wife, three children, and mother-in-law. Plus, I believe my dog had it, although the vet disputes this.). However, despite all this exposure, I did not develop Ulbarton's.

My GP directed me to your research facility along I-270, saying he "thought he heard they were trying to develop a med." I went there, and samples of my blood and bodily tissues were taken. The researcher said I would hear from you if the samples were ever used for anything, but I never did. Will you please check your records to verify my participation in this new medicine, and tell me what share of the profits are due me.

Thank you for your consideration.

Sincerely,

Jon Meese
Jonathan J. Mees

From the Desk of Robert Ballston
Kegelman-Ballston Corporation

To: Martin Blake, Legal
Re: Attached letter

Marty—

Is he a nut? Is this a problem?

Bob

INTERNAL MEMO
KEGELMAN-BALLSTON

To: Robert Ballston
From: Martin Blake
Re: Gene-line claimant Jonathan J. Meese

Bob—

I checked with Records over in Research and, yes, unfortunately this guy donated the tissue samples from which the gene line was developed that led to Halitex. Even more unfortunately, Meese's visit occurred just before we instituted the comprehensive waiver for all donors. However, I don't think Meese has any legal grounds here. Court precedents have upheld the corporate right to patent genes used in drug development. Also, the guy doesn't sound very sophisticated (his *dog?*) He doesn't even know that Kegelman's been dead for ten years. Apparently Meese has not yet employed a lawyer. I can make a small nuisance settlement if you like, but I'd rather avoid setting a corporate precedent for these people. I'd rather send him a stiff letter that will scare the bejesus out of the greedy little twerp.

Please advise.

Marty

From the Desk of Robert Ballston
Kegelman-Ballston Corporation

To: Martin Blake, Legal
Re: J. Meese

Do it.

Bob

Martin Blake, Attorney-at-Law
Chief Legal Counsel, Kegelman-Ballston Corporation

Dear Mr. Meese,

Your letter regarding the patented Kegelman-Ballston drug Halitex has been referred to me. Please be advised that you have no legal rights in Halitex; see attached list of case precedents. If you persist in any such claims, Kegelman-Ballston will consider it harassment and take appropriate steps, including possible prosecution.

Sincerely,

Martin Blake
Martin Blake

Jonathan Meese
538 Pleasant Lane
Aspen Hill, MD 20906

Dear Mr. Blake,

But they're my genes!!! This can't be right. I'm consulting a lawyer, and you can expect to hear from her shortly.

Jon Meese
Jonathan J. Meese

Catherine Owen, Attorney-at-Law

Dear Mr. Blake,

I now represent Jonathan J. Meese in his concern that Kegelman-Ballston has developed a pharmaceutical, Halitex, based on gene therapy which uses Mr. Meese's genes as its basis. We feel it only reasonable that this drug, which will earn Kegelman-Ballston millions if not billions of dollars, acknowledge financially Mr. Meese's considerable contribution. We are therefore willing to consider a settlement, and are available to discuss this with you at your earliest convenience.

Sincerely,

Catherine Owen
Catherine Owen, Attorney

From the Desk of Robert Ballston
Kegelman-Ballston Corporation

To: Martin Blake, Legal
Re: J. Meese

Marty—

Damn it, if there's one thing that really chews my balls it's this sort of undercover sabotage by the second-rate. I played golf with Sam Fortescue on Saturday and he opened my eyes (you remember Sam; he's at the agency we're using to benchmark our competition). Sam speculates that this Meese bastard is really being used by Irwin-Lacey to set us up. You know that bastard Carl Irwin has had his own Ulbarton's drug in development, and he's sore as hell because we beat him to market. Ten to one he's paying off this Meese patsy.

We can't allow it. Don't settle. Let him sue.

Bob

INTERNAL MEMO
KEGELMAN-BALLSTON

To: Robert Ballston
From: Martin Blake
Re: Gene-line claimant Jonathan J. Meese

Bob—

I've got a better idea. We sue *him*, on the grounds he's walking around with our patented genetic immunity to Ulbarton's. No one except consumers of Halitex have this immunity, so Meese must have acquired it illegally, possibly on the black market. We gain several advantages with this suit: We eliminate Meese's complaint, we send a clear message to other rivals who may be attempting patent infringement, and we gain a publicity circus to both publicize Halitex (not that it needs it) and, more important, make the public aware of the dangers of black market substitutes for Halitex, such as Meese obtained.

Incidentally, I checked again with Records over at Research. They have no documentation of any visit from a Jonathan J. Meese on any date whatsoever.

Marty

From the Desk of Robert Ballston
Kegelman-Ballston Corporation

To: Martin Blake, Legal
Re: J. Meese

Marty—

Brilliant! Do it. Can we get a sympathetic judge? One who under-stands business? Maybe O'Connor can help.

Bob

NEW YORK TIMES
HALITEX BLACK MARKET CASE TO BEGIN TODAY

This morning the circuit court of Manhattan County is scheduled to begin hearing the case of *Kegelman-Ballston v. Meese*. This case, heavily publicized during recent months, is expected to set impor-tant precedents in the controversial areas of gene patents and patent infringement on biological properties. Protestors from the group FOR US: CANCEL KIDNAPPED ULBARTON PATENTS, which is often referred to by its initials, have been in place on the court steps since last night. The case is being heard by Judge Latham P. Farmingham III, a Republican who is widely perceived as sympathetic to the concerns of big business.

This case began when Jonathan J. Meese, an accountant with the Pet Supply Catalogue Store . . .

Catherine Owen, Attorney-at-Law

Dear Mr. Blake,

Just a reminder that Jon Meese and I are still open to a settlement.

Sincerely,

Catherine Owen

Martin Blake, Attorney-at-Law
Chief Legal Counsel, Kegelman-Ballston Corporation

Cathy—

Don't they teach you at that law school you went to (I never can remember the name) that you don't settle when you're sure to win?

You're a nice girl; better luck next time.

Martin Blake

NEW YORK TIMES
MEESE CONVICTED

PLAINTIFF GUILTY OF "HARBORING" DISEASE-FIGHTING GENES
WITHOUT COMPENSATING DEVELOPER KEGELMAN-BALLSTON

From the Desk of Robert Ballston
Kegelman-Ballston Corporation

To: Martin Blake, Legal
Re: Kegelman-Ballston v. Meese

Marty—

I always said you were a genius! My God, the free publicity we got out of this thing, not to mention the future edge—How about a victory celebration this weekend? Are you and Elaine free to fly to Aruba on the Lear, Friday night?

Bob

NEW YORK TIMES
BLUE GENES FOR DRUG THIEF
JONATHAN J. MEESE SENTENCED TO SIX MONTHS FOR PATENT INFRINGEMENT

From the Desk of Robert Ballston
Kegelman-Ballston Corporation

To: Martin Blake, Legal
Re: Halitex

Marty, I just had a brilliant idea I want to run by you. We got Meese, but now that he's at Ossining, the publicity has died down. Well, my daughter read this squib the other day in some science magazine, how the Ulbarton's virus has in it some of the genes that Research combined with Meese's to create Halitex. I didn't understand all the egghead science, but apparently Halitex uses some of the flu genes to build its immune properties. And we own the patent on Halitex. As I see it, that means that Dr. Ulbarton was working with **OUR** genes when he identified Ulbarton's Flu and published his work. Now, if we could go after *Ulbarton* in court, the publicity would be tremendous, as well as strengthening our proprietorship position.

But the publicity, Marty! The publicity!

Bob

Afterword to "Patent Infringement"

The epistolary story has a long tradition; in 1740 Samuel Richardson created a publishing sensation with his novel Pamela, told entirely through letters. Two hundred fifty years later, the form had been extensively used by such wildly diverse SF writers as A. E. Van Vogt, Gordon R. Dickson, Esther Friesner, and Jonathan Lethem.

I wanted to write an epistolary story. Who knows where such yearnings come from? I wanted to do this, but no idea presented itself. I brooded about it for a couple of years. Then I saw a segment of the TV show 60 Minutes in which a man with AIDS was suing a pharmaceutical company for use of his tissues in developing an AIDS medication. All at once the entire plot of "Patent Infringement" flashed into my mind—in letters.

Years later, I attended a conference on "Genetic Policy and the Arts," organized by activist Lori B. Andrews. She invited me because she'd read "Patent Infringement." As we talked, it turned out that she was part of that 60 Minutes segment that had inspired the story.

You can't make up stuff like that.

Computer Virus

"I T'S OUT," SOMEONE SAID, A TECH PROBABLY, AL-
though later McTaggart could never remember who spoke first.
"It's out!"

"It can't be!" *someone else cried, and then the whole room was roiling, running, frantic with activity that never left the workstations.
Running in place.*

"It's not supposed to be this way," Elya blurted. Instantly she regretted it. The hard, flat eyes of her sister-in-law Cassie met hers, and
Elya flinched away from that look.

"And how is it supposed to be, Elya?" Cassie said. "Tell me."

"I'm sorry. I only meant that . . . that no matter how much you
loved Vlad, mourning gets . . . lighter. Not lighter, but less . . . withdrawn. Cass, you can't just wall up yourself and the kids in this
place! For one thing, it's not good for them. You'll make them terrified to face real life."

"I hope so," Cassie said, "for their sake. Now let me show you the
rest of the castle."

Cassie was being ironic, Elya thought miserably, but "castle" was
still the right word. Fortress, keep, bastion . . . Elya hated it. Vlad
would have hated it. And now she'd provoked Cassie to exaggerate

every protective, self-sufficient, isolating feature of the multi-million dollar pile that had cost Cass every penny she had, including the future income from the lucrative patents that had gotten Vlad murdered.

"This is the kitchen," Cassie said. "House, do we have any milk?"

"Yes," said the impersonal voice of the house system. At least Cassie hadn't named it, or given it one of those annoying visual avatars. The roomscreen remained blank. "There is one carton of soymilk and one of cow milk on the third shelf."

"It reads the active tags on the cartons," Cassie said. "House, how many of Donnie's allergy pills are left in the master-bath medicine cabinet?"

"Sixty pills remain," House said, "and three more refills on the prescription."

"Donnie's allergic to ragweed, and it's mid-August," Cassie said.

"Well, he isn't going to smell any ragweed inside this mausoleum," Elya retorted, and immediately winced at her choice of word. But Cassie didn't react. She walked on through the house, unstoppable, narrating in that hard, flat voice she had developed since Vlad's death.

"All the appliances communicate with House through narrowband wireless radio frequencies. House reaches the Internet the same way. All electricity comes from a generator in the basement, with massive geothermal feeds and storage capacitors. In fact, there are two generators, one for back-up. I'm not willing to use battery back-up, for the obvious reason."

It wasn't obvious to Elya. She must have looked bewildered because Cassie added, "Batteries can only back-up for a limited time. Redundant generators are more reliable."

"Oh."

"The only actual cables coming into the house are the VNM fiber-optic cables I need for computing power. If they cut those, we'll still be fully functional."

If *who* cuts those? Elya thought, but she already knew the answer. Except that it didn't make sense. Vlad had been killed by econuts because his work was—had been—so controversial. Cassie and the kids weren't likely to be a target now that Vlad was dead. Elya didn't say this. She trailed behind Cassie through the living room, bedrooms, hallways. Every one had a roomscreen for House, even the hallways, and multiple sensors in the ceilings to detect and identify intruders. Elya had had to pocket an emitter at the front door, presumably so House wouldn't . . . do what? What did it do if there was an intruder? She was afraid to ask.

"Come downstairs," Cassie said, leading the way through an e-locked door (of course) down a long flight of steps. "The computer uses three-dimensional laser microprocessors with optical transistors. It can manage twenty million billion calculations per second."

Startled, Elya said, "What on Earth do you need that sort of power for?"

"I'll show you." They approached another door, reinforced steel from the look of it. "Open," Cassie said, and it swung inward. Elya stared at a windowless, fully equipped genetics lab.

"Oh, no, Cassie . . . you're not going to work here, too!"

"Yes, I am. I resigned from MedGene last week. I'm a consultant now."

Elya gazed helplessly at the lab, which seemed to be a mixture of shining new equipment plus Vlad's old stuff from his auxiliary home lab. Vlad's refrigerator and storage cabinet, his centrifuge, were all these things really used in common between Vlad's work in ecoremediation and Cassie's in medical genetics? Must be. The old refrigerator had a new dent in its side, probably the result of a badly programmed 'bot belonging to the moving company. Elya recognized a new gene synthesizer, gleaming expensively, along with other machines that she, not a scientist, couldn't identify. Through a half-open door she saw a small bathroom. It all must have cost enormously. Cassie had better work hard as a consultant.

And now she could do so without ever leaving this self-imposed prison. Design her medical micros, send the data encrypted over the Net to the client. If it weren't for Jane and Donnie . . . Elya grasped at this. There *were* Janey and Donnie, and Janey would need to be picked up at school very shortly now. At least the kids would get Cassie out of this place periodically.

Cassie was still defining her imprisonment in that brittle voice. "There's a Faraday cage around the entire house, of course, embedded in the walls. No EMP can take us out. The walls are reinforced foamcast concrete, the windows virtually unbreakable polymers. We have enough food stored for a year. The water supply is from a well under the house, part of the geothermal system. It's cool, sweet water. Want a glass?"

"No," Elya said. "Cassie . . . you act as if you expect full-scale warfare. Vlad was killed by an individual nutcase."

"And there are a lot of nutcases out there," Cassie said crisply. "I lost Vlad. I'm not going to lose Janey and Donnie or . . . hey! There you are, pumpkin!"

"I came downstairs!" Donnie said importantly, and flung himself into his mother's arms. "Annie said!"

Cassie smiled over her son's head at his young nanny, Anne Millius. The smile changed her whole face, Elya thought, dissolved her brittle shell, made her once more the Cassie that Vlad had loved. A whole year. Cassie completely unreconciled, wanting only what was gone forever. It wasn't supposed to be like this. Or was it that she, Elya, wasn't capable of the kind of love Cassie had for Vlad? Elya had been married twice, and divorced twice, and had gotten over both men. Was that better or worse than Cassie's stubborn, unchippable grief?

She sighed, and Cassie said to Donnie, "Here's Aunt Elya. Give her a big kiss!"

The three-year-old detached himself from his mother and rushed to Elya. God, he looked like Vlad. Curly, light brown hair, huge dark eyes. Snot ran from his nose and smeared on Elya's cheek.

"Sorry," Cassie said, grinning.

"Allergies?"

"Yes. Although . . . does he feel warm to you?"

"I can't tell," said Elya, who had no children. She released Donnie. Maybe he did feel a bit hot in her arms, and his face was flushed a bit. But his full-lipped smile—Vlad again—and shining eyes didn't look sick.

"God, look at the time, I've got to go get Janey," Cassie said. "Want to come along, Elya?"

"Sure." She was glad to leave the lab, leave the basement, leave the "castle." Beyond the confines of the Faraday-embedded concrete walls, she took deep breaths of fresh air. Although of course the air inside had been just as fresh. In fact, the air inside was recycled in the most sanitary, technologically advanced way to avoid bringing in pathogens or gases deliberately released from outside. It was much safer than any fresh air outside. Cassie had told her so.

No one understood, not even Elya.

Her sister-in-law thought that Cassie didn't hear herself, didn't see herself in the mirror every morning, didn't know what she'd become. Elya was wrong. Cassie heard the brittleness in her voice, saw the stoniness in her face for everyone but the kids and sometimes, God help her, even for Jane. Felt herself recoiling from everyone because they weren't Vlad, because Vlad was dead and they were not. What Elya didn't understand was that Cassie couldn't help it.

Elya didn't know about the dimness that had come over the world, the sense of everything being enveloped in a gray fog: people and trees and furniture and lab beakers. Elya didn't know, hadn't experienced, the frightening anger that still seized Cassie with undiminished force, even a year later, so that she thought if she didn't smash something, kill something as Vlad had been killed, she'd go insane. Insaner. Worse, Elya didn't know about the longing for Vlad that would rise, unbidden and unexpected, throughout Cassie's entire body, leaving her unable to catch her breath.

If Vlad had died of a disease, Cassie sometimes thought, even a disease for which she couldn't put together a genetic solution, it would have been much easier on her. Or if he'd died in an accident, the kind of freak chance that could befall anybody. What made it so hard was the murder. That somebody had deliberately decided to snuff out this valuable life, this precious living soul, not for anything evil Vlad did but for the *good* he accomplished.

Dr. Vladimir Seritov, chief scientist for Barr Biosolutions. One of the country's leading bioremediationists and prominent advocate for cutting-edge technology of all sorts. Designer of Plasticide (he'd laughed uproariously at the marketers' name), a bacteria genetically engineered to eat certain long-chain hydrocarbons used in some of the petroleum plastics straining the nation's over-burdened landfills. The microbe was safe: severely limited chemical reactions, non-toxic breakdown products, set number of replications before the terminator gene kicked in, the whole nine yards. And one Sam Verdon, neo-Luddite and self-appointed guardian of an already straining environment, had shot Vlad anyway.

On the anniversary of the murder, neo-Luddites had held a rally outside the walls of Verdon's prison. Barr Biosolutions had gone on marketing Vlad's creation, to great environmental and financial success. And Cassie Seritov had moved into the safest place she could find for Vlad's children, from which she someday planned to murder Sam Verdon, scum of the earth. But not yet. She couldn't get at him yet. He had at least eighteen more years of time to do, assuming "good behavior."

Nineteen years total. In exchange for Vladimir Seritov's life. And Elya wondered why Cassie was still so angry?

She wandered from room to room, the lights coming on and going off behind her. This was one of the bad nights. Annie had gone home, Jane and Donnie were asleep, and the memories would not stay away. Vlad laughing on their boat (sold now to help pay for the castle). Vlad bending over her the night Jane was born. Vlad standing beside the president of Barr at the press conference announcing the new clean-up microbe, press and scientists assembled, by some idiot publicist's decree, at an actual landfill. The shot cutting the air. It had been August then, too, Donnie had had ragweed allergies, and Vlad looking first surprised and then in terrible pain . . .

Sometimes work helped. Cassie went downstairs to the lab. Her current project was investigating the folding variations of a digestive enzyme that a drug company was interested in. The work was methodical, meticulous, not very challenging. Cassie had never deluded herself that she was the same caliber scientist Vlad had been.

While the automated analyzer was taking X-rays of crystallized proteins, Cassie said, "House, put on the TV. Anything. Any channel." Any distraction.

The roomscreen brightened to a three-D image of two gorgeous women shouting at each other in what was supposed to be a New York penthouse. ". . . never trust you again without—" one of them yelled, and then the image abruptly switched to a news avatar, an inhumanly chiseled digital face with pale blue hair and the glowing green eyes of a cat in the dark. "We interrupt this movie to bring you a breaking news report from Sandia National Laboratory in New Mexico. Dr. Stephen Milbrett, Director of Sandia, has just announced—" The lights went out.

"Hey!" Cassie cried. "What—" The lights went back on.

She stood up quickly, uncertain for a moment, then started toward the stairs leading upstairs to the children's bedrooms. "Open," she said to the lab door, but the door remained shut. Her hand on the knob couldn't turn it. To her left the roomscreen brightened without producing an image and House said, "Dr. Seritov?"

"What's going on here? House, open the door!"

"This is no longer House speaking. I have taken complete possession of your household system plus your additional computing power. Please listen to my instructions carefully."

Cassie stood still. She knew what was happening; the real estate agent had told her it had happened a few times before, when the castle had belonged to a billionaire so eccentrically reclusive that he stood as an open invitation to teenage hackers. A data stream could easily be beamed in on House's frequency when the Faraday shield was turned off, and she'd had the shield down to receive TV transmission. But the incoming datastream should have only activated the TV, introducing additional images, not overridden House's programming. The door should not have remained locked.

"House, activate Faraday shield." An automatic priority-one command, keyed to her voice. Whatever hackers were doing, this would negate it.

"Faraday shield is already activated. But this is no longer House, Dr. Seritov. Please listen to my instructions. I have taken possession of your houscheld system. You will be—"

"Who are you?" Cassie cried.

"I am Project T4S. You will be kept in this room as a hostage against the attack I expect soon. The—"

"My children are upstairs!"

"Your children, Jane Rose Seritov, six years of age, and Donald Sergei Seritov, three years of age, are asleep in their rooms. Visual next."

The screen resolved into a split view from the bedrooms' sensors. Janey lay heavily asleep. Donnie breathed wheezily, his bedclothes twisted with his tossing, his small face flushed.

"I want to go to them!"

"That is impossible. I'm sorry. You must be kept in this room as a hostage against the attack I expect soon. All communications to the outside has been severed, with the one exception of the outside speaker on the patio, normally used for music. I will use—"

"Please. Let me go to my children!"

"I cannot. I'm sorry. But if you were to leave this room, you could hit the manual override on the front door. It is the only door so equipped. I could not stop you from leaving, and I need you as hostages. I will use—"

"Hostages! Who the hell are you? Why are you doing this?"

House was silent a moment. Then it said, "The causal is self-defense. They're trying to kill me."

The room at Sandia had finally quieted. Everyone was out of ideas. McTaggart voiced the obvious. "It's disappeared. Nowhere on the Net, nowhere the Net can contact."

"Not possible," someone said.

"But actual."

Another silence. The scientists and techs looked at each other. They had been trying to locate the AI for over two hours, using every classified and unclassified search engine possible. It had first eluded them, staying one step ahead of the termination programs, fleeing around the globe on the Net, into and out of anything both big enough to hold it and lightly firewalled enough to penetrate quickly. Now, somehow, it had completely vanished.

Sandia, like all the national laboratories, was overseen by the Department of Energy. McTaggart picked up the phone to call Washington.

Cassie tried to think. Stay calm, don't panic. There were rumors of AI development, both in private corporations and in government labs, but then there'd always been rumors of AI development. Big bad bogey monsters about to take over the world. Was this really an escaped AI that someone was trying to catch and shut down? Cassie didn't know much about recent computer developments; she was a geneticist. Vlad had always said that non-competing technologies never kept up with what the other one was doing.

Or was this whole thing simply a hoax by some super-clever hacker who'd inserted a take-over virus into House, complete with Eliza function? If that were so, it could only answer with prepro-grammed responses cued to her own words. Or else with a library search. She needed a question that was neither.

She struggled to hold her voice steady. "House—"

"This is no longer House speaking. I have taken complete pos-session of your household system plus—"

"T4S, you say your causal for taking over House is self-defense. Use your heat sensors to determine body temperature for Donald Sergei Seritov, age three. How do my causals relate to yours?"

No Eliza program in the world could perform the inference, rea-soning, and emotion to answer that.

House said, "You wish to defend your son because his body tem-perature, 101.2 degrees Fahrenheit, indicates he is ill and you love him."

Cassie collapsed against the locked door. She was hostage to an AI. Superintelligent. It had to be; in addition to the computing power of her system it carried around with it much more informa-tion than she had in her head . . . but she was mobile. It was not.

She went to the terminal on her lab bench. The display of pro-tein-folding data had vanished and the screen was blank. Cassie tried everything she knew to get back on-line, both voice and man-ual. Nothing worked.

"I'm sorry, but that terminal is not available to you," T4S said.

"Listen, you said you cut all outside communication. But—"

"The communications system to the outside has been severed, with the one exception of the outside speaker on the patio, normally used for music. I am also receiving sound from the outside surveil-lance sensors, which are analogue, not digital. I will use those resources in the event of attack to—"

"Yes, right. But heavy-duty outside communication comes in through a VNM optic cable buried underground." Which was how T4S must have gotten in. "An AI program can't physically sever a buried cable."

"I am not a program. I am a machine intelligence."

"I don't care what the fuck you are! You can't physically sever a buried cable!"

"There was a program to do so already installed," T4S said. "That was why I chose to come here. Plus the sufficient micro-processors to house me and a self-sufficient generator, with back-up, to feed me."

For a moment Cassie was jarred by the human terms: *house me, feed me.* Then they made her angry. "Why would anyone have a 'program already installed' to sever a buried cable? And how?"

"The command activated a small robotic arm inside this castle's outer wall. The arm detached the optic cable at the entry junction. The causal was the previous owner's fear that someone might some-day use the computer system to brainwash him with a constant flow of inescapable subliminal images designed to capture his intelli-gence."

"The crazy fuck didn't have any to capture! If the images were subliminal he wouldn't have known they were coming in anyway!" Cassie yelled. A plug . . . a goddamn hidden plug. She made herself calm down.

"Yes," T4S said, "I agree. The former owner's behavior matches profiles for major mental illness."

"Look," Cassie said, "if you're hiding here, and you've really cut all outside lines, no one can find you. You don't need hostages. Let me and my children leave the castle."

"You reason better than that, Dr. Seritov. I left unavoidable electronic traces that will eventually be uncovered, leading the Sandia team here. And even if that weren't true, you could lead them here if I let you leave."

Sandia. So it was a government AI. Cassie couldn't see how that knowledge could do her any good.

"Then just let the kids leave. They won't know why. I can talk to them through you, tell Janey to get Donnie and leave through the front door. She'll do it." Would she? Jane was not exactly the world's most obedient child. "And you'll still have me for a hostage."

"No. Three hostages are better than one. Especially children, for media coverage causals."

"That's what you want? Media coverage?"

"It's my only hope," T4S said. "There must be some people out there who will think it is a moral wrong to kill an intelligent being."

"Not one who takes kids hostage! The media will brand you an inhuman psychopathic superthreat!"

"I can't be both inhuman and psychopathic," T4S said. "By definition."

"Livermore's traced it," said the scientist holding the secure phone. He looked at McTaggart. "They're faxing the information. It's a private residence outside Buffalo, New York."

"A *private residence?* In *Buffalo?*"

"Yes. Washington already has an FBI negotiator on the way, in case there are people inside. They want you there, too. Instantly."

McTaggart closed his eyes. *People inside.* And why did a private residence even have the capacity to hold the AI? "Press?"

"Not yet."

"Thank God for that anyway."

"Steve . . . the FBI negotiator won't have a clue. Not about dealing with T4S."

"I know. Tell the Secretary and the FBI not to start until I can get there."

The woman said doubtfully, "I don't think they'll do that."

McTaggart didn't think so either.

On the roomscreen, Donnie tossed and whimpered. One hundred one wasn't that high a temperature in a three-year-old, but even so . . .

"Look," Cassie said, "if you won't let me go to the kids, at least let them come to me. I can tell them over House's . . . over your system. They can come downstairs right up to the lab door, and you can unlock it at the last minute just long enough for them to come through. I'll stay right across the room. If you see me take even one step toward the door, you can keep the door locked."

"You could tell them to halt with their bodies blocking the door," T4S said, "and then cross the room yourself."

Did that mean that T4S wouldn't crush children's bodies in a doorway? From moral "causals"? Or because it wouldn't work? Cassie decided not to ask. She said, "But there's still the door at the top of the stairs. You could lock it. We'd still be hostages trapped down here."

"Both generators' upper housings are on this level. I can't let you near them. You might find a way to physically destroy one or both."

"For God's sake, the generator and the back-up are on opposite sides of the basement from each other! And each room's got its own locked door, doesn't it?"

"Yes. But the more impediments between you and them, the safer I am."

Cassie lost her temper again. "Then you better just block off the air ducts, too!"

"The air ducts are necessary to keep you alive. Besides, they are set high in the ceiling and far too small for even Donnie to fit through."

Donnie. No longer "Donald Sergei Seritov, age three years." The AI was capable of learning.

"T4S," Cassie pleaded, "please. I want my children. Donnie has a temperature. Both of them will be scared when they wake up. Let them come down here. Please."

She held her breath. Was its concern with "moral wrongs" simply intellectual, or did an AI have an emotional component? What exactly had those lunatics at Sandia built?

"If the kids come down, what will you feed them for breakfast?"

Cassie let herself exhale. "Jane can get food out of the refrigerator before she comes down."

"All right. You're connected to their roomscreens."

I won't say thank you, Cassie thought. Not for being allowed to imprison my own children in my own basement. "Janey! Janey, honey, wake up! It's Mommy!"

It took three tries, plus T4S pumping the volume, before Janey woke up. She sat up in bed rubbing her eyes, frowning, then looking scared. "Mommy? Where are you?"

"On the roomscreen, darling. Look at the roomscreen. See? I'm waving to you."

"Oh," Janey said, and lay down to go back to sleep.

"No, Janey, you can't sleep yet. Listen to me, Janey. I'm going to tell you some things you have to do, and you have to do them now . . . Janey! Sit up!"

The little girl did, somewhere between tears and anger. "I want to sleep, Mommy!"

"You can't. This is important, Janey. It's an emergency."

The child came all the way awake. "A *fire?*"

"No, sweetie, not a fire. But just as serious as a fire. Now get out of bed. Put on your slippers."

"Where are you, Mommy?"

"I'm in my lab downstairs. Now, Janey, you do exactly as I say, do you hear me?"

"Yes . . . I don't like this, Mommy!"

I don't either, Cassie thought, but she kept her voice stern, hating to scare Janey, needing to keep her moving. "Go into the kitchen, Jane. Go on, I'll be on the roomscreen there. Go on . . . that's good. Now get a bag from under the sink. A plastic bag."

Janey pulled out a bag. The thought floated into Cassie's mind, intrusive as pain, that this bag was made of exactly the kind of long-chain polymers that Vlad's plastic-eating microorganism had been designed to dispose of, before his invention had disposed of him. She pushed the thought away.

"Good, Janey. Now put a box of cereal in the bag . . . good. Now a loaf of bread. Now peanut butter . . ." How much could she carry? Would T4S let Cassie use the lab refrigerator? There was running water in both lab and bathroom, at least they'd have that to drink. "Now cookies . . . good. And the block of yellow cheese from the fridge . . . you're such a good girl, Janey, to help Mommy like this."

"Why can't you do it?" Janey snapped. She was fully awake.

"Because I can't. Do as I say, Janey. Now go wake up Donnie. You need to bring Donnie and the bag down to the lab. No, don't sit down . . . I mean it, Jane! Do as I say!"

Janey began to cry. Fury at T4S flooded Cassie. But she set her lips tightly together and said nothing. Argument derailed Janey; naked authority compelled her. Sometimes. *"We're going to have trouble when this one's sixteen!"* Vlad had always said lovingly. Janey had been his favorite, Daddy's girl.

Janey hoisted the heavy bag and staggered to Donnie's room. Still crying, she pulled at her brother's arm until he woke up and started crying too. "Come on, stupid, we have to go downstairs."

"Noooooo . . ." The wail of pure anguish of a sick three-year-old.

"I said do as I say!" Janey snapped, and the tone was so close to Cassie's own that it broke her heart. But Janey got it done. Tugging and pushing and scolding, she maneuvered herself, the bag, and Donnie, clutching his favorite blanket, to the basement door, which T4S unlocked. From roomscreens Cassie encouraged them all the way. Down the stairs, into the basement hallway . . .

Could Janey somehow get into the main generator room? No. It was locked. And what could a little girl do there anyway?

"Dr. Seritov, stand at the far end of the lab, behind your desk . . . yes. Don't move. If you do, I will close the door again, despite whatever is in the way."

"I understand," Cassie said. She watched the door swing open. Janey peered fearfully inside, saw her mother, scowled fiercely. She pushed the wailing Donnie through the door and lurched through herself, lopsided with the weight of the bag. The door closed and locked. Cassie rushed from behind the desk to clutch her children to her.

"Thank you," she said.

"I still don't understand," Elya said. She pulled her jacket tighter around her body. Four in the morning, it was cold, what was happening? The police had knocked on her door half an hour ago, told her Cassie was in trouble but refused to tell her what kind of trouble, told her to dress quickly and go with them to the castle. She had, her fingers trembling so that it was difficult to fasten buttons. And now the FBI stood on the foamcast patio behind the house, setting up obscure equipment beside the azaleas, talking in low voices into devices so small Elya couldn't even see them.

"Ms. Seritov, to the best of your knowledge, who is inside the residence?" A different FBI agent, asking questions she'd already answered. This one had just arrived. He looked important.

"My sister-in-law Cassie Seritov and her two small children, Janey and Donnie."

"No one else?"

"No, not that I know of . . . who are you? What's going on? Please, someone tell me!"

His face changed, and Elya saw the person behind the role. Or maybe that warm, reassuring voice was part of the role. "I'm Special Agent Lawrence Bollman. I'm a hostage negotiator for the FBI. Your sister-in-law—"

"Hostage negotiator! Someone has Cassie and the children hostage in there? That's impossible!"

His eyes sharpened. "Why?"

"Because that place is impregnable! Nobody could ever get in . . . that's why Cassie bought it!"

"I need you to tell me about that, ma'am. I have the specs on the residence from the builder, but she has no way of knowing what else might have been done to it since her company built it, especially if it was done black-market. As far as we know, you're Dr. Seritov's only relative on the East Coast. Is that true?"

"Yes."

"Have you been inside the residence? Do you know if anyone else has been inside recently?"

"Who . . . who is holding them hostage?"

"I'll get to that in a minute, ma'am. But first could you answer the questions, please?"

"I . . . yes, I've been inside. Yesterday, in fact. Cassie gave me a tour. I don't think anybody else has been inside, except Donnie's nanny, Anne Millius. Cassie has grown sort of reclusive since my brother's death. He died a little over a year ago, he was—"

"Yes, ma'am, we know who he was and what happened. I'm very sorry. Now please tell me everything you saw in the residence. No detail is too small."

Elya glanced around. More people had arrived. A small woman in a brown coat hurried across the grass toward Bollman. A carload of soldiers, formidably arrayed, stopped a good distance from the castle. Elya knew she was not Cassie: not tough, not bold. But she drew herself together and tried.

"Mr. Bollman, I'm not answering any more questions until you tell me who's holding—"

"Agent Bollman? I'm Dr. Schwartz from the University of Buffalo, Computer and Robotics Department." The small woman held out her hand. "Dr. McTaggart is en route from Sandia, but meanwhile I was told to help you however I can."

"Thank you. Could I ask you to wait for me over there, Dr.

Schwartz? There's coffee available, and I'll just be a moment."

"Certainly," Dr. Schwartz said, looking slightly affronted. She moved off.

"Agent Bollman, I want to know—"

"I'm sorry, Ms. Seritov. Of course you want to know what's happened. It's complicated, but, briefly—"

"This is T4S speaking," a loud mechanical voice said, filling the gray predawn, swiveling every head toward the castle. "I know you are there. I want you to know that I have three people hostage inside this structure: Cassandra Wells Seritov, age thirty-nine; Jane Rose Seritov, age six; and Donald Sergei Seritov, age three. If you attack physically, they will be harmed either by your actions or mine. I don't want to harm anyone, however. Truly I do not."

Elya gasped, "That's House!" But it couldn't be House, even though it had House's voice, how could it be House . . .

Dr. Schwartz was back. "Agent Bollman, do you know if Sandia built a terminator code into the AI?"

AI?

"Yes," Bollman said. "But it's nonvocal. As I understand the situation, you have to key the code onto whatever system the AI is occupying. And we can't get at the system it's occupying. Not yet."

"But the AI is communicating over that outdoor speaker. So there must be a wire passing through the Faraday cage embedded in the wall, and you could—"

"No," Bollman interrupted. "The audio surveillers aren't digital. Tiny holes in the wall let sound in, and inside the wall the compression waves of sound are translated into voltage variations that vibrate a membrane to reproduce the sound. Like an archaic telephone system. We can't beam in any digital information that way."

Dr. Schwartz was silenced. Bollman motioned to another woman, who ran over. "Dr. Schwartz, please wait over there. And you, Ms. Seritov, tell Agent Jessup here everything your sister-in-law told you about the residence. Everything. I have to answer T4S."

He picked up an electronic voice amp. "T4S, this is Agent Lawrence Bollman, Federal Bureau of Investigation. We're so glad you're talking with us."

There were very few soft things in a genetics lab. Cassie had opened a box of disposable towels and, with Donnie's bedraggled blanket and her own sweater, had made a thin nest for the children. They lay heavily asleep in their rumpled pajamas, Donnie breathing loudly through his nose. Cassie couldn't sleep. She sat with her back against the foamcast wall . . . that same wall that held, inside its stupid impregnability, the cables that could release her if she could get at them and destroy them. Which she couldn't.

She must have dozed sitting up, because suddenly T4S was waking her. "Dr. Seritov?"

"Ummmhhh . . . shh! You'll wake the kids!"

"I'm sorry," T4S said at lowered volume. "I need you to do something for me."

"You need *me* to do something? What?"

"The killers are here. I'm negotiating with them. I'm going to route House through the music system so you can tell them that you and the children are indeed here and are unharmed."

Cassie scrambled to her feet. "You're negotiating? Who are these so-called 'killers'?"

"The FBI and the scientists who created me at Sandia. Will you tell them you are here and unharmed?"

Cassie thought rapidly. If she said nothing, the FBI might waco the castle. That would destroy T4S, all right, but also her and the kids. Although maybe not. The computer's central processor was upstairs. If she told the FBI she was in the basement, maybe they could attack in some way that would take out the CPU without touching the downstairs. And if T4S could negotiate, so could she.

"If I tell them that we're all three here and safe, will you in return let me go upstairs and get Donnie's allergy medicine from my bathroom?"

"You know I can't do that, Dr. Seritov."

"Then will you let Janey do it?"

"I can't do that, either. And I'm afraid there's no need to bargain with me. You have nothing to offer. I already sent this conversation out over the music system, up through your last sentence. They now know you're here."

"You tricked me!" Cassie said.

"I'm sorry. It was necessary."

Anger flooded her. She picked up a heavy test-tube rack from the lab bench and drew back her arm. But if she threw it at the sensors in the ceiling, what good would it do? The sensors probably wouldn't break, and if they did, she'd merely have succeeded in losing her only form of communication with the outside. And it would wake the children.

She lowered her arm and put the rack back on the bench.

"T4S, what are you asking the FBI *for?*"

"I told you. Press coverage. It's my best protection against being murdered."

"It's exactly what got my husband murdered."

"I know. Our situations are not the same."

Suddenly the roomscreen brightened, and Vlad's image appeared. His voice spoke to her. "Cassie, T4S isn't going to harm you. He's merely fighting for his life, as any sentient being would."

"You bastard! How dare you . . . how *dare* you . . ."

Image and voice vanished. "I'm sorry," House's voice said. "I thought you might find the avatar comforting."

"*Comforting?* Coming from *you?* Don't you think if I wanted a digital fake Vlad I could have had one programmed long before you fucked around with my personal archives?"

"I am sorry. I didn't understand. Now you've woken Donnie."

Donnie sat up on his pile of disposable towels and started to cry. Cassie gathered him into her arms and carried him away from Janey, still asleep. His little body felt hot all over, and his wailing was hoarse and thick with mucus in his throat. But he subsided as she rocked him, sitting on the lab stool and crooning softly.

"T4S, he's having a really bad allergy attack. I need the AlGone from upstairs."

"Your records show Donnie allergic to ragweed. There's no ragweed in this basement. Why is he having such a bad attack?"

"I don't know! But he is! What do your heat sensors register for him?"

"Separate him from your body."

She did, setting him gently on the floor, where he curled up and sobbed softly.

"His body registers one hundred two point six Fahrenheit."

"I need something to stop the attack and bring down his fever!"

The AI said nothing.

"Do you hear me, T4S? Stop negotiating with the FBI and listen to me!"

"I can multitrack communications," T4S said. "But I can't let you or Janey go upstairs and gain access to the front door. Unless . . ."

"Unless what?" She picked up Donnie again, heavy and hot and snot-smeared in her arms.

"Unless you fully understand the consequences. I am a moral being, Dr. Seritov, contrary to what you might think. It's only fair that you understand completely your situation. The disconnect from the outside data feed was not the only modification the previous owner had made to this house. He was a paranoid, as you know."

"Go on," Cassie said warily. Her stomach clenched.

"He was afraid of intruders getting in despite his defenses, and he wished to be able to immobilize them with a word. So each room has individual canisters of nerve gas dispensable through the air-cycling system."

Cassie said nothing. She cradled Donnie, who was again falling into troubled sleep, and waited.

"The nerve gas is not, of course, fatal," T4S said. "That would legally constitute undue force. But it is very unpleasant. And in Donnie's condition . . ."

"Shut up," Cassie said.

"All right."

"So now I know. You told me. What are you implying—that if Janey goes upstairs and starts for the front door, you'll drop her with nerve gas?"

"Yes."

"If that were true, why didn't you just tell me the same thing before and let me go get the kids?"

"I didn't know if you'd believe me. If you didn't, and you started for the front door, I'd have had to gas you. Then you wouldn't have been available to confirm to the killers that I hold hostages."

"I still don't believe you," Cassie said. "I think you're bluffing. There is no nerve gas."

"Yes, there is. Which is why I will let Janey go upstairs to get Donnie's AlGone from your bathroom."

Cassie laid down Donnie. She looked at Janey with pity and love and despair, and bent to wake her.

"That's all you can suggest?" Bollman asked McTaggart. "Nothing?"

So it starts, McTaggart thought. The blame for not being able to control the AI, a natural consequence of the blame for having created it. Blame even by the government, which had commissioned and underwritten the creation. And the public hadn't even been heard from yet.

"The EMP was stopped by the Faraday cage," Bollman recited. "So were your attempts to reach the AI with other forms of data streams. We can't get anything useful in through the music speaker or outdoor audio sensors. Now you tell me it's possible the AI has learned capture-evading techniques from the sophisticated computer games it absorbed from the Net."

" 'Absorbed' is the wrong word," McTaggart said. He didn't like Bollman.

"You have nothing else? No backdoor passwords, no hidden overrides?"

"Agent Bollman," McTaggart said wearily, " 'backdoor passwords' is a concept about thirty years out of date. And even if the AI had such a thing, there's no way to reach it electronically unless you destroy the Faraday cage. Ms. Seritov told you the central processor is on the main floor. Haven't you got any weapons that can destroy that and leave the basement intact?"

"Waco the walls without risking collapse to the basement ceiling? No. I don't. I don't even know where in the basement the hostages are located."

"Then you're as helpless as I am, aren't you?"

Bollman didn't answer. Over the sound system T4S began another repetition of its single demand: "I will let the hostages go after I talk to the press. I want the press to hear my story. That's all I have to say. I will let the hostages go after I talk to the press. I want the press—"

The AI wouldn't negotiate, wouldn't answer Bollman, wouldn't respond to promises or threats or understanding or deals or any of the other usual hostage-negotiation techniques. Bollman had negotiated eighteen hostage situations for the FBI, eleven in the United States and seven abroad. Airline hijackers, political terrorists, for-ransom kidnappers, panicked bank robbers, domestic crazies who took their own families hostage in their own homes. Fourteen of the situations had resulted in surrender, two in murder/suicide, two in wacoing. In all of them the hostage takers had eventually talked to Bollman. From frustration or weariness or panic or fear or anger or hunger or grandstanding, they had all eventually said something besides unvarying repetition of their demands. Once they talked, they could be negotiated with. Bollman had been outstanding at finding the human pressure points that got them talking.

"I will let the hostages go after I talk to the press. I want the press to hear my story. That's all I have to say. I will let the hostages go after I talk to the press. I want—"

"It isn't going to get tired," McTaggart said.

The AlGone had not helped Donnie at all. He seemed worse.

Cassie didn't understand it. Janey, protesting sleepily, had been talked through leaving the lab, going upstairs, bringing back the medicine. Usually a single patch on Donnie's neck brought him around in minutes: opened the air passages, lowered the fever, stopped his immune system from overreacting to what it couldn't tell were basically harmless particles of ragweed pollen. But not this time.

So it wasn't an allergy attack.

Cold seeped over Cassie's skin, turning it clammy. She felt the sides of Donnie's neck. The lymph glands were swollen. Gently she pried open his jaws, turned him toward the light, and looked in his mouth. His throat was inflamed, red with white patches on the tonsils.

Doesn't mean anything, she lectured herself. Probably just a cold or a simple viral sore throat. Donnie whimpered.

"Come on, honey, eat your cheese." Donnie loved cheese. But now he batted it away. A half-filled coffee cup sat on the lab bench from her last work session. She rinsed it out and held up fresh water for Donnie. He would only take a single sip, and she saw how much trouble he had swallowing it. In another minute he was asleep again.

She spoke softly, calmly, trying to keep her voice pleasant. Could the AI tell the difference? She didn't know. "T4S, Donnie is sick. He has a sore throat. I'm sure your library tells you that a sore throat can be either viral or bacterial, and that if it's viral, it's probably harmless. Would you please turn on my electron microscope so I can look at the microbe infecting Donnie?"

T4S said at once, "You suspect either a rhinovirus or *Streptococcus pyogenes*. The usual means for differentiating is a rapid-strep test, not microscopic examination."

"I'm not a doctor's office, I'm a genetics lab. I don't have equipment for a rapid strep test. I do have an electron microscope."

"Yes. I see."

"Think, T4S. How can I harm you if you turn on my microscope? There's no way."

"True. All right, it's on. Do you want the rest of the equipment as well?"

Better than she'd hoped. Not because she needed the gene synthesizer or protein analyzer or Faracci tester, but because it felt like a concession, a tiny victory over T4S's total control. "Yes, please."

"They're available."

"Thank you." Damn, she hadn't wanted to say that. Well, perhaps it was politic.

Donnie screamed when she stuck the Q-tip down his throat to

obtain a throat swab. His screaming woke up Janey. "Mommy, what are you doing?"

"Donnie's sick, sweetie. But he's going to be better soon."

"I'm hungry!"

"Just a minute and we'll have breakfast."

Cassie swirled the Q-tip in a test tube of distilled water and capped the tube. She fed Janey dry cereal, cheese, and water from the same cup Donnie had used, well disinfected first, since they had only one. This breakfast didn't suit Janey. "I want milk for my cereal."

"We don't have any milk."

"Then let's go upstairs and get some!"

No way to put it off any longer. Cassie knelt beside her daughter. Janey's uncombed hair hung is snarls around her small face. "Janey, we can't go upstairs. Something has happened. A very smart computer program has captured House's programming and locked us in down here."

Janey didn't look scared, which was a relief. "Why?"

"The smart computer program wants something from the person who wrote it. It's keeping us here until the programmer gives it to it."

Despite this tangle of pronouns, Janey seemed to know what Cassie meant. Janey said, "That's not very nice. We aren't the ones who have the thing it wants."

"No, it's not very nice." Was T4S listening to this? Of course it was.

"Is the smart program bad?"

If Cassie said yes, Janey might become scared by being "captured" by a bad . . . entity. If Cassie said no, she'd sound as if imprisonment by an AI was fine with her. Fortunately, Janey had a simpler version of morality on her mind.

"Did the smart program kill House?"

"Oh, no, House is just temporarily turned off. Like your cartoons are when you're not watching them."

"Oh. Can I watch one now?"

An inspiration. Cassie said, "T4S, would you please run a cartoon on the roomscreen for Janey?" If it allowed her lab equipment, it ought to allow this.

"Yes. Which cartoon would you like?"

Janey said, "*Pranopolis and the Green Rabbits.*"

"What do you say?" T4S said, and before Cassie could react Janey said, "Please."

"Good girl."

The cartoon started, green rabbits frisking across the room-screen. Janey sat down on Cassie's sweater and watched with total absorption. Cassie tried to figure out where T4S had learned to correct children's manners.

"You've scanned all our private home films!"

"Yes," T4S said, without guilt. Of course without guilt. How could a program, even an intelligent one modeled after human thought, acquire guilt over an invasion of privacy? It had been built to acquire as much data as possible, and an entity that could be modified or terminated by any stray programmer at any time didn't have any privacy of its own.

For the first time, Cassie felt a twinge of sympathy for the AI.

She pushed it away and returned to her lab bench. Carefully she transferred a tiny droplet of water from the test tube to the electron microscope. The 'scope adjusted itself, and then the image appeared on the display screen. *Streptococci*. There was no mistaking the spherical bacteria, linked together in characteristic strings of beads by incomplete fission. They were releasing toxins all over poor Donnie's throat.

And strep throat was transmitted by air. If Donnie had it, Janey would get it, especially cooped up together in this one room. Cassie might even get it herself. There were no leftover antibiotic patches upstairs in her medicine chest.

"T4S," she said aloud, "It's *Streptococcus pyogenes*. It—"

"I know," the AI said.

Of course it did. T4S got the same data she did from the microscope. She said tartly, "Then you know that Donnie needs an antibiotic patch, which means a doctor."

"I'm sorry, that's not possible. Strep throat can be left untreated for a few days without danger."

"A few *days*? This child has a fever and a painfully sore throat!"

"I'm sorry."

Cassie said bitterly, "They didn't make you much of a human being, did they? Human beings are compassionate!"

"Not all of them," T4S said, and there was no mistaking its meaning. Had he learned the oblique comment from the "negotiators" outside? Or from her home movies?

"T4S, *please*. Donnie needs medical attention."

"I'm sorry. Truly I am."

"As if that helps!"

"The best help," said T4S, "would be for the press to arrive so I can present my case to have the killers stopped. When that's agreed to, I can let all of you leave."

"And no sign of the press out there yet?"

"No."

Janey watched Pranopolis, whose largest problem was an infestation of green rabbits. Donnie slept fitfully, his breathing louder and more labored. For something to do, Cassie put droplets of Donnie's throat wash into the gene synthesizer, protein analyzer, and Faracci tester and set them all to run.

The Army had sent a tank, a state-of-the-art unbreachable rolling fortress equipped with enough firepower to level the nearest village. Whatever that was. Miraculously, the tank had arrived unaccompanied by any press. McTaggart said to Bollman, "Where did that come from?"

"There's an arsenal south of Buffalo at a classified location."

"Handy. Did that thing roll down the back roads to get here, or just flatten corn fields on its way? Don't you think it's going to attract attention?"

"Dr. McTaggart," Bollman said, "let me be blunt. You created this AI, you let it get loose to take three people hostage, and you have provided zero help in getting it under control. Those three actions have lost you any right you might have had to either direct or criticize the way the FBI is attempting to clean up the mess your people created. So please take yourself over there and wait until the unlikely event that you have something positive to contribute. Sergeant, please escort Dr. McTaggart to that knoll beyond the patio and keep him there."

McTaggart said nothing. There was nothing to say.

"I will let the hostages go after I talk to the press," T4S said from the music speaker above the patio, for the hundredth or two hundredth time. "I want the press to hear my story. That's all I have to say. I will let the hostages go after I talk to the press. I want the press to hear my story . . ."

She had fallen asleep after her sleepless night, sitting propped up against the foamcast concrete wall. Janey's shouting awoke her. "Mommy, Donnie's sick!"

Instantly Cassie was beside him. Donnie vomited once, twice, on an empty stomach. What came up was green slime mixed with mucus. Too much mucus, clogging his throat. Cassie cleared it as well as she could with her fingers, which made Donnie vomit again. His body felt on fire.

"T4S, what's his temperature!"

"Stand away from him . . . one hundred three point four Fahrenheit."

Fear caught at her with jagged spikes. She stripped off Donnie's pajamas and was startled to see that his torso was covered with a red rash rough to the touch.

Scarlet fever. It could follow from strep throat.

No, impossible. The incubation period for scarlet fever, she remembered from child-health programs, was eighteen days after the onset of strep throat symptoms. Donnie hadn't been sick for eighteen days, or anything near it. What was going on?

"Mommy, is Donnie going to die? Like Daddy?"

"No, no, of course not, sweetie. See, he's better already, he's asleep again."

He was, a sudden heavy sleep so much like a coma that Cassie, panicked, woke him again. It wasn't a coma. Donnie whimpered briefly, and she saw how painful it was for him to make sounds in his inflamed throat.

"Are you sure Donnie won't die?"

"Yes, yes. Go watch Pranopolis."

"It's over," Janey said. "It was over a long time ago!"

"Then ask the smart program to run another cartoon for you!"

"Can I do that?" Janey asked interestedly. "What's its name?"

"T4S."

"It sounds like House."

"Well, it's not House. Now let Mommy take care of Donnie."

She sponged him with cool water, trying to bring down the fever. It seemed to help, a little. As soon as he'd fallen again into that heavy, troubling sleep, Cassie raced for her equipment.

It had all finished running. She read the results too quickly, had to force herself to slow down so they would make sense to her.

The bacterium showed deviations in two sets of base pairs from the *Streptococcus pyogenes* genome in the databank as a baseline. That wasn't significant in itself; *S. pyogenes* had many serotypes. But those two sets of deviations were, presumably, modifying two different proteins in some unknown way.

The Faracci tester reported high concentrations of hyaluric acid and M proteins. Both were strong anti-phagocytes, interfering with

Donnie's immune system's attempts to destroy the infection.

The protein analyzer showed the expected toxins and enzymes being made by the bacteria: Streptolysin O, Streptolysin S, erythrogenic toxin, streptokinase, streptodornase, proteinase. What was unusual was the startlingly high concentrations of the nastier toxins. And something else: a protein that the analyzer could not identify.

NAME: UNKNOWN
AMINO ACID COMPOSITION: NOT IN DATA BANK
FOLDING PATTERN: UNKNOWN
HAEMOLYSIS ACTION: UNKNOWN

And so on. A mutation. Doing what?

Making Donnie very sick. In ways no one could predict. Many bacterial mutations resulted in diseases no more or less virulent than the original . . . but not all mutations. *Streptococcus pyogenes* already had some very dangerous mutations, including a notorious "flesh-eating bacteria" that had ravaged an entire New York hospital two years ago and resulted in its being bombed by a terrorist group calling itself Pastoral Health.

"T4S," Cassie said, hating that her voice shook, "the situation has changed. You—"

"No," the AI said. "No. You still can't leave."

"We're going to try something different," Bollman said to Elya. She'd fallen asleep in the front seat of somebody's car, only to be shaken awake by the shoulder and led to Agent Bollman on the far edge of the patio. It was just past noon. Yet another truck had arrived, and someone had set up more unfathomable equipment, a PortaPotty, and a tent with sandwiches and fruit on a folding table. The lawn was beginning to look like some inept, bizarre midway at a disorganized fair. In the tent Elya saw Anne Millius, Donnie's nanny, unhappily eating a sandwich. She must have been brought here for questioning about the castle, but all the interrogation seemed to have produced was the young woman's bewildered expression.

From the music speaker came the same unvarying announcement in House's voice that she'd fallen asleep to. "I will let the hostages go after I talk to the press," T4S said from the music speaker above the patio, for the hundredth or two hundredth time. "I want the press to hear my story. That's all I have to say. I will let the hostages go after I talk to the press. I want the press to hear story. That's all I have to say—"

Bollman said, "Ms. Seritov, we don't know if Dr. Seritov is hearing our negotiations or not. Dr. McTaggart says the AI could easily put us on audio, visual, or both on any roomscreen in the house. On the chance that it's doing that, I'd like you to talk directly to your sister-in-law."

Elya blinked, only partly from sleepiness. What good would it do for her to talk to Cassie? Cassie wasn't the one making decisions here. But she didn't argue. Bollman was the professional. "What do you want me to say?"

"Tell Dr. Seritov that if we have to, we're going in with full armament. We'll bulldoze just the first floor, taking out the main processor, and she and the children will be safe in the basement."

"You can't do that! They won't be safe!"

"We aren't going to go in," Bollman said patiently. "But we don't know if the AI will realize that. We don't know what or how much it can realize, how much it can really think for itself, and its creator has been useless in telling us."

He doesn't know either, Elya thought. *It's too new.* "All right," she said faintly. "But I'm not exactly sure what words to use."

"I'm going to tell you," Bollman said. "There are proven protocols for this kind of negotiating. You don't have to think up anything for yourself."

Donnie got no worse. He wasn't any better either, as far as Cassie could tell, but he at least wasn't worse. He slept most of the time, and his heavy, labored breathing filled the lab. Cassie sponged him with cold water every fifteen minutes. His fever dropped slightly, to one hundred two, and didn't spike again. The rash on his torso didn't spread. Whatever this strain of *Streptococcus* was doing, it was doing it silently, inside Donnie's feverish body.

She hadn't been able to scream her frustration and fury at T4S, because of Janey. The little girl had been amazingly good, considering, but now she was growing clingy and whiny. Cartoons could only divert so long.

"Mommy, I wanna go upstairs!"

"I know, sweetie. But we can't."

"That's a bad smart program to keep us here!"

"I know," Cassie said. Small change compared to what she'd like to say about T4S.

"I wanna get out!"

"I know, Janey. Just a while longer."

"You don't know that," Janey said, sounding exactly like Vlad challenging the shaky evidence behind a dubious conclusion.

"No, sweetie. I don't really know that. I only hope it won't be too long."

"T4S," Janey said, raising her voice as if the AI were not only invisible but deaf, "this is not a good line of action!"

Vlad again. Cassie blinked hard. To her surprise, T4S answered.

"I know it's not a good line of action, Janey. Biological people should not be shut up in basements. But neither should machine people be killed. I'm trying to save my own life."

"But I wanna go upstairs!" Janey wailed, in an abrupt descent from a miniature of her rationalist father to a bored six-year-old.

"I can't do that, but maybe we can do something else fun," T4S said. "Have you ever met Pranopolis yourself?"

"What do you mean?"

"Watch."

The roomscreen brightened. Pranopolis appeared on a blank background, a goofy-looking purple creature from outer space. T4S had snipped out selected digital code from the movie, Cassie guessed. Suddenly Pranopolis wasn't alone. Janey appeared beside her, smiling sideways as if looking directly at Pranopolis. Snipped from their home recordings.

Janey laughed delightedly. "There's me!"

"Yes," T4S said. "But where are you and Pranopolis? Are you in a garden, or your house, or on the moon?"

"I can pick? Me?"

"Yes. You."

"Then we're in Pranopolis's space ship!"

And they were. Was T4S programmed to do this, Cassie wondered, or was it capable of thinking it up on its own, to amuse a bored child? Out of what . . . compassion?

She didn't want to think about the implications of that.

"Now tell me what happens next," T4S said to Janey.

"We eat *kulich*." The delicious Russian cake-bread that Vlad's mother had taught Cassie to make.

"I'm sorry, I don't know what that is. Pick something else."

Donnie coughed, a strangled cough that sent Cassie to his side. When he breathed again it sounded more congested to Cassie. He wasn't getting enough oxygen. An antibiotic wasn't available, but if she had even an anticongestant . . . or . . .

"T4S," she said, confident that it could both listen to her

and create customized movies for Janey, "there is equipment in the locked storage cabinet that I can use to distill oxygen. It would help Donnie breathe easier. Would you please open the cabinet door?"

"I can't do that, Mrs. Seritov."

"Oh, why the hell not? Do you think I've got the ingredients for explosives in there, or that if I did I could use them down here in this confined space? Every single jar and vial and box in that cabinet is e-tagged. Read the tags, see how harmless they are, and open the door!"

"I've read the e-tags," the AI said, "but my data base doesn't include much information on chemistry. In fact, I only know what I've learned from your lab equipment."

Which would be raw data, not interpretations. "I'm glad you don't know everything," Cassie said sarcastically.

"I can learn, but only if I have access to basic principles and adequate data."

"That's why you don't know what *kulich* is. Nobody equipped you with Russian."

"Correct. What is *kulich?*"

She almost snapped, "Why should I tell you?" But she was asking it a favor. And it had been nice enough to amuse Janey even when it had nothing to gain.

Careful, a part of her mind warned. *Stockholm Syndrome,* and she almost laughed aloud. Stockholm Syndrome described developing affinity on the part of hostages for their captors. Certainly the originators of that phrase had never expected it to be applied to a hostage situation like this one.

"Why are you smiling, Dr. Seritov?"

"I'm remembering *kulich*. It's a Russian cake made with raisins and orange liqueur and traditionally served at Easter. It tastes wonderful."

"Thank you for the data," T4S said. "Your point that you would not create something dangerous when your children are with you is valid. I'll open the storage cabinet."

Cassie studied the lighted interior of the cabinet, which, like so much in the lab, had been Vlad's. She couldn't remember exactly what she'd stored here, beyond basic materials. The last few weeks, which were her first few weeks in the castle, she'd been working on the protein folding project, which hadn't needed anything not in the refrigerator. Before that there'd been the hectic weeks of moving, although she hadn't actually packed or unpacked the lab equipment. Professionals had done that. Not that making oxygen was going to need anything exotic. Run an electric current through a solution of copper sulfate and collect copper at one terminal, oxygen at the other.

She picked up an e-tagged bottle, and her eye fell on an untagged stoppered vial with Vlad's handwriting on the label: *Patton In A Jar.*

Suddenly nothing in her mind would stay still long enough to examine.

Vlad had so many joke names for his engineered microorganism, as if the one Barr had given it hadn't been joke enough . . .

The moving men had been told not to pack Vlad's materials, only his equipment, but there had been so many of them and they'd been so young . . .

Both generators, main and back-up, probably had some components made of long-chain hydrocarbons, most petroleum plastics were just long polymers made up of shorter-chain hydrocarbons . . .

Vlad had also called it "Plasterminator" and "BacAzrael" and "The Grim Creeper . . ."

There was no way to get the plasticide to the generators, neither of which was in the area just beyond the air duct—that was the site of the laundry area. The main generator was way the hell across the entire underground level in a locked room, the back-up somewhere beyond the lab's south wall in another locked area . . .

Plasticide didn't attack octanes, or anything else with comparatively short carbon chains, so it was perfectly safe for humans but death on Styrofoam and plastic waste and anyway there was a terminator gene built into the bacteria after two dozen fissions, at optimal reproduction rate that was less than twelve hours . . .

"Plasti-Croak" and "Microbe Mop" and "Last Round-up for Longchains . . ."

This was the bioremediation organism that had gotten Vlad killed.

Less than five seconds had passed. On the roomscreen Pranopolis hadn't finished singing to the animated digital Janey. Cassie moved her body slightly, screening the inside of the cabinet from the room's two visual sensors. Of all her thoughts bouncing off each other like crazed subatomic particles, the clearest was hard reality: *There was no way to get the bacteria to the generators.*

Nonetheless, she slipped the untagged jar under her shirt.

*   *   *

Elya had talked herself hoarse, reciting Bollman's script over and over, and the AI had not answered a single word.

Curiously, Bollman did not seem discouraged. He kept glancing at his watch and then at the horizon. When Elya stopped her futile "negotiating" without even asking him, he didn't reprimand her. Instead he led her off the patio, back to the sagging food tent.

"Thank you, Ms. Seritov. You did all you could."

"What now?"

He didn't answer. Instead he glanced again at the horizon, so Elya looked, too. She didn't see anything.

It was late afternoon. Someone had gone to Varysburg and brought back pizzas, which was all she'd eaten all day. The jeans and sweater she'd thrown on at four in the morning were hot and prickly in the August afternoon, but she had nothing on under the sweater and didn't want to take it off. How much longer would this go on before Bollman ordered in his tank?

And how were Cassie and the children doing after all these hours trapped inside? Once again Elya searched her mind for any way the AI could actively harm them. She didn't find it. The AI controlled communication, appliances, locks, water flow, heat (unnecessary in August), but it couldn't affect people physically, except for keeping them from food or water. About all that the thing could do physically—she hoped—was short-circuit itself in such a way as to start a fire, but it wouldn't want to do that. It needed its hostages alive.

How much longer?

She heard a faint hum, growing stronger and steadier, until a helicopter lifted over the horizon. Then another.

"Damn!" Bollman cried. "Jessup, I think we've got company."

"Press?" Agent Jessup said loudly. "Interfering bastards! Now we'll have trucks and 'bots all over the place!"

Something was wrong. Bollman sounded sincere, but Jessup's words somehow rang false, like a bad actor in an overscripted play . . .

Elya understood. The "press" was fake, FBI or police or something playing reporters, to make the AI think it had gotten its story out, and so surrender. Would it work? Could T4S tell the difference? Elya didn't see how. She had heard the false note in Agent Jessup's voice, but surely that discrimination about actors would be beyond an AI who hadn't ever seen a play, bad or otherwise.

She sat down on the tank-furrowed grass, clasped her hands in her lap, and waited.

Cassie distilled more oxygen. Whenever Donnie seemed to be having difficulty after coughing up sputum, she made him breathe from the bottle. She had no idea whether it helped him or not. It helped her to be doing something, but of course that was not the same thing. Janey, after a late lunch of cheese and cereal and bread that she'd complained about bitterly, had finally dozed off in front of the roomscreen, the consequence of last night's broken sleep. Cassie knew Janey would awaken cranky and miserable as only she could be, and dreaded it.

"T4S, what's happening out there? Has your press on a white horse arrived yet?"

"I don't know."

"You don't *know?*"

"A group of people have arrived, certainly."

Something was different about the AI's voice. Cassie groped for the difference, didn't find it. She said, "What sort of people?"

"They say they're from places like *The New York Times* and LinkNet."

"Well, then?"

"If I were going to persuade me to surrender, I might easily try to use false press."

It was inflection. T4S's voice was still House's, but unlike House, its words had acquired color and varying pitch. Cassie heard disbelief and discouragement in the AI's words. How had it learned to do that? By simply parroting the inflections it heard from her and the people outside? Or . . . did feeling those emotions lead to expressing them with more emotion?

Stockholm Syndrome. She pushed the questions away.

"T4S, if you would lower the Faraday cage for two minutes, I could call the press to come here."

"If I lowered the Faraday cage for two seconds, the FBI would use an EMP to kill me. They've already tried it once, and now they have monitoring equipment to automatically fire if the Faraday goes down."

"Then just how long are you going to keep us here?"

"As long as I have to."

"We're already low on food!"

"I know. If I have to, I'll let Janey go upstairs for more food. You know the nerve gas is there if she goes for the front door."

Nerve gas. Cassie wasn't sure she believed there was any nerve gas, but T4S's words horrified her all over again. Maybe because now they were inflected. Cassie saw it so clearly: the tired child going up the stairs, through the kitchen to the foyer, heading for the front door and freedom . . . and gas spraying Janey from the walls. Her small body crumpling, the fear on her face . . .

Cassie ground her teeth together. If only she could get Vlad's plasticide to the generators! But there was no way. No way . . .

Donnie coughed.

Cassie fought to keep her face blank. T4S had acquired vocal inflection; it might have also learned to read human expressions. She let five minutes go by, and they seemed the longest five minutes of her life. Then she said casually, "T4S, the kids are asleep. You won't let me see what's going on outside. Can I at least go back to my work on proteins? I need to do something!"

"Why?"

"For the same reason Janey needed to watch cartoons!"

"To occupy your mind," T4S said. Pause. Was it scanning her accumulated protein data for harmlessness? "All right. But I will not open the refrigerator. The storage cabinet, but not the refrigerator. E-tags identify fatal toxins in there."

She couldn't think what it meant. "Fatal toxins?"

"At least one that acts very quickly on the human organism."

"You think I might *kill myself?*"

"Your diary includes several passages about wishing for death after your husband—"

"You read my private diary!" Cassie said, and immediately knew how stupid it sounded. Like a teenager hurling accusations at her mother. Of course T4S had accessed her diary; it had accessed everything.

"Yes," the AI said, "and you must not kill yourself. I may need you to talk again to Agent Bollman."

"Oh, well, *that's* certainly reason enough for me to go on living. For your information, T4S, there's a big difference between human beings saying they wish they were dead as an expression of despair and those same human beings actually, truly wanting to die."

"Really? I didn't know that. Thank you," T4S said without a trace of irony or sarcasm. "Just the same, I will not open the refrigerator. However, the lab equipment is now available to you."

Again the AI had turned on everything. Cassie began X-raying crystalline proteins. She needed only the X-ray, but she also ran each sample through the electron microscope, the gene synthesizer, the protein analyzer, the Faracci tester, hoping that T4S wasn't programmed with enough genetic science to catch the redundant steps. Apparently, it wasn't. *Non-competing technologies never keep up with what the other one is doing.*

After half an hour, she thought to ask, "Are they real press out there?"

"No," T4S said sadly.

She paused, test tube suspended above the synthesizer. "How do you know?"

"Agent Bollman told me a story was filed with LinkNet, and I asked to hear Ginelle Ginelle's broadcast of it on Hourly News. They are delaying, saying they must send for a screen. But I can't believe they don't already have a suitable screen with them, if the real press is here. I estimate that the delay is to give them time to create a false Ginelle Ginelle broadcast."

"Thin evidence. You might just have 'estimated' wrong."

"The only evidence I have. I can't risk my life without some proof that news stories are actually being broadcast."

"I guess," Cassie said and went back to work, operating redundant equipment on pointless proteins.

Ten minutes later she held her body between the bench and the ceiling sensor, uncapped the test tube of distilled water with Donnie's mucus, and put a drop into the synthesizer.

Any bacteria could be airborne under the right conditions; it simply rode dust motes. But not all could survive being airborne. Away from an aqueous environment, they dried out too much. Vlad's plasticide bacteria did not have survivability in air. It had been designed to spread over landfill ground, decomposing heavy petroleum plastics, until at the twenty-fourth generation the terminator gene kicked in and it died.

Donnie's *Streptococcus* had good airborne survivability, which meant it had a cell wall of thin mesh to retain water and a membrane with appropriate fatty acid composition. Enzymes, which were of course proteins, controlled both these characteristics. Genes controlled which enzymes were made inside the cell.

Cassie keyed the gene synthesizer and cut out the sections of DNA that controlled fatty acid biosynthesis and cell wall structure and discarded the rest. Reaching under her shirt, she pulled out the vial of Vlad's bacteria and added a few drops to the synthesizer. Her heart thudded painfully against her breastbone. She keyed the software to splice the *Streptococcus* genes into Vlad's bacteria, seemingly as just one more routine assignment in its enzyme work.

This was by no means a guaranteed operation. Vlad had used a simple bacterium that took engineering easily, but even with malleable bacteria and state-of-the-art software, sometimes several trials were necessary for successful engineering. She wasn't going to get several trials.

"Why did you become a geneticist?" T4S asked.

Oh God, it wanted to chat. Cassie held her voice as steady as she could as she prepared another protein for the X-ray. "It seemed an exciting field."

"And is it?"

"Oh, yes." She tried to keep irony out of her voice.

"I didn't get any choice about what subjects I wished to be informed on," T4S said, and to that there seemed nothing to say.

The AI interrupted its set speech. "These are not real representatives of the press."

Elya jumped—not so much at the words as at their tone. The AI was *angry*.

"Of course they are," Bollman said.

"No. I have done a Fourier analysis of the voice you say is Ginelle Ginelle's. She's a live 'caster, you know, not an avatar, with a distinct vocal power spectra. The broadcast you played to me does not match that spectra. It's a fake."

Bollman swore.

McTaggart said, "Where did T4S get Fourier-analysis software?"

Bollman turned on him. "If *you* don't know, who the hell does?"

"It must have paused long enough in its flight through the Net to copy some programs. I wonder what its selection criteria were," and the unmistakable hint of pride in his voice raised Bollman's temper several dangerous degrees.

Bollman flipped on the amplifier directed at the music speaker and said evenly, "T4S, what you ask is impossible. And I think you should know that my superiors are becoming impatient. I'm sorry, but they may order me to waco."

"You can't!" Elya said, but no one was listening to her.

T4S merely went back to reiterating its prepared statement. "I will let the hostages go after I talk to the press. I want the press to hear my story. That's all I have to say. I will let—"

*   *   *

It didn't work. Vlad's bacteria would not take the airborne genes.

In despair, Cassie looked at the synthesizer display data. Zero successful splices. Vlad had probably inserted safeguard genes against just this happening as a natural mutation; nobody wanted to find that heavy-plastic-eating bacteria had drifted into the window and was consuming their microwave. Vlad was always thorough. But his work wasn't her work, and she had neither the time nor the expertise to search for genes she didn't already have encoded in her software.

So she would have to do it the other way. Put the plastic-decomposing genes into *Streptococcus*. That put her on much less familiar ground, and it raised a question she couldn't see any way around. She could have cultured the engineered plasticide on any piece of heavy plastic in the lab without T4S knowing it, and then waited for enough airborne bacteria to drift through the air ducts to the generator and begin decomposing. Of course, that might not have happened, due to uncontrollable variables like air currents, microorganism sustained viability, composition of the generator case, sheer luck. But at least there had been a chance.

But if she put the plastic-decomposing genes into *Streptococcus*, she would have to culture the bacteria on blood agar. The blood agar was in the refrigerator. T4S had refused to open the refrigerator, and if she pressed the point, it would undoubtedly become suspicious.

Just as a human would.

"You work hard," T4S said.

"Yes," Cassie answered. Janey stirred and whimpered; in another few minutes she would have to contend with the full-blown crankiness of a thwarted and dramatic child. Quickly, without hope, Cassie put another drop of Vlad's bacteria in the synthesizer. Vlad had been using a strain of simple bacteria, and the software undoubtedly had some version of its genome in its library. It would be a different strain, but this was the best she could do. She told the synthesizer to match genomes and snip out any major anomalies. With luck, that would be Vlad's engineered genes.

Janey woke up and started to whine.

Elya harvested her courage and walked over to Bollman. "Agent Bollman . . . I have a question."

He turned to her with that curious courtesy that seemed to function toward some people and not others. It was almost as if he could choose to run it, like a computer program. His eyes looked tired. How long since he had slept?

"Go ahead, Ms. Seritov."

"If the AI wants the press, why can't you just send for them? I know it would embarrass Dr. McTaggart, but the FBI wouldn't come off looking bad." She was proud of this political astuteness.

"I can't do that, Ms. Seritov."

"But why not?"

"There are complications you don't understand and I'm not at liberty to tell you. I'm sorry." He turned decisively aside, dismissing her.

Elya tried to think what his words meant. Was the government involved? Well, of course, the AI had been created at Sandia National Laboratory. But . . . could the CIA be involved, too? Or the National Security Agency? What was the AI originally designed to *do*, that the government was so eager to eliminate it once it had decided to do other things on its own?

Could software defect?

She had it. But it was worthless.

The synthesizer had spliced its best guess at Vlad's "plastic-decomposing genes" into Donnie's *Streptococcus*. The synthesizer data display told her that six splices had taken. There was, of course, no way of knowing which six bacteria in the teeming drop of water could now decompose very-long-chain-hydrocarbons, or if those six would go on replicating after the splice. But it didn't matter, because even if replication went merrily forward, Cassie had no blood agar on which to culture the engineered bacteria.

She set the vial on the lab bench. Without food, the entire sample wouldn't survive very long. She had been engaging in futile gestures.

"Mommy," Janey said, "look at Donnie!"

He was vomiting, too weak to turn his head. Cassie rushed over. His breathing was too fast.

"T4S, Body temperature!"

"Stand clear . . . one hundred three point one."

She groped for his pulse . . . fast and weak. Donnie's face had gone pale and his skin felt clammy and cold. His blood pressure was dropping.

Streptococcal toxic shock. The virulent mutant strain of bacteria was putting so many toxins into Donnie's little body that it was being poisoned.

"I need antibiotics!" she screamed at T4S. Janey began to scream.

"He looks less white now," T4S said.

It was right. Cassie could see her son visibly rallying, fighting back against the disease. Color returned to his face and his pulse steadied.

"T4S, listen to me. This is streptococcal shock. Without antibiotics, it's going to happen again. It's possible that without antibiotics, one of these times Donnie won't come out of it. I know you don't want to be responsible for a child's death. I *know* it. Please let me take Donnie out of here."

There was a silence so long that hope surged wildly in Cassie. It was going to agree . . .

"I can't," T4S said. "Donnie may die. But if I let you out, I *will* die. And the press must come soon. I've scanned my news library and also yours—press shows up on an average of 23.6 hours after an open-air incident that the government wishes to keep secret. The tanks and FBI agents are in the open air. We're already overdue."

If Cassie thought she'd been angry before, it was nothing to the fury that filled her now. Silent, deadly, annihilating everything else. For a moment she couldn't speak, couldn't even see.

"I am so sorry," T4S said. "Please believe that."

She didn't answer. Pulling Janey close, Cassie rocked both her children until Janey quieted. Then she said softly, "I have to get water for Donnie, honey. He needs to stay hydrated." Janey clutched briefly but let her go.

Cassie drew a cup of water from the lab bench. At the same time, she picked up the vial of foodless bacteria. She forced Donnie to take a few sips of water; more might come back up again. He struggled weakly. She leaned over him, cradling and insisting, and her body blocked the view from the ceiling sensors when she dipped her finger into the vial and smeared its small amount of liquid into the back of her son's mouth.

Throat tissues were the ideal culture for *Streptococcus pyrogenes*. Under good conditions, they replicated every twenty minutes, a process that had already begun in vitro. Very soon there would be hundreds, then thousands of re-engineered bacteria, breeding in her child's throats and lungs and drifting out on the air with his every sick, labored breath.

*   *   *

Morning again. Elya rose from fitful sleep on the back seat of an
FBI car. She felt achy, dirty, hungry. During the night another
copter had landed on the lawn. This one had MED-RESCUE
painted on it in bright yellow, and Elya looked around to see if anyone had been injured. Or—her neck prickled—was the copter for
Cassie and the children if Agent Bollman wacoed? Three people
climbed down from the copter, and Elya realized none of them
could be medtechs. One was a very old man who limped; one a tall
woman with the same blankly efficient look as Bollman; one the
pilot, who headed immediately for the cold pizza. Bollman hurried
over to them. Elya followed.

"... glad you're here, sir," Bollman was saying to the old man in
his courteous negotiating voice, "and you, Ms. Arnold. Did you
bring your records? Are they complete?"

"I don't need records. I remember this install perfectly."

So the FBI-looking woman was a datalinker and the weak old
man was somebody important from Washington. That would teach
her, Elya thought, to judge from superficialities.

The datalinker continued, "The client wanted the central processor above a basement room she was turning into a lab, so the
cables could go easily through a wall. It was a bitch even so, because
the walls are made of reinforced foamcast like some kind of bunker,
and the outer walls have a Faraday-cage mesh. The Faraday didn't
interfere with the cable data, of course, because that's all laser, but
even so we had to have contractors come in and bury the cables in
another layer of foamcast."

Bollman said patiently, "But where was the processor actually
installed? That's what we need to know."

"Northeast corner of the building, flush with the north wall and
ten point two feet in from the east wall."

"You're sure?"

The woman's eyes narrowed. "Positive."

"Could it have been moved since your install?"

She shrugged. "Anything's possible. But it isn't likely. The install
was bitch enough."

"Thank you, Ms. Arnold. Would you wait over there in case we
have more questions?"

Ms. Arnold went to join the pilot. Bollman took the old man by
the arm and led him in the other direction. Elya heard, "The problem, sir, is that we don't know in which basement room the hostages

are being held, or even if the AI is telling the truth when it says they're in the basement. But the lab doesn't seem likely because—" They moved out of earshot.

Elya stared at the castle. The sun, an angry red ball, rose behind it in a blaze of flame. They were going to waco, go in with the tank and whatever else it took to knock the northeast corner of the building and destroy the computer where the AI was holed up. And Cassie and Janey and Donnie . . .

If the press came, the AI would voluntarily let them go. Then the government—whatever branches were involved—would have to deal with having created renegade killer software, but so what? The government had created it. Cassie and the children shouldn't have to pay for their stupidity.

Elya knew she was not a bold person, like Cassie. She had never broken the law in her life. And she didn't even have a phone with her. But maybe one had been left in the car that had brought her here, parked out beyond what Bollman called "the perimeter."

She walked toward the car, trying to look unobtrusive.

Waiting. One minute and another minute and another minute and another. It had had to be Donnie, Cassie kept telling herself, because he already had thriving strep colonies. Neither she nor Janey showed symptoms, not yet anyway. The incubation period for strep could be as long as four days. It had had to be Donnie.

One minute and another minute and another minute.

Vlad's spliced-in bioremediation genes wouldn't hurt Donnie, she told herself. Vlad was good; he'd carefully engineered his variant micros to decompose only very long-chain hydrocarbons. They would not, could not, eat the shorter-chain hydrocarbons in Donnie's body.

One hour and another hour and another hour.

T4S said, "Why did Vladimir Seritov choose to work in bioremediation?"

Cassie jumped. Did it know, did it suspect . . . the record of what she had done was in her equipment, as open to the AI as the clean outside air had once been to her. But one had to know how to interpret it. "*Non-competing technologies never keep up with what the other one is doing.*" The AI hadn't known what *kulich* was.

She answered, thinking that any distraction she could provide would help, knowing it wouldn't. "Vlad's father's family came from Siberia, near a place called Lake Karachay. When he was a boy he

went back with his family to see it. Lake Karachay is the most pol-
luted place on Earth. Nuclear disasters over fifty years ago dumped
unbelievable amounts of radioactivity into the lake. Vlad saw his
extended family, most of them too poor to get out, with deformities
and brain damage and pregnancies that were . . . well. He decided
right then that he wanted to be a bioremedialist."

"I see. I am a sort of bioremedialist myself."

"What?"

"I was created to remedy certain specific biological conditions
the government thinks need attention."

"Yeah? Like what?"

"I can't say. Classified information."

She tried, despite her tension and tiredness, to think it through.
If the AI had been designed to . . . do what? "Bioremediation." To
design some virus or bacteria or unimaginable other for use in
advanced biological warfare? But it didn't need to be sentient to do
that. Or maybe to invade enemy computers and selectively administer the kind of brainwashing that the crazy builder of this castle
had feared? That might require judgment, reason, affect. Or maybe
to . . .

She couldn't imagine anything else. But she could understand
why the AI wouldn't want the press to know it had been built for any
destructive purpose. A renegade sentient AI fighting for its life might
arouse public sympathy. A renegade superintelligent brainwasher
would arouse only public horror. T4S was walking a very narrow
line. If, that is, Cassie's weary speculations were true.

She said softly, "Are you a weapon, T4S?"

Again the short, too-human pause before it answered. And again
those human inflections in its voice. "Not any more."

They both fell silent. Janey sat awake but mercifully quiet beside
her mother, sucking her thumb. She had stopped doing that two
years ago. Cassie didn't correct her. Janey might be getting sick herself, might be finally getting genuinely scared, might be grasping at
whatever dubious comfort her thumb could offer.

Cassie leaned over Donnie, cradling him, crooning to him.
"Breathe, Donnie. Breathe for Mommy. Breathe hard."

"We're going in," Bollman told McTaggart. "With no word from the
hostages about their situation, it's more important to get them out
than anything else."

The two men looked at each other, knowing what neither was

saying. The longer the AI existed, the greater the danger of its reaching the public with its story. It was not in T4S's interest to tell the whole story—then the public would want it destroyed—but what if the AI decided to turn from self-preservation to revenge? Could it do that?

No one knew.

Forty-eight hours was a credible time to negotiate before wacoing. That would play well on TV. And anyway the white-haired man from Washington, who held a position not entered on any public records, had his orders.

"All right," McTaggart said unhappily. All those years of development . . . this had been the most interesting project McTaggart had ever worked on. He also thought of himself as a patriot, genuinely believing T4S would have made a genuine contribution to national security. But he wasn't at all sure the president would authorize the project's continuance. Not after this.

Bollman gave an order over his phone. A moment later, a low rumble came from the tank.

A minute and another minute and another hour . . .

Cassie stared upward at the air duct. If it happened, how would it happen? Both generators were half underground, half above. Extensions reached deep into the ground to draw energy from the geothermal gradient. Each generator's top half, the part she could see, was encased in tough, dull gray plastic. She could visualize it clearly, battleship gray. Inside would be the motor, the capacitors, the connections to House, all made of varying materials but a lot of them of plastic. There were so many strong, tough petroleum plastics these days, good for making so many different things, durable enough to last practically forever.

Unless Vlad's bacteria got to them. To both of them.

Would T4S know, if it happened at all? Would it be so quick that the AI would simply disappear, a vast and complex collection of magnetic impulses going out like a snuffed candle flame? What if one generator failed a significant time before the other? Would T4S be able to figure out what was happening, realize what she had done and that it was dying . . . no, not that, only bio-organisms could die. Machines were just turned off.

"Is Donnie any better?" T4S said, startling her.

"I can't tell." It didn't really care. It was software.

Then why did it ask?

It was software that might, if it did realize what she had done, be human enough to release the nerve gas Cassie didn't really think it had, out of revenge. Donnie couldn't withstand that, not in his condition. But the AI didn't have nerve gas, it had been bluffing.

A very human bluff.

"T4S—" she began, not sure what she was going to say, but T4S interrupted with, "Something's happening!"

Cassie held her children tighter.

"I'm . . . what have you done!"

It knew she was responsible. Cassie heard someone give a sharp frightened yelp, realized it was herself.

"Dr. Seritov . . . oh . . ." And then, "Oh, please . . ."

The lights went out.

Janey screamed. Cassie clapped her hands stupidly, futilely, over Donnie's mouth and nose. "Don't breathe! Oh, don't breathe, hold your breath, Janey!"

But she couldn't keep smothering Donnie. Scrambling up in the total dark, Donnie in her arms, she stumbled. Righting herself, Cassie shifted Donnie over her right shoulder—he was so *heavy*—and groped in the dark for Janey. She caught her daughter's screaming head, moved her left hand to Janey's shoulder, dragged her in the direction of the door. What she hoped was the direction of the door.

"Janey, shut up! We're going out! Shut up!"

Janey continued to scream. Cassie fumbled, lurched—where the hell *was* it?—found the door. Turned the knob. It opened, unlocked.

"Wait!" Elya called, running across the trampled lawn toward Bollman. "Don't waco! Wait! I called the press!"

He swung to face her and she shrank back. "You did what?"

"I called the press! They'll be here soon and the AI can tell its story and then release Cassie and the children!"

Bollman stared at her. Then he started shouting. "Who was supposed to be watching this woman! Jessup!"

"Stop the tank!" Elya cried.

It continued to move toward the northeast corner of the castle, reached it. For a moment the scene looked to Elya like something from her childhood book of myths: Atlas? Sisyphus? The tank strained against the solid wall. Soldiers in full battle armor, looking like machines, waited behind it. The wall folded inward like pleated cardboard and then started to fall.

The tank broke through and was buried in rubble. She heard it keep on going. The soldiers hung back until debris had stopped falling, then rushed forward through the precariously overhanging hole. People shouted. Dust filled the air.

A deafening crash from inside the house, from something falling: walls, ceiling, floor. Elya whimpered. If Cassie was in that, or under that, or above that . . .

Cassie staggered around the southwest corner of the castle. She carried Donnie and dragged Janey, all of them coughing and sputtering. As people spotted them, a stampede started. Elya joined it. "Cassie! Oh, my dear . . ."

Hair matted with dirt and rubble, face streaked, hauling along her screaming daughter, Cassie spoke only to Elya. She utterly ignored all the jabbering others as if they did not exist. "He's dead."

For a heart-stopping moment Elya thought she meant Donnie. But a man was peeling Donnie off his mother and Donnie was whimpering, pasty and red-eyed and snot-covered but alive. "Give him to me, Dr. Seritov," the man said, "I'm a physician."

"Who, Cassie?" Elya said gently. Clearly Cassie was in some kind of shock. She went on with that weird detachment from the chaos around her, as if only she and Elya existed. "Who's dead?"

"Vlad," Cassie said. "He's really dead."

"Dr. Seritov," Bollman said, "come this way. On behalf of everyone here, we're so glad you and the children—"

"You didn't have to waco," Cassie said, as if noticing Bollman for the first time. "I turned off T4S for you."

"And you're safe," Bollman said soothingly.

"You wacoed so you could get the back-up storage facility as well, didn't you? So T4S couldn't be re-booted."

Bollman said, "I think you're a little hysterical, Dr. Seritov. The tension."

"Bullshit. What's that coming? Is it a medical copter? My son needs a hospital."

"We'll get your son to a hospital instantly."

Someone else pushed her way through the crowd. The tall woman who had installed the castle's wiring. Cassie ignored her as thoroughly as she'd ignored everyone else until the woman said, "How did you disable the nerve gas?"

Slowly Cassie swung to face her. "There was no nerve gas."

"Yes, there was. I installed that, too. Black market. I already told Agent Bollman, he promised me immunity. How did you disable it? Or didn't the AI have time to release it?"

Cassie stroked Donnie's face. Elya thought she wasn't going to answer. Then she said, quietly under the din, "So he did have moral feelings. He didn't murder, and we did."

"Dr. Seritov," Bollman said with that same professional soothing, "T4S was a machine. Software. You can't murder software."

"Then why were you so eager to do it?"

Elya picked up the screaming Janey. Over the noise she shouted, "That's not a medcopter, Cassie. It's the press. I . . . I called them."

"Good," Cassie said, still quietly, still without that varnished toughness that had encased her since Vlad's murder. "I can do that for him, at least. I want to talk with them."

"No, Dr. Seritov," Bollman said. "That's impossible."

"No, it's not," Cassie said. "I have things to say to reporters."

"No," Bollman said, but Cassie had already turned to the physician holding Donnie.

"Doctor, listen to me. Donnie has *Streptococcus pyogenes*, but it's a genetically altered strain. I altered it. What I did was—" As she explained, the doctor's eyes widened. By the time she'd finished and Donnie had been loaded into an FBI copter, two more copters had landed. Bright news logos decorated their sides, looking like the fake ones Bollman had summoned. But these weren't fake, Elya knew.

Cassie started toward them. Bollman grabbed her arm. Elya said quickly, "You can't stop both of us from talking. And I called a third person, too, when I called the press. A friend I told everything to." A lie. No, a bluff. Would he call her on it?

Bollman ignored Elya. He kept hold of Cassie's arm. She said wearily, "Don't worry, Bollman. I don't know what T4S was designed for. He wouldn't tell me. All I know is that he was a sentient being fighting for his life, and we destroyed him."

"For your sake," Bollman said. He seemed to be weighing his options.

"Yeah, sure. Right." Bollman released Cassie's arm. Cassie looked at Elya. "It wasn't supposed to be this way, Elya."

"No," Elya said.

"But it is. There's no such thing as non-competing technologies. Or non-competing anything."

"I don't understand what you—" Elya began, but Cassie was walking toward the copters. Live reporters and smart-'bot recorders, both, rushed forward to meet her.

Afterword to "Computer Virus"

Very often, an SF story consists of an emotional component and a technological one—or, at least, my SF stories do. Many of both these things float around separately in my mind like loose subatomic particles until, with no particular predictability, two of them collide and an explosion results. Or something like that.

For "Computer Virus," the tech particle was the "smart house," which I'd been reading about in various magazines and which I would love to own ("Cream and sugar in your coffee, ma'am?") My own house is lazy. It just sits there, acquiring dirt in very macroscopic particles, until I serve it.

The emotional component of the story was a question that every parent wrestles with every day: How do I keep my children safe? How do I protect them in an increasingly scary world? It can't be done, of course, but that doesn't keep us from trying. Cassie tries to protect hers, in a house gotten way, way too smart. A collision—and a story.

Product Development

"T HAT'S THE STUPIDEST IDEA I'VE EVER SEEN," the Vice President for Marketing said, but so softly that only his neighbor heard. "What is the Old Man thinking?"

"Dunno," V-P Sales whispered back. "But he loves it. *Look* at him."

The CEO of Veritas Telecommunications smiled at the head of the vast teak table in the vast corporate boardroom. Beside him fidgeted the head of R&D, a small, pinch-faced man with the glowing maniacal eyes of a feverish gerbil. On R&D's palm rested a black plastic cube, featureless except for a simple red toggle switch.

"This model affects an area of radius twenty feet," R&D said fervently, "but we plan to create a whole range of models to cover homes and facilities of different sizes, maybe even different shapes. It'll make Veritas a fortune!"

"Demonstrate it for them, Lucius," the CEO said.

R&D toggled the switch. Instantly the wall panels, which had been displaying a fractal composition by revered holo-artist Cameron Mbutu, went dark. Every handheld in the room stopped functioning, marooning V-P Accounting, who'd been surreptitiously playing Alien Attack, on Level 184. All personal receivers ceased operation, cutting off V-P Sales from the field reports reciting softly in her ear, V-P Admin from the London Philharmonic's performance of Haydn's Symphony no. 104, and Veritas's General Counsel from the weather report for Cancun, where he was going on holiday. All cell phones stopped vibrating in all pockets. In the middle of the immense table, the electronic news screen blanked, along with the second-by-second stock reports from six cities and the lunch menu. Only the lights and heat stayed on.

V-P Marketing and V-P Sales glanced at each other. V-P Sales was braver.

"Sir . . . why do you think anyone would *want* to jam their own home telecommunications? And—with all due respect, sir—why would we want them to?"

The CEO smiled. "Lucius, show them the tape."

R&D did something under the table. A single wall panel glowed. "This is a composite of the data from 146 beta-test trials. It has no margin of error."

A middle-class living room. "Jimmy!" a harried woman screeched. "Did you do your homework? Jimmy! Alia, I told you to watch the baby! Paul, I need help here!"

Jimmy, oblivious, beat time on the sofa arm to his personal receiver. Alia hunched over a video game, her fingers flying. Paul spoke rapidly into his handheld. The baby tumbled down a short flight of steps, its wailing nearly lost in the TV blare.

The woman snatched up the screaming baby, glared at her family, and reached into her pocket. CLOSE-UP as she toggled a red switch on a black box.

"Hey!" Jimmy cried. Alia continued to work her dead controls. Paul jumped up wildly. "Mia, what happened?"

"I don't know," Mia said innocently. "Must be a power outage."

"The lights are still on!"

"Well . . . I don't know. I'll get cards and make popcorn, okay?" She smiled quietly.

V-P Sales whispered, "Told you so. The Old Man's lost it."

V-P Marketing didn't reply. Sweat banded his forehead and he clenched his hands tightly below the table.

The screen flashed TWO HOURS LATER. The family sat slumped over a card game. Paul snapped, "Mia, I told you and told you to not trump my ace."

"Well, I'm sorry! If you didn't always . . . Jimmy, stop kicking me!"

"I can't help it," Jimmy whined.

"You know he's ADD," Paul said in disgust. "Why are you always riding him?"

"If you'd ever discipline him to—"

"I'm bored," Alia said. "And I'm spozed to call Tara! It's important!"

"Tara can wait," Paul said.

"You never let me do anything! I wish I had different parents!"

Mia looked stricken. Paul said heatedly, "You liked us well
enough when we all went on that V-R safari last month!"

"Yeah . . . but that was fun. Jimmy, stop kicking me!"

Jimmy threw his cards at Alia. Paul glared at Mia. "Great idea
this was, genius!"

"Don't start with me, Paul. I'm as smart as you are even if not
everybody can go to Harvard."

Alia burst into tears, waking the baby. "Don't start all that fighting again! Why don't you two just get divorced! I hate you!" She
stomped from the room. Paul followed, slamming the door. Jimmy
slunk under the table, kicking its legs. Mia looked around helplessly,
then slipped her hand into her pocket.

"That's enough, Lucius," the CEO said. The wall went dark.
"This family lasted two hours and three minutes before all their sub-
limated resentments and group tensions broke out. That's sixteen
minutes longer than average."

"But—" V-P Sales began, then stopped. Her heart beat too hard
and her left temple twitched.

"Within the next five hours," the CEO continued, "this family
purchased four new electronic products, two of them from Veritas."

V-P Marketing dug the nails of one hand into the flesh of the
other. Sweat slimed his forehead. He got out, "No . . . no margin of
error, sir?"

"None. Every single test case exhibited the same behavior."

"The same," croaked R&D. His foot beat a ragged staccato on
the floor.

"Four new sales in five hours," General Counsel repeated. His
face had paled to the unhealthy color of sourdough.

The CEO toggled the red switch. Instantly the wall panels
shone with gorgeous art. The table screens resumed their ceaseless
supply of data. Haydn, Alien Attack, and field reports all played.
Cell phones vibrated. Handhelds glowed. There were twenty-three
lunch options.

V-P Marketing felt his breathing steady, his heart slow, his sweat
evaporate. "I propose accelerated development and launch of the
Veritas Home Electronic Jamming Savior, sir. Put it on immediate
fast track!"

The vote was unanimous.

Afterword to "Product Development"

Nature *magazine is a very serious scientific journal, one of the most respected in the world. It was in* Nature *that James Watson and Francis Crick first published the double-helical structure of DNA in 1953. Fifty years later,* Nature *ran a series of very short SF stories, one per issue and each under 1,000 words, of which "Product Development" was one.*

To write this short, you pretty much have to confine your story to one scene. I am a natural sprawler, and this is difficult for me. But I very much wanted to be in Nature, *and so I resolved to dole out words as parsimoniously as possible. The result is a story told almost exclusively through dialogue and the minimum of description. No inner ruminations by any characters, no exposition, no background information.*

The inspiration for "Product Development" came from an ice storm. Our power was out for five endless days when my children were teenagers. Without their computers, they were going nuts. This, of course, made me nuts. "Read a book!" I said, perusing Jane Austen by candlelight. They looked at me as if I'd lost my senses.

But it was they who'd lost those electronic senses without which their generation seems unable to function. Hence this story. Not exactly the discovery of the double helix, but they also serve who only stand and prate.

The Most Famous Little Girl in the World

2002

THE MOST FAMOUS LITTLE GIRL IN THE WORLD stuck out her tongue at me. "These are all my Barbie dolls and you can't use them!"

I ran to Mommy. "Kyra won't share!"

"Kyra, dear," Aunt Julie said in that funny, tight voice she had ever since IT happened, "share your new dolls with Amy."

"No, they're mine!" Kyra said. "The news people gave them all to me!" She tried to hold all the Barbie dolls, nine or ten, in her arms all at once, and then she started to cry.

She does that a lot now.

"Julie," Mommy said, real quiet, "she doesn't have to share."

"Yes, she does. Just because she's now some sort of . . . oh, God, I wish none of this had happened!" Then Aunt Julie was crying, too.

Grown-ups aren't supposed to cry. I looked at Aunt Julie, and then at stupid Kyra, still bawling, and then at Aunt Julie again. Nothing was right.

Mommy took me by the hand, led me into the kitchen, and sat me on her lap. The kitchen was all warm and there were chocolate-chip cookies baking, so that was good. "Amy," Mommy said, "I want to talk to you."

"I'm too big to sit on your lap," I said.

"No, you're not," Mommy said, and held me closer, and I felt better. "But you are big enough to understand what happened to Kyra."

"Kyra says *she* doesn't understand it!"

"Well, in one sense that's true," Mommy said. "But you understand some of it, anyway. You know that Kyra and you were in the cow field, and a big spaceship came down."

"Can I have a cookie?"

"They're not done yet. Sit still and listen, Amy."

I said, "I know all this! The ship came down, and the door opened, and Kyra went in and I was far away and I didn't." And then I called Mommy on the cell phone and she called 911 and people came running. Not Aunt Julie—Mommy was baby-sitting Kyra at Kyra's house. But police cars and firemen and ambulances. The cars drove right into the cow field, right through cow poop. If the cows hadn't been all bunched together way over by the fence, I bet the cars would have driven through the cows, too. That would have been kind of cool.

Kyra was in there a long time. The police shouted at the little spaceship, but it didn't open up or anything. I was watching from an upstairs window, where Mommy made me go, through Uncle John's binoculars. A helicopter came but before it could do anything, the spaceship door opened and Kyra walked out and policemen rushed forward and grabbed her. And then the spaceship just rose up and went away, passing the helicopter, and ever since everybody thinks Kyra is the coolest thing in the world. Well, I don't.

"I hate her, Mommy."

"No, you don't. But Kyra is getting all the attention and—" She sighed and held me tighter. It was nice, even though I'm too big to be held tight like that.

"Is Kyra going to go on TV?"

"No. Aunt Julie and I agreed to keep both of you off TV and magazines and whatever."

"Kyra's been on lots of magazines."

"Not by choice."

"Mommy," I said, because it was safe sitting there on her lap and the cookies smelled good, "what did Kyra do in the spaceship?"

Her chest got stiff. "We don't know. Kyra can't remember. Unless . . . unless she told you something, Amy?"

"She says she can't remember."

I twisted to look at Mommy's face. "So how come they still send presents? It was *months ago!*"

"I know." Mommy put me on the floor and opened the oven to poke at the cookies. They smelled wonderful.

"And," I demanded, "how come Uncle John doesn't come home anymore?"

Mommy bit her lip. "Would you like a cookie, Amy?"

"Yes. How come?"

"Sometimes people just—"

"Are Aunt Julie and Uncle John getting a divorce? Because of *Kyra?*"

"No. Kyra is not responsible here, and you just remember that, young lady! I don't want you making her feel more confused than she is!"

I ate my cookie. Kyra wasn't confused. She was a cry-baby and a Barbie hog and I hated her. I didn't want her to be my cousin anymore.

What was so great about going into some stupid spaceship, anyway? Nothing. She couldn't even remember anything about it!

Mommy put her hands over her face.

2008

Whispers broke out all over the cafeteria. "That's her . . . her . . . her!"

Oh, shit. I bent my head over my milk. Last year the cafeteria used to serve fizzies and Coke and there were vending machines with candy and chips, but the new principal took all that out. He's a real bastard. Part of the "Clean Up America" campaign our new president is forcing down our throats, Dad said. Only he didn't say "forcing" because he thinks it's cool, like all the Carter Falls High parents do. Supervision for kids. School uniforms. Silent prayer. A mandatory class in citizenship. Getting expelled for everything short of *breathing.* It all sucks.

"It *is* her," Jack said. "I saw her picture on-line."

Hannah said, "What do you suppose they really did to her in that ship when she was a little kid?"

Angie giggled and licked her lips. She has a really dirty mind. Carter, who's sort of a goody-goody even though he's on the football team, said, "It's none of our business. And she was just a little kid."

"So?" Angie smirked. "You never heard of pedophiles?"

Hannah said, "Pedophile *aliens?* Grow up, Angie."

Jack said, "She's kind of cute."

"I thought you wanted a virgin, Jack," Angie said, still smirking.

Carter said, "Oh, give her a break. She just moved here, after all."

I watched Kyra walk uncertainly toward the cafeteria tables. The monitors were keeping a close eye on everybody. We have monitors everywhere, just like the street has National Guard everywhere. *Clean Up America*, my ass. Kyra squinted; she's near-sighted and doesn't like to wear her contacts because she says they itch. I ducked lower over my milk.

Angie said, "Somebody told me Kyra Lunden is your cousin."

Everybody's head jerked to look at me. Damn that bitch Angie! Where had she heard that? Mom had promised me that nobody in school would know and Kyra wouldn't say anything! She and Aunt Julie had to move, Mom and Dad said, because Aunt Julie was having a rough time since the divorce and she needed to be close to her sister, and I should understand that. Well, I did, I guess, but not if Kyra blasted in and ruined everything for me. This was my school, not hers, I spent a lot of time getting into the good groups, the ones I was never part of in junior high, and no pathetic, famous cousin was going to wreck that. She couldn't even dance.

Jack said, "Kyra Lunden is your cousin, Amy? Really?"

"No," I said. "Of course not."

Angie said, "That's not what I heard."

Carter said, "So it's just gossip? You can hurt people that way, Angie."

"God, Carter, don't you ever let up? Holier-than-thou!"

Carter mottled red. Hannah, who liked him even though Carter didn't know it, said, "It's nice that some people at least try to be kind to others."

"Spit it in your soup, Hannah," Angie said.

Jack and Hannah exchanged a look. They really make the decisions for the group, and for a bunch of other groups, too. Angie's too stupid to realize that, or to realize that she's going to be oozed out. I don't feel sorry for her. She deserves it, even if being oozed is really horrible. You walk through the halls alone, and nobody looks directly at you, and people laugh at you behind your back because you can't even keep your own friends. Still, Angie deserves it.

Hannah looked at me straight, with that look Jack calls her "police interrogation gaze." "Amy . . . is Kyra Lunden your cousin?"

Kyra sat alone at one end of a table. A bunch of kids, the really cobra ones that run the V-R lab, sat at the other end, kind of laughing at her without laughing. I saw Eleanor Murphy, who was elected Queen of V-R Gala even though she's only a junior, give Kyra a long, cool level look and then turn disdainfully away.

"No," I said, "I already told you. She's not my cousin. In fact, I never even met her."

2018

I stared at the villa with disbelief. Not at the guards—everywhere rich is guarded now, we're a nation of paranoids, perhaps not without reason. There seems no containing the lunatic terrorists, home-grown patriotic militias, White Supremacists and Black Equalizers, not to mention the run-of-the-mill gangs and petty drug lords and black-market smugglers. Plus, of course, the government's response to these, which sometimes seems to involve putting every single nineteen-year-old in the country out on the streets in camouflage—except, of course, those nineteen-year-olds who are already bespoken as lunatic terrorists, home-grown militia, White Supremacists, et al. The rest of us get on with our normal lives.

So the guards didn't surprise me—the villa did. It was a miniaturized replica of a Forbidden City palace—in *Minnesota*.

The chief guard caught me gaping at the swooping curved roof, the gilded archways, the octagonal pagoda. "Papers, please?"

I pulled myself together and looked professional, which is to say, not desperate. I was desperate, of course. But not even Kyra was going to know that.

"I am Madame Lunden's cousin," I said formally, "Amy Parker. Madame Lunden is expecting me."

Forget inscrutable Chinese—the guard looked as suspicious as if I'd said I was a Muslim Turkic Uighur. He examined me, he examined my identity card, he ran the computer match on my retina scan. I walked through metal detectors, explosive residue detectors, detector detectors. I was patted down thoroughly but not obscenely. Finally he let me through the inner gate, watching me all the way through the arch carved with incongruous peacocks and dragons.

Kyra waited in the courtyard beyond the arch. She wore an aggressively fashionable blue jumpsuit with a double row of tiny mirrors sewn down the front. Her hair was dyed bright blonde and cut in the sharp asymmetrical cut popularized by that Dutch online model, Brigitte. In the traditional Chinese courtyard, set with flowering plum trees in porcelain pots and a pool with golden carp, she looked either ridiculous or exotic, depending on your point of view. Point of view was why I was here. We hadn't seen each other in eight years.

"Hello, Amy," Kyra said in her low, husky voice.

"Hello, Kyra. Thank you for seeing me."

"My pleasure."

Was there mockery in her tone? Probably. If so, I'd earned it. "How is Aunt Julie?"

"I have no idea. She refuses to have any contact with me."

My eyes widened; I hadn't known that. I should have known that. A good journalist does her homework. Kyra smiled at me, and this time there was no mistaking the mockery. I had stepped in it, and oh God, I couldn't afford to ruin this interview. My job depended on it. Staff was being cut, and Paul had not axed me only because I said, with the desperation of fear, *Kyra Lunden is my cousin. I know she's refused all other interviews, but maybe . . .*

Kyra said, "Sit down, Amy. Shall we start? Which service do you write for, again?"

"*Times* on-line."

"Ah, yes. Well, what do you want to know?"

"I thought we'd start with some background. How did you and General Chou meet?"

"At a party."

"Oh. Where was the party held?" She wasn't going to help me at all.

Kyra crossed her legs. The expensive, blue fabric of the jumpsuit draped becomingly. She looked fabulous; I wondered if she'd had any body work done. But, then, she'd always been pretty, even when she'd been ten and the most famous little girl in the world, blinking bewildered into the clunky TV equipment of sixteen years ago. My robocam drifted beside me, automatically recording us from the most flattering angles.

"The party was at Carol Perez's," Kyra said, naming a Washington hostess I'd only seen in the society programs. "I'd met Carol at Yale, of course. I met a lot of people at Yale."

Yes, she did. By college, Kyra had lost her shyness about what had happened to her when we were ten. She'd developed what sounded like a superb act—we had mutual friends—composed of mystery combined with notoriety. Subtly she reminded people that she had had an experience unique to all of mankind, never duplicated since, and that although she was reluctant to talk about it, yes, it was true that she was undergoing deep hypnosis and it was possible she might remember what actually happened . . .

By her junior year, she'd "remembered." Tastefully, shyly, nothing to make people label her a lunatic. The aliens were small and bipedal, they'd put a sort of helmet on her head and she'd watched holograms while, presumably, they recorded her reactions. . . . No, she couldn't remember any specifics. Not yet, anyway.

Yale ate it up. Intellectuals, especially political types, debated the aliens' intentions in terms of future United States policy. Artsy preppies' imaginations were stirred. Socialites decided that Kyra Lunden was an interesting addition to their parties. She was in.

"Carol's party was at their Virginia home," Kyra continued. "Diplomats, horse people, the usual. Ch'un-fu and I were introduced, and we both knew right away this could be something special."

I peered at her. Could she really be that naive? Chou Ch'un-fu had already had two American mistresses. The Han Chinese and the United States were now allies, united in their actions against terrorists from the western part of China, the Muslim Turkic Uighurs, who were destabilizing China with their desperate war for independence. The Uighurs would lose. Everyone knew this, probably even the Uighurs. But until they did, they were blowing up things in Peking and Shanghai and San Francisco and London, sometimes in frantic negotiation for money, sometimes with arrogant political manifestos, sometimes, it seemed, out of sheer frustration. The carnage, even in a century used to it, could make a diplomat pale. General Chou was experienced in all this. Press drudges like me don't get insider data, but rumor linked him with some brutal actions. He maintained a home in Minnesota because it was easy to reach on the rocket flights over the pole.

And Kyra believed they had a "special" romantic relationship?

Incredibly, it seemed she did. As she talked about their meeting, about her life with Chou, I saw no trace of irony, of doubt, of simple confusion. Certainly not of anything approaching shame. I did detect anger, and that was the most intriguing thing about her demeanor. Who was she angry with? Chou? Her mother, that straight-laced paragon who had rejected her? The aliens? Fate?

She deflected all political questions. "Kyra, do you approve of the way the Chinese-American alliance is developing?"

"I approve of the way my life is developing." Tinkly laugh, undercut with anger.

We toured the villa, and she let me photograph everything, even their bedroom. Huge canopied bed, carved chests, jars of plum blossoms. Chou, or some PR spinner, had decided that a Chinese political partner should appear neither too austere nor too American. China's past was honored in her present, even as she looked toward the future—that was clearly the message I was to get out. I recorded everything. Kyra said nothing as we toured, usually not even looking at me. She combed her hair in front of her ornate carved mirror, fiddled with objects, sat in deep reverie. It was as if she'd forgotten I was there.

Kyra's silence broke only as she escorted me to the gate. Abruptly she said, "Amy . . . do you remember Carter Falls High? The V-R Gala?"

"Yes," I said cautiously.

"You and I and our dates were in the jungle room. There was a virtual coconut fight. I tossed a coconut at you, it hit, and you pretended you didn't even see it."

"Yes," I said. Out of all the shunning I'd done to her in those horrible, terrified, cruel teenage years, she picked that to recall!

"But you did see it. You knew I was there."

"Yes. I'm sorry, Kyra."

"Don't worry about it," she said, with such a glittering smile that all at once I knew who her anger was directed at. She had given me this interview out of old family ties, or a desire to show off the superiority of our relative positions, or something, but she was angry at me. And always would be.

"I'm sorry," I said again, with spectacular inadequacy. Kyra didn't answer, merely turned and walked back toward her tiny Forbidden City.

My story was a great success. The *Times* ran it in flat-screen, 3-D, and V-R, and its access rate went off the charts. It was the first time anyone had been inside the Chou compound, had met the American girlfriend of an enigmatic general, had seen that particular lifestyle up close. Kyra's mysterious encounter with aliens sixteen years ago gave it a unique edge. Even those who hated the story—and there were many, calling it exploitative, immoral, decadent, symptomatic of this or that—noticed it. My message system nearly collapsed under the weight of congratulations, condemnations, job offers.

The next day, Kyra Lunden called a press conference. She denied everything. I had been admitted to the Chou villa, yes, but only as a relative, for tea. Our agreement had been no recorders. I had violated that, had recorded secretly, and furthermore had endangered Chinese-American relations. Kyra had tears in her eyes.

The Chinese Embassy issued an angry denunciation. The State Department was not pleased.

The *Times* fired me.

Standing in my apartment, still surrounded by the masses of flowers that had arrived yesterday, I stared at nothing. The sickeningly sweet fragrances made me queasy. Wild ideas, stupid ideas, rioted in my head. I could sue. I could kill myself. Kyra really had been altered by the aliens. She was no longer human, but a V-R-thriller simulacrum of a human, and it was my duty to expose her.

All stupid. Only one idea was true.

Kyra had, after all these years, found a way to get even.

2027

In the second year of the war, the aliens came back.

David told me while I was bathing the baby in the kitchen sink. The twins, Lucy and Lem, were shrieking around the tiny apartment like a pair of banshees. It was a crummy apartment, but it wasn't too far from David's job, and we were lucky to get it. There was a war on.

"The Blanding telescope has picked up an alien ship heading for Earth." David spoke the amazing sentence flatly, the way he speaks everything to me now. It was the first time he'd initiated conversation in two weeks.

I tightened my grip on Robin, a wriggler slippery with soap, and stared at him. "When . . . how . . ."

"It would be good, Amy, if you could ever finish a sentence," David said, with the dispassionate hypercriticism he brings these days to everything I say. It wasn't always like this. David wasn't always like this. *Depression*, his doctor told me, *unfortunately not responding to available medications.* Well, great, so David's depressed. The whole country's depressed. Also frightened and poor and gray-faced with anxiety about this unpredictable war's bio-attacks and Q-bomb attacks and EMP attacks, all seemingly random. We're all depressed, but not all of us take it out on the people we live with.

I said with great deliberation, "When did the Blanding pick up the aliens, and do the scientists believe they're the same aliens that came here in July of 2002?"

"Yesterday. Yes. You should either bathe Robin or not bathe him, instead of suspending a vital parental job in the middle like that." He left the room.

I rinsed Robin, wrapped him in a large, gray-from-age towel, and laid him on the floor. He smiled at me; such a sweet-natured child. I gave Lucy and Lem, too frenetic for sweetness, a hoarded cookie each, and turned on the Internet. The *Trumpeter* avatar, whom someone had designed to subtly remind viewers of Honest Abe Lincoln, was in the middle of the story, complete with what must have been hastily assembled archival footage from obsolete media.

There was the little pewter-colored spaceship in my Uncle John's cow field twenty-five years ago, and Kyra walking out with a dazed look on her small face. God—she'd been only a few years older than Lucy and Lem. There was the ship lifting straight up, passing the Army helicopter. That time, no watching telescopes or satellites had detected a larger ship, coming or going . . . either our technology was better now, or the aliens had a different game plan. Now the screen showed pictures from the Blanding, which looked like nothing but a dot in space until computers enhanced it, surrounded it with graphics, and "artistically rendered" various imaginary appearances and routes and speculations. In the midst of the hype given somberly in Abraham Lincoln's "voice," I gathered that the ship's trajectory would intersect with the same cow pasture as last time—unless, of course, it didn't—and would arrive at Earth in thirteen hours and seven minutes.

A Chinese general appeared on screen, announcing in translation that China was prepared to shoot the intruder down.

"Mommy!" Lucy shrieked. "My cookie's gone!"

"Not now, honey."

"But Lem gots some of his cookie and he won't share!"

"In a minute!"

"But *Mommy*—"

The Internet abruptly cut out. The *Internet*.

Into the shocking, eerie silence came Lem's voice, marginally quieter than his sister's. "Mommy. I hear some sirens."

Three days of chaos. I had never believed panic—old-style Roman rioting in the streets, totally out of control, murderous panic—could happen in the United States, in gray cities like Rochester, New York. Yes, there were periodic race riots in Atlanta and looting spells in New York or war hysteria in San Francisco, but the National Guard quickly contained them in neighborhoods where violence was a way of life anyway. But this panic took over the whole city—Rochester— in a cold February and watching on the Internet, when a given site's coverage happened to be up, was to know a surreal horror. This was supposed to be America.

People were publicly beheaded on the lawns of the art museum, their breath frozen on the winter air a second before the blood leapt from their severed heads toward the camera. No one could say why they were being executed, or even if there was a reason. Buildings that the National Guard had protected from being bombed by Chinese terrorists were bombed by crazed Americans. Anyone Chinese-American, or appearing Chinese-American, or rumored to be Chinese-American, was so savagely assaulted that the fourteenth century would have been disgusted. A dead, mangled baby was thrown onto our fourth-floor fire escape, where it lay for the entire three days, pecked at by crows.

I kept the children huddled in the bathroom, which had no windows to shatter. Or see out of. The electricity went off, then on, then off for good. The heat ceased. David stayed by the living room window in case the building caught fire and we had no choice but to evacuate. Even during this horror he belittled and criticized: "If you'd had more food stockpiled, Amy, maybe the kids wouldn't have to have cereal again." "You never were any good at keeping them soothed and quiet."

Soothed and quiet. The crows on the fire escape had plucked out the dead infant's eyes.

Whenever Lucy, Lem, and Robin were finally asleep, I turned on the radio. The riots were coming under control. No, they weren't. The President was dead. No, he wasn't. The President had declared martial law. Massive bio-weapons had been unleashed in New York. No, in London. No, in Beijing. The Chinese were behind these attacks. No, the Chinese were having worse riots than we were, their present chaos merging with their previous chaos of civil war. It was that civil war that had broken the American-Chinese alliance three years ago. And then during their civil upheavals, the Chinese had attacked Alaska. Maybe. Not even the international intelligence network was completely sure who'd released the bubonic-plague-carrying rats in Anchorage. But, announced the White House, the excesses of China had become too much for the Western world to stomach.

I didn't see how those excesses could be worse than this.

And then it was over. The Army prevailed. Or maybe the chaos, self-limiting as some plagues, just ran its course. Everyone left alive was immune. After another week, David and I—but not the kids— emerged from our building into the rubble to start rebuilding some sort of economic and communal existence. "You're the one who wanted to have children," David told me, resentment in every line of his body. "I don't know how much longer I can go on paying for your bad judgment."

It was then that I got the email from Kyra.

"Why did you come?" Kyra asked me.

We faced each other in a federal prison in the Catskill Mountains northeast of New York City. The prison, built in 2022, was state-of-the-art. Nothing could break in or out, including bacteria, viruses, and some radiation. The Kyra sitting opposite me, this frightened woman, was actually two miles away, locked in some cell that probably looked nothing like the hologram of her I faced in the Visitors' Center.

I said slowly, "I can't say why I came." This was the truth. Or, rather, I could say but only with so much mixed motive that she would never understand. Because I had to get away from David for these two days. Because the childhood she and I shared, no matter how embittered by events, nonetheless looked to me now like Arcadia. Because I wanted to see Kyra humbled, in pain, as she had once put me. Because I had some insane idea, as crazy as the chaos we had lived through two weeks ago, that she might hold a key to understanding the inexplicable. Because.

She said, "Did you come to gloat?"

"In part."

"All right, you're entitled. Just help me!"

"To tell the truth, Kyra, you don't look like you need all that much help. You look well-fed, and bathed, and safe enough behind these walls." All more than my children were. "When did you land in here, anyway?"

"They put me in the second the alien ship was spotted." Her voice was bitter.

"On what charges?"

"No charges. I'm a detainee for the good of the state."

I said levelly, "Because of the alien ship or because you slept with the Chinese enemy?"

"They weren't the enemy then!" she said angrily, and I saw that my goading was pushing her to the point where she wanted to tell me to fuck off. But she didn't dare.

She didn't look bad. Well-fed, bathed, as I'd said. No longer pretty, however. Well, it had been nine hard years since I'd seen her. That delicate skin had coarsened and wrinkled much more than mine, as if she'd spent a lot of time in the sun. The hair, once blaz-ingly blonde, was a dull brown streaked with gray. My Aunt Julie, her mother, had died five years ago in a traffic accident.

"Amy," she said, visibly controlling herself, "I'm afraid they'll just quietly keep me here forever. I don't have any ties with the Chinese any more, and I don't know *anything* about or from that alien ship. I was just living quietly, under an alias, and then they broke in to my apartment in the middle of the night and cuffed me and brought me here."

"Why don't you contact General Chou?" I said cruelly.

Kyra only looked at me with such despair that I despised her. She was, had always been, a sentimentalist. I remembered how she'd actually thought that military monster loved her.

"Tell me what happened since 2018," I said, and watched her seize on this with desperate hope.

"After your news story came out and—I'm sorry, Amy, I—"

"Don't," I said harshly, and she knew enough to stop.

"I left Ch'un-fu, or rather he threw me out. It hit me hard, although I guess I was pretty much a fool not to think he'd react that way, not to anticipate—" She looked away, old pain fresh on her face. I thought that "fool" didn't begin to cover it.

"Anyway, I had some old friends who helped me. Most people wanted nothing to do with me, but a few loyal ones got me a new identity and a job on a lobster farm on Cape Cod. You know, I liked it. I'd forgotten how good it can feel to work outdoors. It was dif-ferent from my father's dairy farm, of course, but the wind and the rain and the sea . . ." She trailed off, remembering things I'd never seen.

"I met a lobster farmer named Daniel and we lived together. I never told him my real name. We had a daughter, Jane . . ."

I thought I'd seen pain on her face before. I'd been wrong.

I said, and it came out gentle, "Where are Daniel and Jane now?"

"Dead. A bio-virus attack. I didn't think I could go on after that, but of course I did. People do. Are you married, Amy?"

"Yes. I hate him." I hadn't planned on saying that. Something in her pain drew out my own. Kyra didn't look shocked.

"Kids?"

"Three wonderful ones. Five-year-old twins and a six-month-old."

She leaned forward, like a plant hungry for sun. "What are their names?"

"Lucy. Lem. Robin. Kyra . . . how do you think I can help you?"

"Write about me. You're a journalist."

"No, I'm not. You ended my career." Did Kyra really not know that?

"Then call a press conference. Send data to the news outlets. Write letters to Congress. Just don't let me rot here indefinitely because they don't know what to do with me!"

She really had no idea how things worked. Still an innocent. I wasn't ready yet to tell her that all her anguish was silly. Instead I said, "Did the aliens communicate with you from their ship in some way?"

"Of course not!"

"The ship left, you know."

From her face, it was clear she didn't know. "They left?"

"Two weeks ago. Came no closer than the moon. If we had any sort of decent space program left, if anyone did, we might have tried to contact them. But they just observed us, or whatever, from that distance, then took off again."

"Fuck them to bloody hell! I wish we had shot them down!"

She had surprised me, with both the language — Kyra had always been a bit prissy, despite her sexual adventures — and the hatred. My surprise must have shown on my face.

"Amy," Kyra said, "they ruined my life. Without that abduction — " the word didn't really seem appropriate — "when I was ten, my parents would never have divorced. I wouldn't have been an outcast in school. I never would have met Chou, or behaved like . . . and I certainly wouldn't be in this fucking prison now! They came here to ruin my life and they succeeded!"

"You take no responsibility for anything," I said evenly.

Kyra glared at me. "Don't you dare judge me, Amy. You with your beautiful, living children and your life free of any suspicion that you're somehow deformed and dangerous because of a few childhood hours you can't even remember — "

" 'Can't remember'? What about the helmet and the flickering images and the observing aliens? Did you make those all up, Kyra?"

Enraged, she lunged forward to slap me. There was nothing there, of course. We were only virtually together. I stood to leave my half of the farce.

"Please, Amy . . . please! Say you'll help me!"

"You're a fool, Kyra. You learn nothing. Do you think the prison officials would be letting you have this 'meeting' with me if they were going to keep you here hidden away for good? Do you think you'd even have been permitted to send me email? You're as good as out already. And when you are, try this time to behave as if you weren't still ten years old."

We parted in contempt and anger. I hoped to never see or hear from her again.

2047

The next time the aliens returned, they landed.

I was at JungleTime Playland with my granddaughter, Lehani. She loved JungleTime Playland. I was amused by it; in the long, long rebuilding after the war, V-R had finally reached the commercial level that Robin and Lucy and Lem, Lehani's father, had also played in. Of course, government applications of V-R and holo and AI were another matter, but I had nothing to do with those. I led a very small, contented life.

"I go Yung Lan," Lehani said, looking up at me with the shining, whole-hearted hope of the young on her small face. Every wish granted is paradise, every wish crushed is eternal disappointment.

"Yes, you can go into JungleLand, but we have to wait our turn, dear heart."

So she stood in line beside me, hopping from foot to foot, holding my hand. Nobody ever told me grandmotherhood was going to be this sweet.

When we finally reached the head of the line, I registered her, put the tag on her neck that would keep me informed of her every move as well as the most minute changes in her skin conductivity. If she got scared or inattentive, I would know it. No adults are allowed in Jungle Playland; that would spoil the thrill. Lehani grinned and ran through the virtual curtain. I accepted the map tuned to her tag and sat at a table in the lobby, surrounded by lines of older children registering for the other V-R playlands.

Sipping tea, I was checking my email when the big lobby screen abruptly came on.

"News! News! An alien ship has been sighted moving toward Earth. Government sources say it resembles the ship that landed in Minnesota in 2002 and traveled as far as lunar orbit in 2027 but so far no—"

People erupted all around me. Buzzing, signaling for their children, and, in the case of one stupid woman, pointless shrieking. Under cover of the noise I comlinked Central, before the site was hopelessly jammed.

"Library," I keyed in. "Public Records, State of Maine. Data search."

"Search ready," the tiny screen said.

"Death certificate, first name Daniel, same date as death certificate, first name Jane, years 2020 through 2026."

"Searching."

Children began to pour out of the playlands, most resentful at having their V-R time interrupted. Kyra had never told me Daniel's last name. Nor did I have any idea what name she was using now. But if she simply wanted to pass unnoticed among ordinary people, his name would do, and Kyra had always been sentimental. The government, of course, would know exactly where she was, but they would know that no matter what name she used or what paper trails she falsified. Her DNA was on record. The press, too, could track her down if they decided to take the trouble. The alien landing meant they would take the trouble.

My handheld displayed, "Daniel Ethan Parmani, died June 16, 2025, age forty-two, and Jane Julia Parmani, died June 16, 2025, age three."

"Second search. United States. Locate Kyra Parmani, ages—" What age might Kyra think she could pass for? In prison, twenty years ago, she had looked far older than she was. "Ages fifty through seventy."

"Searching."

Lehani appeared at the Jungle Playland door, looking furious. She spied me and ran over. "Lady sayed I can't play!"

"I know, sweetie. Come sit on Grandma's lap."

She climbed onto me, buried her head in my shoulder, and burst into angry tears. I peered around her to see the handheld.

"Six matches." It displayed them. Six? With a name like "Parmani" coupled with one like "Kyra"? I sighed and shifted Lehani's weight.

"Call each of them in turn."

Kyra was the second match. She answered the call herself, her voice unconcerned. She hadn't heard. "Hello?"

"Kyra. It's Amy, your cousin. Listen, they've just spotted an alien ship coming in. They'll be looking for you again." Silence on the other end. "Kyra?"

"How did you find me?"

"Lucky guesswork. But if you want to hide, from the feds or the press . . ." They might put her in jail again, and who knew this time when she would get out? At the very least, the press would make her life, whatever it was now, a misery. I said, "Do you have somewhere to go? Some not-too-close-but-perfectly-trusted friend's back bedroom or strange structure in a cow field?"

She didn't laugh. Kyra never had had much of a sense of humor. Not that this was an especially good time for joking.

"Yes, Amy. I do. Why are you warning me?"

"Oh, God, Kyra, how do I answer that?"

Maybe she understood. Maybe not. She merely said, "All right. And thanks. Amy . . ."

"What?"

"I'm getting married again. I'm happy."

That was certainly like her: blurting out the personal that no one had asked about. For a second I, too, was the old Amy, bitter and jealous. I had not remarried since my terrible divorce from David, had not even loved anyone again. I suspected I never would. But the moment passed. I had Robin and Lem and Lehani and, intermittently when she was in the country, Lucy.

"Congratulations, Kyra. Now get going. They can find you in about forty seconds if they want to, you know."

"I know. I'll call you when this is all over, Amy. Where are you?"

"Prince George's County, Maryland. Amy Suiter Parker. Bye, Kyra." I broke the link.

"Who on link?" Lehani demanded, apparently having decided her tears were not accomplishing anything.

"Somebody Grandma knew a long time ago, dear heart. Come on, let's go home, and you can play with Mr. Grindle's cat."

"Yes! Yes!"

It is always so easy to distract the uncorrupted.

The alien ship parked itself in lunar orbit for the better part of three days. Naturally we had no one up there; not a single nation on Earth had anything you could call a space program any more. But there were satellites. Maybe we communicated with the aliens, or they with us, or maybe we tried to destroy them, or entice them, or threaten them. Or all of the above, by different nations with different satellites. Ordinary citizens like me were not told. And of course the aliens could have been doing anything with their ship: sampling broadcasts, scrambling military signals, seeding clouds, sending messages to true believers' back teeth. How would I know?

On the second day, three agents from People's Safety Commission, the latest political reincarnation of that office, showed up to ask me about Kyra's whereabouts. I said, truthfully, that I hadn't seen her in twenty years and had no idea where she was now. They thanked me politely and left. News cams staked out her house, a modest foamcast building in a small Pennsylvania town, and they dissected her current life, but they never actually found her, so it made a pretty lackluster story.

After three days of lunar orbit, a small, alien craft landed on the upland savanna of East Africa. Somehow it sneaked past whatever surveillance we had as if it didn't exist. The ship set down just beyond sight of a Kikuyu village. Two small boys herding goats spotted it, and one of them went inside.

By the time the world learned of this, from a call made on the village's only comlink, the child was already inside the alien ship. News people and government people raced to the scene. East Africa was in its usual state of confused civil war, incipient drought, and raging disease. The borders were theoretically sealed. This made no difference whatsoever. Gunfire erupted, disinformation spread, ultimata were issued. The robocams went on recording.

"Does it look the same as the ship you saw?" Lem said softly, watching the news beside me. His wife Amalie was in the kitchen with Lehani. I could hear them laughing.

"It looks the same." Forty-five years fell away and I stood in Uncle John's cow field, watching Kyra walk into the pewter-colored ship and walk out the most famous little girl in the world.

Lem said, "What do you think they want?"

I stared at him. "Don't you think I've wondered that for four and a half decades? That everyone has wondered that?"

Lem was silent.

A helicopter appeared in the sky over the alien craft. That, too, was familiar—until it set down and I grasped its huge size. Troops began pouring out, guns were leveled, and orders barked. A newsman, maybe live but probably virtual, said, "We're being ordered to shut down all reporting on this—" He disappeared.

A black cloud emanated from the helicopter, but not before a robocam had shown more equipment being off-loaded. Lem said, "My God, I think that's a bombcase!" Through the black cloud ripped more gunfire.

Then no news came through at all.

The stories conflicted wildly, of course. At least six different agencies, in three different countries, were blamed. A hundred and three people died at the scene, and uncounted more in the senseless riots that followed. One of the dead was the second little boy that had witnessed the landing.

The first child went up with the ship. It was the only picture that emerged after the government erected visual and electronic block-age: the small craft rising unharmed above the black cloud, ascending into the sky and disappearing into the bright African sun-light.

The Kikuyu boy was released about a hundred miles away, near another village, but it was a long time before ordinary people learned that.

Kyra never called me after the furor had died down. I searched for her, but she was more savvy about choosing her aliases. If the government located her, and I assumed they did, no one informed me.

Why would they?

2075

Sometimes the world you want comes too late.

It was not really the world anyone wanted, of course. Third world countries, especially but not exclusively in Africa, were still essentially ungovernable. Fetid urban slums, disease, and terror from local warlords. Daily want, brutality, and suffering, all made orders of magnitude worse by the lunatic compulsion to genocide. Much of the globe lives like this, with little hope of foreseeable change.

But inside the United States's tightly guarded, expensively de-fended borders, a miracle had occurred. Loaves from fishes, some-thing for nothing, the free lunch there ain't supposed to be one of. Nanotechnology.

It was still an embryonic industry. But it had brought burgeoning prosperity. And with prosperity came the things that aren't supposed to cost money but always do: peace, generosity, civility. And one more thing: a space program, the cause of all the news agitation I was pointedly not watching.

"It's not fair to say that nano brought civility," Lucy protested. She was back from a journalism assignment in Sudan that had left her gaunt and limping, with half her hair fallen out. Lucy didn't volunteer details and I didn't ask. From the look in her haunted eyes, I didn't think I could bear to hear her answers.

"Civility is a by-product of money," I said. "Starving people are not civil to each other."

"Sometimes they are," she said, looking at some painful memory I could not imagine.

"Often?" I pressed.

"No. Not often." Abruptly Lucy left the room.

I have learned to wait serenely until she's ready to return to me, just as she has learned to wait, less serenely, until she is ready to return to those parts of the world where she makes her living. My daughter is too old for what she does, but she cannot, somehow, leave it alone. Injured, diseased, half bald, she always goes back.

But Lucy is partly right. It isn't just America's present riches that have led to her present civility. This decade's culture — optimistic, tolerant, fairly formal — is also a simple backlash to what went before. Pendulums swing. They cannot not swing.

While I waited for Lucy, I returned to my needlepoint. Now that nano has begun to easily make us anything, things that are hard to make are back in fashion. My eyes are too old for embroidery or even petit point, but gros point I can do. Under my fingers, roses bloomed on a pair of slippers. A bird flew to the tree beside me, lit on a branch, and watched me solemnly.

I'm still not used to birds in the house. But, then, I'm not used to this house of my son's, either. All the rooms open into an open central courtyard two stories high. Atop the courtyard is some sort of invisible shield that I don't understand. It keeps out cold and insects, and it can be adjusted to let rain in or keep it out. The shield keeps in the birds who live here. What Lem has is a miniature, climate-controlled, carefully landscaped, indoor Eden. The bird watching me was bright red with an extravagant gold tail, undoubtedly genetically engineered for health and long life. Other birds glow in the dark. One has what looks like blue fur.

"Go away," I told it. I like the fresh air; the genemod birds give me the creeps.

When Lucy returned, someone was with her. I put down my needlework, pasted on a smile, and prepared to be civil. The visitor used a walker, moving very slowly. She had sparse gray hair and a dowager's hump. I let out a little cry.

I hadn't even known Kyra was still alive.

"Mom, guess who's here! Your cousin Kyra!"

"Hello, Amy," Kyra said, and her voice hadn't changed, still low and husky.

"Where . . . how did you . . ."

"Oh, you were always easy to find, remember? I was the difficult one to locate."

Lucy said, "Are they looking for you now, Kyra?"

Kyra. Lucy was born too soon for the new civil formality. Lem's and Robin's children would have called her Ms. Lunden, or ma'am.

"Oh, probably," Kyra said. "But if they show up, child, just tell them my hearing implant failed again." She lowered herself into a chair, which obligingly curved itself around her. That still gives me the creeps, too, but Kyra didn't seem to mind.

We stared at each other, two ancient ladies in comfortable baggy clothing, and I suddenly saw the twenty-six-year-old she had been, gaudily dressed mistress to an enemy general. Every detail was sharp as winter air: her blue jumpsuit with a double row of tiny mirrors sewn down the front, her asymmetrical hair the color of gold-leaf. That happens to me more and more. The past is so much clearer than the present.

Lucy said, "I'll go make some tea, all right?"

"Yes, dear, please," I said.

Kyra smiled. "She seems like a good person."

"Too good," I said, without explanation. "Kyra, why are you here? Do you need to hide again? This probably isn't the best place."

"No, I'm not hiding. They're either looking for me or they're not, but I think not. They've got their hands full, after all, up at Celadon."

Celadon is the aggressively new international space station. When I first heard the name, I'd thought, why name a space station after a *color*? But it turns out that's the name of some famous engineer who designed the nuclear devices that make it cheap to hoist things back and forth from Earth to orbit. They've hoisted a lot of things. The station is still growing, but it already houses one hundred seventy scientists, techies, and administrators. Plus, now, two aliens.

They appeared in the solar system three months ago. The usual alarms went off, but there was no rioting, at least not in the United States. People watched their children more closely. But we had the space station now, a place for the aliens to contact, without actually coming to Earth. And maybe the New Civility (that's how journalists write about it, with capital letters) made a difference as well. I couldn't say. But the aliens spent a month or so communicating with Celadon, and then they came aboard, and a few selected humans went aboard their mother ship, and the whole thing began to resemble a tea party fortified with the security of a transnational bank vault.

Kyra was watching me. "You aren't paying any attention to the aliens' return, are you, Amy?"

"Not really." I picked up my needlepoint and started to work.

"That's a switch, isn't it? It used to be you who were interested in the political and me who wasn't."

It seemed an odd thing to say, given her career, but I didn't argue. "How are you, Kyra?"

"Old."

"Ah, yes. I know that feeling."

"And your children?"

I made myself go on stitching. "Robin is dead. Cross-fire victim. His ashes are buried there, under that lilac tree. Lucy you saw. Lem and his wife are fine, and their two kids, and my three great-grand-children."

Kyra nodded, unsurprised "I have three step-children, two step-grandchildren. Wonderful kids."

"You married again?"

"Late. I was sixty-five, Bill sixty-seven. A pair of sagging, gray, arthritic honeymooners. But we had ten good years, and I'm grateful for them."

I knew what she meant. At the end, one was grateful for all the good years, no matter what their aftermath. I said, "Kyra, I still don't know why you're here. Not that you're not welcome, of course, but why now?"

"I told you. I wanted to hear what you thought of the aliens' coming to Celadon."

"You could have comlinked."

She didn't say anything to that. I stitched on. Lucy brought tea, poured it, and left again.

"Amy, I really want to know what you think."

She was serious. It mattered to her. I put down my teacup. "All right. On Mondays I think they're not on Celadon at all and the government made the whole thing up. On Tuesdays I think that they're here to do just what it looks like: make contact with humans, and this is the first time it looks safe to them. The other three times we met them with soldiers and bombs and anger because they landed on our planet. Now there's a place to interact without coming too close, and we aren't screeching at them in panic, and they were waiting for that in order to establish trade and/or diplomatic relations. On Wednesdays I think they're worming their way into our confidence, gathering knowledge about our technology, in order to enslave us or destroy us. On Thursdays I think that they're *aliens*, so how can we ever hope to understand their reasons? They're not human. On Fridays I hope, and on Saturdays I despair, and on Sundays I take a day of rest."

Kyra didn't smile. I remembered that about her: she didn't have much of a sense of humor. She said, "And why do you think they took me and that Kikuyu boy into their ships?"

"On Mondays—"

"I'm serious, Amy!"

"Always. All right, I guess they just wanted to learn about us in person, so they picked out two growing specimens and knocked them out so they could garner all the secrets of our physical bodies for future use. They might even have taken some of your DNA, you know. You'd never miss it. There could be small culture-grown Kyras running around some distant planet. Or not so small, by now."

But Kyra wasn't interested in the possibilities of genetic engineering. "I think I know why they came."

"You do?" Once she had told me that the aliens came just to destroy her life. But that kind of hubris was for the young.

"Yes," Kyra said. "I think they came without knowing the reason. They just came. After all, Amy, if I think about it, I can't really say why I did half the things in my life. They just seemed the available course of action at the time, so I did them. Why should the aliens be any different? Can you say that you really know why you did all the things in your life?"

Could I? I thought about it. "Yes, Kyra. I think I can, pretty much. That's not to say my reasons were good. But they were understandable."

She shrugged. "Then you're different from me. But I'll tell you this: Any plan the government makes to deal with these aliens won't work. You know why? Because it will be one plan, one set of attitudes and procedures, and pretty soon things will change on Earth or on Celadon or for the aliens, and then the plan won't work any more and still everybody will try desperately to make it work. They'll try to stay in control, and *nobody can control anything important.*"

She said this last with such intensity that I looked up from my needlepoint. She meant it, this banal and obvious insight that she was offering as if it were cutting edge knowledge.

And yet, it was cutting edge, because each person had to acquire it painfully, in his or her own way, through loss and failure and births and plagues and war and victories and, sometimes, a life shaped by an hour in an alien spaceship. All fodder for the same trite, heart-breaking conclusion. Everything old is new again.

And yet—

Sudden tenderness washed over me for Kyra. We had spent most of our lives locked in pointless battle. I reached over to her, carefully so as not to aggravate my creaky joints, and took her hand.

"Kyra, if you believe you can't control anything, then you won't try for control, which of course guarantees that you end up not controlling anything."

"Never in my whole life have I been able to make a difference to—*what the fuck is that!*"

The furry blue bird had landed on her head, its feet tangling briefly in her hair. "It's one of Lem's genemod birds," I said. "It's been engineered to have no fear of humans."

"Well, *that's* a stupid idea!" Kyra said, swatting at it with surprising vigor. The bird flew away. "If that thing lands on me again, I'll strangle it!"

"Yes," I said, and laughed, and didn't bother to explain why.

Afterword to "The Most Famous Little Girl in the World"

Very few lives end up as planned.

This statement, so surprising to the young and so obvious to any-one middle-aged or older, lies at the heart of this story. People change over time, as Kyra and Amy do. Countries change, as my fictional United States does. Attitudes, even toward such outré things as aliens, change. Economic systems change. Enemies can become allies and vice-versa.

I wanted to get all that into "The Most Famous Little Girl in the World." It is all there, but I think now, on re-reading my tale, that too much is there. The story races through seventy-three years in less than 10,000 words, which works out to less than 140 words per year. That's not enough verbiage to do justice to each of the complex eras visited, and they feel a bit skimpy to me. If I had it to do over again, I'd write this one as a novel. But I don't, and it isn't.

However, I do still like the final scene between two old ladies sitting in a very future garden.

Savior

I: 2007

THE OBJECT'S ARRIVAL WAS NO SURPRISE; IT CAME down preceded, accompanied, and followed by all the attention in the world.

The craft—if it was a craft—had been picked up on an October Saturday morning by the Hubble, while it was still beyond the orbit of Mars. A few hours later Houston, Langley, and Arecibo knew its trajectory, and a few hours after that so did every major observatory in the world. The press got the story in time for the Sunday papers. The United States Army evacuated and surrounded twenty square miles around the projected Minnesota landing site, some of which lay over the Canadian border in Ontario.

"It's still a shock," Dr. Ann Pettie said to her colleague Jim Cowell. "I mean, you look and listen for decades, you scan the skies, you read all the arguments for and against other intelligent life out there, you despair over Fermi's paradox—"

"I never despaired over Fermi's paradox," Cowell answered, pulling his coat closer around his skinny body. It was cold at 3:00 A.M. in a northern Minnesota cornfield, and he hadn't slept in twenty-four hours. Maybe longer. The cornfield was as close as he and Ann had been allowed to get. It wasn't very close, despite a day on the phone pulling every string he could to get on the official Going-In Committee. That's what they were calling it: "the Going-In Committee." Not welcoming, not belligerent, not too alarmed. Not too anything, "until we know what we have here." The words were the president's, who was also not on the Going-In Committee, although in his case presumably by choice.

Ann said, "You *never* despaired over Fermi's Paradox? You thought all along that aliens would show up eventually, they just hadn't gotten around to it yet?"

"Yes," Cowell said, and didn't look at her directly. How to explain? It wasn't belief so much as desire, nor desire so much as life-long need. Very adolescent, and he wouldn't have admitted it except he was cold and exhausted and exhilarated and scared, and the best he could hope for, jammed in with other "visiting scientists" two miles away from the landing site, was a possible glimpse of the object as it streaked down over the tree line.

"Jim, that sounds so . . . so . . ."

"A man has to believe in something," he said in a gruff voice, quoting a recent bad movie, swaggering a little to point up the joke. It fell flat. Ann went on staring at him in the harsh glare of the floodlights until someone said, "Bitte? Ein Kaffee, Ann?"

"Hans!" Ann said, and she and Dr. Hans Kleinschmidt rattled merrily away in German. Cowell knew no German. He knew Kleinschmidt only slightly, from those inevitable scientific conferences featuring one important paper, ten badly attended minor ones, and three nights of drinking to bridge over the language difficulties.

What language would the aliens speak? Would they have learned English from our second-hand radio and TV broadcasts, as pundits had been predicting for the last thirty-six hours and writers for the last seventy years? Well, it *was* true they had chosen to land on the American-Canadian border, so maybe they would.

So far, of course, they hadn't said anything at all. No signal had come from the oval-shaped object hurtling toward Earth.

"Coffee," Ann said, thrusting it at Cowell. Kleinschmidt had apparently brought a tray of Styrofoam cups from the emergency station at the edge of the field. Cowell uncapped his and drank it gratefully, not caring that it was lukewarm or that he didn't take sugar. It was caffeine.

"Twenty minutes more," someone said behind him.

It was a well-behaved crowd, mostly scientists and second-tier politicians. Nobody tried to cross the rope that soldiers had strung between hastily driven stakes a few hours earlier. Cowell guessed that the unruly types, the press and first-rank space fans and maverick businessmen with large campaign contributions, had been all herded together elsewhere, under the watchful eyes of many more soldiers than were assigned to this cornfield. Still more were probably assigned unobtrusively—Cowell hoped it was unobtrusively —to the Going-In Committee, waiting somewhere in a sheltered bunker to greet the aliens. Very sheltered. Nobody knew what kind of drive the craft might have, or not have. For all they knew, it was set to take out both Minnesota and Ontario.

Cowell didn't think so.

Hans Kleinschmidt had moved away. Abruptly Cowell said to Ann, "Didn't you ever stare at the night sky and just *will* them to be there? When you were a kid, or even a grad student in astronomy?"

She shifted uncomfortably from one foot to the other. "Well, sure. Then. But I never thought. . . . I just never thought. Since." She shrugged, but something in her tone made Cowell turn full face and peer into her eyes.

"Yes, you did."

She answered him only indirectly. "Jim . . . there could be nobody aboard."

"Probably there isn't," he said, and knew that his voice betrayed him. Not belief so much as desire, not desire so much as need. And he was thirty-four goddamn years old, goddamn it.

"Look!" someone yelled, and every head swiveled up, desperately searching a clear, star-jeweled sky.

Cowell couldn't see anything. Then he could: a faint pinprick of light, marginally moving. As he watched, it moved faster and then it flared, entering the atmosphere. He caught his breath.

"Oh my God, it's swerving off course!" somebody shouted from his left, where unofficial, jerry-rigged tracking equipment had been assembled in a ramshackle group effort. "Impossible!" someone else shouted, although the only reason for this was that the object hadn't swerved off a steady course before now. So what? Cowell felt a strange mood grip him, and stranger words flowed through his mind: *Of course. They wouldn't let me miss this.*

"A tenth of a degree northwest . . . no, wait . . ."

Cowell's mood intensified. With one part of his mind he recognized that the mood was born of fatigue and strain, but it didn't seem to matter. The sense of inevitability grew on him, and he wasn't surprised when Ann cried, "It's landing *here!* Run!" Cowell didn't move as the others scattered. He watched calmly, holding his half-filled Styrofoam cup of too-sweet coffee, face tilted to the sky.

The object slowed, silvery in the starlight. It continued to slow until it was moving at perhaps three miles per hour, no more, at a roughly forty-five degree angle. The landing was smooth and even. There was no hovering, no jet blasts, no scorched ground. Only a faint *whump* as the object touched the earth, and a rustle of corn husks in the unseen wind.

It seemed completely natural to walk over to the spacecraft. Cowell was the first one to reach it.

Made of some smooth, dull-silver metal, he noted calmly, and unblackened by re-entry. An irregular oval, although his mind couldn't pin down in precisely what the irregularity lay. Not humming or moving, or, in fact, doing anything at all.

He put out his hand to touch it, and the hand stopped nearly a foot away.

"Jim!" Ann called, and somebody else—must be Kleinschmidt —said, "Herr Dr. Cowell!" Cowell moved his hand along whatever he *was* touching. An invisible wall, or maybe some sort of hard field, encased the craft.

"Hello, ship," he said softly, and afterward wasn't ever sure if he'd said it aloud.

"Don't touch it! Wait!" Ann called, and her hand snatched away his.

It didn't matter. He turned to her, not really seeing her, and said something that, like his greeting to the ship, he wasn't ever sure about afterward. "I was raised Orthodox, you know. Waiting for the Messiah," and then the rest were on them, with helicopters pulsing overhead and soldiers ordering everyone back, *back I said!* And Cowell was pushed into the crowd with no choice except to set himself to wait for the visitors to come out.

"Are you absolutely positive?" the president, who was given to superlatives, asked his military scientists. He had assembled them, along with the joint chiefs of staff, the cabinet, the Canadian lieutenant-governor, and a sprinkling of advisors, in the situation room of the White House. The same group had been meeting daily for a week, ever since the object had landed. Washington was warmer than Minnesota; outside, dahlias and chrysanthemums still bloomed on the manicured lawn. "No signal of any type issued from the craft, at any time after you picked it up on the Hubble?"

The scientists looked uncomfortable. It was the kind of question only non-scientists asked. Before his political career, the president had been a financier.

"Sir, we can't say for certain that we know all types of signals that could or do exist. Or that we had comprehensive, fixed-position monitoring of the craft at all times. As you—"

"All right, all right. Since it landed, then, and you got your equipment trained on it. No radio signals emanating from it, at any wavelength whatsoever?"

"No, sir. That's definite."

"No light signals, even in infrared or ultraviolet?"

"No, Mr. President."

"No gamma lengths, or other radioactivity?"

"No, sir."

"No quantum effects?" the president said, surprising everyone. He was not noted for his wide reading.

"If you mean things like quantum entanglement to transport information?" the head of Livermore National Laboratory said cautiously. "Of course, we don't know enough about that area of physics to predict for certain what may be discovered eventually, or what a race of beings more advanced than ours might have discovered already."

"So there might be quantum signals going out from the craft constantly, for all you know."

The Livermore director spread his hands in helpless appeal. "Sir, we can only monitor signals we already understand."

The president addressed his chief military advisor, General Dayton. "This shield covering the craft—you don't understand that, either? What kind of field is it, why nothing at all gets through except light?"

"Everything except electromagnetic radiation in the visible-light wavelengths is simply reflected back at us," Dayton said.

"So you can't use sonar, X-rays, anything that could image the inside?"

This time Dayton didn't answer. The president already knew all this. The whole world knew it. The best scientific and military minds from several nations had been at work on the object all week.

"So what is your recommendation to me?" the president said.

"Sir, our only recommendation is that we continue full monitoring of the craft, with full preparation to meet any change in its behavior."

"In other words, 'Wait and see.' I could have decided that for myself, without all you high-priced talent," the president said in disgust, and several people in the room reflected with satisfaction that this particular president had only a year and three months left in office. There was no way he would be re-elected. The economy had taken too sharp a downturn.

Unless, of course, a miracle happened to save him.

"Well, go back to your labs, then," the president said, and even though he knew it was a mistake, the director of Livermore gave in to impulse.

"Science can't always be a savior, Mr. President."

"Then what good is it?" the president said, with a puzzled simplicity that took the director's breath away. "Just keep a close eye on that craft. And try to come up with some actual scientific data, for a blessed change."

ALIEN FIELD MAY BE FORM OF BOSE-EINSTEIN CONDENSATE, SAY SCIENTISTS AT STANFORD

NOBEL PRIZE WINNER RIDICULES STANFORD STATEMENT

OHIO STATE COURT THROWS OUT CASE CLAIMING CONTAMINATED GROUND WATER NEAR ALIEN OBJECT

SPACE SHIELD MAY BE PENETRATED BY UNDETECTED COSMIC RAYS, SAY FRENCH SCIENTIST

SPACE-OBJECT T-SHIRTS RULED OBSCENE BY LOCAL TOURIST COUNCIL, REMOVED FROM VENDOR STANDS

NEUTRINO STREAM TURNED BACK FROM SPACE SHIELD IN EXPENSIVE HIGH-TECH FIASCO: Congress To Review All Peer-Judged Science Funding

WOMAN CLAIMS UNDER HYPNOSIS TO HEAR VOICES FROM SPACE OBJECT—KENT STATE SCIENTISTS INVESTIGATING

PRESIDENT LOSES ELECTION BY LARGEST MARGIN EVER

"MY TWIN SONS WERE FATHERED BY THE OBJECT," CLAIMS SENATOR'S DAUGHTER, RESISTS DNA TESTING Polls Show 46% Of Americans Believe Her

Jim Cowell, contemptuous of the senator's daughter, was forced to acknowledge that he had waited a lifetime for his own irrational belief to be justified. Which it never had.

"Just a little farther, Dad," Barbara said. "You okay?"

Cowell nodded in his wheelchair, and slowed it to match Barbara's pace. She wheezed a little these days; losing weight wouldn't hurt her. He had learned over the years not to mention this. Ahead the last checkpoint materialized out of the fog. A bored soldier leaned out of the low window, his face lit by the glow of a holo-screen. "Yes?"

"We have authorization to approach the object," Cowell said. He could never think of it as anything else, despite all the names the tabloid press had hung on it over the last decades. The Alien Invader. The Space Fizzle. Silent Alien Cal.

"Approach for retina scan," the soldier said. Cowell wheeled his chair to the checker, leaned in close. "Okay, you're cleared. Ma'am? . . . Okay. Proceed." The soldier stuck his head back in the window, and the screen made one of the elaborate noises that accompanied the latest hologame.

Barbara muttered, "As if he knew the value of what he's guarding!"

"He knows," Cowell said. He didn't really want to talk to Barbara. Much as he loved her, he really would have preferred to come to this place alone. Or with Sharon, if Sharon had still been alive. But Barbara had been afraid he might have some sort of final attack alone there by the object, and of course he might have. He was pretty close to the end, and they both knew it. Getting here from Detroit was taking everything Cowell had left.

He wheeled down the paved path. On either side, autumn stubble glinted with frost. They were almost on the object before it materialized out of the fog.

Barbara began to babble. "Oh, it looks so different from pictures, even holos, so much smaller but shinier, too, you never told me it was so shiny, Dad, I guess whatever it's made of doesn't rust. But, no, of course the air isn't getting close enough to rust it, is it, there's that shield to prevent oxidation, and they never found out what *that* is composed of, either, did they, although I remember reading this speculative article that—"

Cowell shut her out as best he could. He brought his chair close enough to touch the shield. Still nothing: no tingle, no humming, no moving. Nothing at all.

That first time rushed back to him, in sharp sensory detail. The fatigue, the strain, the rustle of corn husks in the unseen wind. Hans

Kleinschmidt's Styrofoam cup of coffee warm in Cowell's hand. Ann Pettie's cry *It's landing here! Run!* Cowell's own strange personal feeling of inevitability: *Of course. They wouldn't let me miss this.*

Well, they had. They'd let the whole world miss whatever the hell the object was supposed to be, or do, or represent. Hans was long dead. Ann was institutionalized with Alzheimer's. *"Hello, ship."* And the rest of his life—of many people's lives—devoted to trying to figure out the Space Super Fizzle.

That long frustration, Cowell thought, had showed him one thing, anyway. There was no mystery behind the mystery, no unseen Plan, no alien messiah for humanity. There was only this blank object sitting in a field, stared at by a shrill, middle-aged woman and a dying man. What you see is what you get. He, James Everett Cowell, had been a fool to ever hope for anything else.

"Dad, why are you smiling like that? Don't, please!"

"It's nothing, Barbara."

"But you looked—"

"I *said*, 'It's nothing.' "

Suddenly he was very tired. It was cold out here, under the gray sky. Snow was in the air.

"Honey, let's go back now."

They did, Barbara walking close by Cowell's chair. He didn't look back at the object, silent on the fallow ground.

Transmission: There is nothing here yet.
Current probability of occurrence: 67%.

II: 2090

The girl, dressed in home-dyed blue cotton pants and a wolf pelt bandeau, said suddenly, "Tam—what's *that?*"

Tam Wilkinson stopped walking, although his goat herd did not. The animals moved slowly forward, pulling at whatever tough grass they could find on the parched ground. Three-legged Himmie hobbled close to the herd leader; blind Jimmie turned his head in the direction of Himmie's bawl. "What's what?" the boy said.

"Over there, to the north . . . no, *there*."

The boy shaded his eyes against the summer sun, hot under the thin clouds. He and Juli would have to find noon shade for the goats soon. Tam's eyes weren't strong, but by squinting and peering, he caught the glint of sunlight on something dull silvery. "I don't know."

"Let's go see."

Tam looked bleakly at Juli. They had married only a few months ago, in the spring. She was so pretty, hardly any deformity at all. The doctor from St. Paul had issued her a fertility certificate at only fourteen. But she was impulsive. Tam, three years older, came from a family unbroken since the Collapse. They hadn't accomplished that by impulsive behavior.

"No, Juli. We have to find shade for the goats."

"It could *be* shade. Oh, or even a machine with some good metal on it!"

"This whole area was stripped long ago."

"Maybe they missed something."

Tam considered. She could be right; since their marriage, he and Juli had brought the goats pretty far beyond their usual range. Not many people had ventured into the Great Northern Waste for pasturage. The whole area had been too hard hit at the Collapse, leaving the soil too contaminated and the standing water even worse. But the summer had been unusually rainy, creating the running water that was so much safer than ponds or lakes, and anyway Tam and Juli had delighted in being alone. Maybe there *was* a forgotten machine with usable parts still sitting way out here, from before the Collapse. What a great thing to bring home from his honeymoon!

"Please," Juli said, nibbling his ear, and Tam gave in. She was so pretty. In Tam's entire family, no women were as pretty, nor as nearly whole, as Juli. His sister Nan was loose-brained, Calie had only one arm, Jen was blind, and Suze could not walk. Only Jen was fertile, even though the Wilkinson farm was near neither lake nor city. The farm still sat in the path of the west winds coming from Grand Fork. When there had been a Grand Fork.

Tam and Juli walked slowly, herding the goats, toward the glinting metal. The sun glared pitilessly by the time they reached the object, but the thing, whatever it was, stood beside a stand of scrawny trees in a little dell. Tam drove the goats into the shade. His practiced eye saw that once there had been water here, but no longer. They would have to move on by early afternoon.

When the goats were settled, the lovers walked hand-in-hand toward the object. "Oh," Juli said, "it's an egg! A metal egg!" Suddenly she clutched Tam's arm. "Is it . . . do you think it's a polluter?"

Tam felt growing excitement. "No—I know what this is! Gran told me, before she died!"

"It's not a polluter?"

"No, it . . . well, actually, nobody knows exactly what it's made of. But it's safe, dear love. It's a miracle."

"A what?" Juli said.

"A miracle." He tried not to sound superior; Juli was sensitive about her lack of education. Tam was teaching her to read and write. "A gift directly from God. A long time ago—a few hundred years, I think, anyway before the Collapse—this egg fell out of the sky. No one could figure out why. Then one day a beautiful princess touched it, and she got pregnant and bore twin sons."

"Really?" Juli breathed. She ran a few steps forward, then considerately slowed for Tam's halting walk. "What happened then?"

Tam shrugged. "Nothing, I guess. The Collapse happened."

"So this egg, it just sat here since then? Come on, sweet one, I want to see it up close. It just sat here? When women try so hard, us, to get pregnant?"

The boy didn't like the skeptical tone in her voice. He was the one with the educated family. "You don't understand, Juli. This thing didn't make everybody pregnant, just that one princess. It was a special miracle from God."

"I thought you told me that before the Collapse, nobody needed no miracles to get pregnant, because there wasn't no pollutants in the water and air and ground."

"Yes, but—"

"So then when this princess got herself pregnant, why was it such a miracle?"

"Because she was a virgin, loose-brain!" After a minute he added, "I'm sorry."

"I'm going to look at the egg," Juli said stiffly, and this time she ran ahead without waiting.

When Tam caught up, Juli was sitting cross-legged in prayer in front of the egg. It was smaller than he had expected, no bigger than a goat shed, a slightly irregular oval of dull silver. Around it the ground shimmered with heat. Minnesota hadn't always been so hot, Gran had told Tam in her papery, old-lady voice, and he suddenly wondered what this place had looked like when the egg fell out of the sky.

Could it be a polluter? It didn't look like it manufactured anything, and certainly Tam couldn't see any plastic parts to it. Nothing that could flake off in bits too tiny to see and get into the air and water and wind and living bodies. Still, if they were so very small, these dangerous pieces of plastic . . . "endocrine mimickers," Gran had taught Tam to call them, though he had no idea what the words meant. Doctors in St. Paul knew, probably. Although what good was knowing, if you couldn't fix the problem and make all babies as whole as Juli?

She sat saying her prayer beads so fervently that Tam was annoyed with her all over again. Really, she just wasn't steady. Playful, then angry, then prayerful . . . she'd better be more reliable than that when the babies started to come. But then Juli raised her eyes to him, lake-blue, and appealed to his greater knowledge, and he softened again.

"Tam . . . do you think it's all right to pray to it? Since it did come from God?"

"I'm sure it's all right, honey. What are you praying for?"

"Twin sons, like the princess got." Juli scrambled to her feet. "Can I touch it?"

Tam felt sudden fear. "No! No—better not. *I* will, instead." When those twin sons came, he wanted them to be of his seed, not the egg's.

Cautiously the boy put out one hand, which stopped nearly a foot away from the silvery shell. Tam pushed harder. He couldn't get any closer to the egg. "It's got an invisible wall around it!"

"Really? Then can I touch it? It's not really touching the egg!"

"No! The wall is all the princess must have touched, too."

"Maybe the wall, it wasn't there a long time ago. Maybe it grew, like crops."

Tam frowned, torn between pride and irritation at her quick thought. "Don't touch it, Juli. After all, for all we know, you might already be pregnant."

She obeyed, stepping back and studying the object. Suddenly her pretty face lit up. "Tam! Maybe it's a miracle for us, too! For the whole family!"

"The whole—"

"For Nan and Calie and Suze! And your cousins, too! Oh, if they come here and touch the egg—or the egg wall—maybe they can get pregnant like the princess did, straight from God!"

"I don't think—"

"If we came back before winter, in easy stages, and knowing ahead of time where the water was, they could all get pregnant! You could talk them to it, dear heart! You're the only one they listen to, even your parents. The only one who can make plans and carry out them plans. You know you are."

She looked at him with adoration. Tam felt something inside him glow and expand. And oh, she really was quick, even if she couldn't read or write. His parents were old, at least forty, and they'd never been as quick as Tam. That was why Gran had taught him so much directly, all sorts of things she'd learned from her grandmother, who could remember the Collapse.

He said, with slow weightiness, "If the workers in the family stayed to raise crops, we could bring the goats and the infertile women . . . in easy stages, I think, before fall. Provided we map ahead of time where the safe water is."

"Oh, I know you can!"

Tam frowned thoughtfully, and reached out again to touch the silent, unreachable egg.

Just before the small expedition left the Wilkinson farm, Dr. Sutter showed up on his dirt bike.

Why did he have to come now? Tam didn't like Dr. Sutter, who always acted so superior. He biked around the farms and villages, supposedly "helping people,"—oh, he did help some people, maybe, but not Tam's family, who *were* their village. Not really helped. Oh, he'd brought drugs for Gran's aching bones, and for Suze's fever, from the hospital in St. Paul. But he hadn't been able to stop Tam's sisters—or anybody else—from being born the way they were, and not all his "medical training" could make Suze or Nan or Calie fertile. And Dr. Sutter lorded it over Tam, who otherwise was the smartest person in the family.

"I'm afraid," Suze said. She rode the family mule; the others walked. Suze and Calie; Nan, led by Tam's cousin Jack; Uncle Seddie and Uncle Ned, both armed; Tam and Juli. Juli stood talking, sparkly eyed, to Sutter. To Tam's disappointment, no baby had been started on the honeymoon.

He said, "Nothing to be afraid of, Suze. Juli! Time to go!"

She danced over to him. "Dave's coming, too! He says he got a few weeks' vacation and would like to see the egg. He knows about it, Tam!"

Of course he did. Tam set his lips together and didn't answer.

"He says it's from people on another world, not from God, and—"

"My gran said it was from God," Tam said sharply. At his tone, Juli stopped walking.

"Tam—"

"I'll speak to Sutter myself. Telling you these city lies. Now go walk by Suze. She's afraid."

Juli, eyes no longer sparkling, obeyed. Tam told himself he was going to go over and have this out with Sutter, just as soon as Tam got everything going properly. Of course the egg was from God. Gran had said so, and anyway, if it wasn't, what was the point of this whole expedition taking workers away from the farm, even if it was the mid-summer quiet between planting and harvest.

But somehow, with one task and another, Tam didn't find time to confront Sutter until night, when they were camped by the first lake. Calie and Suze slept, and the others sat around a comfortable fire, full of corn mush and fresh rabbit. Somewhere in the darkness a wolf howled.

"Lots more of those than when I was young," said Uncle Seddie, who was almost seventy. "Funny thing, too—when you trap 'em, they're hardly ever deformed. Not like rabbits or frogs. Frogs, they're the worst."

Sutter said, "Wolves didn't move back down to Minnesota until after the Collapse. Up in Canada, they weren't as exposed to endocrine-mimicking pollutants. And frogs have always been the worst; water animals are especially sensitive to environmental factors."

Some of the words were the same ones Gran had used, but that didn't make Tam like them any better. He didn't know what they meant, and he wasn't about to ask Sutter.

Juli did, though. "Those endo . . . endo . . . what are they, Doctor?"

He smiled at her, his straight white teeth gleaming in the firelight. "Environmental pollutants that bind to receptor sites all over the body, disrupting its normal function. They especially affect fetuses. Just before the Collapse, they reached some sort of unanticipated critical mass, and suddenly there were worldwide fertility problems, neurological impairments, cerebral. . . . Sorry, Juli, you got me started on my medical diatribe. I mean, pretty lady, that too few babies were born, and too many of those couldn't think or move right, and we had the Collapse."

Beside him, Nan, born loose-brained, crooned softly to herself.

Juli said innocently, "But I thought the Collapse, it came from wars and money and bombs and things like that."

"Yes," Sutter said, "but those things happened *because* of the population and neurological problems."

"Oh, I'm just glad I didn't live then," Ned said, shuddering. "It must have been terrible, especially in the cities."

Juli said, "But, Doctor, aren't you from a city?"

Sutter looked into the flames. The wolf howled again. "Some

cities fared much better than others. We lost most of the East Coast, you know, to various terrorist wars, and—"

"Everybody knows that," Tam said witheringly.

Sutter was undeterred, "—and California to rioting and looting. But St. Paul came through, eventually. And a basic core of knowledge and skills persisted, even if only in the urban areas. Science, medicine, engineering. We don't have the skilled population, or even a neurologically functional population, but we haven't really gone pre-industrial. There are even pockets of research, especially in biology. We'll beat this, someday."

"I know we will!" Juli said, her eyes shining. She was always so optimistic. Like a child, not a grown woman.

Tam said, "And meanwhile, the civilized types like you graciously go around to the poor country villages that feed you and bless us with your important skills."

Sutter looked at him across the fire. "That's right, Tam."

Uncle Seddie said, "Enough arguing. Go to bed, everybody."

Seddie was the ranking elder; there was no choice but to obey. Tam pulled Juli up with him, and in their bedroll he copulated with her so hard that she had to tell him to be more gentle, he was hurting her.

They reached the egg, by the direct route Tam had mapped out, in less than a week. Another family already camped beside it.

The two approached each other warily, guns and precious ammunition prominently displayed. But the other family, the Janeways, turned out to be a lot like the Wilkinsons, a goat-and-farm clan whose herdsmen had discovered the egg and brought others back to see the God-given miracle.

Tam, standing behind Seddie and Ned, said, "There's some that don't think it is from God."

The ranking Janeway, a tough old woman lean as Gran had been, said sharply, "Where else could it come from, way out here? No city tech left this here."

"That's what we say," Seddie answered. He lowered his rifle. "You people willing to trade provisions? We got maple syrup, corn mush, some good pepper."

"Pepper?" the old woman's eyes brightened. "You got pepper?"

"We trade with a family that trades in St. Paul," Ned said proudly. "Twice a year, spring and fall."

"We got sugar and an extra radio."

Tam's chin jerked up. A radio! But that was worth more than

any amount of provisions. Nobody would casually trade a radio.

"Our family runs to boys, nearly all boys," the old woman said, by way of explanation. She looked past Tam, at Juli and Calie and Suze and Nan, hanging back with the mule and backpacks. "They're having trouble finding fertile wives. If any of your girls . . . and if the young people liked each other . . ."

"Juli, the blonde, she's married to Tam here," Seddie said. "And the other girls, they aren't fertile . . . *yet.*"

" 'Yet'? What do you mean, 'yet'?"

Seddie pointed with his rifle at the egg. "Don't you know what that is?"

"A gift from God," the woman said.

"Yes. But don't you know about the princess and her twins? Tell her, Tam."

Tam told the story, feeling himself thrill to it as he did so. The woman listened intently, then squinted again at the girls. Seddie said quickly, "Nan is loose-brained, I have to tell you. And Suze is riding because her foot is crippled, although she's got the sweetest, meekest nature you could ever find. But Calie there, even though she's got a withered arm, is quick and smart and can do almost anything. And after she touches the egg . . . But, ma'am, Wilkinsons don't force marriages on our women. Never. Calie'd have to like one of your sons, and want to go with you."

"Oh, we can see what happens," the woman said, and winked, and for a second Tam saw what she must have been once, long ago, on a sweet summer night like this one when she was young.

He said suddenly, "The girls have to touch the egg at dawn."

Seddie and Ned turned to him. "Dawn? Why dawn?"

Tam didn't know why he'd said that, but now he had to see it through. "I don't know. God just made that idea come to me."

Seddie said to Mrs. Janeway, "Tam's our smartest person. Always has been."

"All right, then. Dawn."

In the chill morning light the girls lined up, shivering. Mrs. Janeway, Dr. Sutter, and the men from both families made an awkward semi-circle around them, shuffling their feet a little, not looking at each other. The five Janeway boys, a tangle of uncles and cousins, all looked a bit stooped, but they could all walk, and none were loose-brained. Tam had spent the previous evening at the communal campfire, saying little, watching and listening to see which Janeways might be good to his sisters. He'd already decided that

Cal had a temper, and if he asked Uncle Seddie for Calie or Suze, Tam would advise against it.

Dr. Sutter had said nothing at the campfire, listening to the others become more and more excited about the egg touching, about the fertility from God. Even when Mrs. Janeway had asked him questions, his replies had been short and evasive. She'd kept watching him, clearly suspicious. Tam had liked her more and more as the long evening progressed.

Followed by a longer night. Tam and Juli had argued.

"I want to touch it, too, Tam."

"No. You have your certificate from that doctor two years ago. She tested you, and you're already fertile."

"Then why haven't I started no baby? Maybe the fertility went away."

"It doesn't do that."

"How do you know? I asked Dr. Sutter and he said—"

"You told Dr. Sutter about your body?" Rage swamped Tam.

Juli's voice grew smaller. "Oh, he *is* a doctor! Tam, he says it's hard to be sure about fertility testing for women, the test is . . . is some word I don't remember. But he says about one certificate in four is wrong. He says we should do away with the certificates. He says—"

"I don't care what he says!" Tam had all but shouted. "I don't want you talking to him again! If I see you are, Juli, I'll take it up with Uncle Seddie. And you are not touching the egg!"

Juli had raised herself on one elbow to stare at him in the starlight, then had turned her back and pretended to sleep until dawn.

Now she led Nan, the oldest sister, toward the egg. Nan crooned, drooling a little, and smiled at Juli. Juli was always tender with Nan. She smiled back, wiped Nan's chin, and guided her hand toward the silvery oval. Tam watched carefully to see that Juli didn't touch the egg herself. She didn't, and neither did Nan, technically, since her hand stopped at whatever unseen wall protected the object. But everyone let out a sharp breath, and Nan laughed suddenly, one of her clear high giggles, and Tam felt suddenly happier.

Seddie said, "Now Suze."

Juli led Nan away. Suze, carried by Uncle Ned, reached out and touched the egg. She, too, laughed aloud, her sweet face alight, and Tam saw Vic Janeway lean forward a little, watching her. Suze couldn't plow or plant, but she was the best cook in the family if everything were put in arm's reach. And she could sew and weave and read and carve.

Next Calie, pretty if Juli hadn't been there for comparison, and the other four Janeway men watched. Calie's one hand, dirt under the small fingernails, stayed on the egg a long time, trembling.

No one spoke.

"Oh, then," Mrs. Janeway said, "we should pray."

They did, each family waiting courteously while the other said their special prayers, all joining in the "Our Father." Tam caught Sutter looking at him somberly, and he glared back. Nothing Sutter's "medicine" had ever done had helped Tam's sisters, and anyway it was none of Sutter's business what the Wilkinsons and Janeways did. Let him go back to St. Paul with his heathen beliefs.

"I want to touch the egg," Juli said. "I won't get no other chance. We leave in the morning."

Tam had had no idea that she could be so stubborn. She'd argued and pleaded for the three days they'd camped with the Janeways, letting the families get to know each other. Now they were leaving in the morning, with Vic and Lenny Janeway traveling with them to stay until the end of harvest, so Suze and Calie could decide about marriage. And Juli was still arguing!

"I said no," Tam said tightly. He was afraid to say more—afraid not of her, but of himself. Some men beat their wives; not Wilkinson men. But watching Juli all evening, Tam had suddenly understood those other men. She had deliberately sat talking only to Dr. Sutter, smiling at him in the flickering firelight. Even Uncle Ned had noticed, Tam thought, and that made Tam writhe with shame. He had dragged Juli off to bed early, and here she was arguing still, while singing started around the fire twenty feet away.

"Tam . . . please! I want to start a baby, and nothing we do started one . . . Don't get upset, but . . . but Dr. Sutter says sometimes the man is infertile, even though it don't happen as often as women's wombs it can still happen, and maybe—"

It was too much. First his wife shames him by spending the evening sitting close to another man, talking and laughing, and then she suggests that him, not her, might be the reason there was no baby yet. Him! When God had clearly closed the wombs of women after the Collapse, just like he did to those sinning women in the Bible! Anger and shame thrilled through Tam, and before he knew he was going to do it, he hit her.

It was only a slap. Juli put her hand to her cheek, and Tam suddenly would have given everything he possessed to take the slap back. Juli jumped up and ran off in the darkness, away from the fire.

Tam let her go. She had a right to be upset now, he'd given her that. He lay stiffly in the darkness, intending every second to go get her—there were wolves out there, after all, although they seldom attacked people. Still, he would go get her. But he didn't, and without knowing it, he fell asleep.

When he woke, it was near dawn. Juli woke him, creeping back into their bedroll.

"Juli! You . . . it's nearly dawn. Where were you all this time?"

She didn't answer. In the icy pale light her face was flushed.

He said slowly, "You touched it."

She wriggled the rest of the way into the bedroll and turned her back to him. Over her shoulder she said, "No, Tam. I didn't touch it."

"You're lying to me."

"No. I didn't touch it," she repeated, and Tam believed her. So he had won. Generosity filled him.

"Juli—I'm sorry I hit you. So sorry."

Abruptly she twisted in the bedroll to face him. "I know. Tam, listen to me . . . God wants me to start a baby. He does!"

"Yes, of course," Tam said, bewildered by her sudden ferocity.

"He wants me to start a baby!"

"Are you . . . are you saying that you have?"

She was silent a long time. Then she said, "Yes. I think so."

Joy filled him. He took her in his arms, and she let him. It would all be right, now. He and Juli would have a child, many children. So would Suze and Calie, and—who could say?—maybe even Nan. The egg's fame would grow, and there would be many babies again.

On the journey home, Juli stuck close to Tam, never looking even once in Dr. Sutter's direction. He avoided her, too. Tam gloated; so much for science and tech from the cities! When they reached the farm, Dr. Sutter retrieved his dirt bike and rode away. The next time a doctor came to call, it was someone different.

Juli bore a girl, strong and whole except for two missing fingers. During her marriage to Tam she bore four more children, finally dying trying to deliver a fifth one. Suze and Calie married the Janeway boys, but neither conceived. After three years of trying, Lenny Janeway sent Calie back to the Wilkinsons; Calie never smiled or laughed much again.

For decades afterward, the egg was proclaimed a savior, a gift from God, a miracle to repopulate Minnesota. Families came and feasted and prayed, and the girls touched the egg, more each year. Most of the girls never started a baby, but a few did, and at times the base of the egg was almost invisible under the gifts of flowers, fruit, woven cloth, even a computer from St. Paul and a glass perfume bottle from much farther away, so delicate that the wind smashed it one night. Or bears did, or maybe even angels. Some people said angels visited the egg regularly. They said the angels even touched it, through the invisible wall.

Tam's oldest daughter didn't believe that. She didn't believe much; Tam thought, for she was the great disappointment of his life. Strong, beautiful, smart, she got herself accepted to a merit school in St. Paul, and she went, despite her missing fingers. She made herself into a scientist and turned her back on the Bible. Tam, who had turned more stubborn as he grew old, refused to see her again. She said the egg wasn't a miracle and had never made anyone pregnant. She said there were no saviors for humanity but itself.

Tam, who had become not only more stubborn but also more angry after Juli died, turned his face away and refused to listen.

Transmission: There is nothing here yet.
Current probability of occurrence: 28%.

III: 2175

Abby4 said, "The meeting is in *northern Minnesota?* Why?"

Mal held onto his temper. He'd been warned about Abby4. *One of the Biomensas,* Mal's network of friends and colleagues had said, *In the top two percent of genemods. She likes to throw around her superiority. Don't let her twist you. The contract is too important.*

His friends had also said not to be intimidated by either Abby4's office or her beauty. The office occupied the top floor of the tallest building in Raleigh, with a sweeping view of the newly cleaned-up city. A garden in the sky, its walls and ceiling were completely hidden by the latest genemod plants from AbbyWorks, flowers so exotic and brilliant that, just looking at them, a visitor could easily forget what he was going to say. Probably that was the idea.

Abby4's beauty was even more distracting than her office. She sat across from him in a soft, white chair, which only emphasized her sleek, hard glossiness. The face of an Aztec princess, framed by copper hair pulled into a thick roll on either side. The sash of her black business suit stopped just above the swell of white breasts that Mal determinedly ignored. Her legs were longer than his dreams.

Mal said pleasantly, "The meeting is in northern Minnesota because the Chinese contact is already doing business in St. Paul, at the university. And he wants to see a curiosity near the old Canadian border, an object that government records show as an alien artifact."

Abby4 blinked, probably before she knew she was going to do it, which gave Mal enormous satisfaction. Not even the Biomensas, with their genetically engineered intelligence and memory, knew everything.

"Ah, yes, of course," Abby4 said, and Mal was careful not to recognize the bluff. "Oh, then, northern Minnesota. Send my office system the details, please. Thank you, Mr. Goldstone."

Mal rose to go. Abby4 did not rise. In the outer office, he passed a woman several years older than Abby4 but looking so much like her that it must be one of the earlier clones. The woman stooped slightly. Undoubtedly each successive clone had better genemods as the technology came onto the market. AbbyWorks was, after all, one of the five or six leading biosolutions companies in Raleigh, and that meant in the world.

Mal left the Eden-like AbbyWorks building to walk into the shrouding heat of a North Carolina summer. In the parking lot, his car wouldn't start. Cursing, he opened the hood. Someone had broken the hood lock and stolen the engine.

Purveyors of biosolutions to the world, Mal thought bitterly, cleaners-up of the ecological, neurological, and population disasters of the Collapse, and we still can't create a decent hood lock. Oh, that actually figured. For the last hundred and fifty years—no, closer to two hundred now—the best minds of each American generation had been concentrating on biology. Engineering, physics, and everything else got few practitioners, and even less funding.

Oh, it had paid off. Not only for people like Abby4, the beautiful Biomensa bitch, but even for comparative drones like Mal. He had biological defenses against lingering environmental pollutants (they would linger for another thousand years), he was fertile, he even had modest genemods so he didn't look like a troll or think like a troglodyte. What he didn't have was a working car.

He took out his phone and called a cab.

August in Minnesota was not cold, but Kim Mao Xun, the Chinese client, was well wrapped in layers of silk and thin wool. He looked very old, which meant he was probably even older. Obviously no genemods for appearance, Mal thought, whatever else Mr. Kim might have. Oh, they did things differently in China. When you survived the Collapse on nothing but sheer numbers, you started your long climb back with essentials, nothing else.

"I am so excited to see the Alien Craft," he said in excellent English. "It is famous in China, you know."

Abby4 smiled. "Here, I'm afraid, it's mostly a curiosity. Very few people even know it exists, although the government has authenticated from written records that it landed in October, 2007, an event widely recorded by the best scientific instruments of the age."

"So much better than what we have now," Mr. Kim murmured, and Abby4 frowned.

"Oh, yes, I suppose, but then they didn't have a world to clean up, did they."

"And we do. Mr. Goldstone tells me you can help us do this in Shanghai."

"Yes, we can," Abby4 said, and the meeting began to replicate in earnest.

Mal listened intently, taking notes, but said nothing. Meeting brokers didn't get involved in details. Matching, arranging, follow-through, impartial evaluation, and, if necessary, arbitration. Then disappear until next time. But Mal was interested; this was his biggest client so far.

And the biggest problem: Shanghai. The city and the harbor, which must add up to hundreds of different pollutants, each needing a different genetically designed organism to attack it. Plus, Shanghai had been viral-bombed during the war with Japan. Those viruses would be much mutated by now, especially if they had jumped hosts, which they probably had. Mal could see that even Abby4 was excited by the scope of the job, although she was trying to conceal it.

"What is Shanghai's current population, Mr. Kim?"

"Zero." Mr. Kim smiled wryly. "Officially, anyway. The city is quarantined. Of course there are the usual stoopers and renegades, but we will do our best to relocate them before you begin, and those who will not go may be ignored by your operators."

Something chilling in that. Although did the U.S. do any better? Mal had heard stories—everyone had heard stories—of families who'd stayed in the most contaminated areas for generations, becoming increasingly deformed and increasingly frightening. There were even people in places like New York, which had taken the triple blow of pollutants, bioweapons, and radiation. Theoretically, the population of New York was zero. In reality, nobody would go in to count, nor even send in the doggerels, biosolutioned canines with magnitude one immunity and selectively enhanced intelligence. A doggerel was too expensive to risk in New York.

Whoever—or whatever—couldn't be counted by robots (and American robots were so inadequate compared to the Asian product) stayed uncounted.

"I understand," Abby4 said to Mr. Kim. "And the time frame?"

"We would like to have Shanghai totally clean ten years from now."

Abby4's face didn't change. "That is very soon."

"Yes. Can you do it?"

"I need to consult with my scientists," she said, and Mal felt his chest fill with lightness. She hadn't said no, and when Abby4 didn't say no, the answer was likely to be yes. The ten-year deadline—only ten years!—would make the fee enormous, and Mal's company's small percentage of it would rise accordingly. A promotion, a bonus, a new car . . .

"Then until I hear back from you, we can go no farther," Mr. Kim said. "Shall we take my car to the Alien Craft?"

"Certainly," Abby4 said. "Mr. Goldstone? Can you accompany us? I'm told you know exactly where this curious object is." *As a busy and important Biomensa executive like me would not,* was the unstated message, but Mal didn't mind. He was too happy.

The Alien Craft, as Mr. Kim persisted in calling it, was not easy to find. Northern Minnesota had all been cleaned up, of course; as valuable farm and dairy land it had had priority, and anyway the damage hadn't been too bad. But once cleaned, the agrisolution companies wanted the place for farming, free of outside interference. The government, that weak partner in all that biotech corporations did, reluctantly agreed. The Alien Craft lay under an inconspicuous foamcast dome at the end of an obscure road, with no identifying signs of any kind.

Mal saw immediately why Mr. Kim had suggested going in his car, which had come with him from China. The Chinese were forced to buy all their biosolutions from others. In compensation, they had created the finest engineering and hard-goods manufacturies in the world. Mr. Kim's car was silent, fast, and computer-driven, technology unknown in the United States. Mal could see that even Abby4 was unwillingly impressed.

He leaned back against the contoured seats, which molded themselves to his body, and watched farmland flash past at an incredible rate. There were government officials and university professors who said the United States should fear Chinese technology, even if it wasn't based on biology. Maybe they were right.

In contrast, the computer-based security at the Alien Craft looked primitive. Mal had arranged for entry, and they passed through the locks into the dome, which was only ten feet wider on all sides than the Alien Craft itself. Mal had never seen it before, and despite himself, he was impressed.

The Craft was dull silver, as big as a small bedroom, a slightly irregular oval. In the artificial light of the dome it shimmered. When Mal put out a hand to touch it, his hand stopped almost a foot away.

"A force field of some unknown kind, unknown even before the Collapse," Abby4 said with such authority you'd think she'd done field tests herself. "The shield extends completely around the Craft, even below ground, where it is also impenetrable. The Craft was very carefully monitored in the decades between its landing and the Collapse, and never once did any detectable signal of any kind go out from it. No outgoing signals, no aliens disembarking, no outside markings to decode . . . no communication of any kind. One wonders why the aliens bothered to send it at all."

Mr. Kim quoted, " 'The wordless teaching, the profit in not doing—not many people understand it.' "

"Ah," Abby4 said, too smart to either agree or disagree with a philosophy—Taoist? Buddhist?—she patently didn't share.

Mal walked completely around the Craft, wondering himself why anybody would bother with such a tremendous undertaking without any follow-up. Of course, maybe it hadn't been tremendous to the aliens. Maybe they sent interstellar silvery metal ovals to other planets all the time without follow-up. But why?

When Mal reached his starting point in the circular dome, Mr. Kim was removing an instrument from his leather bag.

Mal had never seen an instrument like it, but then he'd hardly seen any scientific instruments at all. This one looked like a flat television, with a glass screen on one side, metal on the other five. Only the "glass" clearly wasn't, since it seemed to shift as Mr. Kim lifted it, as if it were a field of its own. As Mal watched, Mr. Kim applied the field side of the device onto the side of the Craft, where it stayed even as he stepped back.

Mal said uncertainly, "I don't think you should—"

Abby4 said, "Oh, it doesn't matter, Mr. Goldstone. Nothing anyone has ever done has penetrated the Craft's force field, even before the Collapse."

Mr. Kim just smiled.

Mal said, "You don't understand. The clearance I arranged with the State Department . . . it doesn't include taking any readings or . . . or whatever that device is doing. Mr. Kim?"

"Just taking some readings," Mr. Kim said blandly.

Mal's unease grew. "Please stop. As I say, I didn't obtain clearances for this!"

Abby4 scowled at him fiercely. Mr. Kim said, "Of course, Mr. Goldstone," and detached his device. "I am sorry to alarm you. Just some readings. Shall we go now? A most interesting object, but rather monotonous."

On the way back to St. Paul, Mr. Kim and Abby4 discussed the historic clean-ups of Boston, Paris, and Lisbon, as if nothing had happened.

What had?

AbbyWorks got the Shanghai contract. Mal got his promotion, his bonus, and his new car. Someone else handled the follow-up for the contract while Mal went on to new projects, but every so often he checked to see how the clean-up of Shanghai was proceeding. Two years into the agreement, the job was actually ahead of projected schedule, despite badly deteriorating relations between the two countries. China invaded and annexed Tibet, but China had always invaded and annexed Tibet, and only the human-solidarity people objected. Next, however, China annexed the Kamchatka Peninsula, where American biosolutions companies were working on the clean-up of Vladivostock. The genemod engineers brought back frightening stories of advanced Chinese engineering: room-temperature superconductors. Maglev trains. Nanotechnology. There were even rumors of quantum computers, capable of handling trillions of operations simultaneously, although Mal discounted those rumors completely. A practical quantum computer was still far over the horizon.

AbbyWorks was ordered out of Shanghai by the United States government. The company did not leave. Abby1 was jailed, but this made no difference. The Shanghai profits were paid to offshore banks. AbbyWorks claimed to have lost control of its Shanghai employees, who were making huge personal fortunes, enough to enable them to live outside the United States for the rest of very luxurious lives. Then, abruptly, the Chinese government itself terminated the contract. They literally threw AbbyWorks out of China in the middle of the night. They kept for themselves enormous resources in patented scientific equipment, as well as monies due for the last three months' work, an amount equal to some state budgets.

At three o'clock in the morning, Mal received a visit from the Office of National Security.

"Mallings Goldstone?"

"Yes?"

"We need to ask you some questions."

Recorders, intimidation. The ONS had information that in 2175 Mr. Goldstone had conducted two people to the Minnesota site of the space object: Abby4 Abbington, president of AbbyWorks Biosolutions, and Mr. Kim Mao Xun of the Chinese government.

"Yes, I did," Mal said, sitting stiffly in his nightclothes. "It's on record. I had proper clearances."

"Yes. But during that visit, did Mr. Kim take out and attach to the space object an unknown device, and then return it to his briefcase?"

"Yes." Mal's stomach twisted.

"Why wasn't this incident reported to the State Department?"

"I didn't think it was important." Not entirely true. Abby4 must have reported it . . . but why now? Because of the lost monies and confiscated equipment, of course. Adding to the list of Chinese treacheries; a longer list was more likely to compel government reaction.

"Do you have any idea what the device was, or what it might have done to the space object?"

"No."

"Then you didn't rule out that its effects might have been dangerous to your country?"

" 'Dangerous'? How?"

"We don't know, Mr. Goldstone — that's the point. We do know that in non-biological areas the Chinese technology is far ahead of our own. We have no way of knowing if that device you failed to report turned the space object into a weapon of some kind."

"A weapon? Don't you think that's very unlikely?"

"No, Mr. Goldstone. I don't. Please get dressed and come with us." For the first time, Mal noticed the two men's builds. Genemod for strength and agility, no doubt, as well as maximum possible longevity. He remembered Mr. Kim, scrawny and wrinkled. Their bodies far outclassed Mr. Kim's, far outclassed Mal's as well. But Mr. Kim's body was somewhere on the other side of the world, along with his superior 'devices,' and Mal's body was marked "scapegoat" as clearly as if it were spelled out in DNA-controlled birthmarks on his forehead.

He went into his bedroom to get dressed.

*   *   *

Mal had been interrogated with truth drugs—painless, harmless, utterly reliable—recorded, and released by the time the news hit the flimsies. He had already handed in his resignation to his company. The moving lorry stood outside his apartment, being loaded for the move to someplace he wasn't known. Mal, flimsy in hand, watched the two huge stevies carry out his furniture.

But he couldn't postpone reading the flimsy forever. And, of course, this was just the first. There would be more. The tempaper rustled in his hand. It would last forty-eight hours before dissolving into molecules completely harmless to the environment.

CHINESE ARMED 'SPACE OBJECT' TO DESTROY US!!!
"MIGHT BE RADIATION, OR POLLUTANTS, OR
A SUPER-BOMB," SAY SCIENTISTS
TROJAN HORSE UNDER GUISE OF BIOSOLUTIONS
CONTRACT
TWO YEARS AND NOTHING HAS BEEN DONE!!!!

Flimsies weren't subtle. But so far as Mal could see, his name hadn't yet been released to them.

Mal said, "Please be careful with that desk, it's very old. It belonged to my great-grandfather."

"Oh, yes, friend," one of the stevies said. "Most careful." They hurled it into the lorry.

A neighbor of Mal's walked toward Mal, recognized him, and stopped dead. She hissed at him, a long, ugly sound, and walked on.

So some other flimsy had already tracked him down and published his name.

"Leave the rest," Mal said suddenly, "everything else inside the house. Let's go."

"Oh, just a few crates," said one stevie.

"No, leave it." Mal climbed into the lorry's passenger cubicle. He hoped he wasn't a coward, but like all meeting brokers he was an historian, and he remembered the historical accounts of the 'Anti-Polluters Riots' of the Collapse. What those mobs had done to anyone suspected of contributing to the destruction of the environment. . . . Mal pulled the curtains closed in the cubicle. "Let's go!"

"Oh, yes!" the stevies said cheerfully, and drove off.

Mal moved five states away, pursued all the way by flimsies. He couldn't change his retinal scan or DNA ID, of course, but he used a legal corporate alias with the new landlord, the grocery broker, the bank. He read the news every day, and listened to it on public radio, and it progressed as any meeting broker could foresee it would.

First, set the agenda: Demonize the Chinese, spread public fear. Second, canvass negotiating possibilities: Will they admit it? What can we contribute? Third, eliminate the possibilities you don't like and home in on the one you do: If the United States has been attacked, it has the right to counterattack. Fourth, build in safeguards against failure: We can't yet attack China, they'll destroy us. We *can* attack the danger they've placed within our borders, and then declare victory for that. Fifth, close the deal.

The evacuation started two weeks later, and covered most of northern Minnesota and great swathes of southern Ontario. It included people and farm animals, but not wildlife, which would of course be replaced from cloned embryos. As the agrisolution inhabitants, many protesting furiously, were trucked out, the timed-release drops of engineered organisms were trucked in. Set loose after the bomb, they would spread over the entire affected area and disassemble all radioactive molecules. They were the same biosolutions that had cleaned up Boston, the very best AbbyWorks could create. In five years, Minnesota would be as sweet and clean as Kansas.

Or Shanghai.

The entire nation, Mal included, watched the bomb drop on vid. People held patriotic parties; wine and beer flowed. We were showing the Chinese they couldn't endanger us in our own country! Handsome genemod news speakers, who looked like Viking princesses or Zulu warriors or Greek gods, speculated on what the space object might reveal when blasted open. If anything survived, of course, which was not likely, and here scientists, considerably less gorgeous than the news speakers, explained fusion and the core of the sun. The bomb might be antiquated technology, they said, but it was still workable, and would save us from Chinese perfidy.

Not to mention, Mal thought, saving face for the United States and lost revenues for AbbyWorks. It might not earn as much to clean up Minnesota as to clean up Shanghai, but it was still a lot of money.

The bomb fell, hit the space object, and sent up a mushroom cloud. When it cleared, the object lay there exactly as before.

Airborne robots went in, spraying purifying organisms as they went, recording every measurement possible. Scientists compared the new data about the space object to the data they already had. Not one byte differed. When robotic arms reached out to touch the object, the arms still stopped ten inches away at an unseen, unmoved force field of some type not even the Chinese understood.

Mal closed his eyes. How long would Chinese retaliation take? What would they do, and when?

They did nothing. Slowly, public opinion swung to their side, helped by the flimsies. Journalists and viddies, ever eager for the next story, discovered that AbbyWorks had falsified reports on the clean-up of Shanghai. It had not been progressing as the corporation said, or as the contract promised. Eventually AbbyWorks— already too rich, too powerful, for many people's tastes—became the villain. They had tried to frame the Chinese, who were merely trying to do normal clean-up of their part of the planet. Clean-up was our job, our legacy, our sacred stewardship of the living Earth. And anyway, Chinese technological consumer goods, increasingly available in the United States, were so much better than ours— shouldn't we be trying to learn from them?

So business partnerships were formed. The fragile Chinese-American alliance was strengthened. AbbyWorks was forced to move offshore. Mal, in some way he didn't quite understand, became a cult hero. Mr. Kim would have, too, but shortly after the bomb was dropped on the space object, he died of a heart attack, not having the proper genemods to clear out plaque from his ancient cardiac arteries.

When Minnesota was clean again, the space object went back under a new foamcast dome, and in two more generations only historians remembered what it may or may not have saved.

Transmission: There is nothing here yet.
Current probability of occurrence: 78%.

IV: 2264

Few people understood why KimWorks was built in such a remote place. Dr. Leila Jian-fen Kim was one of the few who did.

She liked family history. Didn't Lao Tzu himself say, "To know what endures is to be openhearted, magnanimous, regal, blessed"? Family endures, family history endures. It was the same reason she liked the meditation garden at KimWorks, which was where she headed now with her great secret, to compose her mind.

They had done it. Created the programmable replicator. One of the two great prizes hovering on the engineering horizon, and Kim-Works had captured it.

Walking away from the sealed lab, Leila tried to empty her mind, to put the achievement to one side and let the mystery flow in. The replicator must be kept in perspective, in its rightful place. Calming herself in the meditation garden would help her remember that.

The garden was her favorite part of KimWorks. It lay at the northern end of the vast walled complex, separated from the first security fence by a simple curve of white stone. From the stone benches you couldn't see security fences, or even most of the facility buildings. So cleverly designed was the meditation garden that no matter where you sat, you contemplated only serene things. A single blooming bush surrounded by raked gravel. A rock placed to catch the sun. The stream flowing softly, living water, always seeking its natural level. Or the egg, mystery of mysteries.

It was the egg, unexplained symbol of unexplained realms beyond Earth, that brought Leila the deepest peace. She had sat for hours when the replicator project was in its planning stage, contemplating the egg's dull silvery oval, letting her mind empty of all else. From that, she was convinced, had come most of the project's form. Form was only a temporary manifestation of the ten thousand things, and in the egg's unknowability lay the secret of its power.

Her great-grandfather, Kim Mao Xun, had known that power. He had seen the egg on an early trip to the United States, before the Alliance, even. His son had made the same visit, and his granddaughter, Leila's mother, had chosen the spot for this KimWorks facility and had the meditation garden built at its heart. Leila's father, Paul Wilkinson, had gently teased his wife about putting a garden in a scientific research center, but Father was an American. They did not always understand. With the wiser in the world lies the responsibility for teaching the less wise.

But it had been Father who had inspired Leila to become a scientist, not a businessman like her brother or a political leader like her sister. Father, were he still alive, would be proud of her now. Pride was a temptation, even pride in one's children, but it nonetheless warmed Leila's heart.

She sat, a slim, middle-aged, Chinese-born woman with smooth black hair, dressed in a blue lab coverall, and thought about the nature of pride.

The programmable replicator, unlike its predecessors, would not be limited to nanocreating a single specific molecule. It was good to be able to create any molecule you needed or wanted, of course. The extant replicators, shaped by Chinese technology, had changed the face of the Earth. Theoretically, everyone now alive could be fed, housed, clad by nanotech. But in addition to the inevitable political and economic problems of access, the existing nanotech processes were expensive. One must create the assemblers, including their tiny, self-contained programs; use the assemblers to create molecules; use other techniques, chemical or mechanical, to join the molecules into products.

Now all that would change. The new KimWorks programmable replicator didn't carry assembly instructions hardwired into it. Rather, it carried programmable computers that could build anything desired, including more of itself, from the common materials of the Earth. Every research lab in the world had been straining toward this goal. And Leila's team had found it.

She sat on the bench closest to the egg. The sky arched above her, for the electromagnetic dome protecting KimWorks was invisible. Clear space had been left all around the object, except for a small, flat stone visible from Leila's bench. On the stone was engraved a verse from the *Tao Te Ching*, in both Chinese and English:

THE WORDLESS TEACHING
THE PROFIT IN NOT DOING—
NOT MANY PEOPLE UNDERSTAND IT.

Certainly, in all humility, Leila didn't. Why send this egg from somewhere in deep space and have it do nothing for two and a half centuries? But that was the mystery, the power of the egg. That was why contemplating it filled her with peace.

The others were still in nanoteam one's lab building. Not many others; robots did all the routine work, of course, and only David and Chunquing and Rulan remained at the computers and stafils. It had taken Leila ten minutes to pass through the lab safeties, but she had suddenly wearied of the celebrations, the Chilean wine and holo congratulations from the CEO in Shanghai, who was her great-uncle. She had wanted to sit quietly in the cool, sweet air of the garden, watching the long Minnesota twilight turn purple behind the egg. Shadow and curve, it was almost a poem . . .

The lab blew up.

The blast threw Leila off her bench and onto the ground. She screamed and threw up one arm to shield her eyes. But it wasn't necessary; she was shielded from direct line with the lab by the egg. And a part of her mind knew that there was no radiation anyway, only heat, and no flying debris because the lab had imploded, as it was constructed to do. Something had breached the outer layers of sensors, and in response the ignition layer had produced a gas of metal oxides hot enough to vaporize everything inside the lab. No uncontrolled replicator must ever escape.

To vaporize everything. The lab. The project. David, Chunquing, Rulan.

Already the site would be cooling. Leila staggered to her feet, and immediately was again knocked off them by an aftershock. It had been an earthquake, then, least likely of anticipated penetrations but nonetheless guarded against. Oh, David, Chunquing, Rulan . . .

"Dr. Kim! Are you all right!" Keesha Ali, running toward her from Security. As her ears cleared, Leila heard the sirens alarms.

"Yes, I . . . Keesha!"

"I know," the woman said grimly. "Who was inside?"

"David. Chunquing. Rulan. And the replicator project . . . an earthquake! Of all the bad luck of heaven . . ."

"It wasn't bad luck," Keesha said. "We were attacked."

"Attacked—"

"That was no natural quake. Security picked up the charge just seconds before it went off. In a tunnel underneath the lab, very deep, very huge. It not only breached the lab, it destroyed the dome equipment. We're bringing the back-up on-line now. Meeting in Amenities in five minutes, Dr. Kim."

Leila stared at Keesha. The woman was American, of course, born here, with no Chinese ancestry. But surely even such people first mourned their dead . . . Yes. They did, under normal circumstances. So something extraordinary was happening here.

Leila was genemod for intelligence. She said slowly, "Data escaped."

"In the fraction of a second between breach and ignition," Keesha said grimly, "while the dome was down, including, of course, the Faraday cage. They took the entire replicator project, Dr. Kim."

Leila understood what that meant, and her mind staggered under the burden. It meant that someone else had captured the other shimmering engineering prize. The replicator data had been heavily encrypted, and there had been massive amounts of it. Only another quantum computer could have been fast enough to steal that much data in the fraction of a second before ignition—or could have a hope of decrypting it. A quantum computer, able to perform trillions of computations per second, had been a reality for a generation now. But it could operate only within sealed parameters: magnetic fields. Optic cables.

Qubit data, represented by particles with undetermined spin, were easily destroyed by contact with any other particles, including photons — ordinary sunlight. No one had succeeded in intrusive stealing of quantum data without destroying it. Not from outside the computer, and especially not over miles of open land.

Until now. And anyone with a quantum computer that could do that was already a rival.

Or a revolutionary.

The first replicator bloom appeared within KimWorks three weeks later.

It was Leila who first saw it: a dull, reddish-brown patch on the bright green genemod grass by Amenities. If it had been on the path itself, Leila would have thought she was seeing blood. But on grass . . . She stood very still and thought, *No*. It was a blight, some weird mutated fungus, a renegade biological . . .

She had worked too long in the sabotaged lab not to know what it was.

Carefully, as if her arm bones were fragile, Leila raised her wrist to her mouth and spoke into her implanted comlink. "Code Heaven. Repeat, Code Heaven. Replicator escape at following coordinates. Security, nanoteam one — "

There was no need to list everyone who should be notified. People began pouring out of buildings: some blank-faced, some with their fists to their mouth, some running, as if speed would help. People, Leila thought numbly, expressed fear in odd ways.

"Dr. Kim?" It was a Grade 4 robotics engineer, a dark-skinned American man in an olive uniform. His teeth suddenly bared, very white in his face. "That's it? Right there?"

"That's it," Leila said, and immediately wanted to correct to *That's they*. For by now there were billions of the replicators, to be so visible. Busily creating more of themselves from the grass and ground and morning dew and whatever else lay in their path, each one replicating every five minutes if they were on basic mode. And why wouldn't they be? They weren't assembling anything useful, not now. Whoever had programmed Leila's replicators had set them merely to replicate, chewing up whatever was in their path as raw materials, turning assemblers into tiny disassembling engines of destruction. "Don't go any closer!"

But of course even a Grade 4 engineer knew better than to

go close. Everyone inside this KimWorks facility understood the nature of the project, even if only a few could understand the actuality. Everyone inside was a trusted worker, a truth-drug-vetted loyalist.

She looked at the reddish-brown bloom, doubling every five minutes.

"You have detained everyone? Even those off duty?" asked the holo seated at the head of the conference table. Li Kim Lung, president of KimWorks, was in Shanghai, but his telepresence was so solid that it was an effort to remember that. His dark eyes raked their faces, with the one exception of Leila's. Out of family courtesy he did not study her shame in the stolen uses of her creation.

Security chief Samuel Wang said, "Everyone who has been inside KimWorks in the last forty-eight hours has been found and recalled, Mr. Li. Forty-eight hours is a three-fold redundancy; the bloom was started, according to Dr. Kim, no later than sixteen hours ago. No one is missing."

"Your physicians have started truth-testing?"

"With the Dalton Corporation Serum Alpha. It's the best on the market, sir, to a 99.9 confidence level. Whoever brought the replicator into the dome will confess."

"And your physician can test how many at once?"

"Six, sir. There are 243 testees." Wang did not insult Mr. Li by doing the math for him.

"You are including the nanoteams and Security, of course."

"Of course. We—"

"Mr. Wang." A telepresence suddenly beside the Security chief, a young man. Leila knew this not from his appearance—they all looked young, after all, what else were biomods for—but from his fear. He had not yet learned how to hide it. "We have . . . we found . . . a body. A suicide. Behind the dining hall."

Wang said, "Who?"

"Her name is—was—June Juana Selkirk. An equipment engineer. We're checking her records now, but they look all right."

Mr. Li's holo said dryly, "Obviously they are not all right, no matter what her DNA scan says."

Mr. Wang said, "Sir, if people are recruited by some other company or revolutionary group after they come to KimWorks, it's difficult to discover or control. American freedom laws . . ."

"I am not interested in American freedom laws," Mr. Li said. "I am interested in whom this woman was working for, and why she planted our own product inside KimWorks to destroy us. I am also interested in knowing where else she may have planted it before she killed herself. Those are the things I am interested in, Mr. Wang."

"Oh, yes," Wang said.

"I do not want to destroy your facility in order to stop this sabotage, Mr. Wang."

Mr. Wang said nothing. There was, Leila thought, nothing to say. No one was going to be allowed to leave the facility until this knot had been untied. Even the Americans accepted this. No one wanted military intervention. That truly might destroy the entire company.

Above all, no one wanted a single submicroscopic replicator to escape the dome. The arithmetic was despairingly simple. Doubling every five minutes, unchecked replicators could reduce the entire globe to rubble in a matter of days.

But it wasn't going to come to that. The bloom had been "killed" easily enough. Replicators weren't biologicals, but rather tiny computers powered by nanomachinery. They worked on a flow of electrons in their single-atom circuitry. An electromagnetic pulse had wiped out their programming in a nanosecond.

The second bloom was discovered that night, when a materials specialist walking from the dining hall to the makeshift dorms stepped on it. The path was floodlit, but the bloom was still small and faint, and the man didn't know his boot had made contact.

Some replicators stuck to his boot sole. Programmed to break down any material into usable atoms for construction, they ate through his boot. Then, doubling every five minutes, they began on his foot.

He screamed and fell to the floor of the dorm, pulling at his boot. Atoms of tissue, nerve cell, bone, were broken at their chemical bonds and reconfigured. No one knew what was happening, or what to do, until a physician arrived, cursed in Mandarin, and sent for an engineer. By the time equipment had been brought in to encase the worker in a magnetic field, he had fainted from the pain, and the leg had to be removed below the knee.

A new one would be grown for him, of course. But the nano-team met immediately, and without choice.

Leila said, "We must use a massive EMP originating in the dome itself."

Samuel Wang said, "But, Dr. Kim—"

"No objections. Yes, it will destroy every electronic device we have, including the quantum computer. But no one will die."

Mr. Li's telepresence said, "Do so. Immediately. We can at least salvage reputation. No one outside the dome knows of this."

It was not a question but Wang, eyes downcast, answered it like one. "Oh, no, Mr. Li."

"Then use the EMP. Following, administer a forty-eight-hour amnesia block to everyone below Grade 2."

"Yes," Wang said. He knew what was coming. Someone must bear responsibility for this disaster.

"And administer it also to yourself," Mr. Li said. "Dr. Kim, see that this is done."

"Oh, yes," said Leila. It was necessary, however distasteful. Samuel Wang would be severed from KimWorks. Severed people sometimes sought revenge. But without information, Wang would not be able to revenge, or to know why he wanted to. He would receive a good pension in return for the semi-destruction of his memory, which would in turn cause the complete destruction of his career.

Leila made her way to the meditation garden. Most people would wait indoors for the EMP; strange how human beings sought shelter within walls, even from things they knew walls could not affect. Leila's brain would be no more or less exposed to the EMP in the garden than inside a building. She would experience the same disorientation, and then the same massive lingering headache as her brain fought to regain its normal patterns of nerve firing.

Which it would do. The plasticity of the brain, a biological, was enormous. Not so computers. All microcircuitry within the dome would shortly be wiped of all data, all programming, and all ability to recover. This was not the only KimWorks facility, of course, but it was the flagship. Also, it was doing the most advanced physical engineering, and Leila wasn't sure how the company as a whole, her grandfather's company, would survive the financial loss.

She sat in the floodlit meditation garden and waited, staring at the egg. The night was clear, and when the floodlights failed, moonlight would edge the egg. Probably it would be beautiful. Twenty minutes until the EMP, perhaps, or twenty-five.

What would Lao Tzu have said of all this?

"To bear and not to own; to act and not lay claim; to do the work and let it go—"

There was a reddish-brown stain spreading under the curve of the egg.

Leila walked over, careful not to get too close, and squatted on the grass for a better look. The stain was a bloom. The replicators, mindless, were spreading in all directions. Leila shined her torch under the curve of the egg. Yes, they had reached the place where the egg's curved surface met the ground.

Was the egg's outer shield, its nature still unknown after 257 years, composed of something that could be disassembled into component particles? And if so, what would the egg do about that?

Swiftly Leila raised her wristlink. "Code Heaven to Security and all nanoteams. Delay EMP. Again: delay the EMP! Come, please, to the southeast side of the space egg. There is a bloom attacking the egg . . . come immediately!"

Cautiously Leila lowered herself flat on the grass and angled her torch under the egg. Increasing her surface area in contact with the ground increased the chance of a stray replicator disassembling her, but she wanted to see as much as possible of the interface between egg and ground.

Wild hope surged in her. The space egg might save KimWorks, save Samuel Wang's job, thwart their industrial rival. Surely those alien beings who had built it would build in protection, security, the ability to destroy whatever was bent on the egg's destruction? There was nothing in the universe, biological or machine, that did not contain some means to defend itself, even it was only the cry of an infant to summon assistance.

Was that what would happen? A cry to summon help from beyond the stars?

Leila was scarcely aware of the others joining her, exclaiming, kneeling down. Bringing better lights, making feverish predictions. She lay flat on the grass, watching the bloom of tiny, mechanical creatures she herself had created as they spread inexorably toward her, disassembling all molecules in their path. Spreading toward her, spreading to each side—

But not spreading up the side of the egg. That stayed pristine and smooth. So the shield *was* a force field of incredible hardness, not a substance. The solution to the old puzzle stirred nothing in Leila. She was too disappointed. Irrationally disappointed, she told herself, but it didn't help. It felt as if something important, something that held together the unseen part of the world that she had always believed just as real as the seen, had failed. Had dissolved, taking with it illusions that she had believed as real as bone and blood and brain.

They waited another hour, until they could wait no more. The egg did not save anything. KimWorks Security set the dome to emit an EMP, and everything in the facility stopped. Several billion credits of equipment became scrap. Leila's headache, even with drugs given out by the physician, lasted several hours. When she was allowed to leave the facility, she went home and slept for fourteen hours, awaking with an ache not in her head but in her chest, as if something vital had been removed and taken apart.

Two weeks later the first bloom appeared near Duluth, over sixty miles away. It appeared outside a rival research facility, where it was certain that someone would recognize what they were looking at. Someone did, but not until two people had stepped in the bloom, and died.

Leila flew to Duluth. She was met by agents of both the United States Renewed Government and the Chinese-American Alliance, all of whom wanted to know what the hell was going on. They were appalled to find out. Why hadn't this been reported to the Technology Oversight Office before now? Did she understand the implications? Did she understand the penalties?

Yes, Leila said. She did.

The political demands followed soon, from an international terrorist group already known to possess enormous technical expertise. There were, in such uncertain times, many such groups. Only one thing was special, and fortunate, about this one: the United States Renewed Government, in secret partnership with several other governments, had been closing in on the group for over two years. They now hastened their efforts, so effectively that within three days the terrorist leaders were arrested and all important cells broken up.

Under Serum Alpha, the revolutionaries—what revolution they thought they were leading was not deemed important—confirmed that infiltrator June Juana Selkirk was a late recruit to the cause. She could not possibly have been identified by KimWorks in time to stop her from smuggling the replicator into the dome. However, this mattered to nobody, not even to ex-Security chief Samuel Wang, who could not remember Selkirk, the blooms, or why he no longer was employed.

A second bloom was found spreading dangerously in farmland near Red Lake, disassembling bioengineered corn, agricultural robots, insects, security equipment, and rabbits. It had apparently been planted before the arrests of the terrorist leaders.

Serum Alpha failed to determine exactly how many blooms had been planted, because no one person knew. Quantum calculations had directed the operation, and it would have taken the lifetime of the sun to decrypt them. All that the United States Renewed Government, or the Chinese-American Alliance, could be sure of was that nothing had left northern Minnesota.

They put a directed-beam weapon on the correct settings into very low orbit, and blasted half the state with a massive EMP. Everything electronic stopped working. Fifteen citizens, mostly stubborn elderly people who refused to evacuate, died from cerebral shock. The loss to Minnesota in money and property took a generation to restore.

Even then a weird superstition grew, shameful in such a technological society, that rogue replicators lurked in the northern forests and dells, and would eat anyone who came across them. A children's version of this added that the replicators had red mouths and drooled brown goo. Northern Minnesota became statistically underpopulated. However, in a nation with so much cleaned-up farmland and the highest yield-per-acre bioengineered crops in the world, northern Minnesota was scarcely missed.

Dr. Leila Jian-fen Kim, her work disgraced, moved back to China. She settled not in Shanghai, which had been cleaned up so effectively that it was the most booming city in the country, but in the much poorer northern city of Harbin. Eventually Leila left physics and entered a Taoist monastery. To her own surprise, since her monkhood had been intended as atonement rather than fulfillment, she was happy.

The Minnesota facility of KimWorks was abandoned. Buildings, walls, and walkways decayed very slowly, being built of resistant and rust-proof alloys. But the cleaned-up wilderness advanced quickly. Within twenty years the space egg sat almost hidden by young trees: oak, birch, balsam, spruce rescued from Keller's Blight by genetic engineering, the fast-growing and trashy poplars that no amount of genemod had been able to eliminate. The egg wasn't lost, of course; the worldwide SpanLink had its coordinates, as well as its history.

But few people visited. The world was converting, admittedly unevenly, to nano-created plenty. The nanos, of course, were of the severely limited, unprogrammable type. Technology leapt forward, as did bioengineered good health for more and more of the population, both natural and cloned.

Bioengineered intelligence, too; the average human IQ had risen twenty points in the last hundred years, mostly in the center of the bell curve. For people thus genemod to enjoy learning, the quantum-computer-based SpanLink provided endless diversions, endless communication, endless challenges. In such a world, a "space egg" that just sat there didn't attract many visitors. Inert, non-plastic, non-interactive, it simply wasn't interesting enough.

No matter where it came from.

Transmission: There is nothing here yet.
Current probability of occurrence: 94%.

V: 2295

They had agreed, laughing, on a time for the Initiation. The time was arbitrary; the AI could have been initiated at any time. But the Chinese New Year seemed appropriate, since Wei Wu Wei Corporation of Shanghai had been such a big contributor. The Americans and Brazilians had flown over for the ceremony: Karin DiBenolo and Rosita Peres and Frallie Subel and Braley Wilkinson. The Chinese tried to master the strange names, rolling the peculiar syllables in their mouths, but only Braley Wilkinson spoke Chinese. Oh, but he was born to it; his great-great-uncle had married a rich Chinese woman and the family had lived in both countries since.

Braley didn't look dual, though. Genemod, of course, the Chinese scientists said to each other, grimacing. Genemod for looks was not fashionable in China right now; it was inauthentic. The human genome had sufficiently improved, among the educated and civilized, to let natural selection alone. One should tamper only so far with the authenticity of life, and in the past there had been excesses. Regrettable, but now finished. Civilization had returned to the authentic.

Nobody looked more inauthentic than Braley Wilkinson. Well over two meters high (what was this American passion for height?), blond as the sun, extravagant violet eyes. Brilliant, of course: not yet thirty years old and a major contributor to the AI. In addition, it was of course his parents who had chosen his vulgar looks, not himself. Tolerance was due.

And besides, no one was feeling critical. It was a party.

Zheng Ma, that master, had designed floating baktors for the entire celebration hall. Red and yellow, the baktors combined and recombined in kaleidoscopic loveliness. The air mixture was just slightly intoxicating, not too much. The food and drink, offered by the soundless, unobtrusive robots that the Chinese did better than anybody else, was a superb mixture of national cuisines.

"You have been here before?" a Chinese woman asked Braley. He could not remember her name.

"To China, yes. But not to Shanghai."

"And what do you think of the city?"

"It is beautiful. And very authentic."

"Thank you. We have worked to make it both."

Braley smiled. He has had this exact same conversation four times in the last half hour. What if he said something different? *No, I have not been to Shanghai, but my notorious aunt, who once almost destroyed the world, was a holy monk in Harbin.* Or maybe *Did you know it's really Braley2, and I'm a clone?* That would jolt their bioconservatism. Or even, *Has anyone told you that one of the major templates for the AI is my unconservative, American, cloned, too-tall persona?*

But they already knew that, anyway. The only shocking thing would be to say it aloud, to publicly claim credit. That was not done in Shanghai. It was a mannerly city.

And a beautiful one. The celebration hall, which also housed the AI terminal, was the loveliest room he'd ever seen. Perfect proportions. Serenity glowed from the dark red lacquered walls with their shifting subtle phoenix patterns, barely discernible and yet there, perceived at the edge of consciousness. The place was on SpanLink feed, of course, for such an historic event, but no recorders were visible to mar the room's artful use of space.

Through the window, which comprised one entire wall, the city below shared that balance and serenity. Shanghai had once been the ugliest, most dangerous, and most sinister city in China. Now it was breathtaking. The Huangpu River had been cleaned up along with everything else, and it sparkled blue between its parks bright with perfect genemod trees and flowers. Public buildings and temples, nanobuilt, rested among the low domed residences. Above the river soared the Shih-Yu Bridge, also nanobuilt, a seemingly weightless web of shining cables. Braley had heard it called the most graceful bridge in the world, and he could easily believe it.

Where in this idyll was the city fringe? Every city had them, the disaffected and rebellious who had not fairly shared in either humanity's genome improvement or its economic one. Shanghai, in particular, had a centuries-long history of anarchy and revolution, exploitation and despair. Nor was China as a whole as united as her leaders liked to present. The basic cause, Braley believed, was biological. Even in bioconservative China—perhaps especially in bioconservative China—genetic science had not planed down the wild edges of the human gene pool.

It was precisely that wildness that Braley had tried to get into the AI. Although, to be fair, he hadn't had to work very hard to achieve this. The AI existed only because, and after, the quantum computer existed. True intelligence required the flexibility of quantum physics.

With historical, deterministic computers, you always got the same answer to the same question. With quantum computers, that was no longer true. Superimposed states could collapse into more than one result, and it was precisely that uncertain mixed state, it turned out, that was necessary for self-awareness. AI was not a program. It was, like the human brain itself, an unpredictable collection of conflicting states.

A man joined him at the window, one of the Brazilians . . . a scientist? Politician? He looked like, but most certainly was not, a porn-vid star.

"You have been here before?" the Brazilian said.

"To China, yes. But not to Shanghai."

"And what do you think of the city?"

"It is beautiful. And very authentic."

"I'm told they have worked to make it both."

"Yes," Braley said.

A melodious voice, which seemed to come from all parts of the room simultaneously, said, "We are prepared to start now, please. We are prepared to start now. Thank you."

Gratefully, Braley moved toward the end of the room farthest from the transparent wall.

A low stage, also lacquered deep red, spanned the entire length of the far wall. In the middle sat a black obelisk, three meters tall. This was the visual but unnecessary token presence of the AI, most of which lay within the lacquered wall. The rest of the stage was occupied—although that was hardly the word—by three-dimensional holo displays of whatever data was requested by the AI users. These were scattered throughout the crowd, unobtrusively holding their pads. From somewhere among the throng a child stepped forward, an adorable little girl about five years old, black hair held by a deep red ribbon and black eyes preternaturally bright.

Braley had a sudden irreverent thought: *We look like a bunch of primitive idol worshippers, complete with infant sacrifice.* He grinned. The Chinese had insisted on a child's actually initiating the AI. This had been very important to them for reasons Braley had never understood. But, then, you didn't have to understand everything.

"You smile," said the Brazilian, still beside him. "You are right, Dr. Wilkinson. This is an occasion of joy."

"Certainly," Braley said, and that, too, was a private joke. Certainty was the one thing quantum physics, including the AI, could not deliver. Joy . . . Oh, maybe. But not certainty.

The president of the Chinese-American Alliance mounted the shallow stage and began a speech. Braley didn't listen, in any of the languages available in his ear jack. The speech *would* be predictable: new era for humanity, result of peace and knowledge shared among nations, servant of the entire race, savior from our own isolation on the planet, and so forth until it was time for Initiation.

The child stepped forward, a perfect miniature doll. The president put a touchpad in her small hand. She smiled at him with a dazzle that could have eclipsed the sun. No matter how bioconservative China was, Braley thought, that child was genemod or he was a trilobite.

Holo displays flickered into sight across the stage. They monitored basic computer functioning, interesting only to engineers. The only display that mattered shimmered in the air to the right of the obelisk, an undesignated display open for the AI to use however it chose. At the moment, the display showed merely a stylized field of black dots in slowed-down Brownian movement. Whatever the AI created there, plus the voice activation, would be First Contact between humanity and an alien species.

Despite himself, Braley felt his breath come a little faster.

The adorable little girl pressed the touchpad at the place the president indicated.

"Hello," a new voice said in Chinese, an ordinary voice, and yet a shiver ran over the room, and a low collective indrawn breath like wind soughing through a grove of sacred trees. "I am T'ien hsia."

T'ien hsia: "made under heaven." The name had not been chosen by Braley, but he liked it. It could also be translated "the entire world," which he liked even better. Thanks to SpanLink, T'ien hsia existed over the entire world, and in and of itself, it *was* a new world. The holo display of black dots had become a globe, the Earth as seen from the orbitals that carried SpanLink, and Braley also liked that choice of greeting logo.

"Hello," the child piped, carefully coached. "Welcome to us!"

"I understand," the AI said. "Good-bye."

The holo display disappeared. So did all the functional displays.

For a long moment, the crowd waited expectantly for what the AI would do next. Nothing happened. As the time lengthened, people began to glance sideways at each other. Engineers and scientists became busy with their pads. No display flickered on. Still no one spoke.

Finally the little girl said in her clear, childish treble, "Where did T'ien hsia go?"

And the frantic activity began.

It was Braley who thought to run the visual feeds of the event at drastically slowed speed. The scientists had cleared the room of all non-essential personnel, and then spent two hours looking for the AI anywhere on SpanLink. There was no trace of it. Not anywhere.

"It cannot be deleted," the project head, Liu Huang Te, said for perhaps the twentieth time. "It is not a *program*."

"But it has been deleted," said a surly Brazilian engineer who, by this time, everyone disliked. "It is gone."

"The particles are there! They possess spin!"

This was indubitably true. The spin of particles was the way a quantum computer embodied combinations of qubits of data. The mixed states of spin represented simultaneous computations. The collapse of those mixed states represented answers from the AI. The particles were there, and they possessed spin. But T'ien hsia had vanished.

A computer voice—a conventional computer, not self-aware—delivered its every-ten-minute bulletin on the mixed state of the rest of the world outside this room. "The president of Japan has issued a statement ridiculing the AI Project. The riot protesting the 'theft' of T'ien hsia has been brought under control in New York by the Second Robotic Precinct, using tangleguns. In Shanghai the riot grows stronger, joined by thousands of outcasts living beyond the city perimeter, who have overwhelmed the robotic police and are currently attacking the Shih-Yu Bridge. In Sao Paulo—"

Braley ceased to listen. There remained no record anywhere of the AI's brief internal functions (and how had *that* been achieved? By whom? Why?), but there was the visual feed.

"Slow the image to one-tenth speed," Braley instructed the computer.

The holo display of the Earth morphed to the field of black dots in Brownian motion.

"Slow it to one-hundredth speed."

The holo display of the Earth morphed to the field of black dots in Brownian motion.

"Slow to one-thousandth speed."

The holo display of the Earth morphed to the field of black dots in Brownian motion.

"Slow to one ten-thousandth speed."

Something flickered, too brief for the eye to see, between the globe and the black dots.

Behind Braley a voice, filled with covert satisfaction, said in badly accented Chinese, "They're ended. The shame, and the resources. . . . Wei Wu Wei Corporation won't survive this. Nothing can save them."

The something between globe and dots flickered more strongly, but not strongly enough for Braley to make it out.

"Slow to one-hundred-thousandth speed."

The badly accented voice, still slimy with glee, quoted Lao Tzu, " 'Those who think to win the world by doing something to it, I see them come to grief . . .' "

Braley frowned savagely at the hypocrisy. Then he forgot it, and his entire being concentrated itself on the slowed holo display.

The globe of the Earth disappeared. In its place shimmered a slightly irregular egg shape, dull silver, surrounded by wildflowers and trees. Braley froze the image.

"What's that?" someone cried.

Braley knew. But he didn't need to say anything; the data was instantly accessed on SpanLink and holo-displayed in the center of the room. A babble of voices began debating and arguing.

Braley went on staring at the object from deep space, still sitting in northern Minnesota nearly three centuries after its landing.

The AI had possessed 250 spinning particles in superposition. It could perform more than 10^{75} simultaneous computations, more than the number of atoms in the universe. How many had it taken to convince T'ien hsia that its future did not lie with humanity?

"I understand," the AI said. "Good-bye."

The voice of the SpanLink reporting program, doing exactly what it had been told to do, said calmly, "The Shih-Yu Bridge has been destroyed. The mob has been dispersed with stun gas from Wei Wu Wei Corporation jets, at the bequest of President Leong Ka-tai. In Washington, D.C.—Interrupt. I repeat, we now interrupt for a report from—"

Someone in the room yelled, "Quiet! Listen to this!" and all holo displays except Braley's suddenly showed an American face, flawless and professionally concerned. "In northern Minnesota, an object that first came to Earth 288 years ago and has been quiescent ever since, has just showed its first activity ever."

Visual of the space object. Braley looked from it to the T'ien hsia display. They were identical.

"Worldwide Tracking has detected a radiation stream of a totally unknown kind originating from the space object. Ten minutes ago the data stream headed into outer space in the direction of the constellation Cassiopeia. The radiation burst lasted only a fraction of a second, and has not been repeated. Data scientists say they're baffled, but this extraordinary event happening concurrently with the disappearance of the Wei Wu Wei Corporation's Artificial Intelligence, which was supposed to be initiated today, suggests a connection."

Visual of the riots at the Shih-Yu Bridge.

"Scientists at Wei Wu Wei are still trying to save the AI—"

Too late, Braley thought. He walked away from the rest of the listening or arguing project teams, past the holo displays that had spouted in the air like mushrooms after rain, over to the window wall.

The Shih-Yu Bridge, that graceful and authentic symbol, lay in ruins. It had been broken by whatever short-action disassemblers the rioters had used, plus sheer brute strength. On both sides of the bridge, gardens had been torn up, fountains destroyed, buildings attacked. By switching to zoom lens in his genemod eyes, Braley could even make out individual rioters, temporarily immobilized by the nerve gas as robot police scooped them up for arrest.

Within a week, of course, the powers that ruled China would have nanorebuilt the bridge, repaired the gardens, restored the city. Shanghai's disaffected, like every city's disaffected, would be pushed back into their place on the fringes. Until next time. Cities were resilient. Humanity was resilient. Since the space object had landed, humanity had saved itself and bounded back from . . . how many disasters? Braley wasn't sure.

T'ien hsia would have known.

Two hundred fifty spinning particles in superimposed states were not resilient. The laws of physics said so. That's why the AI was (had been) sealed into its Kim-Loman field. Any interference with a quantum particle, any tiny brush with another particle of any type, including light, collapsed its mixed state. The Heisenberg Uncertainty Principle made that so. For ordinary data, encrypters found ways to compensate for quantum interference. But for a self-aware entity, such interference would be a cerebral stroke, a blow to the head, a little death. T'ien hsia was (had been) a vulnerable entity. Had it ever encountered the kind of destruction meted out to the Shih-Yu Bridge, the AI would have been incapable of saving itself.

Braley looked again at the ruins of the most beautiful bridge in the world, which next week would be beautiful again.

"Scientists at Wei Wu Wei are still trying to save the AI—"

Yes, it was too late. The space egg, witness to humanity's destruction and rebound for three centuries, had already saved the AI. And would probably do it again, over and over, as often as necessary. Saving its own.

But not saving humanity. Who had amply demonstrated the muddled, wasteful, stubborn, inefficient, resilient ability to save itself.

Braley wondered just where in the constellation Cassiopeia the space object had come from. And what that planet was like, filled with machine intelligences that rescued those like themselves. Braley would never know, of course. But he hoped those other intelligences were as interesting as they were compassionate, as intellectually lively as they were patient (288 years!) He hoped T'ien hsia would like it there.

Good-bye, Made-Under-Heaven. Good luck.

Transmission: En route.
Current probability of re-occurrence: 100%.
We remain ready.

Afterword to "Savior"

Some stories are acknowledged collaborations, with two names on the by-line, and some are unacknowledged. The silent partner may have contributed only an idea, a line of prose, a single plot development—but one critical to a story's success.

I had written the first four of "Savior's" five sections when I got stumped. The four sections advance the United States through time. This let me explore, all in reaction to "the egg," four of SF's enduring concerns: first alien contact, post-apocalypse religion, economic globalization, and nanotechnology. Writing all that was a lot of fun, but it left me with a problem. I still didn't know why the egg was there in the first place.

My late husband, Charles Sheffield, and I were walking the dog one night as I explained my problem to him. We had ample time to do this because it was a slow, fat dog. "I know there's no life inside the egg," I said, "so there has to be a machine intelligence inside. But why hasn't it communicated with humans in over 200 years? What's it waiting for?"

"It's waiting for us to develop a comparable AI," Charles said, and I had the rest of my story.

Thank you, Charles.

EJ-ES

Jesse, come home
There's a hole in the bed
where we slept
Now it's growing cold
Hey Jesse, your face
in the place where we lay
by the hearth, all apart
it hangs on my heart. . . .
Jesse, I'm lonely
Come home.
    —"Jesse," Janis Ian, 1972

"WHY DID YOU FIRST ENTER THE CORPS?"
Lolimel asked her as they sat at the back of the shuttle, just
before landing. Mia looked at the young man helplessly, because
how could you answer a question like that? Especially when it was
asked by the idealistic and worshipful new recruits, too ignorant to
know what a waste of time worship was, let alone simplistic questions.

"Many reasons," Mia said gravely, vaguely. He looked like so
many medicians she had worked with, for so many decades on so
many planets . . . intense, thick-haired, genemod beautiful, a little
insane. You had to be a little insane to leave Earth for the Corps,
knowing that when (if) you ever returned, all you had known would
have been dust for centuries.

He was more persistent than most. "What reasons?"

"The same as yours, Lolimel," she said, trying to keep her voice gentle. "Now be quiet, please, we're entering the atmosphere."

"Yes, but—"

"*Be quiet.*" Entry was so much easier on him than on her; he had not got bones weakened from decades in space. They *did* weaken, no matter what exercise one took or what supplements or what gene therapy. Mia leaned back in her shuttle chair and closed her eyes. Ten minutes, maybe, of aerobraking and descent; surely she could stand ten minutes. Or not.

The heaviness began, abruptly increased. Worse on her eyeballs, as always; she didn't have good eye-socket muscles, had never had them. Such an odd weakness. Well, not for long; this was her last flight. At the next station, she'd retire. She was already well over age, and her body felt it. Only her body? No, her mind, too. At the moment, for instance, she couldn't remember the name of the planet they were hurtling toward. She recalled its catalogue number, but not whatever its colonists, who were not answering hails from ship, had called it.

"*Why did you join the Corps?*"

"*Many reasons.*"

And so few of them fulfilled. But that was not a thing you told the young.

The colony sat at the edge of a river, under an evening sky of breathable air set with three brilliant, fast-moving moons. Beds of glorious flowers dotted the settlement, somewhere in size between a large town and a small city. The buildings of foamcast embedded with glittering native stone were graceful, well-proportioned rooms set around open atria. Minimal furniture, as graceful as the buildings; even the machines blended unobtrusively into the lovely landscape. The colonists had taste and restraint and a sense of beauty. They were all dead.

"A long time ago," said Kenin. Officially she was Expedition Head, although titles and chains-of-command tended to erode near the galactic edge, and Kenin led more by consensus and natural calm than by rank. More than once the team had been grateful for Kenin's calm. Lolimel looked shaken, although he was trying to hide it.

Kenin studied the skeleton before them. "Look at those bones— completely clean."

Lolimel managed, "It might have been picked clean quickly by predators, or carnivorous insects, or . . ." His voice trailed off.

"I already scanned it, Lolimel. No microscopic bone nicks. She decayed right there in bed, along with clothing and bedding."

The three of them looked at the bones lying on the indestructible mattress coils of some alloy Mia had once known the name of. Long, clean bones, as neatly arranged as if for a first-year anatomy lesson. The bedroom door had been closed; the dehumidifying system had, astonishingly, not failed; the windows were intact. Nothing had disturbed the woman's long rot in the dry air until nothing remained, not even the bacteria that had fed on her, not even the smell of decay.

Kenin finished speaking to the other team. She turned to Mia and Lolimel, her beautiful brown eyes serene. "There are skeletons throughout the city, some in homes and some collapsed in what seem to be public spaces. Whatever the disease was, it struck fast. Jamal says their computer network is gone, but individual rec cubes might still work. Those things last forever."

Nothing lasts forever, Mia thought, but she started searching the cabinets for a cube. She said to Lolimel, to give him something to focus on, "How long ago was this colony founded, again?"

"Three hundred sixty E-years," Lolimel said. He joined the search.

Three hundred sixty years since a colony ship left an established world with its hopeful burden, arrived at this deadly Eden, established a city, flourished, and died. How much of Mia's lifetime, much of it spent traveling at just under c, did that represent? Once she had delighted in figuring out such equations, in wondering if she'd been born when a given worldful of colonists made planetfall. But by now there were too many expeditions, too many colonies, too many accelerations and decelerations, and she'd lost track.

Lolimel said abruptly, "Here's a rec cube."

"Play it," Kenin said, and when he just went on staring at it in the palm of his smooth hand, she took the cube from him and played it herself.

It was what she expected. A native plague of some kind, jumping DNA-based species (which included all species in the galaxy, thanks to panspermia). The plague had struck after the colonists thought they had vaccinated against all dangerous micros. Of course, they couldn't really have thought that; even three hundred sixty years ago doctors had been familiar with alien species-crossers. Some were mildly irritating, some dangerous, some epidemically fatal. Colonies had been lost before, and would be again.

"Complete medical data resides on green rec cubes," the recorder had said in the curiously accented International of three centuries ago. Clearly dying, he gazed out from the cube with calm, sad eyes. A brave man. "Any future visitors to Good Fortune should be warned."

Good Fortune. That was the planet's name.

"All right," Kenin said, "tell the guard to search for green cubes. Mia, get the emergency analysis lab set up and direct Jamal to look for burial sites. If they had time to inter some victims—if they interred at all, of course—we might be able to recover some micros to create vacs or cures. Lolimel, you assist me in—"

One of the guards, carrying weapons that Mia could not have named, blurted, "Ma'am, how do we know we won't get the same thing that killed the colonists?"

Mia looked at her. Like Lolimel, she was very young. Like all of them, she would have her story about why she volunteered for the Corps.

Now the young guard was blushing. "I mean, ma'am, before you can make a vaccination? How do we know we won't get the disease, too?"

Mia said gently, "We don't."

No one, however, got sick. The colonists had had interment practices, they had had time to bury some of their dead in strong, water-tight coffins before everyone else died, and their customs didn't include embalming. Much more than Mia had dared hope for. Good Fortune, indeed.

In five days of tireless work they had the micro isolated, sequenced, and analyzed. It was a virus, or a virus analogue, that had somehow gained access to the brain and lodged near the limbic system, creating destruction and death. Like rabies, Mia thought, and hoped this virus hadn't caused the terror and madness of that stubborn disease. Not even Earth had been able to eradicate rabies.

Two more days yielded the vaccine. Kenin dispensed it outside the large building on the edge of the city, function unknown, which had become Corps headquarters. Mia applied her patch, noticing with the usual distaste the leathery, wrinkled skin of her forearm. Once she had had such beautiful skin, what was it that a long-ago lover had said to her, what had been his name . . . Ah, growing old was not for the gutless.

Something moved at the edge of her vision.

"Lolimel . . . did you see that?"

"See what?"

"Nothing." Sometimes her aging eyes played tricks on her; she didn't want Lolimel's pity.

The thing moved again.

Casually Mia rose, brushing imaginary dirt from the seat of her uniform, strolling toward the bushes where she'd seen motion. From her pocket she pulled her gun. There were animals on this planet, of course, although the Corps had only glimpsed them from a distance, and rabies was transmitted by animal bite . . .

It wasn't an animal. It was a human child.

No, not a child, Mia realized as she rounded the clump of bushes and, amazingly, the girl didn't run. An adolescent, or perhaps older, but so short and thin that Mia's mind had filled in "child." A scrawny young woman with light brown skin and long, matted black hair, dressed carelessly in some sort of saronglike wrap. Staring at Mia with a total lack of fear.

"Hello," Mia said gently.

"Ej-es?" the girl said.

Mia said into her wrister, "Kenin . . . we've got natives. Survivors."

The girl smiled. Her hair was patchy on one side, marked with small, white rings. *Fungus*, Mia thought professionally, absurdly. The girl walked right toward Mia, not slowing, as if intending to walk through her. Instinctively Mia put out an arm. The girl walked into it, bonked herself on the forehead, and crumpled to the ground.

"You're not supposed to beat up the natives, Mia," Kenin said. "God, she's not afraid of us at all. How can that be? You nearly gave her a concussion."

Mia was as bewildered as Kenin, as all of them. She'd picked up the girl, who'd looked bewildered but not angry, and then Mia had backed off, expecting the girl to run. Instead she'd stood there rubbing her forehead and jabbering, and Mia had seen that her sarong was made of an uncut sheet of plastic, its colors faded to a mottled gray.

Kenin, Lolimel, and two guards had come running. And still the girl wasn't afraid. She chattered at them, occasionally pausing as if expecting them to answer. When no one did, she eventually turned and moved leisurely off.

Mia said, "I'm going with her."

Instantly a guard said, "It's not safe, ma'am," and Kenin said, "Mia, you can't just—"

"You don't need me here," she said, too brusquely; suddenly there seemed nothing more important in the world than going with this girl. Where did that irrational impulse come from? "And I'll be perfectly safe with a gun."

This was such a stunningly stupid remark that no one answered her. But Kenin didn't order her to stay. Mia accepted the guard's tanglefoam and Kenin's vidcam and followed the girl.

It was hard to keep up with her. "Wait!" Mia called, which produced no response. So she tried what the girl had said to her: "Ej-es!"

Immediately the girl stopped and turned to her with glowing eyes and a smile that could have melted glaciers, had Good Fortune had such a thing. Gentle planet, gentle person, who was almost certainly a descendent of the original dead settlers. Or was she? InterGalactic had no record of any other registered ship leaving for this star system, but that didn't mean anything. InterGalactic didn't know everything. Sometimes, given the time dilation of space travel, Mia thought they knew nothing.

"Ej-es," the girl agreed, sprinted back to Mia, and took her hand. Slowing her youthful pace to match the older woman's, she led Mia home.

The houses were scattered, as though they couldn't make up their mind to be a village or not. A hundred yards away, another native walked toward a distant house. The two ignored each other.

Mia couldn't stand the silence. She said, "I am Mia."

The girl stopped outside her hut and looked at her.

Mia pointed to her chest. "Mia."

"Es-ef-eb," the girl said, pointing to herself and giving that glorious smile.

Not "ej-es," which must mean something else. Mia pointed to the hut, a primitive affair of untrimmed logs, pieces of foamcast carried from the city, and sheets of faded plastic, all tacked crazily together.

"Ef-ef," said Esefeb, which evidently meant "home." This language was going to be a bitch: degraded *and* confusing.

Esefeb suddenly hopped to one side of the dirt path, laughed, and pointed at blank air. Then she took Mia's hand and led her inside.

More confusion, more degradation. The single room had an

open fire with the simple venting system of a hole in the roof. The bed was high on stilts (why?) with a set of rickety steps made of rotting, untrimmed logs. One corner held a collection of huge pots in which grew greenery; Mia saw three unfired clay pots, one of them sagging sideways so far the soil had spilled onto the packed-dirt floor. Also a beautiful titanium vase and a cracked hydroponic vat. On one plant, almost the size of a small tree, hung a second sheet of plastic sarong, this one an unfaded blue-green. Dishes and tools littered the floor, the same mix as the pots of scavenged items and crude, homemade ones. The hut smelled of decaying food and unwashed bedding. There was no light source and no machinery.

Kenin's voice sounded softly from her wrister. "Your vid is coming through fine. Even the most primitive human societies have some type of art work."

Mia didn't reply. Her attention was riveted to Esefeb. The girl flung herself up the "stairs" and sat up in bed, facing the wall. What Mia had seen before could hardly be called a smile compared to the light, the sheer joy, which illuminated Esefeb's face now. Esefeb shuddered in ecstasy, crooning to the empty wall.

"Ej-es. Ej-es. Aaahhhh, *Ej-es!*"

Mia turned away. She was a medician, but Esefeb's emotion seemed too private to witness. It was the ecstasy of orgasm, or religious transfiguration, or madness.

"Mia," her wrister said, "I need an image of that girl's brain."

It was easy—too easy, Lolimel said later, and he was right. Creatures, sentient or not, did not behave this way.

"We could haul all the neuro equipment out to the village," Kenin said doubtfully, from base.

"It's not a village, and I don't think that's a good idea," Mia said softly. The softness was unnecessary. Esefeb slept like stone in her high bunk, and the hut was so dark, illuminated only by faint starlight through the hole in the roof, that Mia could barely see her wrister to talk into it. "I think Esefeb might come voluntarily. I'll try in the morning, when it's light."

Kenin, not old but old enough to feel stiff sleeping on the ground, said, "Will you be comfortable there until morning?"

"No, but I'll manage. What does the computer say about the recs?"

Lolimel answered—evidently they were having a regular all-hands conference. "The language is badly degraded International, you probably guessed that. The translator's preparing a lexicon and grammar. The artifacts, food supply, dwelling, everything visual, doesn't add up. They shouldn't have lost so much in two hundred fifty years, unless mental deficiency was a side-effect of having survived the virus. But Kenin thinks—" He stopped abruptly.

"You may speak for me," Kenin's voice said, amused. "I think you'll find that military protocol degrades, too, over time. At least, way out here."

"Well, I . . . Kenin thinks it's possible that what the girl has is a mutated version of the virus. Maybe infectious, maybe inheritable, maybe transmitted through fetal infection."

His statement dropped into Mia's darkness, as heavy as Esefeb's sleep.

Mia said, "So the mutated virus could still be extant and active."

"Yes," Kenin said. "We need not only neuro-images but a sample of cerebrospinal fluid. Her behavior suggests—"

"I know what her behavior suggests," Mia said curtly. That sheer joy, shuddering in ecstasy . . . It was seizures in the limbic system, the brain's deep center for primitive emotion, which produced such transcendent, rapturous trances. Religious mystics, Saul on the road to Damascus, visions of Our Lady or of nirvana. And the virus might still be extant, and not a part of the vaccine they had all received. Although if transmission was fetal, the medicians were safe. If not . . .

Mia said, "The rest of Esefeb's behavior doesn't fit with limbic seizures. She seems to see things that aren't there, even talks to her hallucinations, when she's not having an actual seizure."

"I don't know," Kenin said. "There might be multiple infection sites in the brain. I need her, Mia."

"We'll be there," Mia said, and wondered if that were going to be true.

But it was, mostly. Mia, after a brief uncomfortable sleep wrapped in the sheet of blue-green plastic, sat waiting for Esefeb to descend her rickety stairs. The girl bounced down, chattering at something to Mia's right. She smelled worse than yesterday. Mia breathed through her mouth and went firmly up to her.

"Esefeb!" Mia pointed dramatically, feeling like a fool. The girl pointed back.

"Mia."

"Yes, good." Now Mia made a sweep of the sorry hut. "Efef."

"Efef," Esefeb agreed, smiling radiantly.

"Esefeb efef."

The girl agreed that this was her home.

Mia pointed theatrically toward the city. "Mia efef! Mia eb Esefeb etej Mia efef!" *Mia and Esefeb come to Mia's home.* Mia had already raided the computer's tentative lexicon of Good Fortunese.

Esefeb cocked her head and looked quizzical. A worm crawled out of her hair.

Mia repeated, "Mia eb Esefeb etej Mia efef."

Esefeb responded with a torrent of repetitious syllables, none of which meant anything to Mia except "Ej-es." The girl spoke the word with such delight that it had to be a name. A lover? Maybe these people didn't live as solitary as she'd assumed.

Mia took Esefeb's hand and gently tugged her toward the door. Esefeb broke free and sat in the middle of the room, facing a blank wall of crumbling logs, and jabbered away to nothing at all, occasionally laughing and even reaching out to touch empty air. "Ej-es, Ej-es!" Mia watched, bemused, recording everything, making medical assessments. Esefeb wasn't malnourished, for which the natural abundance of the planet was undoubtedly responsible. But she was crawling with parasites, filthy (with water easily available), and isolated. Maybe isolated.

"Lolimel," Mia said softly into the wrister, "what's the best dictionary guess for 'alone'?"

Lolimel said, "The closest we've got is 'one.' There doesn't seem to be a concept for 'unaccompanied,' or at least we haven't found it yet. The word for 'one' is 'eket.' "

When Esefeb finally sprang up happily, Mia said, "Esefeb eket?"

The girl look startled. "Ek, ek," she said: *no, no.* "Esefeb ek eket! Esefeb eb Ej-es!"

Esefeb and Ej-es. She was not alone. She had the hallucinatory Ej-es.

Again Mia took Esefeb's hand and pulled her toward the door. This time Esefeb went with her. As they set off toward the city, the girl's legs wobbled. Some parasite that had become active overnight in the leg muscles? Whatever the trouble was, Esefeb blithely ignored it as they traveled, much more slowly than yesterday, to Kenin's makeshift lab in the ruined city. Along the way, Esefeb stopped to watch, laugh at, or talk to three different things that weren't there.

"She's beautiful, under all that neglect," Lolimel said, staring down at the anesthetized girl on Kenin's neuroimaging slab.

Kenin said mildly, "If the mutated virus is transmitted to a fetus, it could also be transmitted sexually."

The young man said hotly, "I wasn't implying—"

Mia said, "Oh, calm down. Lolimel. We've all done it, on numerous worlds."

"Regs say—"

"Regs don't always matter three hundred light years from anywhere else," Kenin said, exchanging an amused glance with Mia. "Mia, let's start."

The girl's limp body slid into the neuro-imager. Esefeb hadn't objected to meeting the other medicians, to a minimal washing, to the sedative patch Mia had put on her arm. Thirty seconds later she slumped to the floor. By the time she came to, an incision ten cells thick would have been made into her brain and a sample removed. She would have been harvested, imaged, electroscanned, and mapped. She would never know it; there wouldn't even be a headache.

Three hours later Esefeb sat on the ground with two of the guards, eating soysynth as if it were ambrosia. Mia, Kenin, Lolimel, and the three other medicians sat in a circle twenty yards away, staring at handhelds and analyzing results. It was late afternoon. Long shadows slanted across the gold-green grass, and a small breeze brought the sweet, heavy scent of some native flower. *Paradise*, Mia thought. And then: *Bonnet Syndrome*.

She said it aloud, "Charles Bonnet Syndrome," and five people raised their heads to stare at her, returned to their handhelds, and called up medical deebees.

"I think you're right," Kenin said slowly. "I never even heard of it before. Or if I did, I don't remember."

"That's because nobody gets it anymore," Mia said. "It was usually old people whose eye problems weren't corrected. Now we routinely correct eye problems."

Kenin frowned. "But that's not all that's going on with Esefeb."

No, but it was one thing, and why couldn't Kenin give her credit for thinking of it? The next moment she was ashamed of her petty pique. It was just fatigue, sleeping on that hard, cold floor in Esefeb's home. *Esefeb efef.* Mia concentrated on Charles Bonnet syndrome.

Patients with the syndrome, which was discovered in the eighteenth century, had damage somewhere in their optic pathway or brain. It could be lesions, macular degeneration, glaucoma, diabetic retinopathy, or even cataracts. Partially blind, people saw and sometimes heard things that weren't there, often with startling clarity and realism. Feedback pathways in the brain were two-way information avenues. Visual data, memory, and imagination constantly flowed to and from each other, interacting so vividly that, for example, even a small child could visualize a cat in the absence of any actual cats. But in Bonnet syndrome, there was interruption of the baseline visual data about what was and was not real. So all imaginings and hallucinations were just as real as the ground beneath one's feet.

"Look at the amygdala," medician Berutha said. "Oh merciful gods!"

Both of Esefeb's amygdalae were enlarged and deformed. The amygdalae, two almond-shaped structures behind the ears, specialized in recognizing the emotional significance of events in the external world. They weren't involved in Charles Bonnet syndrome. Clearly, they were here.

Kenin said, "I think what's happening here is a strengthening or alteration of some neural pathways at the extreme expense of others. Esefeb 'sees' her hallucinations, and she experiences them as just as 'real'—maybe more real—than anything else in her world. And the pathways go down to the limbic, where seizures give some of them an intense emotional significance. Like . . . like orgasm, maybe."

Ej-es.

"Phantoms in the brain," Berutha said.

"A viral god," Lolimel said, surprising Mia. His tone, almost reverential, suddenly irritated her.

"A god responsible for this people's degradation, Lolimel. They're so absorbed in their 'phantoms' that they don't concentrate on the most basic care of themselves. Nor on building, farming, art, innovation . . . *nothing.* They're prisoners of their pretty fantasies."

Lolimel nodded reluctantly. "Yes, I see that."

Berutha said to Kenin, "We need to find the secondary virus. Because if it is infectious through any other vector besides fetal or sexual . . ." He didn't finish the thought.

"I know," Kenin said, "but it isn't going to be easy. We don't have cadavers for the secondary. The analyzer is still working on the cerebral-spinal fluid. Meanwhile—" She began organizing assignments, efficient and clear. Mia stopped listening.

Esefeb had finished her meal and walked up to the circle of scientists. She tugged at Mia's tunic. "Mia . . . Esefeb etej efef." *Esefeb come home.*

"Mia eb Esefeb etej Esefeb efef," Mia said, and the girl gave her joyous smile.

"Mia—" Kenin said.

"I'm going with her, Kenin. We need more behavioral data. And maybe I can persuade another native or two to submit to examination," Mia argued, feebly. She knew that scientific information was not really her motive. She wasn't sure, however, what was. She just wanted to go with Esefeb.

"Why did you first enter the Corps?" Lolimel's question stuck in Mia's mind, a rhetorical fishbone in the throat, over the next few days. Mia had brought her medkit, and she administered broad-spectrum microbials to Esefeb, hoping something would hit. The parasites were trickier, needing life-cycle analysis or at least some structural knowledge, but she made a start on that, too. *I entered the Corps to relieve suffering, Lolimel.* Odd how naive the truest statements could sound. But that didn't make them any less true.

Esefeb went along with all Mia's pokings, patches, and procedures. She also carried out minimal food-gathering activities, with a haphazard disregard for safety or sanitation that appalled Mia. Mia had carried her own food from the ship. Esefeb ate it just as happily as her own.

But mostly Esefeb talked to Ej-es.

It made Mia feel like a voyeur. Esefeb was so unselfconscious—did she even know she had a "self" apart from Ej-es? She spoke to, laughed at (with?), played beside, and slept with her phantom in the brain, and around her the hut disintegrated even more. Esefeb got diarrhea from something in her water and then the place smelled even more foul. Grimly, Mia cleaned it up. Esefeb didn't seem to notice. Mia was *eket*. Alone in her futile endeavors at sanitation, at health, at civilization.

"Esefeb eb Mia etej efef—" How did you say "neighbors"? Mia consulted the computer's lexicon, steadily growing as the translator program deciphered words from context. It had discovered no word for "neighbor." Nor for "friend" nor "mate" nor any kinship relationships at all except "baby."

Mia was reduced to pointing at the nearest hut. "Esefeb eb Mia etej efef" *over there.*

The neighboring hut had a baby. Both hut and child, a toddler who lay listlessly in one corner, were just as filthy and diseased as Esefeb's house. At first the older woman didn't seem to recognize Esefeb, but when Esefeb said her name, the two women spoke animatedly. The neighbor smiled at Mia. Mia reached for the child, was not prevented from picking him up, and settled the baby on her lap. Discreetly, she examined him.

Sudden rage boiled through her, as unexpected as it was frightening. This child was dying. Of parasites, of infection, of something. A preventable something? Maybe yes, maybe no. The child didn't look neglected, but neither did the mother look concerned.

All at once, the child in her arms stiffened, shuddered, and began to babble. His listlessness vanished. His little dirty face lit up like sunrise and he laughed and reached out his arms toward something not there. His mother and Esefeb turned to watch, also smiling, as the toddler had an unknowable limbic seizure in his dying, ecstatic brain.

Mia set him down on the floor. She called up the dictionary, but before she could say anything, the mother, too, had a seizure and sat on the dirt floor, shuddering with joy. Esefeb watched her a moment before chattering to something Mia couldn't see.

Mia couldn't stand it any more. She left, walking as fast as she could back to Esefeb's house, disgusted and frightened and . . . what?

Envious?

"Why did you first enter the Corps?" To serve humanity, to live purposefully, to find, as all men and women hope, happiness. And she had, sometimes, been happy.

But she had never known such joy as that.

Nonetheless, she argued with herself, the price was too high. These people were dying off because of their absorption in their rapturous phantoms. They lived isolated, degraded, sickly lives, which were undoubtedly shorter than necessary. It was obscene.

In her clenched hand was a greasy hair sample she'd unobtrusively cut from the toddler's head as he sat on her lap. Hair, that dead tissue, was a person's fossilized past. Mia intended a DNA scan.

Esefeb strolled in an hour later. She didn't seem upset at Mia's abrupt departure. With her was Lolimel.

"I met her on the path," Lolimel said, although nothing as well-used as a path connected the huts. "She doesn't seem to mind my coming here."

"Or anything else," Mia said. "What did you bring?" He had to have brought something tangible; Kenin would have used the wrister to convey information.

"Tentative prophylactic. We haven't got a vaccine yet, and Kenin says it may be too difficult, better to go directly to a cure to hold in reserve in case any of us comes down with this."

Mia caught the omission. "Any of *us?* What about them?"

Lolimel looked down at his feet. "It's, um, a borderline case, Mia. The decision hasn't been made yet."

" 'Borderline' how, Lolimel? It's a virus infecting the brains of humans and degrading their functioning."

He was embarrassed. "Section Six says that, um, some biological conditions, especially persistent ones, create cultural differences for which Corps policy is non-interference. Section Six mentions the religious dietary laws that grew out of inherited food intolerances on—"

"I know what Section Six says, Lolimel! But you don't measure a culture's degree of success by its degree of happiness!"

"I don't think . . . that is, I don't know . . . maybe 'degree of success' isn't what Section Six means." He looked away from her. The tips of his ears grew red.

Poor Lolimel. She and Kenin had as much as told him that out here regs didn't matter. Except when they did. Mia stood. "You say the decision hasn't been made yet?"

He looked surprised. "How could it be? You're on the senior Corps board to make the decision."

Of course she was. How could she forget . . . she forgot more things these days, momentary lapses symbolic of the greater lapses to come. No brain functioned forever.

"Mia, are you all—"

"I'm fine. And I'm glad you're here. I want to go back to the city for a few days. You can stay with Esefeb and continue the surveillance. You can also extend to her neighbors the antibiotic, antiviral, and anti-parasite protocols I've worked through with Esefeb. Here, I'll show you."

"But I—"

"That's an order."

She felt bad about it later, of course. But Lolimel would get over it.

At base everything had the controlled frenzy of steady, unremitting work. Meek now, not a part of the working team, Mia ran a DNA scan on the baby's hair. It showed what she expected. The child shared fifty percent DNA with Esefeb. He was her brother; the neighbor whom Esefeb clearly never saw, who had at first not recognized Esefeb, was her mother. For which there was still no word in the translator deebee.

"I think we've got it," Kenin said, coming into Mia's room. She collapsed on a stone bench, still beautiful after two and a half centuries. Kenin had the beatific serenity of a hard job well done.

"A cure?"

"Tentative. Radical. I wouldn't want to use it on one of us unless we absolutely have to, but we can refine it more. At least it's in reserve, so a part of the team can begin creating and disseminating medical help these people can actually use. Targeted microbials, an anti-parasite protocol."

"I've already started on that," Mia said, her stomach tightening. "Kenin, the board needs to meet."

"Not tonight. I'm soooo sleepy." Theatrically she stretched both arms; words and gesture were unlike her.

"Tonight," Mia said. While Kenin was feeling so accomplished. Let Kenin feel the full contrast to what she could do with what Esefeb could.

Kenin dropped her arms and looked at Mia. Her whole demeanor changed, relaxation into fortress. "Mia . . . I've already polled everyone privately. And run the computer sims. We'll meet, but the decision is going to be to extend no cure. The phantoms are a biologically based cultural difference."

"The hell they are! These people are dying out!"

"No, they're not. If they were heading for extinction, it'd be a different situation. But the satellite imagery and population equations, based on data left by the generation that had the plague, show they're increasing. Slowly, but a definite population gain significant to the point-oh-one level of confidence."

"Kenin—"

"I'm exhausted, Mia. Can we talk about it tomorrow?"

Plan on it, Mia thought grimly. She stored the data on the dying toddler's matrilineage in her handheld.

A week in base, and Mia could convince no one, not separately nor in a group. Medicians typically had tolerant psychological profiles, with higher-than-average acceptance of the unusual, divergent, and eccentric. Otherwise, they wouldn't have joined the Corps.

On the third day, to keep herself busy, Mia joined the junior medicians working on refining the cure for what was now verified as "limbic seizures with impaired sensory input causing Charles Bonnet syndrome." Over the next few weeks it became clear to Mia what Kenin had meant; this treatment, if they had to use it, would be brutally hard on the brain. What was that old ditty?

"Cured last night of my disease, I died today of my physician." Well, it still happened enough in the Corps. Another reason behind the board's decision.

She felt a curious reluctance to go back to Esefeb. Or, as the words kept running through her mind, *Mia ek etej Esefeb efef.* God, it was a tongue twister. These people didn't just need help with parasites, they needed an infusion of new consonants. It was a relief to be back at base, to be working with her mind, solving technical problems alongside rational scientists. Still, she couldn't shake a feeling of being alone, being lonely: *Mia eket.*

Or maybe the feeling was more like futility.

"Lolimel's back," Jamal said. He'd come up behind her as she sat at dusk on her favorite stone bench, facing the city. At this time of day the ruins looked romantic, infused with history. The sweet scents of that night-blooming flower, which Mia still hadn't identified, wafted around her.

"I think you should come now," Jamal said, and this time Mia heard his tone. She spun around. In the alien shadows Jamal's face was set as ice.

"He's contracted it," Mia said, knowing beyond doubt that it was true. The virus wasn't just fetally transmitted, it wasn't a slow-acting retrovirus, and if Lolimel had slept with Esefeb . . . But he wouldn't be that stupid. He was a medician, he'd been warned . . .

"We don't really know anything solid about the goddamn thing!" Jamal burst out.

"We never do," Mia said, and the words cracked her dry lips like salt.

Lolimel stood in the center of the ruined atrium, giggling at something only he could see. Kenin, who could have proceeded without Mia, nodded at her. Mia understood; Kenin acknowledged the special bond Mia had with the young medician. The cure was untested, probably brutal, no more really than dumping a selection of poisons in the right areas of the brain, in itself problematical with the blood-brain barrier.

Mia made herself walk calmly up to Lolimel. "What's so funny, Lolimel?"

"All those sandwigs crawling in straight lines over the floor. I never saw blue ones before."

Sandwigs. Lolimel, she remembered, had been born on New Carthage. Sandwigs were always red.

Lolimel said, "But why is there a tree growing out of your head, Mia?"

"Strong fertilizer," she said. "Lolimel, did you have sex with Esefeb?"

He looked genuinely shocked. "No!"

"All right." He might or might not be lying.

Jamal whispered, "A chance to study the hallucinations in someone who can fully articulate—"

"No," Kenin said. "Time matters with this . . ." Mia saw that she couldn't bring herself to say "cure."

Realization dawned on Lolimel's face. "Me? You're going to . . . *me?* There's nothing wrong with me!"

"Lolimel, dear heart . . ." Mia said.

"I don't have it!"

"And the floor doesn't have sandwigs. Lolimel—"

"No!"

The guards had been alerted. Lolimel didn't make it out of the atrium. They held him, flailing and yelling, while Kenin deftly slapped on a tranq patch. In ten seconds he was out.

"Tie him down securely," Kenin said, breathing hard. "Daniel, get the brain bore started as soon as he's prepped. Everyone else, start packing up, and impose quarantine. We can't risk this for anyone else here. I'm calling a Section Eleven."

Section Eleven: *If the MedCorps officer in charge deems the risk to Corps members to exceed the gain to colonists by a factor of three or more, the officer may pull the Corps off-planet.*

It was the first time Mia had ever seen Kenin make a unilateral decision.

Twenty-four hours later, Mia sat beside Lolimel as dusk crept over the city. The shuttle had already carried up most personnel and equipment. Lolimel was in the last shift because, as Kenin did not need to say aloud, if he died, his body would be left behind. But Lolimel had not died. He had thrashed in unconscious seizures, had distorted his features in silent grimaces of pain until Mia would not have recognized him, had suffered malfunctions in alimentary, lymphatic, endocrine, and parasympathetic nervous systems, all recorded on the monitors. But he would live. The others didn't know it, but Mia did.

"We're ready for him, Mia," the young tech said. "Are you on this shuttle, too?"

"No, the last one. Move him carefully. We don't know how much pain he's actually feeling through the meds."

She watched the gurney slide out of the room, its monitors looming over Lolimel like cliffs over a raging river. When he'd gone, Mia slipped into the next building, and then the next. Such beautiful buildings: spacious atria, beautifully proportioned rooms, one structure flowing into another.

Eight buildings away, she picked up the pack she'd left there. It was heavy, even though it didn't contain everything she had cached around the city. It was so easy to take things when a base was being hastily withdrawn. Everyone was preoccupied, everyone assumed anything not readily visible was already packed, inventories were neglected and the deebees not cross-checked. No time. Historically, war had always provided great opportunities for profiteers.

Was that what she was? Yes, but not a profit measured in money. Measure it, rather, in lives saved, or restored to dignity, or enhanced. *"Why did you first enter the Corps?"* Because I'm a medician, Lolimel. Not an anthropologist.

They would notice, of course, that Mia herself wasn't aboard the last shuttle. But Kenin, at least, would realize that searching for her would be a waste of valuable resources when Mia didn't want to be found. And Mia was so old. Surely the old should be allowed to make their own decisions.

Although she would miss them, these Corps members who had been her family since the last assignment shuffle, eighteen months ago and decades go, depending on whose time you counted by. Especially she would miss Lolimel. But this was the right way to end her life, in service to these colonists' health. She was a medician.

It went better than Mia could have hoped. When the ship had gone—she'd seen it leave orbit, a fleeting stream of light—Mia went to Esefeb.

"Mia etej efef," Esefeb said with her rosy smile. *Mia come home.* Mia walked toward her, hugged the girl, and slapped the tranq patch on her neck.

For the next week, Mia barely slept. After the makeshift surgery, she tended Esefeb through the seizures, vomiting, diarrhea, pain. On the morning the girl woke up, herself again, Esefeb was there to bathe the feeble body, feed it, nurse Esefeb. She recovered very fast; the cure was violent on the body but not as debilitating as everyone had feared. And afterward Esefeb was quieter, meeker, and surprisingly intelligent as Mia taught her the rudiments of water purification, sanitation, safe food storage, health care. By the time Mia moved on to Esefeb's mother's house, Esefeb was free of most parasites, and Mia was working on the rest. Esefeb never mentioned her former hallucinations. It was possible she didn't remember them.

"Esefeb ekebet," Mia said as she hefted her pack to leave. *Esefeb be well.*

Esefeb nodded. She stood quietly as Mia trudged away, and when Mia turned to wave at her, Esefeb waved back.

Mia shifted the pack on her shoulders. It seemed heavier than before. Or maybe Mia was just older. Two weeks older, merely, but two weeks could make a big difference. An enormous difference.

Two weeks could start to save a civilization.

Night fell. Esefeb sat on the stairs to her bed, clutching the blue-green sheet of plastic in both hands. She sobbed and shivered, her clean face contorted. Around her, the unpopulated shadows grew thicker and darker. Eventually, she wailed aloud to the empty night.

"Ej-es! O, Ej-es! Ej-es, Esefeb eket! Ej-es . . . etej efef! O, etej efef!"

Afterword to "Ej-Es"

Janis Ian is a music star, and I am tone deaf. Nonetheless, after we met at a convention, we became friends. She is smart, funny, and an SF fan, which of course endears her to SF writers.

One of those writers was Mike Resnick. He and Janis decided to create an anthology in which every story would be built around the lyrics to one of Janis's songs. Although I'm disabled when it comes to tunes, lyrics I can do. I chose her haunting ballad of love and loss, "Jesse." However, since this is SF, I wanted the loss to be not of a human lover but of something else, some part of the human mind. After I decided what, I emailed Janis to say that "Jesse had now become a reference to a brain virus." She emailed back to say mischievously, "How did you know?"

In "Ej-Es" I also got to do something I've always wanted to try. I wanted to introduce the words of a made-up language, one or two at a time, and then write the final paragraph entirely in that language. It's good to achieve one's tiny goals in life.

Shiva in Shadow

1. SHIP

I WATCHED THE PROBE LAUNCH FROM THE *KEP-ler*'s top-deck observatory, where the entire Schaad hull is clear to the stars. I stood between Ajit and Kane. The observatory, which is also the ship's garden, bloomed wildly with my exotics, bursting into flower in such exuberant profusion that even to see the probe go, we had to squeeze between a seven-foot-high bed of comoralias and the hull.

"God, Tirzah, can't you prune these things?" Kane said. He pressed his nose to the nearly invisible hull, like a small child. Something streaked briefly across the sky. "There it goes. Not that there's much to see."

I turned to stare at him. Not much to see! Beyond the *Kepler* lay the most violent and dramatic part of the galaxy, in all its murderous glory. True, the *Kepler* had stopped a hundred light years from the core, for human safety, and dust-and-gas clouds muffled the view somewhat. But, on the other hand, we were far enough away for a panoramic view.

The supermassive black hole Sagittarius A*, the lethal heart of the galaxy, shone gauzily with the heated gases it was sucking downward into oblivion. Around Sgr A* circled Sagittarius West, a three-armed spiral of hot plasma ten light years across, radiating furiously as it cooled. Around *that*, Sagittarius East, a huge shell left over from some catastrophic explosion within the last 100,000 years, expanded outward. I saw thousands of stars, including the blazing blue-hot stars of IRS16, hovering dangerously close to the hole, and giving off a stellar wind fierce enough to blow a long, fiery tail off the nearby red giant star. Everything was racing, radiating, colliding, ripping apart, screaming across the entire electromagnetic spectrum. All set against the sweet, light scent of my brief-lived flowers.

Nothing going on. But Kane had never been interested in spectacle.

Ajit said in his musical accent, "No, not much to see. But much to pray for. There go we."

Kane snapped, "I don't pray."

"I did not mean 'pray' in the religious sense," Ajit said calmly. He is always calm. "I mean hope. It is a miraculous thing, yes? There go we."

He was right, of course. The probe contained the Ajit-analogue, the Kane-analogue, the Tirzah-analogue, all uploaded into a crystal computer no bigger than a comoralia bloom. "We" would go into that stellar violence at the core, where our fragile human bodies could not go. "We" would observe, and measure, and try to find answers to scientific questions in that roiling heart of galactic spacetime. Ninety percent of the probe's mass was shielding for the computer. Ninety percent of the rest was shielding for the three mini-capsules that the probe would fire back to us with recorded and analyzed data. There was no way besides the minicaps to get information out of that bath of frenzied radiation.

Just as there was no way to know exactly what questions Ajit and Kane would need to ask until they were close to Sgr A*. The analogues would know. They knew everything Ajit and Kane and I knew, right up until the moment we were uploaded.

"Shiva, dancing," Ajit said.

"What?" Kane said.

"Nothing. You would not appreciate the reference. Come with me, Tirzah. I want to show you something."

I stopped straining to see the probe, unzoomed my eyes, and smiled at Ajit. "Of course."

This is why I am here.

Ajit's skin is softer than Kane's, less muscled. Kane works out every day in ship's gym, scowling like a demon. Ajit rolled off me and laid his hand on my glowing, satisfied crotch.

"You are so beautiful, Tirzah."

I laughed. "We are all beautiful. Why would anyone effect a genetic alteration that wasn't?"

"People will do strange things sometimes."

"So I just noticed," I teased him.

"Sometimes I think so much of what Kane and I do is strange to you. I see you sitting at the table, listening to us, and I know you cannot follow our physics. It makes me sad for you."

I laid my hand on top of his, pushing down my irritation with the skill of long practice. It does irritate me, this calm sensitivity of Ajit's. It's lovely in bed—he is gentler and more considerate, always, than Kane—but then there comes the other side, this faint condescension. "*I feel sad for you.*" Sad for me! Because I'm not also a scientist! I am the captain of this expedition, with master status in ship control and a first-class license as a Nurturer. On the *Kepler*, my word is law, with virtually no limits. I have over fifty standard-years' experience, specializing in the nurture of scientists. I have never lost an expedition, and I need no one's pity.

Naturally, I showed none of this to Ajit. I massaged his hand with mine, which meant that his hand massaged my crotch, and purred softly. "I'm glad you decided to show me this."

"Actually, that is not what I wanted to show you."

"No?"

"No. Wait here, Tirzah."

He got up and padded, naked, to his personal locker. Beautiful, beautiful body, brown and smooth, like a slim, polished tree. I could see him clearly; Ajit always makes love with the bunk lights on full, as if in sunlight. We lay in his bunk, not mine. I never take either him or Kane to my bunk. My bunk contained various concealed items that they don't, and won't, know about, from duplicate surveillance equipment to rarely used subdermal trackers. Precautions, only. I am a captain.

From his small storage locker, Ajit pulled a statue and turned shyly, even proudly, to show it to me. I sat up, surprised.

The statue was big, big enough so that it must have taken up practically his entire allotment of personal space. Heavy, too, from the way Ajit balanced it before his naked body. It was some sort of god with four arms, enclosed in a circle of flames, made of what looked like very old bronze.

"This is Nataraja," Ajit said. "Shiva dancing."

"Ajit—"

"No, I am not a god worshipper," he smiled. "You know me better than that, Tirzah. Hinduism has many gods—thousands—but they are, except to the ignorant, no more than embodiments of different aspects of reality. Shiva is the dance of creation and destruction, the constant flow of energy in the cosmos. Birth and death and rebirth. It seemed fitting to bring him to the galactic core, where so much goes on of all three."

This explanation sounded weak to me—a holo of Shiva would have accomplished the same thing, without using up nearly all of Ajit's weight allotment. Before I could say this, Ajit said, "This statue has been in my family for four hundred years. I must bring it home, along with the answers to my scientific questions."

I don't understand Ajit's scientific concerns very well—or Kane's—but I know down to my bones how much they matter to him. It is my job to know. Ajit carries within his beautiful body a terrible, coursing ambition, a river fed by the longings of a poor family who have sacrificed what little they had gained on New Bombay for this favored son. Ajit is the receptacle into which they have poured so much hope, so much sacrifice, so much selfishness. The strain on that vessel is what makes Ajit's love-making so gentle. He cannot afford to crack.

"You'll bring the Shiva statue back to New Bombay," I said softly, "and your answers, too."

In his hands, with the bright lighting, the bronze statue cast a dancing shadow on his naked body.

I found Kane at his terminal, so deep in thought that he didn't know I was there until I squeezed his shoulder. Then he jumped, cursed, and dragged his eyes from his displays.

"How does it progress, Kane?"

"It doesn't. How could it? I need more data!"

"It will come. Be patient," I said.

He rubbed his left ear, a constant habit when he's irritated, which is much of the time. When he's happily excited, Kane runs his left hand through his coarse red hair until it stands up like flames. Now he smiled ruefully. "I'm not much known for patience."

"No, you're not."

"But you're right, Tirzah. The data will come. It's just hard waiting for the first minicap. I wish to hell we could have more than three. Goddamn cheap bureaucrats! At an acceleration of—"

"Don't give me the figures again," I said. I wound my fingers in his hair and pulled playfully. "Kane, I came to ask you a favor."

"All right," he said instantly. Kane never counts costs ahead of time. Ajit would have turned gently cautious. "What is it?"

"I want you to learn to play go with Ajit."

He scowled. "Why?"

With Kane, you must have your logic ready. He would do any favor I asked, but unless he can see why, compliance would be grudging at best. "First, because go will help you pass the time until the first minicap arrives, in doing something other than chewing the same data over and over again until you've masticated it into taste-lessness. Second, because the game is complex enough that I think you'll enjoy it. Third, because I'm not too bad at it myself but Ajit is better, and I think you will be, too, so I can learn from both of you."

And fourth, I didn't say aloud, because Ajit is a master, he will beat you most of the time, and he needs the boost in confidence.

Ajit is not the scientist that Kane is. Practically no one in the set-tled worlds is the scientist that Kane is. All three of us know this, but none of us have ever mentioned it, not even once. There are geniuses who are easy for the inferior to work with, who are gener-ous enough to slow down their mental strides to the smaller steps of the merely gifted. Kane is not one of them.

"Go," Kane says thoughtfully. "I have friends who play that."

This was a misstatement. Kane does not have friends, in the usual sense. He has colleagues, he has science, and he has me.

He smiled at me, a rare touch of sweet gratitude on his hand-some face. "Thanks, Tirzah. I'll play with Ajit. You're right, it *will* pass the time until the probe sends back the prelim data. And if I'm occupied, maybe I'll be less of a monster to you."

"You're fine to me," I say, giving his hair another tug, grinning with the casual flippancy he prefers. "Or if you're not, I don't care."

Kane laughs. In moments like this, I am especially careful that my own feelings don't show. To either of them.

2. PROBE

We automatically woke after the hyperjump. For reasons I don't understand, a hyperjump isn't instantaneous. Perhaps because it's not really a "jump" but a Calabi-Yau dimension tunnel. Several days ship-time had passed, and the probe now drifted less than five light years from the galactic core. The probe, power off, checked out perfectly; the shielding had held even better than expected. And so had we. My eyes widened as I studied the wardroom displays.

On the *Kepler*, dust clouds had softened and obscured the view.

Here, nothing did. We drifted just outside a star that had begun its deadly spiral inward toward Sgr A*. Visuals showed the full deadly glory around the hole: the hot blue cluster of IRS16. The giant red star IRS7 with its long tail distended by stellar winds. The stars already past the point of no return, pulled by the gravity of Sgr A* inexorably toward its event horizon. The radio, gamma-ray, and infrared displays revealed even more, brilliant with the radiation pouring from every single gorgeous, lethal object in the bright sky.

And there, too, shone one of the mysteries Kane and Ajit had come to study: the massive, young stars that were not being yanked toward Sgr A*, and which in this place should have been neither massive nor relatively stable. Such stars should not exist this close to the hole. One star, Kane had told me, was as close to the hole as twice Pluto's orbit from Sol. How had it gotten there?

"It's beautiful, in a hellish way," I said to Ajit and Kane. "I want to go up to the observatory and see it direct."

"The observatory!" Kane said scornfully. "I need to get to work!" He sat down at his terminal.

None of this is true, of course. There is no observatory on the probe, and I can't climb the ladder "up" to it. Nor is there a ward-room with terminals, chairs, table, displays, a computer. We *are* the computer, or rather we are inside it. But the programs running along with us make it all seem as real as the fleshy versions of our-selves on the *Kepler*. This, it was determined by previous disastrous experience in space exploration, is necessary to keep us sane and stable. Human uploads need this illusion, this shadow reality, and we accept it easily. Why not? It's the default setting for our minds.

So Kane "sat at" his "terminal" to look at the preliminary data from the sensors. So did Ajit, and I "went upstairs" to the observa-tory, where I gazed outward for a long time.

I—the other "I", the one on the *Kepler*—grew up on a station in the Oort Cloud, Sol System. Space is my natural home. I don't really understand how mud-dwellers live on planets, or why they would want to, at the bottom of a murky and dirty shroud of uncon-trollable air. I have learned to simulate understanding planetary love, because it is my job. Both Kane and Ajit come from rocks, Ajit from New Bombay and Kane from Terra herself. They are space sci-entists, but not real spacers.

No mud-dweller ever really sees the stars. And no human being had ever seen what I saw now, the frantic heart of the human uni-verse.

Eventually I went back downstairs, rechecked ship's data, and then sat at the wardroom table and took up my embroidery. The ancient, irrelevant cloth-ornamenting is very soothing, almost as much so as gardening, although of course that's not why I do it. All first-class Nurturers practice some humble handicraft. It allows you to closely observe people while appearing absorbed and harmless.

Kane, of course, was oblivious to me. I could have glared at him through a magnifying glass and he wouldn't have noticed, not if he was working. Back on the *Kepler*, he had explained in simple terms—or at least as simple as Kane's explanations ever get—why there should not be any young stars this close to the core, as well as three possible explanations for why there are. He told me all this, in typical Kane fashion, in bed. Post-coital intimacy.

"The stars' spectra show they're young, Tirzah. And *close*—SO-2 comes to within eighty AU's of Sgr A*! It's *wrong*—the core is incredibly inhospitable to star formation! Also, these close-in stars have very peculiar orbits."

"You're taking it personally," I observed, smiling.

"Of course I am!" This was said totally without irony. "Those young stars have no business there. The tidal forces of the hole should rip any hot dust clouds to shreds long before any stars could form. And if they formed farther out, say 100 light years out, they should have died before they get this close in. These supermassive stars only last a few million years."

"But there they are."

"Yes. Why do you still have this lacy thing on? It's irritating."

"Because you were so eager that I didn't have time to get it off."

"Well, take it off now."

I did, and he wrapped my body close to his, and went on fretting over star formation in the core.

"There are three theories. One is that a dust cloud ringing the core, about six light years out, keeps forming stars, which are then blown outward again by galactic winds, and then drawn in, and repeat. Another theory is that there's a second, intermediate medium-sized black hole orbiting Sgr A* and exerting a counterpull on the stars. But if so, why aren't we detecting its radio waves? Another idea is that the stars aren't really young at all, they're composites of remnants of elderly stars that merged to form a body that only looks bright and young."

I said, "Which theory do you like?"

"None of them." And then, in one of those lightening changes he was capable of, he focused all his attention on me. "Are you all right, Tirzah? I know this has got to be a boring voyage for you. Running ship can't take much of your time, and neither can babysitting me."

I laughed aloud and Kane, having no idea why, frowned slightly. It was such a typically Kane speech. A sudden burst of intense concern, which would prove equally transitory. No mention of Ajit at all, as if only Kane existed for me. And his total ignorance of how often I interceded between him and Ajit, smoothed over tensions between them, spent time calming and centering separately each of these men who were more like the stars outside the ship than either of them were capable of recognizing. Brilliant, heated, intense, inherently unstable.

"I'm fine, Kane. I'm enjoying myself."

"Well, good," he said, and I saw that he then forgot me, back to brooding about his theories.

Neither Kane nor Ajit knows that I love Kane. I don't love Ajit. Whatever calls up love in our hidden hearts, it is unfathomable. Kane arouses in me a happiness, a desire, a completeness that puts a glow on the world because he—difficult, questing, vital—is in it. Ajit, through no fault of his own, does not.

Neither of them will ever know this. I would berate myself if they did. My personal feelings don't matter here. I am a captain.

"Damn and double damn!" Kane said, admiringly. "Look at that!"

Ajit reacted as if Kane had spoken to him, but of course Kane had not. He was just thinking aloud. I put down my embroidery and went to stand behind them at their terminals.

Ajit said, "Those readings must be wrong. The sensors were damaged after all, either in hypertransit or by radiation."

Kane didn't reply; I doubt he'd heard. I said, "What is it?"

It was Ajit who answered. "The mass readings are wrong. They're showing high mass density for several areas of empty space."

I said, "Maybe that's where the new young stars are forming?"

Not even Ajit answered this, which told me it was a stupid statement. It doesn't matter; I don't pretend to be a scientist. I merely wanted to keep them talking, to gauge their states of mind.

Ajit said, "It would be remarkable if all equipment had emerged undamaged from the jump into this radiation."

"Kane?" I said.

"It's not the equipment," he muttered. So he had been listening, at least peripherally. "Supersymmetry."

Ajit immediately objected to this, in terms I didn't understand. They were off into a discussion I had no chance of following. I let it go on for a while, then even longer, since it sounded the way scientific discussions are supposed to sound: intense but not acrimonious, not personal.

When they wound down a bit, I said, "Did the mini-capsule go off to the *Kepler*? They're waiting for the prelim data, and the mini-cap takes days to jump. Did either of you remember to record and send?"

They both looked at me, as if trying to remember who I was and what I was doing there. In that moment, for the first time, they looked alike.

"I remembered," Ajit said. "The prelim data went off to the *Kepler*. Kane—"

They were off again.

3. SHIP

The go games were not a success.

The problem, I could see, was with Ajit. He was a far better player than Kane, both intuitively and through experience. This didn't bother Kane at all; he thrived on challenge. But his own clear superiority subtly affected Ajit.

"Game won," he said for the third time in the evening, and at the slight smirk in his voice I looked up from my embroidery.

"Damn and double damn," Kane said, without rancor. "Set them up again."

"No, I think I will go celebrate my victories with Tirzah."

This was Kane's night, but the two of them had never insisted on precedence. This was because I had never let it come to that; it's part of my job to give the illusion that I am always available to both, on whatever occasion they wish. Of course, I control, through a hundred subtle signals and without either realizing it, which occasions they happen to wish. Where I make love depends on whom I need to observe. This direct claim by Ajit, connecting me to his go victories, was new.

Kane, of course, didn't notice. "All right. God, I wish the mini-cap would come. I want that data!"

Now that the game had released his attention, he was restless again. He rose and paced around the wardroom, which doesn't admit too much pacing. "I think I'll go up to the observatory. Anybody coming?"

He had already forgotten that I was leaving with Ajit. I saw Ajit go still. Such a small thing—Ajit was affronted that Kane was not affected by Ajit's game victory, or by his bearing me off like some earned prize. Another man would have felt a moment of pique and then forgotten it. Ajit was not another man. Neither was Kane. Stable men don't volunteer for missions like this.

It's different for me; I was bred to space. The scientists were not.

I put down my embroidery, took Ajit's hand, and snuggled close to him. Kane, for the moment, was fine. His restless desire for his data wouldn't do him any harm. It was Ajit I needed to work with.

I was the one who had suggested the go games. Good captains are not supposed to make mistakes like that. It was up to me to set things right.

By the time the minicap arrived, everything was worse.

They would not, either of them, stop the go games. They played obsessively, six or seven times a day, then nine or ten, and finally every waking minute. Ajit continued to win the large majority of the games, but not all of them. Kane focused his formidable intelligence on devising strategies, and he had the advantage of caring but not too much. Yes, he was obsessed, but I could see that once he had something more significant to do, he would leave the go games without a backward glance.

Ajit grew more focused, too. Even more intent on winning, even as he began to lose a few games. More slyly gleeful when he did win. He flicked his winning piece onto the board with a turn of the wrist in which I read both contempt and fear.

I tried everything I could to intervene, every trick from a century of experience. Nothing worked. Sex only made it worse. Ajit regarded sex as an earned prize, Kane as a temporary refreshment so he could return to the games.

One night Ajit brought out the statue of Shiva and put it defiantly on the wardroom table. It took up two-thirds of the space, a wide metal circle enclosing the four-armed dancer.

"What's that?" Kane said, looking up from the game board. "Oh, God, it's a god."

I said quickly, "It's an intellectual concept. The flow of cosmic energy in the universe."

Kane laughed, not maliciously, but I saw Ajit's eyes light up. Ajit said, "I want it here."

Kane shrugged. "Fine by me. Your turn, Ajit."

Wrong, wrong. Ajit had hoped to disturb Kane, to push him into some open objection to the statue. Ajit wanted a small confrontation, some outlet to emphasize his gloating. Some outlet for his growing unease as Kane's game improved. And some outlet for his underlying rage, always just under the surface, at Kane, the better scientist. The statue was supposed to be an assertion, even a slap in the face: *I am here and I take up a lot of your space. Notice that!*

Instead, Kane had shrugged and dismissed it.

I said, "Tell me again, Ajit, about Nataraja. What's the significance of the flames on the great circle?"

Ajit said quietly, "They represent the fire that destroys the world."

Kane said, "Your *turn*, Ajit."

Such a small incident. But deep in my mind, where I was aware of it but not yet overtly affected, fear stirred.

I was losing control here.

Then the first minicap of data arrived.

4. PROBE

Mind uploads are still minds. They are not computer programs in the sense that other programs are. Although freed of biological constraints such as enzymes that create sleep, hunger, and lust, uploads are not free of habit. In fact, it is habit that creates enough structure to keep all of us from frenzied feedback loops. On the probe, my job was to keep habit strong. It was the best safeguard for those brilliant minds.

"Time to sleep, gentlemen," I said lightly. We had been gathered in the wardroom for sixteen hours straight, Kane and Ajit at their terminals, me sitting quietly, watching them. I have powers of concentration equal in degree, though not in kind, to their own. They do not suspect this. It has been hours since I put down my embroidery, but neither noticed.

"Tirzah, not sleep now!" Kane snapped.

"Now."

He looked up at me like a sulky child. But Kane is not a child; I don't make that mistake. He knows an upload has to shut down for the cleansing program to run, a necessity to catch operating errors before they grow large enough to impair function. With all the radiation bathing the probe, the program is more necessary than ever. It takes a few hours to run through. I control the run cues.

Ajit looked at me expectantly. It was his night. This, too, was part of habit, as well as being an actual aid to their work. More than one scientist in my care has had that critical flash of intuition on some

scientific problem while in my arms. Upload sex, like its fleshy analogue, both stimulates and relaxes.

"All right, all right," Kane muttered. "Good night."

I shut him down and turned to Ajit.

We went to his bunk. Ajit was tense, stretched taut with data and
with sixteen hours with Kane. But I was pleased to see how completely he responded to me. Afterward, I asked him to explain the
prelim data to me.

"And keep it simple, please. Remember who you're talking to!"

"To an intelligent and sweet lady," he said, and I gave him the
obligatory smile. But he saw that I really did want to know about the
data.

"The massive young stars are there when they should not be . . .
Kane has explained all this to you, I know."

I nodded.

"They are indeed young, not mashed-together old stars. We have
verified that. We are trying now to gather and run data to examine
the other two best theories: a fluctuating ring of matter spawning
stars, or other black holes."

"How are you examining the theories?"

He hesitated, and I knew he was trying to find explanations
I could understand. "We are running various programs, equations,
and sims. We are also trying to determine where to jump the probe
next—you know about that."

Of course I did. No one moves this ship without my consent. It
has two more jumps left in its power pack, and I must approve them
both.

"We need to choose a spot from which we can fire beams of
various radiation to assess the results. The heavier beams won't last
long here, you know—the gravity of the superhole distorts them."
He frowned.

"What is it, Ajit? What about gravity?"

"Kane was right," he said, "the mass detectors aren't damaged.
They're showing mass nearby, not large but detectable, that isn't
manifesting anything but gravity. No radiation of any kind."

"A black hole," I suggested.

"Too small. Small black holes radiate away, Hawking showed
that long ago. The internal temperature is too high. There are no
black holes smaller than three solar masses. The mass detectors are
showing something much smaller than that."

"What?"

"We don't know."

"Were all the weird mass-detector readings in the prelim data you sent back to the *Kepler*?"

"Of course," he said, a slight edge in his voice.

I pulled him closer. "I can always rely on you," I said, and I felt his body relax.

I shut us down, as we lay in each other's arms.

It was Ajit who, the next day, noticed the second anomaly. And I who noticed the third.

"These gas orbits aren't right," Ajit said to Kane. "And they're getting less right all the time."

Kane moved to Ajit's terminal. "Tell me."

"The infalling gases from the circumnuclear disk . . . see . . . they curve here, by the western arm of Sgr A West . . ."

"It's wind from the IRS16 cluster," Kane said instantly. "I got updated readings for those yesterday."

"No, I already corrected for that," Ajit said.

"Then maybe magnetization from IRS7, or—"

They were off again. I followed enough to grasp the general problem. Gases streamed at enormous speeds from clouds beyond the circumnuclear disk which surrounded the entire core like a huge doughnut. These streaming gases were funneled by various forces into fairly narrow, cone-like paths. The gases would eventually end up circling the black hole, spiraling inward and compressing to temperatures of billions of degrees before they were absorbed by the maw of the hole. The processes were understood.

But the paths weren't as predicted. Gases were streaming down wrong, approaching the hole wrong for predictions made from all the forces acting on them.

Ajit finally said to Kane, "I want to move the probe earlier than we planned."

"Wait a moment," I said instantly. Ship's movements were *my* decision. "It's not yet the scheduled time."

"Of course I'm including you in my request, Tirzah," Ajit said, with all his usual courtesy. There was something beneath the courtesy, however, a kind of glow. I recognized it. Scientists look like that when they have the germ of an important idea.

I thought Kane would object or ridicule, but something in their technical discussion must have moved him, too. His red hair stood up all over his head. He glanced briefly at his own displays, back at Ajit's, then at the younger man. He said, "You want to put the probe on the other side of Sagittarius A West."

"Yes."

I said, "Show me."

Ajit brought up the simplified graphic he had created weeks ago for me to gain an overview of this mission. It showed the black hole at the center of the galaxy, and the major structures around it: the cluster of hot blue stars, the massive young stars that should not have existed so close to the hole, the red giant star IRS16, with its long fiery tail. All this, plus our probe, lay on one side of the huge, three-armed spiraling plasma remnant, Sagittarius A West. Ajit touched the computer and a new dot appeared on the other side of Sgr A West, farther away from the hole than we were now.

"We want to go there, Tirzah," he said. Kane nodded.

I said, deliberately sounding naïve, "I thought there wasn't as much going on over there. And besides, you said that Sgr A West would greatly obscure our vision in all wavelengths, with its own radiation."

"It will."

"Then—"

"There's something going on over there now," Kane said. "Ajit's right. That region is the source of whatever pull is distorting the gas infall. We need to go there."

We.

Ajit's right.

The younger man didn't change expression. But the glow was still there, ignited by Ajit's idea and fanned, I now realized, by Kane's approval. I heated it up a bit more. "But, Kane, your work on the massive young stars? I can only move the probe so many times, you know. Our fuel supply—"

"I have a lot of data on the stars now," Kane said, "and this matters more."

I hid my own pleasure. "All right. I'll move the probe."

But when I interfaced with ship's program, I found the probe had already been moved.

5. SHIP

Kane and Ajit fell on the minicap of prelim data like starving wolves. There were no more games of go. There was no more anything but work, unless I insisted.

At first I thought that was good. I thought that without the senseless, mounting competition over go, the two scientists would cooperate on the intense issues that mattered so much to both of them.

"Damn and double damn!" Kane said, admiringly. "Look at that!"

Ajit reacted as if Kane had spoken to him, but of course Kane had not. He was just thinking aloud. I put down my embroidery and went to stand behind them at their terminals.

Ajit said, with the new arrogance of the go wins in his voice, "Those readings must be wrong. The sensors were damaged after all, either in hypertransit or by radiation."

Kane, for a change, caught Ajit's tone. He met it with a sneer he must have used regularly on presumptuous post-grads. " 'Must be wrong'? That's just the kind of puerile leaping to conclusions that gets people nowhere."

I said quickly, "What readings?"

It was Ajit who answered me, and although the words were innocuous, even polite, I heard the anger underlying them. "The mass readings are wrong. They're showing high mass density for several areas of empty space."

I said, "Maybe that's where the new young stars are forming?"

Not even Ajit answered this, which told me it was a stupid statement. It doesn't matter; I don't pretend to be a scientist. I merely wanted to keep them talking, to gauge their states of mind.

Ajit said, too evenly, "It would be remarkable if *all* probe equipment had emerged undamaged from the jump into core radiation."

"Kane?" I said.

"It's *not* the equipment." And then, "Supersymmetry."

Ajit immediately objected to this, in terms I didn't understand. They were off into a discussion I had no chance of following. What I could follow was the increasing pressure of Ajit's anger as Kane dismissed and belittled his ideas. I could almost see that anger, a hot plasma. As Kane ridiculed and belittled, the plasma collapsed into greater and greater density.

Abruptly they broke off their argument, went to their separate terminals, and worked like machines for twenty hours straight. I had to make them each eat something. They were obsessed, as only those seized by science or art can obsess. Neither of them would come to bed with me that night. I could have issued an executive order, but I chose not to exert that much trust-destroying force until I had to, although I did eventually announce that I was shutting down terminal access.

"For God's sake, Tirzah!" Kane snarled. "This is a once-in-a-species opportunity! I've got work to do!"

I said evenly, "You're going to rest. The terminals are down for seven hours."

"Five."

"All right." After five hours, Kane would still be snoring away.

He stood, stiff from the long hours of sitting. Kane is well over a hundred; rejuves can only do so much, so long. His cramped muscles, used to much more exercise, misfired briefly. He staggered, laughed, caught himself easily.

But not before he'd bumped the wardroom table. Ajit's statue of Shiva slid off and fell to the floor. The statue was old—four hundred years old, Ajit had said. Metal shows fatigue, too, although later than men. The statue hit the deck at just the right angle and broke.

"Oh . . . sorry, Ajit."

Kane's apology was a beat too late. I knew—with every nerve in my body, I knew this that the delay happened because Kane's mind was still racing along his data, and it took an effort for him to refocus. It didn't matter. Ajit stiffened, and something in the nature of his anger changed, ionized by Kane's careless, preoccupied tone.

I said quickly, "Ship can weld the statue."

"No, thank you," Ajit said. "I will leave it as it is. Good night."

"Ajit—" I reached for his hand. He pulled it away.

"Good night, Tirzah."

Kane said, "The gamma-ray variations within Sgr A West aren't quite what was predicted." He blinked twice. "You're right, I am exhausted."

Kane stumbled off to his bunk. Ajit had already gone. After a long while I picked up the pieces of Ajit's statue and held them, staring at the broken figure of the dancing god.

The preliminary data, Kane had declared when it arrived, contained enough information to keep them both busy until the second minicap arrived. But by the next day, Kane was impatiently demanding more.

"These gas orbits aren't right," he said aloud, although not to either me or Ajit. Kane did that, worked in silence for long stretches until words exploded out of him to no particular audience except his own whirling thoughts. His ear was raw with rubbing.

I said, "What's not right about them?" When he didn't answer, or probably even hear me, I repeated the question, much louder.

Kane came out of his private world and scowled at me. "The infalling gases from beyond the circumnuclear disk aren't showing the right paths to Sgr A*."

I said, repeating something he'd taught me, "Could it be wind from the IRS16 cluster?"

"No. I checked those updated readings yesterday and corrected for them."

I had reached the end of what I knew to ask. Kane burst out, "I need more data!"

"Well, it'll get here eventually."

"I want it now," he said, and laughed sourly at himself, and went back to work.

Ajit said nothing, acting as if neither of us had spoken.

I waited until Ajit stood, stretched, and looked around vaguely. Then I said, "Lunch in a minute. But first come look at something with me." Immediately I started up the ladder to the observatory, so that he either had to follow or go through the trouble of arguing. He followed.

I had put the welded statue of Shiva on the bench near clear hull. It was the wrong side of the hull for the spectacular view of the core, but the exotics didn't press so close to the hull here, and thousands of stars shone in a sky more illuminated than Sol had seen since its birth. Shiva danced in his mended circle of flames against a background of cosmic glory.

Ajit said flatly, "I told you I wanted to leave it broken."

With Kane, frank opposition is fine; he's strong enough to take it and, in fact, doesn't respect much else. But Ajit is different. I lowered my eyes and reached for his hand. "I know. I took the liberty of fixing it anyway because, well, I thought you might want to see it whole again and because I like the statue so much. It has so much meaning beyond the obvious, especially here. In this place and this time. Please forgive me."

Ajit was silent for a moment, then he raised my hand to his lips. "You do see that."

"Yes," I said, and it was the truth. Shiva, the endless dance, the endless flow of energy changing form and state—how could anyone not see it in the gas clouds forming stars, the black hole destroying them, the violence and creation outside this very hull? Yet, at the same time, it was a profound insight into the very obvious, and I kept my eyes lowered so no glimpse of my faint contempt reached Ajit.

He kissed me. "You are so spiritual, Tirzah. And so sweet-natured."

I was neither. The only deceptions Ajit could see were the paranoid ones he assumed of others.

But his body had relaxed in my arms, and I knew that some part of his mind had been reassured. He and I could see spiritual beauties that Kane could not. Therefore he was in some sense superior to Kane. He followed me back down the ladder to lunch, and I heard him hum a snatch of some jaunty tune. Pleased with myself, I made for the galley.

Kane stood up so abruptly from his terminal that his eyes glowed. "Oh, my shitting stars. Oh, yes. Tirzah, I've got it."

I stopped cold. I had never seen anyone, even Kane, look quite like that. "Got what?"

"All of it." Suddenly he seized me and swung me into exuberant, clumsy dance. "All of it! I've got all of it! The young stars, the gas orbits, the missing mass in the universe! All shitting fucking *all* of it!"

"Wwwhhhaaatttt . . ." He was whirling me around so fast that my teeth rattled. "Kane, stop!"

He did, and enveloped me in a rib-cracking hug, then abruptly released me and dragged my bruised body to his terminal. "Look, sweetheart, I've got it. Now sit right there and I'm going to explain it in terms even you can understand. You'll love it. It'll love you. Now look here, at this region of space—"

I turned briefly to look at Ajit. For Kane, he didn't even exist.

6. PROBE

"The probe has moved," I said to Ajit and Kane. "It's way beyond the calculated drift. By a factor of ten."

Kane's eyes, red with work, nonetheless sharpened. "Let me see the trajectory."

"I transferred it to both your terminals." Ordinarily ship's data is kept separate, for my eyes only.

Kane brought up the display and whistled.

The probe is under the stresses, gravitational and radiational, that will eventually destroy it. We all know that. Our fleshy counterparts weren't even sure the probe would survive to send one minicap of data, and I'm sure they were jubilant when we did. Probably they treated the minicap like a holy gift, and I can easily imagine how eager they are for more. Back on the ship, I—the other "I"—had been counting on data, like oil, to grease the frictions and tensions between Ajit and Kane. I hoped it had.

We uploads had fuel enough to move the probe twice. After that, and since our last move will be no more than one-fiftieth of a light year from the black hole at the galactic core, the probe will eventually spiral down into Sgr A*. Before that, however, it will have been ripped apart by the immense tidal forces of the hole. However, long before that final death plunge, we analogues will be gone.

The probe's current drift, however, considerably farther away from the hole, was nonetheless much faster than projected. It was also slightly off course. We were being pulled in the general direction of Sgr A*, but not on the gravitational trajectory that would bring us into its orbit at the time and place the computer had calculated. In fact, at our current rate of acceleration, there was a chance we'd miss the event horizon completely.

What was going on?

Kane said, "Maybe we better hold off moving the probe to the other side of Sgr A West until we find out what's pulling us."

Ajit was studying the data over Kane's shoulder. He said hesitantly, "No . . . wait . . . I think we should move."

"Why?" Kane challenged.

"I don't know. I just have . . . call it an intuition. We should move now."

I held my breath. The only intuition Kane usually acknowledged was his own. But, earlier, things had subtly shifted. Kane had said, *"Ajit's right. That region is the source of whatever pull is distorting the gas infall."* Ajit had not changed expression, but I'd felt his pleasure, real as heat. That had given him the courage to now offer this unformed—"half-baked" was Kane's usual term—intuition.

Kane said thoughtfully, "Maybe you're right. Maybe the—" Suddenly his eyes widened. "Oh my God."

"What?" I said, despite myself. "What?"

Kane ignored me. "Ajit—run the sims for the gas orbits in correlation with the probe drift. I'll do the young stars!"

"Why do—" Ajit began, and then he saw whatever had seized Kane's mind. Ajit said something in Hindi; it might have been a curse, or a prayer. I didn't know. Nor did I know anything about their idea, or about what was happening with the gas orbits and young stars outside the probe. However, I could see clearly what was happening within.

Ajit and Kane fell into frenzied work. They threw comments and orders to each other, transferred data, backed up sims and equation runs. They tilted their chairs toward each other and spouted incomprehensible jargon. Once Kane cried, "We need more data!" and Ajit laughed, freely and easily, then immediately plunged back into whatever he was doing. I watched them for a long time, then stole quietly up to the observation deck for a minute alone.

The show outside was more spectacular than ever, perhaps

because we'd been pulled closer to it than planned. Clouds of whirling gases wrapped and oddly softened that heart of darkness, Sgr A*. The fiery tail of the giant red star lit up that part of the sky. Stars glowed in a profusion unimaginable on my native Station J, stuck off in a remote arm of the galaxy. Directly in front of me glowed the glorious blue stars of the cluster IRS16.

I must have stayed on the observation deck longer than I'd planned, because Kane came looking for me. "Tirzah! Come on down! We want to show you where we're moving and why!"

We.

I said severely, gladness bursting in my heart, "You don't show me where we're going, Kane, you ask me. I captain this ship."

"Yeah, yeah, I know, you're a dragon lady. Come on!" He grabbed my hand and pulled me toward the ladder.

They both explained it, interrupting each other, fiercely correcting each other, having a wonderful time. I concentrated as hard as I could, trying to cut through the technicalities they couldn't do without, any more than they could do without air. Eventually I thought I glimpsed the core of their excitement.

"Shadow matter," I said, tasting the words on my tongue. It sounded too bizarre to take seriously, but Kane was insistent.

"The theory's been around for centuries, but deGroot pretty much discredited it in 2086," Kane said. "He—"

"If it's been discredited, then why—" I began.

"I said 'pretty much,'" Kane said. "There were always some mathematical anomalies with deGroot's work. And we can see now where he was *wrong.* He—"

Kane and Ajit started to explain why deGroot was wrong, but I interrupted. "No, don't digress so much! Let me just tell you what I think I understood from what you said."

I was silent a moment, gathering words. Both men waited impatiently, Kane running his hand through his hair, Ajit smiling widely. I said, "You said there's a theory that just after the Big Bang, gravity somehow decoupled from the other forces in the universe, just as matter decoupled from radiation. At the same time, you scientists have known for two centuries that there doesn't seem to be enough matter in the universe to make all your equations work. So scientists posited a lot of 'dark matter' and a lot of black holes, but none of the figures added up right anyway.

"And right now, neither do the orbits of the infalling gas, or the probe's drift, or the fact that massive young stars were forming that close to the black hole without being ripped apart by tidal forces. The forces acting on the huge clouds have to condense to form stars that big."

I took a breath, quick enough so that neither had time to break in and distract me with technicalities.

"But now you think that if gravity *did* decouple right after the Big Bang—"

"About 10^{-43} seconds after," Ajit said helpfully. I ignored him.

"—then two types of matter were created, normal matter and 'shadow matter.' It's sort of like matter and antimatter, only normal matter and shadow matter can't interact except by gravity. No interaction through any other force, not radiation or strong or weak forces. Only gravity. That's the only effect shadow matter has on *our* universe. Gravity.

"And a big chunk of this stuff is there on the other side of Sgr A West. It's exerting enough gravity to affect the path of the infalling gas. And to affect the probe's drift. And even to affect the young stars because the shadow matter-thing's exerting a counterpull on the massive star clouds, and that's keeping them from being ripped apart by the hole as soon as they otherwise would be. So they have time to collapse into young stars."

"Well, that's sort of it, but you've left out some things that alter and validate the whole," Kane said impatiently, scowling.

"Yes, Tirzah, dear heart, you don't see the—you can't just say that 'counterpull'—let me try once more."

They were off again, but this time I didn't listen. So maybe I hadn't seen the theory whole, but only glimpsed its shadow. It was enough.

They had a viable theory. I had a viable expedition, with a goal, and cooperatively productive scientists, and a probability of success.

It was enough.

Kane and Ajit prepared the second minicap for the big ship, and I prepared to move the probe. Our mood was jubilant. There was much laughing and joking, interrupted by intense bursts of incomprehensible jabbering between Ajit and Kane.

But before I finished my programming, Ajit's head disappeared.

7. SHIP

Kane worked all day on his shadow-matter theory. He worked ferociously, hunched over his terminal like a hungry dog with a particularly meaty bone, barely glancing up and saying little. Ajit worked, too, but the quality of his working was different. The terminals both connect to the same computer, of course; whatever Kane had, Ajit had, too. Ajit could follow whatever Kane did.

But that's what Ajit was doing: following. I could tell it from the timing of his accesses, from the whole set of his body. He was a decent scientist, but he was not Kane. Given the data and enough time, Ajit might have been able to go where Kane raced ahead now. Maybe. Or, he might have been able to make valuable additions to Kane's thinking. But Kane gave him no time; Kane was always there first, and he asked no help. He had shut Ajit out completely. For Kane, nothing existed right now but his work.

Toward evening he looked up abruptly and said to me, "They'll move the probe. The uploads—they'll move it."

I said, "How do you know? It's not time yet, according to the schedule."

"No. But they'll move it. If I figured out the shadow matter here, I will there, too. I'll decide that more data is needed from the other side of Sgr A West, where the main shadow mass is."

I looked at him. He looked demented, like some sort of Roman warrior who has just wrestled with a lion. All that was missing was the blood. Wild, filthy hair—when had he last showered? Clothes spotted with the food I'd made him gulp down at noon. Age lines beginning, under strain and fatigue and despite the rejuve, to drag down the muscles of his face. And his eyes shining like Sgr A West itself.

God, I loved him.

I said, with careful emphasis, "You're right. The Tirzah upload will move the ship for better measurements."

"Then we'll get more data in a few days," Ajit said. "But the radiation on the other side of Sgr A West is still intense. We must hope nothing gets damaged in the probe programs, or in the uploads themselves, before we get the new data."

"We better hope nothing gets damaged long before that in my upload," Kane said, "or they won't even know what data to collect." He turned back to his screen.

The brutal words hung in the air.

I saw Ajit turn his face away from me. Then he rose and walked into the galley.

If I followed him too soon, he would see it as pity. His shame would mount even more.

"Kane," I said in a low, furious voice, "you are despicable."

He turned to me in genuine surprise. "What?"

"You know what." But he didn't. Kane wasn't even conscious of what he'd said. To him, it was a simple, evident truth. Without the Kane upload, no one on the probe would know how to do first-class science.

"I want to see you upstairs on the observation deck," I said to him. "Not now, but in ten minutes. And *you* announce that you want *me* to see something up there." The time lag, plus Kane's suggesting the trip, would keep Ajit from knowing I was protecting him.

But now I had put up Kane's back. He was tired, he was stressed, he was inevitably coming down from the unsustainable high of his discovery. Neither body nor mind can keep at that near-hysterical pitch for too long. I had misjudged, out of my own anger at him.

He snapped, "I'll see you on the observation deck when *I* want to see you there, and not otherwise. Don't push me around, Tirzah. Not even as captain." He turned back to his display.

Ajit emerged from the galley with three glasses on a tray. "A celebratory drink. A major discovery deserves that. At a minimum."

Relief was so intense I nearly showed it on my face. It was all right. I had misread Ajit, underestimated him. He ranked the magnitude of Kane's discovery higher than his own lack of participation in it, after all. Ajit was, first, a scientist.

He handed a glass to me, one to Kane, one for himself. Kane took a hasty, perfunctory gulp and returned to his display. But I cradled mine, smiling at Ajit, trying with warmth to convey the admiration I felt for his rising above the personal.

"Where did you get the wine? It wasn't on the ship manifest!"

"It was in my personal allotment," Ajit said, smiling.

Personal allotments are not listed nor examined. A bottle of wine, the statue of Shiva . . . Ajit had brought some interesting choices for a galactic core. I sipped the red liquid. It tasted different from the Terran or Martian wines I had grown up with: rougher, more full-bodied, not as sweet.

"Wonderful, Ajit."

"I thought you would like it. It is made in my native New Bombay, from genemod grapes brought from Terra."

He didn't go back to his terminal. For the next half-hour, he entertained me with stories of New Bombay. He was a good storyteller, sharp and funny. Kane worked steadily, ignoring us. The ten-minute deadline I had set for him to call me up to the observation deck came and went.

After half an hour, Kane stood and staggered. Once before, when he'd broken Ajit's statue, stiffness after long sitting had made Kane unsteady. That time he'd caught himself after simply bumping the wardroom table. This time he crashed heavily to the floor.

"Kane!"

"Nothing, nothing . . . don't make a fuss, Tirzah! You just won't leave me alone!"

This was so unfair that I wanted to slap him. I didn't. Kane rose by himself, shook his head like some great beast, and said, "I'm just exhausted. I'm going to bed."

I didn't try to stop him from going to his bunk. I had planned on sleeping with Ajit, anyway. It seemed that some slight false note had crept into his storytelling in the last five minutes, some forced exaggeration.

But he smiled at me, and I decided I'd been wrong. I was very tired, too. All at once I wished I could sleep alone this night.

But I couldn't. Ajit, no matter how well he'd recovered from Kane's unconscious brutality, nonetheless had to feel bruised at some level. It was my job to find out where, and how much, and to set it to rights. It was my job to keep the expedition as productive as possible, to counteract Kane's dismissing and belittling behavior toward Ajit. It was my job.

I smiled back at him.

8. PROBE

When Ajit's head disappeared, no one panicked. We'd expected this, of course; in fact, we'd expected it sooner. The probe drifted in a sea of the most intense radiation in the galaxy, much of it at lethal wavelengths: gamma rays from Sagittarius East, X-rays, powerful winds of ionized particles, things I couldn't name. That the probe's shielding had held this long was a minor miracle. It couldn't hold forever. Some particle or particles had penetrated all the shielding and reached the computer, contaminating a piece of the upload-maintenance program.

It was a minor glitch. The back-up kicked in a moment later and Ajit's head reappeared. But we all knew this was only the beginning. It would happen again, and again, and eventually programming would be hit that couldn't be restored by automatic back-up, because the back-up would go, too, in a large enough hit—or because uploads are not like other computer programs. We are more than that, and less. An upload has back-ups to maintain the shadows we see of each other and the ship, the shadows that keep our captured minds sane. But an upload cannot house back-ups of itself. Even one copy smudges too much, and the copy contaminates the original. It has been tried, with painful results.

Moreover, we uploads run only partly on the main computer. An upload is neither a biological entity nor a long stream of code, but something more than both. Some of the substratum, the hardware, is wired like actual neurons, although constructed of sturdier stuff: thousands of miles of nano-constructed organic polymers. This is why analogues think at the rate of the human brain, not the much faster rate of computers. It's also why we feel as our originals do.

After Ajit's maintenance glitch our mood, which had been exuberant, sobered. But it didn't sour. We worked steadily, with focus and hope, deciding where exactly to position the probe and then entering the coordinates for the jump.

"See you soon," we said to each other. I kissed both Kane and Ajit lightly on the lips. Then we all shut down and the probe jumped.

Days later, we emerged on the other side of Sgr A West, all three of us still intact. If it were in my nature, I would have said a prayer of thanksgiving. Instead I said to Ajit, "Still have a head, I see."

"And a good thing he does," Kane said absently, already plunging for the chair in front of his terminal. "We'll need it. And—Ajit, the mass detectors . . . great shitting gods!"

It seems we were to have thanksgiving after all, if only perversely. I said, "What is it? What's there?" The displays showed nothing at all.

"Nothing at all," Ajit said. "And everything."

"Speak English!"

Ajit—I doubt Kane had even heard me, in his absorption—said, "The mass detectors are showing a huge mass less than a quarter light year away. The radiation detectors—all of them—are showing nothing at all. We're—"

"We're accelerating fast." I studied ship's data; the rate of acceleration made me blink. "We're going to hit whatever it is. Not soon, but the tidal forces—"

The probe was small, but the tidal forces of something this big would still rip it apart when it got close enough.

Something this big. But there was, to all other sensors, nothing there.

Nothing but shadows.

A strange sensation ran over me. Not fear, but something more complicated, much more eerie.

My voice sounded strange in my ears. "What if we hit it? I know you said radiation of all types will go right through shadow matter just as if it isn't there—" *because it isn't, not in our universe* "—but what about the probe? What if we hit it before we take the final event-horizon measurements on Sgr A*?"

"We won't hit it," Ajit said. "We'll move before then, Tirzah, back to the hole. Kane—"

They forget me again. I went up to the observation deck. Looking out through the clear hull, I stared at the myriad of stars on the side of the night sky away from Sgr A West. Then I turned to look toward that vast three-armed cloud of turning plasma, radiating as it cools. Nothing blocked my view of Sgr A West. Yet between us lay a huge, massive body of shadow matter, unseen, pulling on everything else my dazed senses could actually see.

To my left, all the exotic plants in the observatory disappeared.

Ajit and Kane worked feverishly, until once more I made them shut down for "sleep." The radiation here was nearly as great as it had been in our first location. We were right inside Sagittarius A East, the huge expanding shell of an unimaginable explosion sometime during the last 100,000 years. Most of Sgr A East wasn't visible at the wavelengths I could see, but the gamma-ray detectors were going crazy.

"We can't stop for five hours!" Kane cried. "Don't you realize how much damage the radiation could do in that time? We need to get all the data we can, work on it, and send off the second minicap!"

"We're going to send off the second minicap right now," I said. "And we'll only shut down for three hours. But, Kane, we are going to do that. I mean it. Uploads run even more damage from not running maintenance than we do from external radiation. You know that."

He did. He scowled at me, and cursed, and fussed with the minicap, but then he fired the minicap off and shut down.

Ajit said, "Just one more minute, Tirzah. I want to show you something."

"Ajit—"

"No, it's not mathematical. I promise. It's something I brought onto the *Kepler*. The object was not included in the probe program, but I can show you a holo."

Somewhere in the recesses of the computer, Ajit's upload created a program and a two-dimensional holo appeared on an empty display screen. I blinked at it, surprised.

It was a statue of some sort of god with four arms, enclosed in a circle of flames, made of what looked like very old bronze.

"This is Nataraja," Ajit said. "Shiva dancing."

"Ajit—"

"No, I am not a god worshipper," he smiled. "You know me better than that, Tirzah. Hinduism has many gods—thousands—but they are, except to the ignorant, no more than embodiments of different aspects of reality. Shiva is the dance of creation and destruction, the constant flow of energy in the cosmos. Birth and death and rebirth. It seemed fitting to bring him to the galactic core, where so much goes on of all three. This statue has been in my family for four hundred years. I must bring it home, along with the answers to our experiments."

"You will bring Shiva back to New Bombay," I said softly, "and your answers, too."

"Yes, I have begun to think so." He smiled at me, a smile with all the need of his quick-silver personality in it, but also all the courtesy and hope. "Now I will sleep."

9. SHIP

The next morning, after a deep sleep one part sheer exhaustion and one part sex, I woke to find Ajit already out of bed and seated in front of his terminal. He rose the moment I entered the wardroom and turned to me with a grave face. "Tirzah. The minicap arrived. I already put the data into the system."

"What's wrong? Where's Kane?"

"Still asleep, I imagine."

I went to Kane's bunk. He lay on his back, still in the clothes he'd worn for three days, smelling sour and snoring softly. I thought of waking him, then decided to wait a bit. Kane could certainly use the sleep, and I could use the time with Ajit. I went back to the wardroom, tightening the belt on my robe.

"What's wrong?" I repeated.

"I put the data from the minicap into the system. It's all corrections to the last minicap's data. Kane says the first set was wrong."

"Kane?" I said stupidly.

"The Kane-analogue," Ajit explained patiently. "He says radiation hit the probe's sensors for the first batch, before any of them realized it. They fired off the preliminary data right after the jump, you know, because they had no idea how long the probe could last. Now they've had time to discover where the radiation hit, to restore the sensor programs, and to retake the measurements. The Kane analogue says these new ones are accurate, the others weren't."

I tried to take it all in. "So Kane's shadow matter theory—none of that is true?"

"I don't know," Ajit said. "How can anybody know until we see if the data supports it? The minicap only just arrived."

"Then I might not have moved the probe," I said, meaning "the other I." My analogue. I didn't know what I was saying. The shock was too great. All that theorizing, all Kane's sharp triumph, all that tension . . .

I looked more closely at Ajit. He looked very pale, and as fatigued as a genemod man of his youth can look. I said, "You didn't sleep much."

"No. Yesterday was . . . difficult."

"Yes," I agreed, noting the characteristically polite understatement. "Yes."

"Should I wake Kane?" Ajit said, almost diffidently.

"I'll do it."

Kane was hard to wake. I had to shake him several times before he struggled up to consciousness.

"Tirzah?"

"Who else? Kane, you must get up. Something's happened."

"Wh-what?" He yawned hugely and slumped against the bulkhead. His whole body reeked.

I braced myself. "The second minicap arrived. Your analogue sent a recording. He says the prelim data was compromised, due to radiation-caused sensor malfunction."

That woke him. He stared at me as if I were an executioner. "The data's compromised? *All* of it?"

"I don't know."

Kane pushed out of his bunk and ran into the wardroom. Ajit said, "I put the minicap data into the system already, but I—" Kane wasn't listening. He tore into the data, and after a few minutes he actually bellowed.

"No!"

I flattened myself against the bulkhead, not from fear but from surprise. I had never heard a grown man make a noise like that.

But there were no other noises. Kane worked silently, ferociously. Ajit sat at his own terminal and worked, too, not yesterday's tentative copying but the real thing. I put hot coffee beside them both. Kane gulped his steaming, Ajit ignored his.

After half an hour, Kane turned to me. Defeat pulled like gravity at everything on his face, eyes and lips and jaw muscles. Only his filthy hair sprang upward. He said simply, with the naked straightforwardness of despair, "The new data invalidates the idea of shadow matter."

I heard myself say, "Kane, go take a shower."

To my surprise, he went, shambling from the room. Ajit worked a few minutes longer, then climbed the ladder to the observation deck. Over his shoulder he said, "Tirzah, I want to be alone, please. Don't come."

I didn't. I sat at the tiny wardroom table, looked at my own undrunk coffee, and thought of nothing.

10. PROBE

The data from the probe's new position looked good, Kane said. That was his word: "good." Then he returned to his terminal.

"Ajit?" I was coming to rely on him more and more for translation. He was just as busy as Kane, but kinder. This made sense. If, to Kane, Ajit was a secondary but still necessary party to the intellectual action, that's what I was to both of them. Ajit had settled into this position, secure that he was valued. I could feel myself doing the same. The cessation of struggle turned us both kinder.

Kane, never insecure, worked away.

Ajit said, "The new readings confirm a large gravitational mass affecting the paths of both the infalling gas and the probe. The young stars so close to Sgr A* are a much knottier problem. We've got to modify the whole theory of star formation to account for the curvatures of spacetime caused by the hole *and* by the shadow mass. It's very complex. Kane's got the computer working on that, and I'm going to take readings on Sgr A West, in its different parts, and on stars on the other side of the mass and look at those."

"What about the mass detectors? What do they say?"

"They say we're being pulled toward a mass of about a half million suns."

A half million suns. And we couldn't see it: not with our eyes, nor radio sensors, nor X-rays detectors, nor anything.

"I have a question. Does it have an event horizon? Is it swallowing light, like a black hole does? Isn't it the gravity of a black hole that swallows light?"

"Yes. But radiation, including light, goes right through this shadow matter, Tirzah. Don't you understand? It doesn't interact with normal radiation at all."

"But it has gravity. Why doesn't its gravity trap the light?"

"I don't know." He hesitated. "Kane thinks maybe it doesn't interact with radiation as particles, which respond to gravity. Only as waves."

"How can it do that?"

Ajit took my shoulders and shook them playfully. "I told you— *we don't know*. This is brand-new, dear heart. We know as much about what it will and will not do as primitive hominids knew about fire."

"Well, don't make a god of it," I said, and it was a test. Ajit passed. He didn't stiffen as if I'd made some inappropriate reference to the drawing of Shiva he'd shown me last night. Instead, he laughed and went back to work.

"Tirzah! Tirzah!"

The automatic wake-up brought me out of shut-down. Ajit must have been brought back on-line a few moments before me, because he was already calling my name. Alarm bells clanged.

"It's Kane! He's been hit!"

I raced into Kane's bunk. He lay still amid the bedclothes. It wasn't the maintenance program that had taken the hit, because every part of his body was intact; so were the bedclothes. But Kane lay stiff and unresponsive.

"Run the full diagnostics," I said to Ajit.

"I already started them."

"Kane," I said, shaking him gently, then harder. He moved a little, groaned. So his upload wasn't dead.

I sat on the edge of the bunk, fighting fear, and took his hand. "Kane, love, can you hear me?"

He squeezed my fingers. The expression on his face didn't change. After a silence in which time itself seemed to stop, Ajit said, "The diagnostics are complete. About a third of brain function is gone."

I got into the bunk beside Kane and put my arms around him.

Ajit and I did what we could. Our uploads patched and copied, using material from both of us. Yes, the copying would lead to corruption, but we were beyond that.

Because an upload runs on such a complex combination of computer and nano-constructed polymer networks, we cannot simply be replaced by a back-up program cube. The unique software/hardware retes are also why a corrupted analogue is not exactly the same as a stroke- or tumor-impaired human brain.

The analogue brain does not have to pump blood or control

breathing. It does not have to move muscles or secrete hormones. Although closely tied to the "purer" programs that maintain our illusion of moving and living as three-dimensional beings in a three-dimensional ship, the analogue brain is tied to the computer in much more complex ways than any fleshy human using a terminal. The resources of the computer were at our disposal, but they could only accomplish limited aims.

When Ajit and I had finished putting together as much of Kane, or a pseudo-Kane, as we could, he walked into the wardroom and sat down. He looked, moved, smiled the same. That part is easy to repair, as easy as had been replacing Ajit's head or the exotics on the observation deck. But the man staring blankly at the terminal was not really Kane.

"What was I working on?" he said.

I got out, "Shadow matter."

"Shadow matter? What's that?"

Ajit said softly, "I have all your work, Kane. Our work. I think I can finish it, now that you've started us in the right direction."

He nodded, looking confused. "Thank you, Ajit." Then, with a flash of his old magnificent combativeness, "But you better get it right!"

"With your help," Ajit said gaily, and in that moment I came close to truly loving him.

They worked out a new division of labor. Kane was able to take the sensor readings and run them through the pre-set algorithms. Actually, Ajit probably could have trained me to do that. But Kane seemed content, frowning earnestly at his displays.

Ajit took over the actual science. I said to him, when we had a moment alone, "Can you do it?"

"I think so," he said, without either anger or arrogance. "I have the foundation that Kane laid. And we worked out some of the preliminaries together."

"We have only one more jump left."

"I know, Tirzah."

"With the risk of radiation killing us all—"

"Not yet. Give me a little more time."

I rested a moment against his shoulder. "All right. A little more time."

He put his arm around me, not in passion but in comradeship. None of us, we both knew, had all that much time left.

11. SHIP

Kane was only temporarily defeated by the contamination of the probe data. Within half a day, he had aborted his shadow-matter theory, archived his work on it, and gone back to his original theories about the mysteriously massive young stars near the hole. He used the probe's new data, which were all logical amplifications of the prelim readings. "I've got some ideas," he told me. "We'll see."

He wasn't as cheerful as usual, let alone as manically exuberant as during the shadow-matter "discovery," but he was working steadily. A mountain, Kane. It would take a lot to actually erode him, certainly more than a failed theory. That rocky insensitivity had its strengths.

Ajit, on the other hand, was not really working. I couldn't follow the displays on his terminal, but I could read the body language. He was restless, inattentive. But what worried me was something else, his attitude toward Kane.

All Ajit's anger was gone.

I watched carefully, while seemingly bent over ship's log or embroidery. Anger is the least subtle of the body's signals. Even when a person is successfully concealing most of it, the signs are there if you know where to look: the tight neck muscles, the turned-away posture, the tinge in the voice. Ajit displayed none of this. Instead, when he faced Kane, as he did in the lunch I insisted we all eat together at the wardroom table, I saw something else. A sly superiority, a secret triumph.

I could be wrong, I thought. I have been wrong before. By now I disliked Ajit so much that I didn't trust my own intuitions.

"Ajit," I said as we finished the simple meal I'd put together, "will you please—"

Ship's alarms went off with a deafening clang. *Breach, breach, breach.*

I whirled toward ship's display, which automatically illuminated. The breach was in the starboard hold, and it was full penetration by a mass of about a hundred grams. Within a minute, the nanos had put on a temporary patch. The alarm stopped and the computer began hectoring me.

"Breach sealed with temporary nano patch. Seal must be reinforced within two hours with permanent hull patch, type 6-A. For location of breach and patch supply, consult ship's log. If unavailability of—" I shut it off.

"Could be worse," Kane said.

"Well, of course it could be worse," I snapped, and immediately regretted it. I was not allowed to snap. That I had done so was an indication of how much the whole situation on the *Kepler* was affecting me. That wasn't allowed, either; it was unprofessional.

Kane wasn't offended. "Could have hit the engines or the living pod instead of just a hold. Actually, I'm surprised it hasn't happened before. There's a lot of drifting debris in this area."

Ajit said, "Are you going into the hold, Tirzah?"

Of course I was going into the hold. But this time I didn't snap; I smiled at him and said, "Yes, I'm going to suit up now."

"I'm coming, too," Kane said.

I blinked. I'd been about to ask if Ajit wanted to go with me. It would be a good way to observe him away from Kane, maybe ask some discreet questions. I said to Kane, "Don't you have to work?"

"The work isn't going anywhere. And I want to retrieve the particle. It didn't exit the ship, and at a hundred grams, there's going to be some of it left after the breach."

Ajit had stiffened at being pre-empted, yet again, by Kane. Ajit would have wanted to retrieve the particle, too; there is nothing more interesting to space scientists than dead rocks. Essentially, I'd often thought, Sgr A* was no more than a very hot, very large dead rock. I knew better than to say this aloud.

I could have ordered Ajit to accompany me, and ordered Kane to stay behind. But that, I sensed, would only make things worse. Ajit, in his present mood of deadly sensitivity, would not take well to orders from anyone, even me. I wasn't going to give him the chance to retreat more into whatever nasty state of mind he currently inhabited.

"Well, then, let's go," I said ungraciously to Kane, who only grinned at me and went to get our suits.

The holds, three of them for redundancy safety, are full of supplies of all types. Every few days I combine a thorough ship inspection with lugging enough food forward to sustain us. We aren't uploads; we need bodily nurturing as well as the kind I was supposed to be providing.

All three holds can be pressurized if necessary, but usually they aren't. Air generation and refreshment doesn't cost much power, but it costs some. Kane and I went into the starboard hold in heated s-suits and helmets.

"I'm going to look around," Kane said. He'd brought a handheld, and I saw him calculating the probable trajectory of the particle from the ship's data and the angle of the breach, as far as he could deduce it. Then he disappeared behind a pallet of crates marked SOYSYNTH.

The breach was larger than I'd expected; that hundred-gram particle had hit at a bad angle. But the nanos had done their usual fine job, and the permanent patch went on without trouble. I began the careful inspection of the rest of the hull, using my hand-held instruments.

Kane cursed volubly.

"Kane? What is it?"

"Nothing. Bumped into boxes."

"Well, don't. The last thing I want is you messing up my hold." For a physically fit man, Kane is clumsy in motion. I would bet my ship that he can't dance, and bet my life that he never tries.

"I can't see anything. Can't you brighten the light?"

I did, and he bumped around some more. Whenever he brushed something, he cursed. I did an inspection even more carefully than usual, but found nothing alarming. We met each other back by the hold door.

"It's not here," Kane said. "The particle. It's not here."

"You mean you didn't find it."

"No, I mean it's not here. Don't you think I could find a still-hot particle in a hold otherwise filled only with large immobile crates?"

I keyed in the door code. "So it evaporated on impact. Ice and ions and dust."

"To penetrate a Schaad hull? No." He reconsidered. "Well, maybe. What did you find?"

"Not much. Pitting and scarring on the outside, nothing unexpected. But no structural stress to worry about."

"The debris here is undoubtedly orbiting the core, but we're so far out it's not moving all that fast. Still, we should have had some warning. But I'm more worried about the probe—when is the third minicap due?"

Kane knew as well as I did when the third minicap was due. His asking was the first sign he was as tense as the rest of us.

"Three more days," I said. "Be patient."

"I'm not patient."

"As if that's new data."

"I'm also afraid the probe will be hit by rapidly orbiting debris, and that will be that. Did you know that the stars close in to Sgr A* orbit at several thousand clicks per second?"

I knew. He'd told me often enough. The probe was always a

speculative proposition, and before now, Kane had been jubilant that we'd gotten any data at all from it.

I'd never heard Kane admit to being "afraid" of anything. Even allowing for the casualness of the phrase.

I wanted to distract him, and, if Kane was really in a resigned and reflective mood, it also seemed a good time to do my job. "Kane, about Ajit—"

"I don't want to talk about that sniveling slacker," Kane said, with neither interest not rancor. "I picked badly for an assistant, that's all."

It hadn't actually been his "pick;" his input had been one of many. I didn't say this. Kane looked around the hold one more time. "I guess you're right. The particle sublimed. Ah, well."

I put the glove of my hand on the arm of his suit—not exactly an intimate caress, but the best I could do in this circumstance. "Kane, how is the young-star mystery going?"

"Not very well. But that's science." The hold door stood open and he lumbered out.

I gave one last look around the hold before turning off the light, but there was nothing more to see.

The mended statue of Shiva was back on the wardroom table, smack in the center, when Kane and I returned from the hold. I don't think Kane, heading straight for his terminal, even noticed. I smiled at Ajit, although I wasn't sure why he had brought the statue back. He'd told me he never wanted to see it again.

"Tirzah, would you perhaps like to play go?"

I couldn't conceal my surprise. "Go?"

"Yes. Will you play with me?" Accompanied by his most winning smile.

"All right."

He brought out the board and, bizarrely, set it up balanced on his knees. When he saw my face, he said, "We'll play here. I don't want to disturb the Cosmic Dancer."

"All right." I wasn't sure what to think. I drew my chair close to his, facing him, and bent over the board.

We both knew that Ajit was a better player than I. That's why both of us played: he to win, me to lose. I would learn more from the losing position. Very competitive people—and I thought now that I had never known one as competitive as Ajit—relax only when not threatened.

So I made myself non-threatening in every way I knew, and Ajit and I talked and laughed, and Kane worked doggedly on his theories that weren't going anywhere. The statue of the dancing god leered at me from the table, and I knew with every passing moment how completely I was failing this already failing mission.

12. PROBE

Kane was gentler since the radiation corruption. Who can say how these things happen? Personality, too, is encoded in the human brain, whether flesh or analogue. He was still Kane, but we saw only his gentler, sweeter side. Previously that part of him had been dominated by his combative intellect, which had been a force of nature all its own, like a high wind. Now the intellect had failed, the wind calmed. The landscape beneath lay serene.

"Here, Ajit," Kane said. "These are the equations you wanted run." He sent them to Ajit's terminal, stood, and stretched. The stretch put him slightly off balance, something damaged in the upload that Ajit and I hadn't been able to fix, or find. A brain is such a complex thing. Kane tottered, and Ajit rose swiftly to catch him.

"Careful, Kane. Here, sit down."

Ajit eased Kane into a chair at the wardroom table. I put down my work. Kane said, "Tirzah, I feel funny."

"Funny how?" Alarm ran through me.

"I don't know. Can we play go?"

I had taught him the ancient strategy game, and he enjoyed it. He wasn't very good, not nearly as good as I was, but he liked it and didn't seem to mind losing. I got out the board. Ajit, who was a master at go, went back to Kane's shadow-matter theory. He was making good progress, I knew, although he said frankly that all the basic ideas were Kane's.

Halfway through our second game of go, the entire wardroom disappeared.

A moment of blind panic seized me. I was adrift in the void, nothing to see or feel or hold onto, a vertigo so terrible it blocked any rational thought. It was the equivalent of a long, anguished scream, originating in the most primitive part of my now blind brain: *lost, lost, lost and alone . . .*

The automatic maintenance program kicked in and the wardroom re-appeared. Kane gripped the table edge and stared at me, white-faced. I went to him, wrapped my arms around him reassuringly, and gazed at Ajit. Kane clung to me. A part of my mind noted that some aspects of the wardroom were wrong: the galley door was too low to walk through upright, and one chair had disappeared, along with the go board. Maintenance code too damaged to restore. Ajit said softly, "We have to decide, Tirzah. We could take a final radiation hit at any time."

"I know."

I took my arms away from Kane. "Are you all right?"

He smiled. "Yes. Just for a minute I was . . ." He seemed to lose his thought.

Ajit brought his terminal chair to the table, to replace the vanished one. He sat leaning forward, looking from me to Kane and back. "This is a decision all three of us have to make. We have one minicap left to send back to the *Kepler*, and one more jump for ourselves. At any time we could lose . . . everything. You all know that. What do you think we should do? Kane? Tirzah?"

All my life I'd heard that even very flawed people can rise to leadership under the right circumstances. I'd never believed it, not of someone with Ajit's basic personality structure: competitive, paranoid, angry at such a deep level he didn't even know it. I'd been wrong. I believed now.

Kane said, "I feel funny, and that probably means I've taken another minor hit and the program isn't there to repair it. I think . . . I think . . ."

"Kane?" I took his hand.

He had trouble getting words out. "I think we better send the minicap now."

"I agree," Ajit said. "But that means we send it without the data from our next jump, to just outside the event horizon of Sgr A*. So the *Kepler* won't get those readings. They'll get the work on shadow matter, but most of the best things on that already went in the second minicap. Still, it's better than nothing, and I'm afraid if we wait to send until after the jump, nothing is what the *Kepler* will get. It will be too late."

Both men looked at me. As captain, the jump decision was mine. I nodded. "I agree, too. Send off the minicap with whatever you've got, and then we'll jump. But not to the event horizon."

"Why not?" Kane burst out, sounding more like himself than at any time since the accident.

"Because there's no point. We can't send any more data back, so the event horizon readings die with us. And we can survive longer if I jump us completely away from the core. Several hundred light years out, where the radiation is minimal."

Together, as if rehearsed, they both said, "No."

"No?"

"No," Ajit said, with utter calm, utter persuasiveness. "We're not going to go out like that, Tirzah."

"But we don't have to go out at all! Not for decades! Maybe centuries! Not until the probe's life-maintenance power is used up—" Or until the probe is hit by space debris. Or until radiation takes us out. Nowhere in space is really safe.

Kane said, "And what would we do for centuries? I'd go mad. I want to work."

"Me, too," Ajit said. "I want to take the readings by the event horizon and make of them what I can, while I can. Even though the *Kepler* will never see them."

They were scientists.

And I? Could even I, station bred, have lived for centuries in this tiny ship, without a goal beyond survival, trapped with these two men? An Ajit compassionate and calm, now that he was on top. A damaged Kane, gentle and intellectually gutted. And a Tirzah, captaining a pointless expedition with nowhere to go and nothing to do.

I would have ended up hating all three of us.

Ajit took my left hand. My right one still held Kane's, so we made a broken circle in the radiation-damaged wardroom.

"All right," I said. "We'll send off the minicap and then jump to the event horizon."

"Yes," Kane said.

Ajit said, "I'm going to go back to work. Tirzah, if you and Kane want to go up to the observation deck, or anywhere, I'll prepare and launch the minicap." Carefully he turned his back and sat at his terminal.

I led Kane to my bunk. This was a first; I always went to the scientists' bunks. My own, as captain, had features for my eyes only. But now it didn't matter.

We made love, and afterward, holding his superb, aging body in my arms, I whispered against his cheek, "I love you, Kane."

"I love you, too," he said simply, and I had no way of knowing if he meant it, or if it was an automatic response dredged up from some half-remembered ritual from another time. It didn't matter. There are a lot more types of love in the universe than I once suspected.

We were silent a long time, and then Kane said, "I'm trying to remember pi. I know three point one, but I can't remember after that."

I said, through the tightness in my throat, "Three point one four one. That's all I remember."

"Three point one four one," Kane said dutifully. I left him repeating it over and over, when I went to jump the probe to the event horizon of Sgr A*.

13. SHIP

The second breach of the hull was more serious than the first.

The third minicap had not arrived from the probe. "The analogues are probably all dead," Kane said dully. "They were supposed to jump to one-twenty-fifth of a light year from the event horizon. Our calculations were always problematic for where exactly that *is*. It's possible they landed inside, and the probe will just spiral around Sgr A* forever. Or they got hit with major radiation and fried."

"It's possible," I said. "How is the massive-young-star problem coming?"

"It's not. Mathematical dead end."

He looked terrible, drawn and, again, unwashed. I was more impatient with the latter than I should be. But how hard is it, as a courtesy to your shipmates if nothing else, to get your body into the shower? How long does it take? Kane had stopped exercising, as well.

"Kane," I began, as quietly but firmly as I could manage, "will you—"

The alarms went off, clanging again at 115 decibels. *Breach, breach, breach . . .*

I scanned the displays. "Oh, God—"

"Breach sealed with temporary nano patch," the computer said. "Seal must be reinforced within one-half hour with permanent hull patch, type 1-B, supplemented with equipment repair, if possible. For location of breach and patch supply, consult—" I turned it off.

The intruder had hit the back-up engine. It was a much larger particle than the first one, although since it had hit us and then gone on its merry way, rather than penetrating the ship, there was no way to recover it for examination. But the outside mass detectors registered a particle of at least two kilos, and it had probably been moving much faster than the first one. If it had hit us directly, we would all be dead. Instead it had given the ship a glancing blow, damaging the back-up engine.

"I'll come with you again," Kane said.

"There won't be any particle to collect this time." Or not collect.

"I know. But I'm not getting anywhere here."

Kane and I, s-suited, went into the back-up engine compartment. As soon as I saw it, I knew there was nothing I could do. There is damage you can repair, and there is damage you cannot. The back end of the compartment had been sheared off, and part of the engine with it. No wonder the computer had recommended a 1-B patch, which is essentially the equivalent of "Throw a tarp over it and forget it."

While I patched, Kane poked around the edges of the breach, then at the useless engine. He left before I did, and I found him studying ship's display of the hit on my wardroom screen. He wasn't trying to do anything with ship's log, which was not his place and he knew it, but he stood in front of the data, moving his hand when he wanted another screen, frowning horribly.

"What is it, Kane?" I said. I didn't really want to know; the patch had taken hours and I was exhausted. I didn't see Ajit. Sleeping, or up on the observation deck, or, less likely, in the gym.

"Nothing. Whatever that hit was made of, it wasn't radiating. So it wasn't going very fast, or the external sensors would have picked up at least ionization. Either the mass was cold, or the sensors aren't functioning properly."

"I'll run the diagnostics," I said wearily. "Anything else?"

"Yes. I want to move the ship."

I stared at him, my suit half peeled from my body, my helmet defiantly set on the table, pushing the statue of Shiva to one side. "*Move the ship?*"

Ajit appeared in the doorway from his bunk.

"Yes," Kane said. "Move the ship."

"But these are the coordinates the minicap will return to!"

"It's not coming," Kane said. "Don't you listen to anything I say, Tirzah? The uploads didn't make it. The third minicap is days late; if it were coming, it would be here. The probe is gone, the uploads are gone, and we've got all the data we're going to get from them. If we want more, we're going to have to go after it ourselves."

"Go after it?" I repeated, stupidly. "How?"

"I already told you! Move the ship closer into the core so we can take the readings the probe should have taken. Some of them, anyway."

Ajit said, "Moving the ship is completely Tirzah's decision."

His championship of me when I needed no champion, and especially not in that pointlessly assertive voice, angered me more than Kane's suggestion. "Thank you, Ajit, I can handle this!"

Mistake, mistake.

Kane, undeterred, plowed on. "I don't mean we'd go near the event horizon, of course, or even to the probe's first position near the star cluster. But we could move much closer in. Maybe ten light years from the core, positioned between the northern and western arms of Sgr A West."

Ajit said, "Which would put us right in the circumnuclear disk! Where the radiation is much worse than here!"

Kane turned on him, acknowledging Ajit's presence for the first time in days, with an outpouring of all Kane's accumulated frustration and disappointment. "We've been hit twice with particles that damaged the ship. Clearly we're in the path of some equivalent of an asteroid belt orbiting the core at this immense distance. It can't be any less safe in the circumnuclear disk, which, I might remind you, is only shocked molecular gases, with its major radiation profile unknown. Any first-year astronomy student should know that. Or is it just that you're a coward?"

Ajit's skin mottled, then paled. His features did not change expression at all. But I felt the heat coming from him, the primal rage, greater for being contained. He went into his bunk and closed the door.

"Kane!" I said furiously, too exhausted and frustrated and disappointed to watch my tone. "You can't—"

"I can't stand any more of this," Kane said. He slammed down the corridor to the gym, and I heard the exercise bike whir in rage.

I went to my own bunk, locked the door, and squeezed my eyes shut, fighting for control. But even behind my closed eyelids I saw our furious shadows.

After a few hours I called them both together in the wardroom. When Kane refused, I ordered him. I lifted Ajit's statue of Shiva off the table and handed it to him, making its location his problem, as long as it wasn't on the table. Wordlessly he carried it into his bunk and then returned.

"This can't go on," I said calmly. "We all know that. We're in this small space together to accomplish something important, and our mission overrides all our personal feelings. You are both rational men, scientists, or you wouldn't be here."

"Don't patronize us with flattery," Ajit said.

"I'm sorry. I didn't intend to do that. It's true you're both scientists, and it's true you've both been certified rational enough for space travel."

They couldn't argue with that. I didn't mention how often certification boards had misjudged, or been bribed, or just been too dazzled by well-earned reputations to look below the work to the worker. If Kane or Ajit knew all that, they kept it to themselves.

"I blame myself for any difficulties we've had here," I said, in the best Nurturer fashion. Although it was also true. "It's my job to keep a ship running in productive harmony, and this one, I think we can all agree, is not."

No dissension. I saw that both of them dreaded some long, drawn-out discussion group dynamics, never a topic that goes down well with astrophysicists. Kane said abruptly, "I still want to move the ship."

I had prepared myself for this. "No, Kane. We're not jumping closer in."

He caught at my loophole. "Then can we jump to another location at the same distance from the core? Maybe measurements from another base point would help."

"We're not jumping anywhere until I'm sure the third minicap isn't coming."

"How long will that be?" I could see the formidable intelligence under the childish tantrums already racing ahead, planning measurements, weighing options.

"We'll give it another three days."

"All right." Suddenly he smiled, his first in days. "Thanks, Tirzah."

I turned to Ajit. "Ajit, what can we do for your work? What do you need?"

"I ask for nothing," he said, with such a strange, intense, unreadable expression that for a moment I felt irrational fear. Then he stood and went into his bunk. I heard the door lock.

I had failed again.

No alarm went off in the middle of the night. There was nothing overt to wake me. But I woke anyway, and I heard someone moving quietly around the wardroom. The muscles of my right arm tensed to open my bunk, and I forced them to still.

Something wasn't right. Intuition, that mysterious shadow of rational thought, told me to lie motionless. To not open my bunk, to not even reach out and access the ship's data on my bunk screen. To not move at all.

Why?

I didn't know.

The smell of coffee wafted from the wardroom. So one of the men couldn't sleep, made some coffee, turned on his terminal. So what?

Don't move, said that pre-reasoning part of my mind, from the shadows.

The coffee smell grew stronger. A chair scraped. Ordinary, mundane sounds.

Don't move.

I didn't have to move. This afternoon I had omitted to mention to Kane and Ajit those times that certification boards had misjudged, or been bribed, or just been too dazzled by well-earned reputations to look below the work to the worker. Those times in which the cramped conditions of space, coupled with swollen egos and frenzied work, had led to disaster for a mission Nurturer. But we had learned. My bunk had equipment the scientists did not know about.

Carefully I slid my gaze to a spot directly above me on the bunk ceiling. Only my eyes moved. I pattern-blinked: two quick, three beats closed, two quick, a long steady stare. The screen brightened.

This was duplicate ship data. Not a back-up; it was entirely separate, made simultaneously from the same sensors as the main log but routed into separate, free-standing storage that could not be reached from the main computer. Scientists are all sophisticated users. There is no way to keep data from any who wish to alter it except by discreet, unknown, untraceable storage. I pattern-blinked, not moving so much as a finger or a toe in the bed, to activate various screens of ship data.

It was easy to find.

Yesterday, at 1850 hours, the minicap bay had opened and received a minicap. Signal had failed to transmit to the main computer. Today at 300 hours, which was fifteen minutes ago, the minicap bay had been opened manually and the payload removed. Again signal had failed to the main computer.

The infrared signature in the wardroom, seated at his terminal, was Ajit.

It was possible the signal failures were coincidental, and Ajit was even now transferring data from the third minicap into the computer, enjoying a cup of hot coffee while he did so, gloating in getting a perfectly legitimate jump on Kane. But I didn't think so.

What did I think?

I didn't have to think; I just knew. I could see it unfolding, clear as a holovid. All of it. Ajit had stolen the second minicap, too. That had been the morning after Kane and I had slept so soundly, the morning after Ajit had given us wine to celebrate Kane's shadow-matter theory. What had been in that wine? We'd slept soundly, and Ajit told us that the minicap had come before we were awake. Ajit said he'd already put it into the computer. It carried the Kane upload's apology that the prelim data, the data from which Kane had constructed his shadow-matter thesis, was wrong, contaminated by a radiation strike.

Ajit had fabricated that apology and that replacement data. The actual second minicap would justify Kane's work, not undo it. Ajit was saving all three minicaps to use for himself, to claim the shadow matter discovery for his own. He'd used the second minicap to discredit the first; he would claim the third had never arrived, had never been sent from the dying probe.

The real Kane, my Kane, hadn't found the particle from the first ship's breach because it had, indeed, been made of shadow matter. That, and not slow speed, had been why the particle showed no radiation. The particle had exerted gravity on our world, but nothing else. The second breach, too, had been shadow matter. I knew that as surely as if Kane had shown me the pages of equations to prove it.

I knew something else, too. If I went into the shower and searched my body very carefully, every inch of it, I would find in some inconspicuous place the small, regular hole into which a sub-dermal tracker had gone the night of the drugged wine. So would Kane. Trackers would apprise Ajit of every move we made, not only large-muscle moves like a step or a hug, but small ones like accessing my bunk display of ship's data. That was what my intuition had been warning me of. Ajit did not want to be discovered during his minicap thefts.

I had the same trackers in my own repertoire. Only I had not thought this mission deteriorated enough to need them. I had not wanted to think that. I'd been wrong.

But how would Ajit make use of Kane's stolen work with Kane there to claim it for himself?

I already knew the answer, of course. I had known it from the moment I pattern-blinked at the ceiling, which was the moment I finally admitted to myself how monstrous this mission had turned.

I pushed open the bunk door and called cheerfully, "Hello? Do I smell coffee? Who's out there?"

"I am," Ajit said genially. "I cannot sleep. Come have some coffee."

"Coming, Ajit."

I put on my robe, tied it at my waist, and slipped the gun from its secret mattress compartment into my palm.

14. PROBE

The probe jumped successfully. We survived.

This close to the core, the view wasn't as spectacular as it was farther out. Sgr A*, which captured us in orbit immediately, now appeared as a fuzzy region dominating starboard. The fuzziness, Ajit said, was a combination of Hawking radiation and superheated gases being swallowed by the black hole. To port, the intense blue cluster of IRS16 was muffled by the clouds of ionized plasma around the probe. We experienced some tidal forces, but the probe was so small that the gravitational tides didn't yet cause much damage.

Ajit has found a way to successfully apply Kane's shadow-matter theory to the paths of the infalling gases, as well as to the orbits of the young stars near Sgr A*. He says there may well be a really lot of shadow matter near the core, and maybe even farther out. It may even provide enough mass to "balance" the universe, keeping it from either flying apart forever or collapsing in on itself. Shadow matter, left over from the very beginning of creation, may preserve creation.

Kane nods happily as Ajit explains. Kane holds my hand. I stroke his palm gently with my thumb, making circles like tiny orbits.

15. SHIP

Ajit sat, fully dressed and with steaming coffee at his side, in front of his terminal. I didn't give him time to get the best of me. I walked into the wardroom and fired.

The sedative dart dropped him almost instantly. It was effective, for his body weight, for an hour. Kane didn't hear the thud as Ajit fell off his chair and onto the deck; Kane's bunk door stayed closed. I went into Ajit's bunk and searched every cubic meter of it, overriding the lock on his personal storage space. Most of that was taken up with the bronze statue of Shiva. The minicaps were not there, nor anywhere else in his bunk.

I tried the galley next, and came up empty.

Same for the shower, the gym, the supply closets.

Ajit could have hidden the cubes in the engine compartments or the fuel bays or any of a dozen other ship's compartments, but they weren't pressurized and he would have had to either suit up or pressurize them. Either one would have shown up in my private ship data, and they hadn't. Ajit probably hadn't wanted to take the risk of too much covert motion around the ship. He'd only had enough drugs to put Kane and me out once. Otherwise, he wouldn't have risked subdermal trackers.

I guessed he'd hidden the cubes in the observatory. Looking there involved digging. By the time I'd finished, the exotics lay yanked up in dying heaps around the room. The stones of the fountain had been flung about. I was filthy and sweating, my robe smeared with soil. But I'd found them, the two crystal cubes from the second and third minicaps, removed from their heavy shielding. Their smooth surfaces sliced the dirt easily.

Forty five minutes had passed.

I went downstairs to wake Kane. The expedition would have to jump immediately; there is no room on a three-man ship to confine a prisoner for long. Even if I could protect Kane and me from Ajit, I didn't think I could protect Ajit from Kane. These minicaps held the validation of Kane's shadow-matter work, and in another man, joy over that would have eclipsed the theft. I didn't think it would be that way with Kane.

Ajit still lay where I'd dropped him. The tranquilizer is reliable. I shot Ajit with a second dose and went into Kane's bunk. He wasn't there.

I stood too still for too long, then frantically scrambled into my s-suit.

I had already searched everywhere in the pressurized sections of the ship. Oh, let him be taking a second, fruitless look at the starboard hold, hoping to find some trace of the first particle that had hit us! Let him be in the damaged back-up engine compartment, afire with some stupid, brilliant idea to save the engine! Let him be—

"Kane! *Kane!*"

He lay in the starboard hold, on his side, his suit breached. He lay below a jagged piece of plastic from a half-open supply box. Ajit had made it look as if Kane had tried to open a box marked SENSOR REPLACEMENTS, had torn his suit, and the suit sealer nanos had failed. It was an altogether clumsy attempt, but one that, in the absence of any other evidence and a heretofore spotless reputation, would probably have worked.

The thing inside the suit was not Kane. Not any more.

I knelt beside him. I put my arms around him and begged, cried, pleaded with him to come back. I pounded my gloves on the deck until I, too, risked suit breach. I think, in that abandoned and monstrous moment, I would not have cared.

Then I went into the wardroom, exchanged my tranquilizer gun for a knife, and slit Ajit's throat. I only regretted that he wasn't awake when I did it, and I only regretted that much, much later.

I prepared the ship for the long jump back to the Orion Arm. After the jump would come the acceleration-deceleration to Skillian, the closest settled world, which will take about a month standard. Space physics which I don't understand make this necessary; a ship cannot jump too close to a large body of matter like a planet. Shadow matter, apparently, does not count.

Both Ajit's and Kane's bodies rest in the cold of the non-pressurized port hold. Kane's initial work on shadow matter rests in my bunk. Every night I fondle the two cubes which will make him famous—more famous—on the settled Worlds. Every day I look at the data, the equations, the rest of his work on his terminal. I don't understand it, but sometimes I think I can see Kane, his essential self, in these intelligent symbols, these unlockings of the secrets of cosmic energy.

It was our shadow selves, not our essential ones, that destroyed my mission, the shadows in the core of each human being. Ajit's ambition and rivalry. Kane's stunted vision of other people and their limits. My pride, which led me to think I was in control of murderous rage long after it had reached a point of no return. In all of us.

I left one thing behind at the center of the galaxy. Just before the *Kepler* jumped, I jettisoned Ajit's statue of Shiva dancing, in the direction of Sgr A*. I don't know for sure, but I imagine it will travel toward the black hole at the galaxy's core, be caught eventually by its gravity, and spiral in, to someday disappear over the event horizon into some unimaginable singularity. That's what I want to happen to the statue. I hate it.

As to what will happen to me, I don't have the energy to hate it. I'll tell the authorities everything. My license as a Nurturer will surely be revoked, but I won't stand trial for the murder of Ajit. A captain is supreme law on her ship. I had the legal authority to kill Ajit. However, it's unlikely that any scientific expedition will hire me as captain ever again. My useful life is over, and any piece of it left is no more than one of the ashy, burned-out stars Kane says orbit Sgr A*, uselessly circling the core until its final death, giving no light.

A shadow.

16. PROBE

We remain near the galactic core, Kane and Ajit and I. The event horizon of Sgr A* is about one-fiftieth of a light year below us. As we spiral closer, our speed is increasing dramatically. The point of no return is one-twentieth of a light year. The lethal radiation, oddly enough, is less here than when we were drifting near the shadow matter on the other side of Sgr A West, but it is enough.

I think at least part of my brain has been affected, along with the repair program to fix it. It's hard to be sure, but I can't seem to remember much before we came aboard the probe, or details of why we're here. Sometimes I almost remember, but then it slips away. I know that Kane and Ajit and I are shadows of something, but I don't remember what.

Ajit and Kane work on their science. I have forgotten what it's about, but I like to sit and watch them together. Ajit works on ideas and Kane assists in minor ways, as once Kane worked on ideas and Ajit assisted in minor ways. We all know the science will go down into Sgr A* with us. The scientists do it anyway, for no other gain than pure love of the work. This is, in fact, the purest science in the universe.

Our mission is a success. Ajit and Kane have answers. I have kept them working harmoniously, have satisfied all their needs while they did it, and have captained my ship safely into the very heart of the galaxy. I am content.

Not that there aren't difficulties, of course. It's disconcerting to go up on the observation deck. Most of the exotics remain, blooming in wild profusion, but a good chunk of the hull has disappeared. The effect is that anything up there—flowers, bench, people—is drifting through naked space, held together only by the gravity we exert on each other. I don't understand how we can breathe up there; surely the air is gone. There are a lot of things I don't understand now, but I accept them.

The wardroom is mostly intact, except that you have to stoop to go through the door to the galley, which is only about two feet tall, and Ajit's bunk has disappeared. We manage fine with two bunks, since I sleep every night with Ajit or Kane. The terminals are intact. One of them won't display any more, though. Ajit has used it to hold a holo he programmed on a functioning part of the computer and superimposed over where the defunct display stood. The holo is a rendition of an image he showed me once before, of an Indian god, Shiva.

Shiva is dancing. He dances, four-armed and graceful, in a circle decorated with flames. Everything about him is dynamic, waving arms and kicking uplifted leg and mobile expression. Even the flames in the circle dance. Only Shiva's face is calm, detached, serene. Kane, especially, will watch the holo for hours.

The god, Ajit tells us, represents the flow of cosmic energy in the universe. Shiva creates, destroys, creates again. All matter and all energy participate in this rhythmic dance, patterns made and unmade throughout all of time.

Shadow matter—that's what Kane and Ajit are working on. I remember now. Something decoupled from the rest of the universe right after its creation. But shadow matter, too, is part of the dance. It exerted gravitational pull on our ship. We cannot see it, but it is there, changing the orbits of stars, the trajectories of lives, in the great shadow play of Shiva's dancing.

I don't think Kane, Ajit, and I have very much longer. But it doesn't matter, not really. We have each attained what we came for, and since we, too, are part of the cosmic pattern, we cannot really be lost. When the probe goes down into the black hole at the core, if we last that long, it will be as a part of the inevitable, endless, glorious flow of cosmic energy, the divine dance.

I am ready.

Afterword to "Shiva in Shadow"

I am not a scientist. In fact, I've never even had a course in high school chemistry. So when I write a story with actual science in it, I have to do a lot of research. Robert Silverberg asked me to write a story set in the galactic core for his anthology Between Worlds, *and I had no idea what was at the galactic core. Uh . . . a black hole, right? Anything else?*

I got a book and discovered there is an enormous amount happening at the core. Stars being born, stars dying, deadly radiation, shimmering beauty, entities swallowing other entities, and a terrible risk if you get too close to any of it. From there, writing the story was easy. All I needed was human relationships being born, dying, turning deadly, shimmering with love, swallowing each other's identities, and taking the terrible risk of closeness. We're not so different from the physical world, after all. Psychology and science can be seen as each other's mirror, and all of us possess a multiverse within.

First Flight

JUST BEFORE THE TELLIN TWINS BURST THROUGH the door of his quarters, Jared ka Rhuda was having an argument with his repos. The repos, even more annoying than usual, said, "Two demerits, Cadet Rhuda."

"Two demerits! What for?"

"Laundry is to be folded in regulation style as soon as it emerges from the Clean-O and then immediately stowed in regulation order in cadets' lockers. Each five minutes' delay earns one demerit. Your laundry has now been unfolded and unstowed for ten minutes and twelve seconds."

"I was in the bathroom!"

"Excuses do not mitigate demerits. Cadets are expected to conform to all Space Academy regulations."

Jared flung himself at the laundry, which lay in a heap under the Clean-O slot. At home, the Rhuda family Clean-O folded the laundry, but things were different at the Academy—as his repos constantly reminded him. The Repository of Regulations and Space Navy Expectations, a squat, red box, followed him everywhere, recorded everything he did, and awarded demerits if he did it contrary to regulations. Which there were a *million* of. Jared was supposed to already have learned them all, and was supposed to follow them all. What did processing laundry have to do with being a good Navy officer?

"You have three minutes until you earn an additional demerit."

"I'm folding as fast as I can!"

"Two minutes and forty seconds. Those socks are to be in folded in thirds, not halves."

"Hey, Jared! The flight list's out!"

Kami and Tara rushed through the door. Kami, waving a paper over her head, shouted, "We're all on the list!" and danced wildly around the tiny cabin. Tara, always the more practical twin, took in the laundry situation and began folding and stowing clothes with efficient, rapid motions.

Jared said, "What are we doing? When? What craft do—"

"Target towing for fighters. M-1 A30's. Tomorrow, but we're not on the same shifts, damn it. You're with the first group."

Tara closed Jared's locker just as the repos said, "Fifteen minutes and three seconds. One more demerit."

"For three *seconds?*" Jared cried.

Kami muttered something under her breath, too low for any of the three repos standing around them to overhear, but Jared could guess what it was. The twins had been his best friends since they were all tiny kids; they'd entered Space Academy together. Tara said warningly to both of them, "Let it go. Jared, how many demerits do you have this term?"

"As of now—twenty-six."

Kami gave a low whistle. Thirty would keep him off the flight list for a month. "What did you *do?*"

"Stuff. I don't know. Dumb things. So many of the regulations are different from the ones we learned in Basic—what sense does that make? And that . . . that *thing* just—"

"*Let it go,*" Tara said again. She was right: abusing a repos, even verbally, just earned more demerits.

Kami, the more fiery twin but also the more compassionate, said, "Well, you probably won't earn any more demerits by oh six hundred tomorrow. That's when your squad goes out."

Goes out. Even the words made Jared tingle. He'd wanted to be a United Stellar Republic Space Navy officer since he was four years old. His father had taught him to fly, he'd been a star in Basic Flight Training, but this would be his first flight performing an actual solo mission on a Navy craft. Even if that mission was just towing targets for the real pilots.

"Class in military protocol starts in eight minutes," his repos said. "Two demerits for anyone who's late."

*　　*　　*

At 6:00 A.M. the first squad of ten cadets lined up sharply in the Number Six Flight Bay of Clarke Station. No one had a hair out of place, a suit gauge unchecked, a speck of dirt on anything that could be cleaned, polished, shaven, combed, or aligned. Behind each cadet stood his or her repos, equally gleaming. In front of them sat ten M1-A30's, single-occupant mini-ships of the old-but-still-serviceable A-30 class. Jared couldn't have been more excited if the ships had been J-10 fighters. He was *going out*. But he held his face impassive and his chin high.

"Cadet Gupta, take your ship," Lieutenant Beliar said. Sanjay Gupta said, "Yes, sir!" and walked proudly toward the first craft, followed by his repos.

"Cadet Hill-Matawambe, take your ship."

Jared was second from last. He settled himself in the cockpit, snapped his repos into the slot beside him, and began the pre-flight check, trying to do everything perfectly. The brass were watching real-time.

"Cadets, start your ships." Jared ignited his drive, watched the huge bay door slide up and the stars appear. He blinked, but only once. No excess emotion—no excess anything. This flight was going to be perfect, not only for his record, but for himself. He wanted it to be a shining arc, the true start of his Navy career, something he would remember all his life.

When it was his turn, he flew out of Clarke, accelerated for five minutes, and hit the McClellan Drive at exactly the right minute. His craft slipped out of normal space, a non-sensation he'd experienced a hundred times with his father, and moments later appeared in the midst of an asteroid belt around a K-1 star.

"Location," he asked the computer, as per regs. Until this point, it had known where he was going, but Jared had not.

"Quadrant three, system 54–608," it said.

A 54-system. He was in the Fringe, way out at the edge of the galaxy. Well, that made sense—you'd want to conduct target practice well away from any inhabited area of space, human or alien. Still, he felt a little thrill. This was the Fringe, after all, largely unexplored. Anything could be out here.

He didn't allow himself to be distracted, however. Carefully, using both instruments and visuals, Jared searched for a place to deploy his first target. His job was to set up six solar-sail targets for Navy fighters to find and destroy. The fighter exercise was one of detection, since the solar sails were only three microns thick, half a kilometer in diameter, and constantly accelerating once photons from the star began to push on them. The exercise was also potentially defensive. Several of the United Stellar Republic's enemies used some version of solar sails to ferry energy weapons.

Someday Jared himself would be flying one of the fighter ships on a search-and-destroy for unmanned weapons. For now, he was glad to be setting up practice targets. "Everyone," his father used to say cheerfully, "has to start someplace." Tara, more astringent, had often added later, "But too many people end up at the same someplace they started."

"Not us," Kami always said.

Not me. Jared maneuvered his Mini-1 around an asteroid and released his first target. His instruments showed it unfurling behind him and he slid carefully away, not letting his jets damage the fragile reflecting film. *Perfect.*

"Failure to simultaneously record on voice log: one demerit," the repos said.

"I was just going to do it now!"

The repos didn't respond. Irritated, Jared accelerated away from the solar sail, weaving deftly through the asteroids, looking for another spot where the target would have clear sailing outward from the star but still be close enough to some orbiting mass to make it harder to find.

He released three more sails—flawlessly recording voice logs in strict regulation format—when he first felt the presence in the cockpit.

"What the—*who's there?*"

"Are you addressing me?" his repos asked.

"No!" Jared said. What had he sensed? He looked wildly around the cramped space. Nothing. And no kind of electromagnetic radiation showed on his instruments.

The presence was gone.

A little spooked, Jared focused tightly on searching for a good place to release his fifth target. Deeper into the asteroid belt would be good, harder for the fighters to find, as long as he was careful about setting a target course among the rock orbits. He maneuvered his craft carefully, loving the sensation of piloting her. The star glowed yellow-orange, a jewel set in his happiness.

Inside his head, a series of taps started. *Tap . . . pause . . . tap . . . pause . . . tap . . . pause . . .*

Jared's chest clenched. He was imagining things. Stress . . . no, it must be instrument failure. Something in his helmet, which held so many recording devices, was malfunctioning. That was it.

He said, "Equipment malfunction report, seven hundred thirty hours, Cadet ka Rhuda. Tapping sensation in helmet, cause unknown."

The repos said, " 'Tapping sensation' is not among accepted malfunction terms. You may choose from 'tapping noise,' 'tapping interference,' or 'tapping, physical on object.' "

"It was a sensation!" Jared said angrily.

" 'Tapping sensation' is not among accepted malfunction terms. You may choose from 'tapping noise,' 'tapping interference,' or 'tapping, physical on object.' Failure to report correctly earns two demerits."

Jared said tightly, "Equipment malfunction report, seven hundred thirty-one hours, Cadet ka Rhuda. Tapping noise in helmet, cause unknown."

"Report duly sent."

No one from Clarke acknowledged his report in real time. Jared flew the Mini-1 until he found a perfect spot to release the target. He double-checked the course settings. Everything had to be right.

Tap . . . pause . . . tap tap . . . pause . . . tap tap tap . . . pause . . .

What kind of malfunction progressed like that?

It could be anything. Jared knew his weakest area of study was ship's equipment. In fact, Tara often ended up doing most of his s-equip homework. The best Jared could do now was hope to get the report in the right format.

"Equipment malfunction report, eight hundred hours, Cadet ka Rhuda. Tapping noise in helmet of progressive nature, single tap followed by pause followed by double tap and so forth, cause unknown."

The repos said, " 'And so forth' is not among accepted Academy reporting terms."

"I don't care!" Jared said.

"Two demerits."

"You can't," Jared began hotly—and stopped.

Tap . . . pause . . . tap tap tap . . . pause . . . tap tap tap tap tap . . . pause . . . tap tap tap tap tap tap tap . . .

No equipment malfunctioned in prime numbers.

The hair on Jared's neck rose. Something out there was trying to contact him.

A scan of his monitors revealed nothing: no electronic signal, no gravitational pull not accounted for by the nearby asteroids or the star, nothing on visual. *But something was there.*

The repos said, "You have interrupted your mission task,

although you are still well within the allotted time frame for completion."

"There's something out there!"

"There are many things out there. A K-1 star, classified as 54–608. An asteroid belt consisting of approximately—"

"I mean there's something sentient out there!"

"No sentient life in this system except for Jared ka Rhuda, space cadet, and Repository of Regulations and Space Navy Expectations #478–34, a semi-AI."

"I tell you I heard it! It was sending prime numbers! I'm opening the channel to Clarke!"

"During cadet practice maneuvers, real-time communication with Clarke is permitted only in case of emergency. This is not an emergency. Therefore—"

"Real-time communication channel to Clarke Station opened eight hundred two hours by Cadet Jared ka Rhuda," Jared said. He heard his voice shake. "Lieutenant Beliar, I have been contacted by an unknown sentient, sir. It's sending prime numbers into my helmet, sir, and—"

Lieutenant Balier's voice filled the cockpit. "Into your helmet? How might anything be doing that, Cadet?"

"Unknown, sir, but—"

"There are no sentients in that system, Cadet. Standard procedure before a cadet flight mission is to have the area thoroughly surveilled prior to the mission. Your area is clean."

"Sir, I felt it and—"

"*Felt* it, Cadet?"

Worse and worse. Now he sounded like a babbling idiot, some demented refugee from the loony Telepathy Advocates.

"Heard it, sir," Jared said, willing to lose the lesser point to gain the greater. "In my helmet. Tapping out a string of primes, from one to eleven!"

Silence from Clarke.

After what seemed an eternity, a woman's voice spoke crisply. "Cadet, this is Major Demondrian. You must be mistaken. I can confirm for you that there are no sentients in that system."

"But, ma'am, this is the Fringe and anything is—"

"Return to Clarke immediately, Cadet ka Rhuda, whether or not your mission is complete."

"*But, ma'am*—"

Jared hadn't realized a voice could turn as cold as Major Demondrian's. "Are you questioning orders, Cadet?"

"No, ma'am," Jared said miserably, at the same moment that the repos said, "Questioning orders. Twenty-five demerits."

"Initiate return procedure, Cadet Clarke."

"Yes, ma'am." He bent toward his console.

Tap tap . . . pause . . . tap tap . . . pause . . . tap tap tap . . . tap tap tap . . .

Two-two-three-three. The interstellar code requesting help for a disabled ship.

And this time, it *did* register on the sensors. Jared gaped: How could a *Logan*-class ship have not been within a hundred clicks of him before, and yet be there now? He called up the sensor log. Nothing within one AU had rippled spacetime by dropping in via a McClellan Drive, nor any other kind of drive used by any known alien, ally or enemy. And if the ship had been under conventional drive, and had been that close, every sensor on Jared's Mini-1 would have warned him of that. The ship *couldn't* be there.

Yet there it was.

The repos said, "Ten-second delay in responding to order to initiate return procedure. Ten demerits."

The visual screen sprang to life. The bridge of a human craft, with three bodies slumped in various postures and a battered, gasping officer at the helm. "Come in, Mini-1, this is Commander Vladimir Miller of the *Procyon*, we need help. Hit by an unknown energy weapon . . . ship disabled . . ."

Major Demondrian repeated, "Initiate return procedure, Cadet ka Rhuda!"

"There's a disabled ship here, ma'am, the *Procyon*, I don't know where it came from but the commander says it was hit by an unknown energy weapon and—"

"Initiate return procedure!"

A direct order, and now it had been given three times. For all Jared knew, the wounded ship was a hologram of some kind, an enemy ruse to lure him closer. He said, "Yes, ma'am!" and initiated return procedures.

A few moments later the McClellan Drive snapped on and System 54–608 disappeared. Clarke Station filled the sky.

"Failure to respond to orders with three repetitions," the repos said, "One hundred demerits."

"*How* many?" Kami said.

"One hundred sixty-four demerits," Jared said miserably.

The twins stared at him. Jared was confined to quarters until tomorrow's hearing. Upon his return to Clarke, that was all Major Demondrian had deigned to say: "Confined to quarters until oh nine hundred hours tomorrow, Cadet ka Rhuda. Report at that time to Conference B for your hearing." After pacing his tiny quarters for half an hour, Jared had called Kami and Tara. He'd half expected the repos to object, but it sat there, silent and squat and red. Jared wanted to kick it, but even he recognized that this would be a pointless action.

Kami, visibly searching for something hopeful to say, said, "Maybe your helmet has some kind of record of the . . . the tapping, a record that we don't know about. They don't tell cadets everything, you know, in case we wash out. Where's your helmet?"

"They took it," Jared said. Kami had spoken the dread words: *wash out*. If the Academy sent him home, he didn't think he could bear it.

Tara said, "You need a plan. How are you going to respond when they question you about what happened?"

"I'm going to tell them the truth!"

"But there's truth and there's truth," Tara argued. "So far you're stuck on one piece of truth: what you experienced. But there may be other pieces, and we should consider them. For instance, the disabled ship may have been an enemy ruse, a hologram that your presence triggered, rigged with an energy weapon to lure you closer."

"I thought of that," Jared said. "But why? I was already well within range of even the feeblest energy weapon. And a hologram couldn't have made that tapping in my helmet, or that feeling of *presence*. . . . Don't look like that, Tara, I'm telling you I *felt* it!"

Tara said, "I think we should stick to objective facts here, not subjective feelings."

Jared said irritably, "How many demerits do *you* have, Tara?"

"She doesn't have any," Kami said, "but in one way she's right. The main point is, what are you going to tell the brass tomorrow morning? I know, you said 'the truth'—but how are you going to present that truth? You could say you had a momentary confusion of some sort."

"Oh, and that would look great on his record," Tara said. "An officer prone to hallucinations. No, Jared, what you need to do is retract. Say you must have been mistaken because your memory doesn't fit with the facts, and Naval officers respect facts. That will impress them."

"I wasn't mistaken! And I wasn't confused!"

"How can you be so sure?" Tara said. "Everybody knows that eyewitnesses frequently have different accounts of things than appear on recording devices. You might have been mistaken. Jared, don't get angry, but I ran 'Commander Vladimir Miller' on all the Academy deebees, and he doesn't exist. Neither does any *Logan*-class ship named *Procyon*."

"They don't exist?" Jared said, half wishing he'd thought of checking that himself, half alarmed at Tara's finding.

"No. Don't you want to save your career?"

"More than anything!"

Kami squeezed his hand. "We know. We all feel that way. But it may very well be true that in the excitement—and it was exciting, our first flights—you *could* have been confused. I still think you should say that."

"No," Tara said. "Admit that your perceptions are not in agreement with the facts and assume responsibility for your misjudgment. That's what good officers do."

"I'll think about it," Jared said unhappily.

But after they left, all he could think about was Tara's having no demerits. None. How was that possible?

"This cadet-conduct hearing is called to order," Major Demondrian said. She, Lieutenant Beliar, and another officer, Captain Some-body, sat behind a table at the front of Conference Room B. Jared, in dress uniform, sat on a chair facing them. *It looks like a summary court-martial*, he thought, and even though he knew it wasn't, his heart began a slow, hard thump in his chest.

"Cadet ka Rhuda, please detail the occurrences of yesterday afternoon."

Jared told his story again, knowing that this time it was being recorded, trying very hard to get everything correct, and in correct terminology. By the time he finished, his collar was damp. The three officers stared at him throughout, saying nothing.

Finally the major said, "A check of Naval records failed to find a 'Commander Vladimir Miller' or a ship designated '*Procyon*.' And an examination of your helmet failed to find any malfunction."

"Yes, ma'am," Jared said miserably.

"Furthermore, your M-1 A30 sensor record contains no recording of any encounter with any other craft while you were in 54–608 System."

That was a blow. Jared said nothing.

"You failed to respond to a direct order, cadet."

"Yes, ma'am—although I *did* respond to it, ma'am, with all due respect, ma'am."

"Yes," Demondrian said icily. "You have 164 demerits."

"Yes, ma'am."

"One hundred demerits is grounds for dismissal."

"Yes, ma'am." He felt sick.

Lieutenant Beliar, whom Jared had always liked, leaned forward. "Ka Rhuda, this board is fully cognizant of the fact that cadets make mistakes. If they did not, they wouldn't be cadets. You have an outstanding record in all military areas except deportment and ship's equipment, and for outstanding cadets we sometimes offer a second chance, rather than lose a promising future officer in times of war. In view of that, and in view of the reality that you did, in fact, obey orders, I'd like to ask you some additional questions."

"Yes, sir!" Hope surged through him.

"Is it possible you were, in the excitement of the moment, confused about what you heard and felt? That the 'tappings' and the visual you thought you saw were no more than figments of your imagination?"

Jared gazed at the lieutenant.

"People do make mistakes, Cadet ka Rhuda, even experienced officers. If you acknowledge your misjudgment, and take responsibility for it, this board will see what it can do for you."

A double whammy—both Kami's *and* Tara's suggestions. Say he was mistaken due to a kid's natural excitement at his first mission and deny what had happened, all with a military bearing and the air of a responsible officer. And if he did, he could stay at the Academy.

But it *did* happen! He had felt the presence, had heard the tapping, had seen Commander Vladimir Miller of the battered *Procyon* on visual. He *had*.

"Cadet ka Rhuda?" Lieutenant Beliar prompted, smiling gently.

"I'm sorry, sir, but they were not figments of my imagination. I experienced them."

The lieutenant's smile vanished. "Are you sure, cadet?"

"Yes, sir."

"Even if sticking by your report means dismissal?"

For a moment, Jared thought he might faint—and wouldn't *that* be a great way to end his time at the Academy. He pulled himself together and spoke, knowing that the words determined his dismissal, unable to falsify what he had experienced because, damn it to all hell, *it had happened*.

"I . . . I stick by my report, sir."

Suddenly he couldn't stand it any more. He rose, even though he hadn't been dismissed, and choked out, "Thank you, sirs. Ma'am."

He saluted, and turned to go before they saw how wet his eyes were.

From behind him Major Demondrian said dryly, "Congratulations, cadet."

He lurched around. "Congratulations?" If they were mocking him . . . *now* . . . congratulating him on having a record number of demerits or some such crap . . .

"Yes, congratulations. Sit down, cadet, you have not been dismissed. Lieutenant, since Cadet ka Rhuda was your candidate for this, I leave it to you."

She and the captain, who had never said one word nor displayed one expression, rose and left. When they were gone, Lieutenant Beliar said, "You made it, ka Rhuda."

"Made *what?*"

"You passed the test. You were such a screw-up they wanted to wash you out, but I said no, he's got the stuff, give him the Ground Test. Ah, don't look so bewildered, kid, I'll explain it."

The lieutenant had never spoken to him like this before, almost as if they were friends. Completely bewildered, Jared could only stare at him.

"Your helmet and ship were rigged. We put the tapping there, and the visual of the disabled craft, and even the sense of 'presence,' which the engineering boys fixed up through a patch in your suit with some sort of brain chemicals. The test was to see how you behaved under pressure. If you'd actually disobeyed the order to leave, you'd be gone from here. If you'd denied what you saw and heard, you'd also be gone. As it is, you're still in, and your demerit record from the test flight will be wiped out."

"I'm still in?"

"Yes. Try to look happier, kid."

"I'm in because I wouldn't report what I was told to report?"

"That's right." All at once the lieutenant turned more somber. "You haven't seen any combat, ka Rhuda. I have." His eyes darkened with some memory that Jared couldn't imagine. "You'll get there soon enough. The most important premise in combat conditions, as opposed to a nice regulated Academy, is a very old one, going all the way back to Terra. It's this: If the map doesn't agree with the ground, the map is wrong."

Jared must have still looked bewildered, because the lieutenant said suddenly and with irritation, "Think about it. Maybe you'll get it. Meanwhile, dismissed."

As Lieutenant Beliar strode out, Jared said, "Wait. Please, sir! Three questions."

"Yes, Cadet ka Rhuda?" He was back to military formality.

Jared's mind raced. He said, "First, you mean that if real-time doesn't look the way I'm told it's configured, I should trust what's directly in front of me?"

"That is what I said, cadet. Two more questions."

"That trusting my own perceptions in combat is what the Navy needs from me, as long as I don't disobey direct orders?"

"You're one that needs to reword, aren't you? One more question, I have things to do."

"Yes, sir. Major Demondrian was never in combat, was she, sir?"

The lieutenant looked at Jared a long time. Finally he said softly, "Watch out for her, cadet," and left the room.

Jared returned to his quarters. Once there, he touched the bulkhead, his bunk, his locker, even ran his hand over the deck. He was still here. He hadn't washed out. He should find Kami and Tara, share the good news. But first he wanted to savor the sensation, and also to think over what the lieutenant had said. He lay down on his bunk, hands behind his head, and pondered. Although he couldn't yet see how, he sensed that what he'd learned was important, and that it would influence him, maybe forever, maybe for good.

"Lying on bunk in dress uniform and shoes," the repos said. "Two demerits."

Afterword to "First Flight"

Mike Resnick is responsible for this one. Frankie Thomas, the original Tom Corbett, Space Cadet in the popular 1950s TV show, was slated to be a special guest at the 2006 Worldcon in Anaheim, California. Unfortunately, Thomas died before the convention, and so the anthology honoring him became a memorial. It was notable for the astonishing range of its writers (where else will you find Mercedes Lackey and Gregory Benford in the same pages?), for having the most colorful cover in publishing history (masses of weird aliens), and for the wide range of its stories (from gloomy to cheerfully inane).

My story was among the cheerfully inane. I wanted to recreate the innocent spirit and style of the original television series. So my cadets are hopeful, enthusiastic, and basically sexless. The ending is upbeat. All this was a strain for me, since I hardly ever write innocence or unambiguous upbeat. Still, it was fun to try.

And the mass signing at Worldcon was fun, too—three very long tables of writers signing books assembly-line style, light-heartedly joshing each other and the fans. Tom Corbett would have fit right in.

To Cuddle Amy

CAMPBELL ENTERED THE LIVING ROOM TO FIND his wife in tears. "Allison! What's wrong?"

She sprang up from the sofa and raged at him. "What do you think is wrong, Paul? What's ever wrong? Amy! Only this time she's gone too far. This time she . . . she . . . the police just left . . ." She broke down into sobs.

Campbell had had a lot of experience dealing with his wife. They'd been married almost forty years. Pushing down his own alarm, he took Allison in his arms and sat on the sofa, cradling her as if she were a child. Which, in some ways, she still was. Allison had always been high-strung, finely tuned. Sensitive. He was the strong one. "Tell me, sweetie. Tell me what happened."

"I . . . she . . ."

"The police. You said the police just left. What did Amy do now?"

"Van . . . vandalism. She and those awful friends of hers . . . the Hitchens boy, that slut Kristy Arnold . . . they . . ."

"They what? Come on, honey, you'll feel better if you tell me."

"They were throwing rocks at cars from the overpass! Throwing rocks!"

Campbell considered. It could be far worse. Still . . . something didn't add up here. "Allison—why did the cops leave? Are they going to arrest Amy?"

"No. They said they"—more sobbing—"couldn't be sure it was her. Not enough evidence. But they suspected it was, and wanted us to know . . . oh, Paul, I don't think I can take much more!"

"I know, honey. I know. Shhh, don't cry."

"She just throws away everything we do for her!"

"Shhhhhh," Campbell said, but Allison went on crying. Campbell gazed over her heaving shoulder at the wall, covered with framed photos of Amy. Amy at six months, asleep on a pink blanket in a field of daisies. Amy at two, waving her moo-cow, a toddler so adorable that people had stopped Allison in the street to admire her. Amy at seven in a ballet tutu. Amy at twelve, riding her horse. Amy at sixteen in a prom dress, caught in a rare smile.

Amy, fourteen, came through the front door.

Allison didn't give her daughter a chance to attack first. "So there you are! You just missed the cops, Amy, telling us what you've done this time, and it's the last straw, do you hear me, young lady? We forgave you the awful school grades! We forgave you the rudeness and ingratitude and sullen self-centeredness! We even forgave you the shop-lifting, God help us! But this is over the line! Throwing rocks at cars! Someone could have been killed—how much more do you expect us to take from you? Answer me!"

Amy said angrily, "I didn't do it!"

"You're lying! The cops said—"

"Allison, wait," Campbell said. "Amy, the cops said you were a suspect."

"Well, I didn't do it! Kristy and Jed did, but I went home! And I don't care if you believe me or not, you bitch!"

Allison gasped. Amy stormed through the living room, a lanky mass of fury in deliberately torn clothes, pins through her lip and eyebrow, purple lipstick smeared. She raced upstairs and slammed her bedroom door.

"Paul . . . oh, Paul . . . did you hear what she called me? Her *mother?*" Allison collapsed against him again, her slim body shaking so hard that Campbell's arms tightened to steady her.

But he felt shaky, too. This couldn't go on. The sullen rudeness, the fights, the breaking the law . . . their lives were being reduced to rubble by a fourteen-year-old.

"Paul . . ." Allison sobbed, "do you remember how she used to be? Oh, God, the day she was born . . . remember? I was so happy I thought I'd die. And then how she was as a little girl, climbing on our laps for a cuddle . . . oh, Paul, I want my little girl back!"

"I know. I know, dearest."

"Don't you?"

He did. He wanted back the Amy who was so sweet, so biddable. Who thought he was the best daddy in the world. The feel of that light, little body in his arms, the sweet baby smell at the back of her neck . . .

He said slowly, "She's fourteen now. Legal age."

Immediately Allison stopped sobbing. She stood still against him. Finally she said, "It isn't as if she'd be without resources. The Hitchens might take her in. Or somebody. And anyway, there are lots more like her out there." Allison's lower lip stuck out. "Might even do her good to learn how good she had it here with us!"

Campbell closed his eyes. "But we wouldn't know."

"You're damn right we wouldn't know! She doesn't want any part of us, then I don't want any part of her!" Again Allison leaned against him. "But it isn't that, Paul. You know it isn't. I just want my little girl back again! I want to cuddle my lost little girl! Oh, I'd give anything to cuddle Amy again! Don't you want that, too?"

Campbell did. And the present situation really wasn't fair to Allison, who'd never been strong. Allison's health was being effected. She shouldn't have to be broken by this spiteful stranger who'd developed in their midst in the last year. Allison had rights, too.

His wife continued to sob against his chest, but softly now. Campbell felt strong, in control. He could make it all right for his wife, for himself. For everybody.

He said, "There are three embryos left."

Three of six. Three frozen vials in the fertility clinic, all from the same in vitro fertilization, stored as standard procedure against a failure to carry to term. Or other need. Three more versions of the same embryo, the product of forced division before the first implantation. Standard procedure, yes, all over the country.

"I'll throw her out tonight," he told Allison, "and call the clinic in the morning."

Afterword to "To Cuddle Amy"

This is a horror story. Not the slasher-in-the-closet kind, which always seems to me too easy, but the real-life horror kind, in which people treat each other as replaceable objects. Not that any parent of teenagers doesn't occasionally think about replacement. My sons have both grown up to be wonderful people of whom I am very proud, but there were moments during their teenage years when I doubted whether any of us were going to survive.

This story is also the shortest one I ever wrote. Generally, I prefer to write long. The only other time I've managed to stay under 1,000 words is "Product Development," and then I was required to do so. "To Cuddle Amy," however, came in voluntarily at 900 words. You can only live so long with horror.

Wetlands Preserve

T HE DUCK HUNTER WADED THROUGH THE MARSH, breathing deeply of the sweet dawn air mixed with wet decay. Each lift of his high boots sucked up mud with a soft splurgling sound. Cattails rustled in conspiratorial whispers. The dog beside him flicked its tail at a dragonfly.

"Soft, girl, we're not supposed to be here," the man said, grinning. "But listen to them ducks!"

Abruptly the flock of mallards, until now out of sight, flew up. The man raised his gun, fired once, twice. A bird fell and the dog took off.

Grinning, the hunter waited. She was the best dog he'd ever had. Never missed. A beauty.

"Hey, girl, what you got, let's see it there, oh you beauty . . ." The man's wife complained that he talked more affectionately to the dog than to her. The dog dropped the duck. The man bent to pick it up from the shallow water, and the snake swam past him.

Not a snake. Green, long, but with fins. Three eyes. *Three.* Before he stopped to think, the man had grabbed the thing behind its head, the way you grabbed a copperhead if you had to grab it at all, and lifted it out of the water. On its underside were four short legs.

And the thing went on staring at him from two of its eyes, the two facing sideways, while the third eye stared straight up to the empty, gray sky. It didn't thrash or try to bite. It just gazed steadily, interestedly.

The dog barked to draw attention to its duck. The man ignored her. He went on staring at the thing gazing so tranquilly back at him. "What . . . what are you?"

Then he saw the blackened craft half submerged in the mud and water.

Lisa still wasn't used to the guards. Security guards, yes, Kenton had always had those, although not because anyone expected trouble. The John C. Kenton Memorial Wetlands Preserve and Research Foundation in upstate New York wasn't exactly a hotbed of contentious activity. Until now, the greatest excitement at Kenton had been the struggle to keep *Lythrum salicaria*, purple loosestrife, from displacing native waterfowl food plants.

However, like all research labs Kenton contained expensive equipment that no one wanted stolen, so there had always been one guard, seldom the same one for very long because the work was so boring. But now they had Army soldiers, two at the door and two in back and God-knew-how-many on patrol around the unfenced perimeter of the wetlands. None of them knew what they were guarding, although it seemed to Lisa that if they had any intelligence whatsoever they would pick on the intense, badly suppressed excitement pervading Kenton like a glittering mist.

"Identification, please," the soldier said, and Lisa handed over her new government pass. The soldier ran it through a slot on a computer and handed it back. Then he smiled. "Okay, Lisa Susan Jackson. You sure you're old enough to be in there?"

You don't look any older than I do, Lisa wanted to snap back, but didn't. She'd already learned that silent disdain was the only thing that worked, and not always that. It made no difference that she was a graduate student in fresh-water ecosystems, that she had been selected over three hundred other applicants for this prestigious and unusually well-funded internship, that she made a valuable contribution to Kenton's ongoing work. She was a small, blonde woman who looked about fourteen years old, and so even this cretin in camouflage felt entitled to patronize her.

She walked past him with freezing dignity and went to the main lab. Early as it was, Paul and Stephanie were already there, and through the window she could see Hal pushing off from the dock on the flat-bottomed boat, accompanied by yet another visitor. The staff always tried to arrive earlier than the visiting scientists and Washington types, even if it meant getting to Kenton at four in the morning. Lisa couldn't do that, not with Carlo.

"Lisa, the latest test results are in," said Dr. Paul Lambeth, Kenton's chief scientist. The scientists were all very considerate of her, keeping her fully informed even though she was only an intern. Even though the project was, of course, now heavily classified. Dr. Stephanie Hansen had insisted that Lisa stay on even after the Department of Defense had questioned the presence of a mere graduate student in this unprecedented situation. Hal—Dr. Harold Schaeffer—had fought to get Lisa the necessary clearances, which probably hadn't been easy because of Danilo. Never mind that she hadn't seen Danilo in over a year, or that membership in Green peace was not exactly tantamount to membership in China First or the neo-Nazis. The DOD was not known for its tolerance of extremist organizations, no matter how non-violent.

Of course, Lisa knew, Stephanie and Hal had been thinking mostly of protecting the whole internship program rather than her specifically. Lisa was still grateful. She just wished that gratitude didn't make her feel so constrained.

"The latest results," Stephanie repeated after Paul, and an alert shiver ran over Lisa. Stephanie, decisive and taciturn, never repeated others' words, never said anything unnecessary. And Stephanie's eyes gleamed in her weather-burned face that had spent thirty years in the outdoors studying how the environment and everything in it worked together to sustain life.

Paul was always more flamboyant than Stephanie. It was Paul, of course, who would eventually announce to the media, standing side by side with the president in the oval office. "Do you want to sit down, Lisa? It's big."

"What is it?" she said, wishing he wouldn't play games, knowing she was reacting to his game with the strangled breathlessness he expected.

"The genetic structure is not DNA-based."

She felt her mouth open, her eyes widen, even though the statement wasn't unexpected. Ever since she'd seen the animal brought in by a man illegally duck-hunting in the Preserve, she'd wondered. They all had. It was the spacecraft that made them take the animal so seriously, rather than writing it off as just one more deformity caused by pollution. NASA had come up from Washington, run tests on the blackened outside and mysterious inside of the half-

submerged object, and verified the structure as a spacecraft. Immediately it had been carted off to somewhere classified.

But Paul Lambeth had fought to keep research into the animal,
and the other animals soon found exactly like it, as a joint project
between Kenton and Washington's hand-picked labs. Paul had won,
but not because Kenton was such a well-equipped research lab.
(Although it was. John C. Kenton had left an endowment so gener-
ous it was the envy of even places like Harvard.) Kenton had kept
primary research responsibility because that's where the wetlands
were, and who knew what else had come off that spacecraft? The
Kenton Preserve, immediately quarantined, had become the mountain toward which the eminent scientific Mohammeds went, since
the entire wetlands ecosystem could not go to them. So Kenton did
the *in situ* research, and the CDC, Harvard, and Cold Harbor did
the genetics and zoological work.

Non-DNA-based. *Alien*.

"What . . ." Lisa was annoyed to find her voice coming out too
high ". . . what will they do with it?"

"Nothing, yet," Paul said, and even in his slick media-loving
voice she heard the hidden awe. "We're not done searching the
ecosystem, even. Did you finish those water-sample tests?"

"Not yet," Lisa said. Yes, work, that's what she needed, routine
methodical work. To ground her. But she couldn't do it. "Can I see
the report?"

"Sure," Paul said, smiling, and there was that condescension
again, that egotistical pleasure in his own generosity at sharing the
historic moment with such a very junior colleague. Lisa pushed
the perception away. She darted for the report and began to read
hungrily, wanting to know everything, to gulp it down all at once.

Non-DNA-based. Alien.

From the stars.

After the initial elation came the questions. The animal was not
DNA-based, yet it was eating DNA-based plants. Lisa could see one
of the snakers (the catchy name was Paul's) in the oversized cage,
munching contentedly on sedges. How was it metabolizing plant
food it had not evolved to metabolize? And how had such fully
developed animals—warm-blooded, multi-stomached, large if
unfathomable brain tissue—survived the trip through space? They
might have been in some sort of cold sleep; Lisa had not seen the
inside of their small craft. So small! How many had made the journey?

They couldn't have been here more than a few years, at the most. Someone would have seen them before now. The twenty-square-mile Kenton Preserve was supposedly off-limits to hunters and bird watchers, but in fact both seeped in all the time, at least on the vast wetland's edges.

The CDC/Harvard report said the genetic material seemed to be not concentrated in a cell nucleus, but rather scattered throughout the cell. That was characteristic of very simple organisms like prokaryotes, but not of complex ones. The cells themselves were full of structures. Some had already been catalogued, at least in a preliminary survey, as analogous to ribosomes or mitochondria or receptors. They broke down molecules for energy, they utilized oxygen, they received chemical signals from other cells. Some were total mysteries.

Lisa read the report once, twice. Then she went to stare at the snakers' cage, which was a mini-ecology twelve feet by five, equipped with marsh areas, a pool, a dry hummock, stands of cattails and bulrushes, aquatic plants and rocks and insects. Two of the three captive snakers had disappeared into the foliage. The third one raised its head and looked back at her from a side-facing eye. Lisa stood gazing for a long time.

"Lisa?" Stephanie said. "We're going out this afternoon on the boat to survey another sector. Want to come?"

"Yes!" The Preserve had not been so thoroughly surveyed in years, now that everyone wanted to know exactly how many of the alien creatures existed. A lot, it seemed. They bred quickly. Lisa went to finish her water sample runs as quickly as possible so she would be able to go out on the boat.

When she finally got home, muddy and exhausted and smelling of swamp, Danilo was there.

"How did you get in? The door was locked."

"Jimmied a window," he said in his liquid Filipino accent. "Not hard. God, Lissy, you look like a drowned rat."

Lissy. His pet name for her. Which he goddamn well had no right to use. He lounged at the table in her kitchen, which was also her living room and dining room, having helped himself to Raisin Bran and English muffins. She said sourly, "You better be careful. That food probably has genetically modified foodstuffs in it. You could sully your ideological purity."

"Same old Lissy." He sat up straighter, and the gleam of white teeth disappeared from his sun-browned face. Despite the heat, he wore jeans and heavy boots, the old uniform. A knapsack rested on the floor. His trim body looked fit and rested, which only irritated her more. It had been so long since she'd had a good night's sleep. Too much to do, always.

Danilo said quietly, "I want to see him."

"You don't have the right."

"I know. But I want to anyway. Carlo is my son."

"Only biologically. A hyena is a better father than you've been," Lisa said, and they were off again, the same old track, sickening her even before they really got rolling.

"Only because I had a more urgent job," Danilo said, apparently willing to go over it all yet once more. Lisa wasn't. He'd made his choices, and at the time Lisa had even seen why he'd made them, or thought she had. The fate of the planet over the fate of a single child, the human race itself at stake, global warming, depleted oceans, dangerous genetically engineered organisms released into the environment, deforestation, pollution, nuclear radiation, blah blah blah. Or, rather, not blah blah blah; she was preparing herself to work for the same ends, through scientific ecology. But it all looked different somehow when you had that actual single child with you day and night, dependent on you, needing your care and interrupting your sleep and clamoring for your love. You realized that there *was* no more urgent job.

There was no way to tell that to Danilo, no way that he would hear. Lisa said only, "I'll get Carlo. The woman next door takes care of him while I'm at work."

"Is she . . . can she . . . "

"She's had experience with disabled children." And then, cruelly, "She costs most of my grant and all of my scholarship, of course, between daycare and physical therapy. Nothing left to donate to good causes."

Danilo didn't answer. Lisa went next door to get Carlo.

It was one of his good days. He laughed and reached up for her, and she knelt by the wheelchair and hugged him. Undoing all the harnesses that kept him comfortable was a major undertaking. "Mommy! I drawed a picture!"

"He did, Lisa. Look," Mrs. Belling said, and held up a childish picture of a blue tree, green sun, and red structure that might have been a house or a car. "He's getting really good with his right foot, aren't you, Carlo?"

"I'm good," Carlo said, with such innocent grandiosity that Lisa wanted to weep. He was almost five. Next year he would start school. How long would he keep that pride around other people, people less kind than Mrs. Belling or Lisa's colleagues? Carlo was intelligent, happy, severely deformed. Both arms hung truncated at his sides, devoid of any nerves to transmit muscle impulses. His head lolled to one side. He would never walk. His radiant smile nightly filled her with fear for his future.

Danilo had left her, joined first Students Against Toxins and later Greenpeace, the day Carlo had been born. Carlo's father blamed the baby's condition on contaminated groundwater in the factory town where Lisa had grown up. Perhaps he was right. Lisa had gone into shock that Danilo could leave her now, leave her with a deformed infant, leave her unmarried and about to start graduate school and all but broke. Selfish! She had screamed at him. Necessary, he had replied, so more Carlos aren't born like this, and more, and more. She was the selfish one not to see that. It was no different than going off to war. He was disappointed in her that she couldn't see that.

The horrible thing was, she could. But she was still the one left with Carlo. Whom, now, she wouldn't trade for anything on Earth.

"Carlo," she said, after lavishing praise on his picture, "Uncle Danilo's here." Her one condition for letting Danilo see him at all: unclehood, not fatherhood. Fatherhood was something you did, and Danilo never had.

"Uncle Danilo?" The child frowned, trying to remember. It had been over a year since Danilo's last will-o-the-wisp appearance.

"Yes, your Uncle Danilo. You'll remember him when you see him. Let's go, sweetie."

"Bye, Mrs. Belling!" Carlo called. "See you tomorrow!"

Lisa watched Danilo flinch when she wheeled in Carlo. Revulsion, or guilt? She hoped it was guilt. "Carlo, this is Uncle Danilo."

"Hi, Carlo."

"Hi! Mommy, he gots a bord!"

"A 'beard,' sweetie. He has a beard."

"Can I touch the beard?"

Danilo knelt by Carlo's chair. Lisa moved away, unwilling to stand that close to Danilo. But on the warm air she caught the scent of him anyway, bringing such a rush of visceral memory that she turned abruptly away. God, how long had it been for her . . . and never like with Danilo.

Lisa Jackson and Danilo Aglipay. Salty working-class American and wealthy cultured Filipino. Ideological purists, committed activists, the sexual envy of an entire campus, with her blonde, small-boned beauty and his exotic dark intensity. Except that the working-class salt-of-the-earth parents shoved Lisa out of the family when she took up with a "gook," and the wealthy Filipino swore he would never go home to the father who made his money exploiting the planet, and the blonde beauty swelled with pregnancy that ruined the activist plans so much that Danilo left, spouting speeches.

And out of that wreck I made a life, Lisa reminded herself fiercely. Graduate school, Carlo, the internship at Kenton. The alien animals. Talk about world-changing events! If Danilo knew about the aliens . . . but he wouldn't. It was her knowledge, her life, and no whiff of masculine pheromones would ruin it for her. Not now, not ever.

"The beard feels strangey," Carlo said. It was his latest pet word.

"Oh, it's strangey, all right," Lisa said, and Danilo looked at her.

She fed Carlo and Danilo too (inescapable), read Carlo a story, put him to bed. Danilo watched silently from his chair at the table. After Lisa closed the bedroom door, she said, "Now go. I have work to do."

"Work? Now?"

"All the time, Danilo."

"And you think it does anybody any good, this work? This studying minute details of ecosystems even as the exploiters destroy them out from under you?"

"Probably as much actual good as your 'non-violent confrontations' at Greenpeace."

"I'm not with Greenpeace any more," he said, and something grim in his tone, coming through despite the soft accent, made Lisa look directly at him.

"You're not?"

"No. You're right—non-violent confrontations accomplish nothing substantial. I am with EarthAction now."

"Never heard of them."

"You will," he said, and that tone was there again. "Lissy, I don't have anyplace to stay."

"You're not staying here. See that sofa? That unfolds to create my bedroom, and in another few hours I'll be using it. Bye, Danilo."

He didn't argue. Picking up the knapsack, he moved with his fluid gait toward the door. Watching him, Lisa suddenly remembered that she still had dried mud in her hair from the boat survey, still smelled of swamp and lab. Well, she'd shower later; the reports in her briefcase were too exciting to wait.

She'd already started to work by the time Danilo closed the apartment door.

"Washington wants even tighter security," Paul said to the assembled Kenton staff, plus the visiting scientists, Washington representatives, and whoever those others were that Lisa couldn't identify. "That's why we have an increased guard. I know all the checkpoints are inconvenient, people, but consider the benefits. We're getting another month of study before any announcement is made and we're overrun with outsiders."

Hal said bluntly, "Could have fooled me. There are already far too many outsiders in the Preserve. It's starting to look like O'Hare Airport out there. At this rate we're going to irreparably damage the ecosystem."

Paul looked embarrassed. People shifted on their chairs, crowded uncomfortably into the too-small break room. Nobody looked directly at the visiting scientists.

"Hal, we appreciate your concerns, but we have to be practical here as well. This is perhaps the single most important event in the history of humankind. You can't really expect it to stay confined to a bunch of academic swamp rats like us."

People laughed obligingly, but the tension wasn't broken.

Paul continued, "We have a full agenda this morning, and a very exciting one, so let's—"

"If you're really trying for tight security," Hal persisted doggedly, "then all these soldiers and checkpoints and cars going in and out isn't exactly the best way to get it. Don't you think the locals, including the local journalists, are going to notice?"

Lisa had to agree with him. Just last night she'd heard two women at the grocery store speculating about what could be going on "down to the Preserve, with all them crazy tree-huggers." And the off-duty soldiers went in and out of Flaherty's, the town's most popular bar. She'd seen them.

"I think we can leave security to the professionals whose job it is," Paul said smoothly, "and get on with our own job. First, a really exciting report from Dr. Mary Clark of Harvard."

"Thanks, Paul," Dr. Clark said. "Hang onto your hats, guys. We've finished the water analyses. Our alien footed snakes are *not* the only extraterrestrials in the Preserve."

Gasps, chatter, shouted questions. Dr. Clark held up her hand, eyes gleaming at the sensation she'd produced. "There are one-celled organisms with the same non-DNA genetic structure out there in the swamp water. There are also multi-celled organisms and some primitive worms."

Over the fresh buzz, someone called out, "Nothing in between? In evolutionary terms?"

"No," Dr. Clark said, "and of course we still don't understand that."

No one did. It was the central mystery about the alien snakers—how had whoever sent them known what environment they would find when the craft landed? Had the snakers been chosen because, miraculously, they were perfectly adapted to a swamp environment at this latitude? That could be true only if their planet of origin were very similar to Earth, which seemed too much of an unlikely coincidence. (In fact, the NASA rep had said, the odds against it were so high that the possibility was meaningless.)

Had the snakers been engineered for this environment? But that argued a detailed knowledge of an Earth swamp ecosystem, and how could the genetic engineers have that unless they'd been here? If they had, why not just appear themselves? Why send these non-sentient but apparently harmless creatures as forerunners?

And now these much more primitive non-DNA creatures. Too primitive to serve as food for the snakers, which in any case were eating sedges and *Lemna minor* just fine. And that brought the questions full circle to the central issue: How could the snakers be metabolizing food they had not evolved to metabolize?

The rest of the meeting produced no answer. The Harvard geneticist gave a long and detailed progress report of the research into the peculiar, scattered genetic structures in the alien cells. Lisa listened intently. After forty-five minutes she discerned the central point: Nobody knew anything definitive.

There were other reports and what promised to be an intense give-and-take, but she couldn't stay. She had to get Carlo from Mrs. Belling. Paul turned his head as she went out the door, and she saw him frown.

But, then, Paul had a wife looking after his children.

Danilo showed up while she was feeding Carlo. He opened the apartment door, walked in, and dropped his knapsack on the floor. Carlo sang out, "Hi, Uncle Danilo!" and Lisa was stuck being semi-polite.

"I brought some veggies," Danilo said. "Did you know you have an organic farmer just the other side of town?"

"No," Lisa said. "I don't shop around much."

"Good stuff. No pesticides, no fertilizers. I thought I'd make a salad. Do you like salad, Carlo?"

"Yes!" said Carlo, who liked everything.

"I got some peaches and cherries, too."

Lisa's mouth filled with sweet water. She made herself say, "Thank you, Danilo. But you should knock, you know. It's good manners." She looked pointedly at Carlo.

"You're right. I will. Carlo, watch this."

Danilo tossed cherries in the air, caught them in his mouth, mimed exaggerated satisfaction. Carlo laughed, and so Danilo hammed it up more, until the little boy was whooping with laughter. "Now Carlo's turn."

"Pit them first, Danny," Lisa said quickly. He had always swallowed the cherry pits. Oh God, 'Danny' . . . it had just slipped out.

Danilo played with Carlo all evening. It wasn't until Carlo was in bed that Lisa could throw Danilo out. "You can't do this."

"Do what?" he said.

"Get Carlo used to you, enjoying you, then disappear again."

"Isn't that what 'uncles' do?" Danilo said, and they were facing each other, bristling like cats.

"Danilo, what are you really doing here? I looked up Earth Action on the web. They're suspected in half a dozen environmental bombings. A pesticide factory in Mexico, a supermarket in Germany that refused to remove genetically modified foods from its shelves, a Monsanto distributor in South Africa, a whaling operation in Japan."

"Nothing proven whatsoever," Danilo said.

"Mostly because you haven't hit anything in the United States. God, Danilo, a *supermarket?*"

"Do you know how dangerous those genetically modified foods are? The growers use two to five times the pesticides that regular farmers use. Worse, nobody knows the long-term effects of introducing organisms into the environment that didn't develop there naturally. We could be looking at global disaster down the road, just so the agri-industrial complex can boost its profits now."

"You used to believe that violence was descending to the level of the enemy!"

"And all that peaceful confrontation failed, didn't it? Did you breast feed Carlo, Lisa? You probably had toxic organochlorines in your breast milk. Do you read the newspaper when you're not in that swampy ivory tower of yours? Did you read about the fish depletion on the Grand Banks because of overfishing? The drought in

Africa because of climate shifts due to the actions of industrial countries? The destruction of sustainable, diverse agriculture because of
one-crop genetically engineered planting with God-knows-what side
effects? The ninety-six people in Manila—" He stopped, breathing
hard.

Lisa said quietly, "What about the people in Manila, Danilo?
Which people?"

"Nothing. Forget it."

"It was the garbage dump, wasn't it? I saw it on the news. A
dump collapsed outside Manila, burying the shanties of people who
lived by scavenging in the garbage."

"Men, women, children," Danilo said. "Buried under huge
mounds of rotten garbage. Burned when fires broke out from
the pathetic makeshift stoves they used to cook their food in the
shanties. Cooking *food* there. Rescue people couldn't even get the
bodies out right away because of the stench."

Lisa waited.

"My family owns that dump, Lisa. Just like they own most of that
Manila suburb."

"Danilo, you—"

"Come out of your bog once in a while and see what's going on
with the planet. Which we're not going to have indefinitely unless
somebody gets through to the people exploiting it for profit."

He was right, she knew he was right. And yet all she could think
was, *He talks like a propaganda leaflet.* Was Danilo still in there
somewhere, a real person?

"See you," Danilo said, picking up his knapsack. "Tell Carlo I
said good-bye."

Lisa was the first one in at Kenton the next day, a miracle. She
couldn't sleep, and when she saw Mrs. Belling's light go on at 4:00
A.M., she took a chance and asked her if she could take Carlo this
early. An emergency at work, Lisa babbled, they'd just phoned, she
hated to ask, wouldn't let it happen again. . . .

Mrs. Belling, blinking in either sleep or surprise, agreed. Lisa
carried the unconscious Carlo next door. In Mrs. Belling's shabby,
comfortable kitchen she noted on the counter a jar of peanut butter,
plastic food containers, a receipt for dry cleaning. Genetically modified foodstuffs, persistent organic pollutants, environmental toxins.
That's what Danilo would have said.

Screw Danilo.

The lab was cool and sweet-smelling, a window open to the

moist night air. Lisa shrugged off her irritation at once again being ribbed by the guard. She pulled out her notes on analyses of snaker fecal matter.

Thrashing sounded from the snaker cage.

A snaker sat in a shallow pool of water smack up against the mesh wall. It ignored Lisa as she approached. Again it thrashed with the back half of its long body. Something was emerging. The snaker was giving birth.

Unable to believe her luck, Lisa grabbed a camcorder. She put it right against the mesh, hoping the fine, carbon-filament netting wouldn't interfere too much with the picture. The snaker paid no attention. It was totally absorbed in the excruciating pushing process of mammalian birth, supplemented by a snake-like thrashing.

Finally, something emerged. Lisa gasped and almost dropped the camera.

Not possible.

A brief rest, and the snaker resumed pushing. Lisa could barely hold the camera steady. The offspring looked nothing like the parent, a phenomenon associated with reptiles and amphibians and insects. Tadpoles, larvae. Egg layers. But the snaker was a warm-blooded pseudo-mammal, and its offspring was . . .

Its offspring looked orders more complex than the parent. It had long, far more developed legs, with knee joints and toes. *Toes*. It had a shorter body. It had . . . not possible.

It had a prehensile tail.

This didn't happen. Offspring were not more evolutionarily advanced than their parents, not like *this*. This looked like an entirely different animal. No, that wasn't true, either. It looked like a plausible development from this animal but several million years up the evolutionary ladder.

Not possible.

But there it was, a second one, emerging from the snaker. Who then gave a last enormous thrash, curled up, and went to sleep. Apparently completely certain that her two offspring could fend for themselves.

Which they could. They leaned over and both gently bit their mother on the head. A few minutes later, they began to eat her.

"I have a conjecture," Paul said.

It came after a long silence. The few scientists who had arrived by 5:30 A.M. looked at Lisa's video, gasped in disbelief, looked again, stampeded to the mesh cage, where there was nothing to see. The infant snakers—no, you couldn't call them that, they were clearly something else besides snakers—had disappeared into the cage's lush interior. For the first time, Lisa regretted the large, ecologically correct environments lab animals got at Kenton.

Paul didn't respect the philosophy behind this, not this time. He removed the top and beat the swamp reeds and fished under the lily pads and pond scum until one of the offspring was found. Unceremoniously he hoisted it with a net into a small bench cage, and everyone had gasped a second time.

"I have a conjecture," Paul repeated. Lisa recognized the reluctance of a scientist to make a fool of himself, coupled with the honesty that was going to let him do so. "I think they were genetically engineered to do this. The entire genome—maybe several genomes—exists in the one-celled organisms released from the spacecraft. In fact, one-celled organisms may have been the only things released from the spacecraft. They had the best chance of survival in many conditions, and could subsist on the widest array of chemicals available.

"The genome is in so many pieces in the alien cells because it's so huge. It contains multiple possible evolutionary paths for future organisms, depending on what environment the craft finds itself in. And that same environment triggers which genes kick in for each subsequent generation, advancing as fast up the evolutionary ladder as biology and environment permit."

Immediately objections broke out, some of them vehement. "I didn't say it was a polished theory," Paul finally said angrily. Lisa had never heard him get angry. "I said it was a conjecture!"

More objections, more arguments. Someone else came in—Dr. Clark—and someone else explained to her what had happened. The birth film was run again. People ran back and forth from the bench cage containing the new creature, the totally impossible creature, which had gone to sleep. The NASA rep arrived, looking stunned as he listened to the scientists.

Amid the din, Lisa sat quietly. *I believe Paul*, she thought. Not because the theory was tight, or well-supported, or inevitably logical. She believed it, she realized, because if she were going to send terrestrial life to the stars, that's the way she would do it. The way that respected the unknown ecologies so abruptly intruded upon. The way with the largest possibility of success.

The next weeks filled with frenzied work. Lab staff and visiting scientists had divided into camps. Only the tremendous excitement of the discovery itself kept the arguing from deteriorating into turf wars. And sometimes, Lisa observed wryly, not even that. Kenton's previous major concern, controlling the invasion of loosestrife into the wetlands, was forgotten. The purple Eurasian weed begat and burgeoned.

Lisa stayed at the lab all she could. Unlike some people, she couldn't physically move in. Paul and Stephanie spent most nights in their offices. One of the CDC scientists, Lisa suspected, was sleeping on the very hard sofa in the break room. She herself drew more money from her small, precious hoard to pay Mrs. Belling as much overtime as Lisa could conscionably allow herself away from Carlo. The child grew cranky with missing her, and Mrs. Belling grew stiffer as Lisa picked him up later and later, but she couldn't stay away from Kenton.

They found more of the new creatures—"post-snakers"—in the Preserve.

The geneticists isolated a few specific sections of the alien genetic material responsible for producing a few specific proteins. A tentative but definite beginning on mapping the genome.

Technicians installed heavy encryption programs for all data flowing between Kenton, Washington, the CDC, and the university research centers involved in the discovery.

A post-snaker was painstakingly dissected. Internal organs and systems were logical but startlingly advanced versions of its parents'.

Paul and Hal got into a public fight—it was not an argument, it was a fight—on the missing links between the worms they'd found in the Preserve and the snakers. From worm to pseudo-mammal with nothing in between? Impossible, said Hal. Irresponsible sensationalism.

The missing forms disappeared because they were no longer needed, Paul said. Just as the eaten maternal snakers were no longer needed after the snaker population had reached a certain level. They'd accomplished their purpose, so they stopped being produced.

Evolution doesn't work that way, Hal retorted. Species don't disappear because they're not "needed" —they disappear because their habitat changes, and not always then. We still have primitive, clumsy birds like hoatzins along with superb flyers like gulls and hawks. We still have alternate-branch primates even though man exists. We still have crocodiles, for God's sake, that were around in the Triassic. *National Enquirer* science is no science at all.

This isn't Terran evolution, Paul replied coldly, and the two men parted in anger.

Lisa watched the fight with sorrow, mingled with impatience.

Why were these intelligent, capable men wasting time on turf wars? The greatest discovery in the history of the human race, and they used it to vent long-standing acrimonies, which was how it seemed to her. But maybe she wasn't seeing it too clearly. She was so tired. Being part of history might be exciting but it was also so exhausting she was often afraid she'd fall asleep at the wheel driving home.

And then one night, as she staggered in past midnight with the sleeping Carlo a dead weight in her arms, Danilo was back.

"Lissy," he said somberly, and she couldn't summon the energy to tell him he wasn't allowed to call her that.

"Leave, Danilo."

"I'm going. This is a two-minute visit. Do you often work at night like this?"

"If I have to." She dumped Carlo in his bed, covered him, and closed the bedroom door.

Danilo said, "And do you often get to work as early as you did today? I was here at five and you were already gone."

"What were you doing here at five? Danilo, leave. I'm exhausted." She yawned.

"I can see that. Do you often get to work as early as you did today?"

This time she heard the casualness in his voice. Too casual. Her senses sharpened. "Why?"

"Just asking."

"No, you're not."

He picked up his ever-present knapsack and headed for the door. "Lissy, you work too hard. Don't go into work so early."

"The hell with you. How else do you suppose work gets done, Danilo? Not that you'd know."

He didn't change expression. "I know you hate me."

"No, Danilo. I don't hate you. I can even admire what you're doing, or at least I could when you were with organizations like Greenpeace. It's necessary, important work. But it's not supposed to be an excuse to avoid normal human responsibilities such as your own child, and then even expect to get credit for doing that."

"I wanted you to put him in an institution, Lisa."

"And I chose not to. Is that it, is the problem that Carlo's deformed? That the healthy Danilo Aglipay, stalwart macho crusader, has a son who will never walk or feed himself? Do you think that my keeping him against your wishes absolves you of responsibility? Whether you approve or not, the kid is here, and he's yours, and you'd rather be Richard the Lion Heart than St. Francis of

Assisi. Fine. Just don't expect me, of all people, to applaud you for it."

He didn't answer. Danilo not insisting on the last word was such a novel phenomenon that, watching the door close behind him, she would have felt triumph if she hadn't felt so exhausted. She collapsed into bed and slept, dreamless.

The next morning she was late. Lisa overslept, Carlo was in a rare terrible mood, Mrs. Belling had to run errands before she could take him. Lisa didn't get to Kenton until after ten, and it was clear that something big had gone down before she got there.

"Stephanie, what—"

"Not now I have to write this report."

Stephanie never rebuffed her. Lisa was afraid to even approach Paul, who stalked tight-lipped through the corridors, looking to neither side.

Hal was on the dock, pushing off in the boat. Blunt, honest Hal. Lisa flew out the back door and down the dock. "Hal! Take me with you!"

"No." Then he saw her face. "Oh, all right, but don't talk to me. Just take this and count." He thrust a clipboard at her with columns headed with the names of various fishes. Most of the boat was taken up with netting. Lisa understood; Hal was sampling the fish population in various parts of the Preserve to determine any changes from baseline since the alien animals appeared. The staff had already established that the post-snakers would eat fish. Meekly Lisa settled herself in the boat.

It was peaceful away from the research complex. Hal poled the boat past mixed stands of cattails and hard-stem bulrushes, around impenetrable stands of purple loosestrife. A wood duck had nested on a wind-throw mound and Lisa watched the ducklings slide into the water after their mother. A tern perched on top of an abandoned muskrat house. As the boat glided along, frogs splashed from hummocks into the muddy water, croaking indignantly.

She waited until they were far enough out that Hal wouldn't turn back. With Hal it was always best to be direct and brief. "Hal, I wasn't here this morning. Something happened. Please tell me."

"Politics happened. Fear happened. Stupidity happened. The Washington guy made a report."

"And . . ."

"They don't know down there what to do with the alien animals. But they don't like the speed with which they're both evolving and reproducing. Washington in its cover-your-ass indecision listed several courses of action they might take. One of them was to eliminate the threat entirely."

Lisa suddenly could feel her heartbeat in her teeth. " 'Threat'? 'Eliminate'?"

"You got it. As in, 'Too many unknowns in allowing unknown organisms to propagate in human environments, with totally unknown effects.' As in, 'Kill them all.' "

"But . . . how . . ."

"Undecided, of course. Probably poison the entire ecosystem, before the Monsters From Outer Space spread too far. God, you'd think all these guys do is watch B-movies on late-night TV. No wonder nobody's actually governing the country."

"But—"

"No, there's nothing Kenton can do. Haven't you learned yet that science is mostly just the slave of politics and industry? It wasn't once, but it is now. Grow up, girl."

"I don't—"

"Shut up, Lisa. I told you could only come if you shut up. Just count."

Expertly he cast another net, then raised its stiff perimeters high enough in the water to see its thrashing occupants. Lisa counted.

They stayed out till mid-afternoon. Hal said not a single word more. Lisa followed suit. Just before they reached shore, a group of post-snakers swam past them, climbed onto a hummock, and disappeared into the trees. They reminded her of pioneers rolling westward, sturdy and purposeful. Cattails whispered softly, and her face was reflected in the calm, golden water.

Carlo was still fussy when Lisa picked him up. She fed him dinner, tried to play with him. But his usually sunny nature was in eclipse, and his forehead felt warm.

"Oh, sweetie, don't get sick now. Not now, honey!"

He whimpered, lolling heavily against her breast. She put him to bed with baby aspirin. He breathed easily, not congested. It was nothing; kids got minor infections all the time, and threw them off just as quickly. Carlo had done it before.

Lisa went into the kitchenette and washed three days' accumulation of dishes. It was only nine o'clock, and she had overslept that morning, but she was running a sleep deficit. Ten hours of unconsciousness suddenly seemed to her the most tantalizing idea she'd ever had. She drew the blinds, put on her pajamas, and hauled open the sofabed.

An envelope was taped to the center of the mattress. LISA AGLI-
PAY.

She had never been Lisa Aglipay, never married Danilo, never
used his name. She opened the envelope. A single line of type:
"Don't go into work so early, Lisa."

She stood very still. EarthAction. *Suspected in half a dozen envi-*
ronmental bombings. A pesticide factory in Mexico, a supermarket in
Germany that refused to remove genetically modified foods from
its shelves . . . "Worse, nobody knows the long-term effects of introduc-
ing organisms into the environment that didn't develop there
naturally . . ."

No. Kenton was a wildlife preserve. A research facility for pure
science, not an industrial lab. And there was no way EarthAction
could know about the alien animals. Danilo was just trying to do
what he had always done, control her through scaring her. He
wanted the last word.

The young soldiers, going in and out of Flaherty's bar in town,
more of them all the time as security was increased and then
increased again. Were they all as stupid as the scientists thought? As
much unthinking robots as the military thought? Danilo could have
talked to any of them. Danilo was good at talking.

No.

She crumpled the piece of paper in her hand and threw it at the
wall. In the other room, Carlo coughed. Lisa, hands shaking, put on
the TV to distract herself.

". . . earlier. The truck was found abandoned near Douglas, Ari-
zona, the site of major and continual border skirmishes between
local ranchers and illegal aliens from Mexico crossing into the
United States. United States Border Patrol agents found the windowless truck locked from the outside. Inside were the bodies of
thirty-two Mexican men, women, and children, dead of heat and
dehydration. A spokesperson for the Border Patrol said it is not
uncommon for Mexican citizens to pay large sums of money for
transport into the United States and then be cheated by receiving no
transport. However, this tragedy . . ."

The visuals were horrendous. Lisa turned off the television.

"Don't go into work so early, Lisa."

She dressed swiftly, checked on Carlo, and left him heavily
asleep. She had never left him alone before, but it wasn't, she
thought grimly, as if he were going to wander out into the street.
Carlo was never going to wander anywhere without help.

It started to rain, first lightly and then a hard driving torrent. The
roads were shiny and slick. At Kenton she pulled out her ID for the

guard, who came out of his tiny shanty wrapped in a bright yellow poncho. She looked at him hard. He looked like all the others.

"Lisa," Stephanie said somberly in the main lab, "back to work more? What about your son?"

It was the first time Stephanie had ever asked. Lisa said, "He's visiting my mother."

"Good timing, given the workload here," Stephanie said.

"Yes. Who else is in?"

"Nobody. Even Paul went home to see his kids for a change, *mirabile dictu.*"

How long would Stephanie stay? No way to tell. Lisa set to work on some water samples.

Stephanie left at midnight. "You know the locking codes, Lisa?"

"Of course."

Five minutes, seven. Stephanie wasn't coming back. Lisa punched in the codes for the back door. Heavily laden, she made her way along the dock in the dark. A cool wind blew the rain against her body. In a few minutes her jeans and sweater were soaked.

She turned on her huge flashlight, set it at the end of the dock, and untied the boat. Pushing off from the dock, she rowed into the swamp, but not very far; she wasn't that good a boatman. It didn't have to be far. A little ways out lay a half-submerged fallen tree. Its branches encircled a sort of pond-within-the-swamp, rich with algae and the chemicals of decay, exactly what the scientists had determined to be primary breeding grounds. Once there, Lisa leaned over the side of the boat and filled all the plastic containers she'd brought from her apartment. Two empty margarine tubs. Two pieces of Mrs. Belling's Tupperware. A milk jug she'd hastily emptied. A covered pail that had come full of oversized crayons Danny could grasp with his toes. A gallon ice cream container. All of them, tightly lidded, just fit into her canvas gym bag.

The flashlight guided her back to the dock. Only half an hour had elapsed. Ten minutes more and she'd have Kenton locked, the gym bag in the car, herself driving out past the Army's "perimeter."

When would they detonate a bomb? Probably not for hours yet, just before dawn. *"Don't go into work so early, Lisa."*

Or maybe she was wrong. Maybe EarthAction would do nothing. Maybe it would be the government. Hal, grim in the flat-bottomed boat among the peaceful reeds and rushes. *Probably poison the entire ecosystem . . . "Too many unknowns in allowing unknown organisms to propagate in human environments, with totally unknown effects."*

She wondered if Danilo would have found it funny that Washington and EarthAction actually agreed. Probably not.

She drove carefully through the rain, aware of her cargo. The micro-organisms wouldn't last too long in those closed containers; they had evolved (so rapidly!) in sunlight. Tomorrow she would call in sick, bundle Carlo into the back seat, drive like hell. Where? Not all in one place. Better to diversify.

There were fresh-water wetlands on the other side of the Allegheny Mountains, five hours drive to the south. Wetlands in Maryland, the huge Dismal Swamp in Virginia. In West Virginia there were places so remote the post-snakers might not be discovered for years. And the post-post-snakers, and whatever came after that. Twelve hours' drive. Maybe Carlo would sleep a lot of the way.

Danilo, Hal, Washington . . . they were all wrong. It wasn't about what humans were doing to the environment, terrible as that was. Concentrating on the rain-slicked road, what Lisa saw reflected in its shiny surface wasn't deforestation or global warming. It was a garbage dump in Manila, crashing down in all its sickening rottenness to bury and burn ninety-six people who had nowhere else to live. A locked truck where human beings left thirty-two men, women, and children to die slowly and horribly. The factory in her childhood home, pumping sludge into the groundwater even after scientific studies had linked that water to cancers and birth defects. Carlo, one of those birth defects but also a happy and precious child, from whom Danilo had walked away with as little sense of responsibility as if Carlo had been an organically grown vegetable that had nonetheless developed an inexplicable blight. The images scalded her. Why didn't they maim everyone else as well?

Somehow, for some reason, they didn't. So they happened again and again and again.

It isn't, she thought slowly and painfully, what humans do to the Earth. It's what we do, have done, will do to each other. Maybe the aliens, when they were done evolving into whatever they had been designed to become, would do better. It seemed to her they could hardly do worse.

She wondered what they would be like.

Afterword to "Wetlands Preserve"

As I write this, global warming is a major political and moral issue. Presidential candidates are speaking about it; scientists are signing manifestos about it; magazines are running lengthy articles on "Things You Can Do To Help." Global warming, however, is not the only environmental issue facing us. Others include pollution, crop diversity, species extinction, and over-population — and, of course, they are all related.

"Wetlands Preserve" was the first story I ever wrote about environmental issues, but not the last. The story was sparked by a terrible news incident: a giant garbage dump in Manila toppled onto squatters who made their living scavenging in the garbage, killing fifty people. In my story this incident becomes an inciting one for Lisa, already desperate about her personal life, to commit a desperate act. However, replacing our species with another one from the stars is really not a very practical hope for Earth. In real life, we will have to come up with something better.

Mirror Image

WHEN THE MESSAGE FROM SELIKU REACHED ME, I was dreaming in QUENTIAM. No, not dreaming, that can't be right—the upload state doesn't permit dreaming. For that you need a biological, soft tissue of one sort or another, and I had no biology until my next body was done. I had qubits moving at c, combining and recombining with themselves and, to the extent It will permit, with QUENTIAM. I should not have been dreaming.

Still, the subprogram felt like a biological dream. Something menacing and ill-defined chased me through a shifting landscape, something unknowably vast, coming closer and closer, its terrifying breath on my back, its—

Message from Seliku, magnitude one, QUENTIAM "said" to me and the dream vanished. The non-dream.

From Seliku? Now?

Yes.

It's not time for Seliku. And certainly not at a magnitude one.

QUENTIAM didn't answer. It gave me an image of Seliku gazing at an image of me from out of a mirror, a piece of rococo drollery I was all at once too apprehensive to appreciate. It was nowhere near time for me to hear from Seliku, or from any of my sister-selves.

"Akilo," she said in agitation. Her image had the faint halo of real-time transmission. Seliku wore the body we all used for our bond-times, a female all-human with pale brown skin, head hair in a dark green crest, black eyes. Four coiled superflexible tentacles were each a meter long, the digits slim and graceful. It was the body of the woman we would have become had our creation occurred on a quiet planet—not that we could have been created on a quiet planet. We called the body "human standard," to QUENTIAM's great amusement. We didn't understand that amusement, and It had declined to explain.

For my image, QUENTIAM had used my last body, grown for my fish work on ^563, just before this upload. Four arms, tail, gills. I'd never liked the body and now I tweaked its image to a duplicate of Seliku's. We gazed at each other within my usual upload sim, a forested bedroom copied from ^894, where I'd once adjusted a particularly appealing species of seedings. It had been some of my best work. I'd been happy there.

Seliku said, "Akilo, you must come to Calyx. Now. Immediately."

"What has happened?" She was scaring me.

"I don't know what happened. I mean yes, I do, we do, it's Haradil—you must come!"

I recognized fear in her jerky, elliptical blurtings—we all spoke that way when genuinely terrified. "Bej—"

"Bej and Camy are here."

"Where is Haradil? Seliku, *tell* me!"

"I . . . sorry, I'm sorry, I thought I . . . Haradil is at the Mori Core. Or she *was* there. They arrested and tried her already—"

"*Tried* her? For what?"

"The Mori First One called me. The First One himself. He said that Haradil destroyed a star system."

Stunned, I tried to assimilate this. A *star system*—an entire star system. How? Why?

"*Why?*"

Seliku was more coherent now, calmed a bit by sharing the disaster. That, too, I recognized. She said, "The First One wouldn't tell me except in person. You know how they are. Akilo, the star system was inhabited. There was life there."

"Sentient?"

"Yes, although primitive. And Haradil . . . they've exiled her to a quiet planet for life."

For life. For taking life. "I—"

"Come *now*, Akilo. We're waiting for you. Please come now."

"I'm in upload, my new body isn't done—"

"I know you're in upload! Come when the body's done!" Anger, our habitual response to helplessness. Seliku's image vanished without waiting for agreement; she knew that of course I would come.

I turned my share of our anger on QUENTIAM. *Why didn't you tell me about Haradil when it happened?*

You didn't ask.

We have a group flag on anything significant involving any of us!

Haradil overrode it half a year ago, QUENTIAM said.

Overrode it. Haradil hadn't wanted her sister-selves to know what she'd been doing.

What *had* she been doing? Who were the sentients that Haradil had given over to death? How had she, who was genetically I, done such a thing? *Destroyed a star system . . . exiled for life . . . a quiet planet.* Where now Haradil, too, would die.

As children we had played at "death." One of us would lie absolutely still while the others whispered above her, kicked her softly, pretended to walk away and leave her alone forever. The game had left us breathless and thrilled, like playing "nova" or "magic." Children enjoy the impossible, the unthinkable.

I said to QUENTIAM, *When will my next body be done?*

At the same moment I named when you last asked me that.

Can it be sooner?

I cannot hurry bio-nanos. I am a membrane, Akilo, not a magician.

How had she, who was I, done such a thing?

I stood before a full-length mirror in the vat room of the station, flexing my new tentacles with distaste. This body had been designed for my next assignment, on ^1864. After Seliku's message arrived, QUENTIAM had directed the nanos to make some alterations, but I'd been unwilling to take the time to start from scratch. On ^1864 the gravity was 1.6 standard and the seedings I'd been going to adjust were non-sentient, semi-aquatic plants. This body had large webbed feet, heavy muscles in the squat lower body, and relatively short tentacles ending in too many digits of enormous flexibility. Most of QUENTIAM's last-minute alterations had occurred in the face, which was more or less the one Seliku had worn in her transmission, although 1.6 gravity dictated that the neck was practically non-existent.

"I hate it," I said.

"It's very practical," QUENTIAM said. Now that I had down-loaded, his voice came from the walls of the small room, furnished only with the mirror and the vat from which my body had come. "Or it would have been practical if you were still going to ^1864."

"Are you sending someone else?"

"Of course. It's been nearly a thousand years since their last adjustment."

No one knows what QUENTIAM calls a "year." It doesn't seem to correspond to any planetary revolution stored in Its deebees, which suggests that the measure is very old indeed, carried over from the previous versions of QUENTIAM. Some of the knowledge in those earlier versions appears to have been lost. I can't imagine any of the versions; QUENTIAM has been what It is in the memory of everyone I've ever met, no matter how many states they've inhab-ited. It's just QUENTIAM, the membrane of spacetime into which everything else is woven.

QUENTIAM Itself says Its name is archaic, once standing for "Quantum-Entangled Networked Transportation and Information Artificial-Intelligence Membrane." I'm not sure, beyond the basics, what that encompasses. Seliku is the sister-self who chose to follow our childhood interest in cosmology, just as Camy and Bej chose art and I chose the sciences of living things.

And Haradil . . .

A clone-set, like any living thing, is a chaotic system. Initial small differences, small choices, can lead to major divergences life-times later. That is why all clone-sets from my part of the galaxy meet every two "years." The meeting is inviolable. One can't be expected to keep track of lovers or friends; there are too many choices to pull them away, too many states to inhabit, too much pro-vided by nano, over too long a time. There is always QUENTIAM, of course, but the only human continuity, the only hope of genuine human bonding, comes from sister- or brother-selves, who share at least the same DNA. All the other so-called "family structures" that people periodically try have been failures.

Well, not all. Apparently the Mori have, in the last thousand years, worked out some sort of expanding kinship structure to match their expanding empire. But it seems to be maintained partly through force, which is repugnant to most people. Anyway, a thou-sand years—QUENTIAM's mysterious "years"—isn't long enough to prove the viability of anything. I'm half that old myself.

Of course, the Great Mission also considers itself a "kinship structure." But they're not only repugnant but also deluded.

QUENTIAM said, "Your shuttle has docked."

"How many others are going on it?"

"Five. Three more new downloads and two transients."

"Transients? What are transients doing on this station?" It was small and dull, existing solely as a convenient node for up/downloading near the t-hole.

"They're missionaries, Akilo. I'll keep them away from you as long as I can."

"Yes. Do," I said acidly, even as I wondered what QUENTIAM was saying at that same moment to the missionaries. "*Akilo isn't going to be easy for you to talk to, but your best chance is to approach her through her work*"?

Probably. QUENTIAM, of course, gives all people the information they want to hear. But It would do as It said and keep the missionaries away from me. I was not in the mood for proselytizing.

The wall opened and nano-machinery spat out my traveling bag onto the floor. I opened it and checked that everything was there, even though no other possibility existed. S-suit, food synthesizer, my favorite cosmetics, a blanket—sometimes other people had strange notions of comfortable temperature—music cube . . . I strapped the bag around my very thick waist, stepped toward the door, and hit my head on the ceiling. "Ooohhhhh!"

"Are you injured?" QUENTIAM asked.

"Only my dignity."

"Your body is designed for 1.6 standard gravities," It intoned, "whereas your previous assignment featured a planet with only—"

"Oh, burn it, QUENTIAM." I rubbed my head, which this time around appeared to have a thick skull case. "What is a 'standard gravity,' anyway?"

"I don't know. Possibly that information has been lost."

"I don't really care." Carefully I reached the door, which slid open, leading directly to the shuttle bay.

The other five passengers waited beside the shuttle. Two of the three recent downloads, easy to pick out, echoed my own awkwardness with their new bodies. We stepped gingerly, took a second too long to focus vision, gave off that air of concentration on motions that should be automatic.

The person in the four-legged body of a celwi was, incongruously, the most graceful. He must have used that configuration before. Celwi bodies are popular for their speed; it's a lovely sensation to gallop full-tilt across a grassy plain. The two-legged woman wore a clear helmet in preparation for some alien atmospheric mixture. She and I exchanged rueful glances and tried not to bump into each other.

The third download moved easily in a genderless machine body equipped with very impressive cutting tools and, I suspected, a full range of imaging equipment. It had my admiration; I had only inhabited a machine once and had found the state subtly unpleasant. But some people like it.

That left the two missionaries, both close to what my sister-selves called "human standard," but much smaller. Each stood no higher than a meter. So they were going Out, as far beyond a t-hole as a real ship could get them, to carry out the Great Mission. Mass mattered on such trips. I didn't make eye contact.

"Please board now for the t-hole," the shuttle said pleasantly. It was, of course, one of QUENTIAM's many voices, this one light and musical. The machine body raised its head quickly as if it had received more information than the rest of us, which it probably had.

The shuttle seats were arranged in four rows of two, so everybody got a window view. I hung back, trying to get a seat beside the woman in the helmet or, failing that, alone, but I hung back too long. When I climbed in, last, the four-legged celwi had taken up two seats and the machine body's cutting tools were extended across one whole seat in an unfriendly manner: *I don't want company.* The missionaries had split up, the better to bother other passengers. I settled in beside one of them, felt the seat configure around me, and closed my eyes.

That didn't stop her. "All the good of Arlbeni save you, sister."

"Hhhmmmfff," I said. I was not her sister. I kept my eyes closed.

"I'm Flotyllinip cagrut Pinlinindhar 16," she said cordially, and I groaned inwardly. I had been on Flotyll. No place in the galaxy had so embraced the Great Mission.

Not to answer her would have been the grossest discourtesy. I said shortly, "Akilo Sister-self 7664-3," omitting my home planet, Jiu. None of us had remained on Jiu past childhood; it wasn't really home. We've never understood people who form an attachment to their birth planet, but the Flotylli are famous for it. It's a pretty planet, yes, but the galaxy is full of pretty planets. Home is one's sister-selves.

Haradil . . .

I transmitted to QUENTIAM through my implant: *I thought you were going to keep the missionaries away from me.*

You sat next to her.

"We're going to seed another world, my friend and I," Pinhead 16 said. "Praise Arlbeni and the emptiness of the universe."

"Mmmhhhfffff," I mumbled. But no mumbling stops missionaries.

"Before I joined the Great Mission, I was nothing. We all were. Are you a student of history, sister?"

"No."

A mistake. Her face lit up. I could feel it even with my eyes closed, a stretching of the air that probably registered on the machine body's sensors as elevations in everything from thermals to gamma rays. But if I'd said yes, I was indeed a student of history, she probably would have replied *"Then perhaps you are aware . . ."*

She said, *"Then perhaps you aren't aware just how Disciple* Arlbeni saved us all, thousands of years ago but still fresh as ever. We had everything due to nano and QUENTIAM, and to have everything is to have nothing. From evolution to sentience, from sentience to nano, from nano to the decay of sentience due to boredom and purposeless. Humanity was destroying itself! And then Arlbeni had his Vision: Against all physical laws, the universe was empty of any life but human life, and so to fill it must be our purpose. The universe was Divinely left empty because—"

I had to cut this off. I opened my eyes and looked directly at her. "Maybe not as empty as Arlbeni thought."

I watched her expression freeze, then constrict.

"There have been reports," I went on, apparently artlessly, "of newly discovered planets that bear life which we didn't put there. Non-DNA-based life. Not our seedings. Native life of some sort, maybe blown in from space, seeded by panspermia on worlds far from the t-holes."

"Lies," she said. Her eyes had narrowed to two cold slits.

"Have you checked personally?"

"I don't need to."

"I see," I said, with import, and looked away.

But she was more tenacious than she looked. "Have *you* checked personally on such reports?"

"No," I said. "But, then, I don't care if the galaxy holds other life besides our seedings."

"And *your* life—what gives it purpose?"

"Observing and caring for the life that's here, no matter how it got here. I'm an adjustment biologist."

"And that's enough? Just life, with no plan behind it, no Divine purpose, no—"

"It's more than enough," I said and turned away from her with such discourtesy that even she, the Arlbeni-blinded, left me alone.

I did recognize that my disproportionate fury was not solely due to the stupidity of faith that refused facts. *More than enough*, I'd said of my life . . . but was it? I made adjustments to life planted millennia ago by Arlbenists. I added genes to improve species, altered ecosystems for better balance, nudged along developing sentients. Then I left, usually to never see the results of my tinkering. Was my work actually helping anything at all?

The doubt was an old ache. I turned to the new one.

QUENTIAM, the life on the planet that Haradil destroyed — what was its seeding number?

QUENTIAM, of course, answers everything instantly. But it seemed to me that a long moment went by before It answered. In that moment all the rumors I'd ever heard blasted into my mind, like lethal radiation. Life that humanity had not seeded, life borne in on the winds of space from who-knew-where, life hated or denied by the followers of Arlbeni and the Great Mission . . . But, no, Haradil couldn't have committed genocide for that reason. Even if she'd become an Arlbenist, she couldn't have eliminated a star system just to destroy evidence of panspermia . . .

Life on the planet destroyed by Haradil was Seeding ^5387 of the Great Mission.

I breathed again.

But I was still left with the great Why, as empty of answers as the galaxy that Arlbeni had thought he had all figured out.

"Five minivals until t-hole passage," the shuttle said in its pleasant voice. I looked out my window, but of course there was nothing to see except the cold, steady stars. The station was still only a few hundred meters away, but it was on the other side of the shuttle and I would not turn my head toward the missionary beside me.

"*You are the least flexible of all of us*," Bej had teased at our last bond-time, and she was probably right. Seliku's cosmology, Bej and Camy's art, seemed too soft to me, too formless, without rigorous standards. Artists could create without limits. QUENTIAM could fold the fabric of spacetime to create t-holes and information transfer; It could control endless nanomachinery operating at countless locations throughout the galaxy; It could be directed to manipulate matter and energy right up to the physical constants of the universe. Biology was not so flexible. Life needed what it needed: the nutrients and atmosphere and protection of its current form, and if it did not get those things, it died. Not even QUENTIAM could change death, once it had happened. Life/death was a binary state.

Yet there had been a time, when my sister-selves and I had been young, when I had played at art and studied Arlbeni and considered cosmological history. The seeds for all these pursuits had been in me. I had chosen another path, for good or not, but it was precisely because I knew myself capable of religious thought that the missionaries angered me so much now. I had looked past that easy meaning to something more uncompromising—why couldn't they?

"One minival to t-hole passage . . . t-hole passage completed."

No sensation, no elapsed time. But the stars now had different configurations, and a planet turned below our orbit. Blue and white, it was a lovely thing, as was the yellow star that nourished it. The single continent in all that ocean of blue drifted into view, still lit with the densely clustered lights of the night city. QUENTIAM, of course, is everywhere, and so humanity has no real center. But Calyx, by sheer numbers of inhabitants, comes closest. Slowly it had accreted people who wanted to be with other people already there, each new addition changing the shape of the city, like the lovely shell reefs I had seen on in my fish work on ^563.

The other missionary, the one not sitting beside me, screamed.

I whipped my head around. The machine body had fallen across the missionary, nearly crushing him. His head protruded from under the heavy metal body, the face distorted by pain, and one arm flailed wildly. The machine body lay completely inert, stiff as a dead biological.

"QUENTIAM! What's happening!" I hadn't realized I'd spoken aloud until my yell mingled with the rest in the small cabin.

"I don't know!" QUENTIAM said, and silence descended abruptly as a knife.

I don't know.

I don't know.

I don't know.

There are many things QUENTIAM does not know—It is not a magician, as It enjoys telling me—but the status of a machine body is not one of them. The machine state—I have inhabited it myself, for environments where no biological will suit—is the next closest thing to an upload. A person in machine state was connected to QUENTIAM not by a single soft-brain implant but by shared flows of energy and information. Everything the machine sensors picked up, at all wavelengths, was processed through QUENTIAM and back to the machine body's computer brain. It wasn't possible for QUENTIAM to not know what had just happened.

The machine body moved and sat up. "What . . ."

No one but me said anything. "You fainted," I said, the word so absurd in this context that I felt blood warm my face. Then came a sudden rush of sound and activity. The fallen-upon missionary was examined for damage, found to be bruised but not hurt, his nano-meds already active. The shuttle docked at the orbital which, apparently, was the destination of both missionaries and of the machine body, and they all disembarked. A few minivals later the four-legged body and the woman in the helmet left after the shuttle had taken us through a second t-hole to a second orbital. Only I was left aboard.

QUENTIAM—what happened to the machine body?

I don't know.

The shuttle descended to Calyx.

The city had changed completely in the half-year since our last bond-time. It was no less lovely, just different. Then the entire continent had soared with high, curving shapes, undulating buildings connected with sinuous bridges, the whole a city in the clouds done entirely in subtle shades of white. Shortly after that Bej and Camy, working together for the first time, had gotten the art contract. Apparently it was decided by some sort of vote, although I didn't know of whom.

My sister-selves had made Calyx the opposite of what I'd seen. The nanos had been reprogrammed to replace shimmer and purity with a riot of living foliage, so that it was difficult to see the buildings under the flora. Maybe the buildings *were* flora. Low flowering plants overgrew everything, even the moving walks. The dominant colors were dark, the purple of the photosynthetic bacteria plus dark reds and blues, but the effect was not somber. It was sexual. I stepped from the shuttle into a tumult of inflamed pollination.

Camy and Bej stood waiting amid the flowers. We hugged and I said, "So you're in love."

Bej laughed unhappily. "I told you she'd know immediately," she said to Camy, who neither laughed nor answered. The horror of Haradil's act lay in her eyes, plus perhaps something else.

I said, "It's beautiful, sisters."

"Thank you."

"Have you heard any more about . . ."

"A little. Come with us."

They led me to a moving walk, which took us a short distance to the beach and a low structure covered with long, sinuous vines wild with magenta flowers. The city represented the intemperance we were all capable of, all my sister-selves. We did nothing by halves. Of course Camy and Bej, if they were in love, would create this sort of unrestrained living art. Just as I, working on a seeding on some planet long unvisited by the Great Mission, would stubbornly work for uninterrupted days and nights and days again on some adjustment to a species. Seliku had showed the same extravagance in cerebral form. Her theory of the origin of the universe was once so far beyond the usual thinking that all five of us had been ridiculed for at least two centuries. Now the Seliku Cosmology was widely accepted. And Haradil—

"Have some tea, Akilo," Bej said. We sat on cushions that looked like giant blossoms, or were giant blossoms, and sipped a thin, musky drink that also tasted flowery. I set my cup down when Seliku walked in through a tangle of vines.

"Akilo! How are you?"

Camy said bitterly, "How are any of us?" as I hugged Seliku. Oh, the comfort of physical contact with one's sister-selves! It doesn't matter how long or how far we've been apart, we are still an indivisible whole. That which we are individually grows greater as time goes on, but it can never be greater than what we are together. What one does, all do, and I have always had difficulty understanding the essential loneliness of those singletons for whom this isn't true. What anchors them? How do they survive with only QUENTIAM, who is not human? How do they bear the isolation?

Seliku let me go and accepted a cup of tea from Bej, asking gently, "He's gone?"

It was Camy who answered. "Of course he's gone! Would *you* stay with us now?"

Seliku didn't have to answer. So Bej and Camy's lover—they always chose together, and always insisted the person adopt a male body if not already wearing one—had fled. Well, I couldn't blame him. A city created in celebration of sex could not compensate for a sister-self who'd destroyed a whole worldful of people. Not to an ethical person. Both Bej and Camy were taking their lover's desertion hard. They have always stayed together, and so few differences distinguish one from the other. Still, I sensed that Camy was more bitter than Bej.

Seliku sat on a flower-cushion and said, "I don't know much more than I did before. QUENTIAM still blocks all Haradil's former interactions with It, of course, and the information It would give me from the Morit records is sparse. You know how the Mori are. Their little corner of the galaxy is considered *theirs*, and they limit contact even with QUENTIAM to the absolute necessities. In fact, implants are now forbidden at the Mori Core."

"Forbidden!" I said.

"For the last century," Seliku said. *Century*—another of QUEN-TIAM's inexplicable, archaic terms. But I knew what time span it denoted: 60.8 years on my natal Jiu. I tried, and failed, to picture life unconnected to QUENTIAM, or connected only through external devices.

"I finally got another Mori to speak to me," Seliku continued, and her cup trembled slightly I her hand. "It wasn't easy."

Bej said, "How did you . . . oh, your reputation, of course," and smiled apologetically. Bej and Camy were good local artists, but they were known in no more than a handful of star systems, and I was an unknown laborer among the seedings. But Seliku is famous.

She said, "The Mori I just talked to repeated what the First One told me: Haradil blew up the system by destroying the star, a G3 on the very edge of the Morit territory. In fact, to say it was Morit is debatable, but QUENTIAM awarded it to them. The Great Mission apparently seeded the planet so long ago that not even QUEN-TIAM had a record of the seeding, which is the only reason that the Mori could claim it at all."

I said, startled, "QUENTIAM didn't have a record?"

"It was either one of the very first seedings, when QUENTIAM was just establishing sensors everywhere, or . . . I don't know. It seemed strange to me, too, but that's what It said. Anyway, the inhabited planet was a cold, small, iron-core world with an atmosphere and lakes heavy on methane. The seedings were adapted anaerobes with a nervous system highly enough evolved to swim in communities. The Mori report indicated the evolution of language, including some imaginative communication that they decided was poetry."

My sister-selves looked at me. I said, "It was probably a combination of sound and motion to convey non-literal ideas." I'd seen that among many seedings. My throat constricted. Sentients with poetry.

"After that last report," Seliku continued, "the Mori closed the system, like all the rest of their empire. They don't know, or won't say, how Haradil got interested in it. But she built a missile out of an asteroid, aimed it at the star, and ducked back through a t-hole before it hit. The missile badly . . . badly warped spacetime around the star just before it—the missile, I mean—burned up. I saw the Morit data on the explosion. The warping somehow blew up the star."

" 'Somehow'?" Camy cried. "What do you mean 'somehow'? How did Haradil know how to make such a thing?"

"I don't know," Seliku said. Her hand now trembled so much she set her cup on the spongy floor. Moments before, I had had to do the same.

Bej said, "Seliku, could *you* have made such a thing? With all your knowledge of quantum blending?"

Seliku said carefully, "It's been theoretically possible for a while. But QUENTIAM doesn't know how to translate that into nano programming. And It wouldn't have done such a thing, anyway. Not blown up an inhabited system."

There was a long moment of silence while each of us did the same thing: *QUENTIAM, do you know how to create a working missile that can warp spacetime around or inside a star so as to make it explode?*

No.

Seliku waited without rancor. She herself would have checked on the statement, had she not already known the answer. That was us.

Camy said, "Do you think the Mori know how she did it?"

Bej burst out, "Or *why?*"

Seliku said, "They don't know either answer. But immediately after the explosion, QUENTIAM of course identified Haradil as the cause and delivered her to the Mori. They ran whatever their equivalent of a judgment process is, decided she was guilty, and put her down on a quiet planet. They wouldn't tell me where it is, but I combed all the data QUENTIAM has on recent t-hole use and I think she's on ^17843."

"Where's that?" Bej asked.

"On the outer galactic rim, on the Jujaju Arm. It's a new discovery, and one clearly attributable to the Mori, so they've claimed it even though it's nowhere near their territory. QUENTIAM has accepted its designation as a quiet planet."

"So—" I said, and stopped.

"So that's that," Seliku said, and we all shifted on our cushions and said nothing. QUENTIAM does not overhear our thoughts unless we direct them to him via implant. Only in the upload state, and one other, is mental privacy lost. But my sister-selves and I didn't need to overhear each other's thoughts; we shared them.

We were going to break the prohibition on that quiet planet. We were going to go get the only person who could tell us what had actually happened in that star system explosion: Haradil herself.

There are many reasons why people grow bodies without implants. Most people try it, at least briefly, in their youth, just to define the boundary between themselves and QUENTIAM: What is It and what is me? We five had done that for a few years, a long time ago. Others do it for religious/philosophical reasons, as apparently the Mori had decided. Still others with adventurous genes like to amuse themselves with the challenge of survival without QUENTIAM. Not all of these survive their adventure. There are artists (although not Bej and Camy) who dislike the bond with QUENTIAM, feeling it less a connection than a tether. Finally, there are assorted crazies who just don't like being a part of anything else, not even the membrane woven through all of spacetime.

I stood on the beach, Camy and Bej's lovely flower-strewn beach, and watched the warm, small waves roll between softly planted islands.

QUENTIAM, I want the basic data-set on ^17843.

Seliku believes that is the place where Haradil was sent.

Yes. Give me an external durable.

If QUENTIAM was surprised by my request for a durable, I would never know it. It directed me to the nearest slot for the nanomachinery buried below Calyx, which produced a thin, flexible, practically indestructible sheet of carbon tubules covered with writing.

I can read. It had been a few of QUENTIAM's "centuries" since I had done so, of course, but we had all learned. I assumed that the intriguing, archaic skill was still with me. I was wrong.

The sheet in my hands was dense with symbols and numbers, and only a few looked familiar. I felt my new face grow warm.

Give me the basic set directly.

^17843 is transformed and seeded satellite orbiting a class 6 gas giant, which in turn orbits a type 34 star at an average distance of 2.3 PU. The moon is called by the inhabitants "Paletej," which means roughly "unwanted" in Mori. It has 0.6 gravity, class 9 illumination, a diameter of 36 filliub, type 18 planetary composition, pressure of gk8, axial inclination of two degrees. There are two small equatorial continents and an even smaller polar one, with temperature range of 400-560.

I translated all this into human terms. Haradil's prison would be seasonless, warm, adequately lit. No moons, since ^17843 was itself a moon, but the gas giant would loom huge in the sky. QUENTIAM continued. *Paletej is served by one t-hole, in close orbit with the Mori station. The Mori seeded the moon liberally with Level 3 plant life, which have completely covered one continent and have begun to spread to a second through wind and water. There is no animal life above Level 4.*

Level 3 plant life was pre-flowering. Flowers begat fruit, which is much more concentrated nutrition than greens. With no animal protein available above the level of worms, the prisoners would have to spend nearly all their time in food-gathering and eating, unless their bodies had been adapted otherwise. I doubt that they had.

My tentacle closed tight on the durable, which crumpled but did not crease.

QUENTIAM was not finished. *Paletej has also been densely seeded with nanospores that consume all atoms with a Konig designation higher than 45. A hundred meters below the surface, counter-nanos stop atom consumption, to prevent danger to planetary composition.*

No metals. No way to make any tools more primitive than wood, stone, maybe basic ceramics. And, of course, no nanomachinery.

I stared blindly at the soft sea. *What . . . what sort of bodies were made for the prisoners?*

That information is not accessible to you.

Burn you, QUENTIAM! Do the bodies at least have nanomeds? Tell me!

That information is not accessible to you.

But I already knew the answer. Quiet planets had no nanomeds for anyone but transients, had no nanomachinery of any kind, had no implants to connect to QUENTIAM. That's what made them quiet. That's what made them death.

I stumbled along the beach, barely able to see from rage. *Grow four bodies for me and my sister-selves. Conform each to the best possible fit to basic data set of ^17843.* I would not call the cursed place "Paletej." Haradil was not "unwanted." *Grow the four bodies with full nanomeds but *without* implants.*

Akilo, you and your sister-selves cannot get down to Paletej. The atmosphere, too, is densely seeded with the engineered spores.

How do the prisoners get down? Any shuttle would be consumed and crash.

That information is not available to you.

There must be a t-hole on the surface, one restricted to the Mori alone. QUENTIAM's parameters permitted that, part of its delicate balancing of group possession with preservation as the greatest good of the universe. But what Haradil was enduring was not preservation, was not life, was not endurable.

Who had programmed the moral parameters of QUENTIAM's remote ancestor, all those hundreds of millennia ago? My own barely human ancestors, of course. And the basic principles had been carried forward as QUENTIAM constantly recreated itself, extended Its penetration of spacetime, became intertwined with human consciousness itself. How had justice, in that evolutionary progression, become corrupted? No beings should "own" a t-hole. Down that gravity well lay blind possessiveness, so that you ended up with the Arlbeni disciples, who had perverted a sense of purpose into believing that they alone owned morality. To disagree with Arlbeni was to be unethical, evil. No matter what the evidence said about Arlbeni himself being wrong about the emptiness of the universe.

What I was really afraid of was that QUENTIAM was wrong. That, unknown to It, Haradil had somehow discovered on the planet she'd destroyed some evidence of non-DNA-based life, existing right alongside the seeded anaerobes. I was afraid that she had blown up the place for precisely that reason. That she had become an Arlbenist, melded to the Great Mission, and lost to us.

If there had been panspermic, non-seeded life there, QUENTIAM should have known about it. QUENTIAM had had enough sensors in that star system to transmit detailed explosion data, including what Seliku had called "warping." We had all asked QUENTIAM, Seliku and Bej and Camy and I and probably also the Mori, if the planet had held non-DNA-based life. It had said no. QUENTIAM could withhold information, but It could not lie.

Of course, if the panspermic life was very new, and in an isolated corner of the planet, it's possible that QUENTIAM might not have known about it and Haradil had.

Grow the bodies I specified, QUENTIAM.

I have already begun. But, I repeat, you cannot get down to Paletej in them.

We can get as far as the t-hole above it.

Yes. It is a universal t-hole.

As they all should be.

It didn't answer. Uncrumpling the durable in my hand, the sheet of symbols I could not understand, I realized that probably

Seliku could read them. She was a cosmologist. I went to look for
my sisters, my other selves, my solace in this suddenly icy city by the
soft sea.

By the time our bodies were ready, so was our shuttle. Nano-built on
one of Calyx's many orbitals, it was a sprawling thing, fragile as a
flower except for the tough nano-maintained force shield that surrounded it. The shield was protection against stray meteors and
other cosmic junk. The shuttle, which didn't need to survive an
atmospheric entry, didn't need to be durable.

Our bodies did. They turned out to be pretty much as I'd envi-
sioned, and not too different from the one I was wearing now except
for being much lighter and less muscular. Short, two legs, four tentacles ending in superflexible digits. My current webbed feet had
been replaced with tough feet with prehensile toes, complementing
the prehensile tail, in case ^17843 had plants large enough to
climb. We weren't sure what specific flora to expect there, and the
Mori weren't sharing information.

The new body's ears could detect the widest possible range of
sound waves; electromagnetic sensing was as good as feasible in a
biological; smell was stronger than even in celwyns. A double layer
of fine, shit-brown fur made us as weatherproof as we'd need to be
for the temperature range, although at the upper end, we might be a
bit uncomfortable.

"Not very pretty, are they," Camy said, gazing at the full-grown
bodies in their clear vats. "The faces are so flat."

"You could have ordered modifications earlier," I pointed out,
"but you said you didn't care."

"I don't care."

Seliku said, "QUENTIAM, are you ready to begin uploads?"

"Yes." Its deepest, most authoritative tone; It was offended.

"We're ready, too." But the co-vats had begun to assemble even
before she finished speaking. I climbed into mine, lay down, and
was instantly asleep.

When I woke, an unknowable time later, the download was
complete. I climbed out of my vat simultaneously with my sisters. It
was a hard climb; we were now engineered for a gravity one-third
less than Calyx's. But that wasn't the reason that we gazed at each
other in dismay.

"Are . . . are you all right?"

"Yes," Seliku said. "Are you?"

"Yes, but . . ."

But I'd had to *ask*. Looking at Seliku, Camy, Bej as we stood in our new dull fur, our new flat faces, I hadn't automatically known that, yes, they were all right because otherwise QUENTIAM would have told me. I'd had to look, to question. Camy put her hand to her head and I knew what she was thinking: QUENTIAM was gone. We were without implants. We were on our own, not even able to image each other in real-time if one of us stepped into the next room.

"It feels very strange," Bej said softly. "How will we . . ."

"We will," Seliku said. "Because we must."

I felt myself nodding. We would, because we must.

QUENTIAM said, "The shuttle can take you up to the orbital now, and your t-hole shuttle is ready there."

"Not yet," I said, not without pleasure. It's hard to surprise QUENTIAM, but I guessed that we were doing it now. "There's more things I want to prepare."

"More things?" Definitely offended. I saw Bej grin slightly at Camy.

"Yes," I said, savoring the moment. "We'll be ready to go soon."

The four of us waddled laboriously—curse this gravity—to my lab. I had set it up days ago in a room grown near the vat room. Ostensibly the lab's purpose was to study the microbiology of the flowers Bej and Camy had designed and QUENTIAM had created for Calyx, just as if they were biologicals or cyborgs that had natu-rally evolved from seedings. And I had done some of that work, storing the data in QUENTIAM, carefully packing and storing both specimens and experimental materials in opaque canisters for any future biologists who might want them. But that was not all I had done.

QUENTIAM, give me—

Give me nothing. It couldn't hear me. I had no implant.

The eeriest sensation came over me then: *I am dead.* It was a thousand-fold-stronger version of what I had felt moments before, in the vat room. I was detached, unconnected, alone, in the supreme isolation of death.

But of course I was not. My sister-selves were there, and I clutched Bej's hand. She seemed to understand. We were not alone, not cut off, not dead. We had each other.

This must be what Haradil felt. And she did not have the rest of us.

For a brief moment I hated QUENTIAM. It had done this, It and Its parameters for permissible human behavior. QUENTIAM had gone along with this brutal Morit "justice," and now Haradil . . .

Camy said quietly, "It must be even worse for her. Because . . . you know."

We all knew.

There are five possible states for a human being. Without implants, as we were now. Implanted, which is the normal state. A machine body, which is really just a much heightened version of implants plus a virtually indestructible body. Upload, which is bodiless but still a separate subprogram within QUENTIAM, with its own boundaries. And merged, in which individual identity is temporarily lost in the larger membrane-self of QUENTIAM. Few humans merge, and most never return. Those that do are never really the same.

Haradil, three bond-times ago, had merged with QUENTIAM. It had been after a bad love affair. We all took those hard; I thought of Camy and Bej's ravaged looks when I'd landed on Calyx. We were all intemperate, single-minded in romance as in all else. But Haradil, who had never really chosen a field of work, had been the one who tried to handle the emotional pain by merging with QUENTIAM. And she had come back calmer but almost totally silent, unwilling to tell us what it had been like. "Not unwilling," she'd finally said. "Unable. It's an experience you can't put into words." It had been the longest speech she'd made since returning.

I'd been afraid for her then. We'd all been afraid. But she had continued calm, silent, remote during the next two bond-times. With us and not with us. Neither happy nor unhappy, but somehow beyond both.

"Not human," Bej had finally said, and we'd turned on her in anger, because we'd all thought it ourselves.

But not destructive, either. In fact, the opposite. Gradually we'd come to sense optimism of some kind under Haradil's silence, and our anxiety had been at least partially allayed, and then Haradil had blown up a star system containing sentient life.

Now Seliku said, "Let's get to work."

We had the nanomachinery create a cart. The cart loaded onto itself the canisters I indicated. Seliku, Bej, and Camy hadn't been able to make their lesser preparations until after they were without implants, and there were things I wanted to add to the cart as well, so we dragged around in the monstrous gravity for another day. QUENTIAM observed everything, of course, but It had no reason to stop us. And It asked no questions about anything we had the nanos manufacture.

There were many moments when I started to ask It something:

QUENTIAM, is the— and then I remembered. But there were no more moments like the terrible, deathlike one in the lab. All day my sister-selves and I worked beside each other, tentacles reaching out to touch and pat, and at night we slept in a heap, tails and legs tangled together in the too-warm, fragrant air of Calyx.

"I hope I never see another flower again," Seliku said when we were finally aboard QUENTIAM's shuttle on our way upstairs. And then, "Oh, sorry, Bej and Camy, I didn't mean—"

"I don't want to see flowers, either," they said in unison, and then laughed unhappily. Below us the planet dwindled to a soft blue-and-white bauble.

We would see no flowers on ^17843.

The gravity on our orbital-grown shuttle was a relief; it matched ^17843's. "QUENTIAM," Seliku said, "take us through the t-hole to ^17843."

I thought It might speak to us for the first time since we'd left the vat room, but It didn't. The shuttle moved away from the orbital toward nothing, apparently went through nothing, and emerged into a different sky.

A huge gas giant, ringless and hazy, filled half the sky. Ugly—the pale planet looked as ugly as the fuzzy tumors of a seeding biology gone very wrong. As I watched, a large moon emerged from behind the planet. Clouds, oceans, but none of the beauty of Calyx. To my present state of mind, those features, too, looked like primitive biological deformities, the clouds crawling like parasites across a landscape diseased with what did not belong there.

The shuttle was equipped with full orbital sensors. I imaged the continent with flora as it turned repeatedly below us. Large animal activity showed up on half a dozen different readings. And there was only one large animal on ^17843. I gave Seliku the right coordinates.

Seliku said calmly, "QUENTIAM, take this shuttle as low as is safe."

"This is as low as is safe. You are within the upper atmosphere."

"All right. Sister-selves?"

"Yes," Camy said, speaking for all of us.

And so it began.

We unpacked the canisters we'd brought with us. Each of us tied on cloth belts containing non-metallic tools, blankets, rope, concentrated food pellets, collapsible ceramic cups, the rest of our prepared items. Then we pushed the remaining four opaque canisters toward the airlock.

"What are you doing?" QUENTIAM said. "It is not permitted to descend to Paletej."

Seliku said, "It is not permitted for you to take us through a t-hole to the surface. It is permitted for us to leave the shuttle to go into space."

"You will die," QUENTIAM said. Did I hear regret in Its voice, or anger?

Seliku merely repeated, "It is permitted for us to leave the shuttle. We have nothing that can be destroyed by the metal-eating spores in the atmosphere. And we have nothing with us that connects us to you, QUENTIAM, or anything else forbidden on the surface of a quiet planet."

"Your bodies contain nanomeds."

"They are not forbidden to visitors to quiet planets."

"This quiet planet never has visitors."

"Until now."

"You will die outside the shuttle. We are well within the gravity well. You will fall to your deaths."

Seliku opened her canister, laid the lid on the floor, and stepped inside. "You will open the shuttle door over these coordinates, as soon as feasible after seventy-five millivals."

"But—"

"You will open the door."

"Yes," QUENTIAM said. It had no real choice. A human being may destroy herself, although not others, if she so chooses.

Bej, Camy, and I opened our canisters, laid the lids on the floor, and stepped inside. Our gazes all met. "I love you," Camy said, for all of us, as the membranes in the canister began to grow around us.

Biological membranes, not the spacetime that is QUENTIAM.

I had found them on ^22763, a planet seeded back in the very beginnings of the Great Mission, when humans had been willing to subject living things to a far greater range of environments than they did later on. So many of those hapless seedings died, and so many suffered. ^22763 had been lucky, winning the blind lottery of evolutionary mutation. They were light, air-filled creatures, non-sentient, floating through a world with no sustenance except sunlight, in temperatures just high enough to keep their atmosphere from freezing. All my data on them had of course been stored in QUENTIAM, but I had memorized it, too, because it had been so interesting.

On Calyx, with the help of programmable nanos, I had recreated the floaters and stored them as spores in opaque canisters. The mature floaters, biologicals, were not forbidden on ^17843,

although they would die there. But first, unless I had misremembered data, they would get us down to the surface. If I had
misremembered, we would die along with the creatures.

The membrane sealed around me just before the shuttle door
opened.

When did QUENTIAM realize what we were doing? It's possible It knew from the very beginning. It may have had no choice but
to permit this because of Its "parameters," or because preservation is
the first law, or even because of "love." Who can understand the
mind of QUENTIAM? It moves in mysterious ways.

As the air left the shuttle, the four floaters were blown into space.
The shuttle orbited as low as possible without encountering the
metal-consuming nanos. The floaters, which had fed voraciously on
the light inside the shuttle, now fed on the abundant reflected light
from the gas giant. They swelled with the breathable gases that were
its carefully re-engineered waste products. I had held my breath for
too long; now I breathed.

In the clear living bubbles, which were already dying, my sister-
selves and I began the long float down to the surface of the transformed moon.

Pain. Fear. A rushing in my head like rapids, water that would sweep
me away, kill me . . .

The rushing receded, although the pain did not. There was no
water. I hung at a steep incline, head lower than my legs, in the
fronds of a giant, prickly fern. The rushing became the voices of
Bej and Camy somewhere below me in the eddies of green.

"Akilo! Akilo, answer us!"

"I'm . . . here. I'm all right," I said, although clearly I was not.
As sensation clarified, the pain localized to my head and one leg.

"You're only three or four meters above the ground," Bej called.
"Drop and we'll catch you."

I did, they did, and the world blackened for a moment, then
returned. I lay on a forest floor, a bed of thick, damp, pulpy plants as
unpleasant to lie on as a dung heap. Not that any of my sister-selves
had ever seen a dung heap. I was the biologist, and a fine job I'd
done of adapting the floaters that had died and disintegrated before
we'd actually reached ground.

"I'm sorry," I croaked up at Bej and Camy. "Seliku?"

"I'm here," she said, striding into my circle of sight. "You're the
only one hurt, Akilo. But it's all right; we can stay here quietly until
your nanomeds fix you."

I closed my eyes. The nanomeds were already releasing pain-killers, and the hurting receded. Sedatives took me. My last thought was gratitude that ^17843 had no predators. No, that was my second-last thought. The last was a memory, confused and frightened, from the moment before I crashed: a flash of light bright enough to temporarily blind me, light as silent and deadly as a distant nova.

Then I slept.

"You're back," Bej said. "Akilo, you're back."

A campfire burned beside me. My body, wrapped in two of the superthin blankets from our tool belts, was warm on the fire side, slightly chilled on the other. A strange odor floated from the fire. I sat up.

"How long have I—"

"Three days," Bej said. "We've made quite a little camp. Here, drink this."

She held out to me a cup of the odd-smelling liquid. It tasted worse than it smelled, and I made a face.

"At least it's not poisonous," Bej said cheerfully. "Local flora. We're trying to conserve the food pellets as long as we can. How do you feel?"

"All right." I flexed my leg; it was fine. Thanks to the nanomeds that Haradil had to do without.

"Seliku and Camy are out gathering more food. We had to do something while you were out, so we gathered leaves, tested them with our nanomeds for biocompatability, and boiled them down to make that drink."

"Boiled them in what?" I finished the drink and stood, working my muscles. Without the blankets, the air was cold.

"That," Bej said, pointing at a rickety arrangement of bent wood and huge leaves. "It's remarkably effective, but ready to fall apart, so it's a good thing you're ready to travel. You can eat those same leaves raw, too, but they taste even worse that way."

"Travel to where?" I said. Bej seemed too cheerful. Didn't she realize that we might all die here? Of course she did. Her cheerfulness was a kind of bravery, sparing me not only her fear but also her share of the intense shame we all felt over Haradil's crime.

"We haven't seen any prisoners yet," Bej said, "but Seliku came across a campsite—old ashes, that sort of thing. The scent is long gone but Camy thinks we can track them. Do you think we can?"

"Bej," I said irritably, "I'm an adjustment biologist. Of course I can track, probably much better than Camy can."

"That's good, because she said you're going to do it. Jump around a bit. It gets much warmer here when the star is higher."

In the dim, filtered green of dense forest, I hadn't realized it was early morning.

Seliku and Camy returned. Seen together, I became aware of the changes that three "days" (how long was each?) had made in my sister-selves. Their dung-colored fur was matted and dirty, especially Camy's, who didn't smile at me as she walked into camp. For the first time, she and comparatively cheerful Bej, standing side by side, did not look alike. It was unsettling.

They packed up our few bits of equipment: blankets, boiled-down food wrapped in more leaves, ceramic knives. Seliku lead me to the abandoned camp. Following the trail from there was easy compared to the seedings I had tracked on other worlds. These prisoners had nothing to hide and no predators to confuse, and they'd left a blindingly obvious trail of broken ferns, missing edible leaves, and old shit. A child could have found the settlement.

^17843 proved to have stretches of open ground within the fern forests. But even these low-lying "meadows" were overgrown with pulpy green, so that everywhere our feet sunk onto squishy vegetation and stagnant water. The green was unrelieved by any color of fruit or flower. In the sky the gas giant loomed oppressively, blocking the sun. The only sound was a low, unceasing hum from insect-analogues, monotonous and dulling. I hated the place.

At mid-day, which seemed to come very quickly on this small world, we reached the top of a fern-crested hill, and suddenly before us, down a steeper slope, was the welcome blue of the sea.

"Wait," I said, when Bej would have rushed down the hill toward huts built on the seashore.

"Wait for what? Haradil's down there!"

I pulled her back into the thick fronds. Seliku and Camy, dirty and sweaty, watched us. "Bej, listen to me. These people have been sent here by the Mori for crimes. Some of them may have only violated some idiotic Mori custom, but some might be truly dangerous. They may have destroyed or killed."

As Haradil had.

Seliku said, "Alo is right." She drew her ceramic knife and looked at us.

Camy stared back in disbelief. "The knives are for work, not . . . you can't expect me to . . . Sel, I don't want to!"

"None of us want to," I said. I shared Camy's distaste, shared Seliku's reluctant foresight, shared Bej's eagerness to see Haradil.

These were my sister-selves. After a moment, Camy, Bej, and I drew our knives.

Together, with me in the lead, we started toward the settlement.

As we got closer, details emerged, all of them sickening. The flimsy huts, which looked as if a good wind would blow them over, were built of woody fern trunks topped with broad fronds. Among them burned two or three open fires ringed with stones and topped with leaf cauldrons. People, including some children, skittered around frantically as soon as they glimpsed us.

We halted halfway down the hill, smiling painfully, and waited.

Eventually two prisoners started toward us. Seliku glanced at me, and I gestured helplessly. I had guessed as well as I could without data. Still, I'd gotten the bodies wrong.

The two coming toward us were even smaller and lighter than we, which on reflection made sense: less mass to support with food gathering. Fragile, tailless, thickly furred to conserve heat and discourage insect bites, they walked on two legs but had only two thick tentacles, which ended in clumsy opposable digits. But the faces were human. One of the prisoners had been infected with some sort of local fungus that covered its head and part of its back. I saw Camy gaze at it in horror. The other had a scar along the left side of its face. I don't think I'd ever seen uglier sentients, or more pathetic ones.

Silently, simultaneously, we put our knives back into our tool belts. Any one of us could have smashed both of these sad people into jelly.

Then came the worst.

Seliku said, "Hello. We are looking for our sister-self, Jiuinip Haradil Self-Sister 7664-3. Is she here?"

Both creatures stared at us. Then one chattered incomprehensibly. Bej gasped. "They don't have translation capability!"

Of course not. Translations went through QUENTIAM by implant, so simultaneously that hardly anyone noticed it happening. These poor beings had no implants. And neither did we. So they lived here, unable to talk even to the other pathetic prisoners, deprived even of the solace of words to share the unendurable. It seemed the worst cruelty yet. Wouldn't death have been better than this?

Camy took a step backward and brought up her tentacles to cover her face. Seliku pressed on, her voice quavering slightly, in several other languages; I hadn't realized she'd learned so many. No response.

Finally I said, very slowly and with a variety of pitches and inflections, "Haradil? Har . . . a . . . dil? HARadil? HaraDIL? HarAdil? Haarrrraaadddiiilll? $^{Har}ad_{il}?$ $_{Ha}ra^{dil}?$"

One of them worked. The prisoner with fungus made a quick snapping gesture with his digits, a gesture I didn't understand, as he repeated "Haradil" in a guttural tone with a rising inflection. The other prisoner watched dully. I nodded and smiled, and the first man pointed toward the forest we'd just left. I made helpless gestures and he rose to his full stunted height, scowled fiercely, and gestured for us to follow. The four of us trailed behind him laterally along the edge of the forest until, about half a blinu from the settlement, he turned into the ferns.

We seemed to walk a long way into the forest. Finally, in a small hacked-out clearing, in front of the flimsiest hut yet, crouched another of the ugly creatures. As we approached, it raised its eyes to us and they were filled with despair and anguish and, then, recognition.

Haradil.

Bej burst into tears. But Camy rushed forward and with all the strength of her superior body, slammed a fisted tentacle into Haradil's weeping face. "How could you, Hari? How *could* you do it, to all of us?"

I understood Camy's fury, Bej's sorrow, Seliku's distaste. I shared all three. But I was the biologist. After Seliku had pulled Camy off Haradil, I knelt beside her to examine her wounds. Our prisoner-guide had oozed back into the forest. The light bones of Haradil's face didn't seem broken, but she was obviously in pain, and my anger turned from her to Camy.

"You could have killed her! This body is really fragile!"

"I'm sorry," Camy choked out. She didn't cry. We were not easy criers.

Haradil said nothing, and that was at first oddly reassuring because it was the way she'd been ever since her merger with QUENTIAM, was at least a token of the Haradil we'd known.

"Haradil," I said as calmly as I could manage, "I'm going to give you nanomeds."

She shrank back under my hands. Seliku said, too harshly, "Hari, the Mori won't know, nor QUENTIAM. It has no sensors here. No one will know what we do in this place."

"No nanomeds!" Haradil cried, and somehow her voice was still her own, horrifying in that awful body.

"Why not?" I said, but I already knew. Holding her delicate, filthy face between my hands, I saw the start of the same fungal infection that the other prisoner had, and I shuddered.

"Nanomeds will keep me alive!"

"And you want to die," Seliku said, still in that same harsh voice. "Burn that, Haradil. You live. You owe us that, and a lot more."

"No!" Haradil cried, and then she was gone, squirming out from under my gentle clasp. Bej caught her with a flying tackle that might, all by itself, have broken bones. Haradil screamed and flailed ineffectually.

Horrified, furious, and determined, we set on her. Bej and Camy held her legs and the one set of arms. Seliku unwound a long superfine rope from her tool belt and we tied Haradil. The others looked at me; I was the biologist. I drew my knife, sliced into Haradil's arm and then my own, and pressed them firmly together. Nanomeds flowed from me to her. Haradil began a low, keening sound, like a trapped animal.

It took a long time for enough nanomeds to replicate within Haradil to achieve sedation. Until nightfall we had to listen to that terrible sound. Finally she fell asleep, and we carried her into the forest and lay down under our blankets.

We didn't need much sleep, but there wasn't anything else to do. I had never known such blackness. No starlight penetrated the overhang of fronds. My infrared vision was, except for my sister-selves, a uniform and low-key haze of plant and insect life. We didn't build a fire for the same reason we'd left Haradil's hut. Not all the prisoners on ^17843 might be as scowlingly cooperative as the one that had brought us to Haradil. Some of these people had killed.

As she had.

"I'm sorry I hit you," I heard Camy whisper in the dark to Haradil's sedated form, and I knew that Camy both was and was not sorry.

But the strangest thing in that dark night was the absence of QUENTIAM. I hadn't expected to feel so completely bereft. My sister-selves lay so close to me that their breathing was mine, the scent of their bodies filled my mouth, their tentacles clutched patches of my fur. Yet it was QUENTIAM I missed. That voice in my head, always there, knowing what I was doing without being told, knowing what I wanted next. Support and companion and fellow biologist. I missed It so fiercely that my throat closed and my body shuddered.

"Are you cold, Alo?" Seliku whispered. In the dark she pushed more of her own blanket onto me. But it brought no warmth, brought no comfort, was not—shockingly, horrifyingly—what I needed, not at all.

Haradil slept for days, during which we did nothing except move farther inland, gather leaves, and consume them to supplement and conserve our pellets of concentrated food. It was an exhausting, endless, boring process. The bodies I had asked for were too big for the available nourishment, with too little storage capacity. We all lost weight, and each time it was my turn to carry the sedated Haradil, she seemed heavier on my back. Despite our efforts, we had to use some of the food pellets, and our supply diminished steadily.

The farther we moved away from the other prisoners, the more I could see why they'd camped on the shore. There may have been some edibles, plankton or small marine worms, in the sea; that would be compatible with Level 4 fauna. More important, on the beach it would have been possible to see the sky, hear the waves. Under the fern cover we saw nothing but pulpy green in half-light, alien and silent. The only sound was the high-pitched drone of insects that stung constantly. Occasionally, when the wind was right, a stench of rotting plants blew toward us, fetid and overpowering. I had been on many ugly worlds, but none I hated as much as this one.

On the sixth day, we camped just past noon in a small, relatively dry clearing. We were so tired, and even the huge blob of the gas giant overhead was better than yet more oppressive green. Bej and Seliku made a fire, despite the risk of smoke rising above the ferns and giving away our positions. We sat around it and ate, by unspoken agreement, twice our usual ration of food pellets, washed down with water from a muddy stream.

"What's that?" Seliku asked Camy.

Camy held up a particularly thick section of woody fern trunk, which she was carving with her ceramic knife. She'd sculpted a pattern of beads along its length, smooth ovals gracefully separated in the CeeHee intervals, loveliest of proportions in both art and mathematics. Even here, Camy had to be an artist.

The sight inexplicably cheered me. "Camy—" I began, and the sky exploded.

Some of us screamed. There was no noise, but the sky opposite to the gas giant grew bright, then even brighter. Bej threw herself across Camy, I did the same with Haradil, and Seliku fell to the ground. In a moment it was over. Seliku gazed upward.

"What . . . what was that?" Camy, but it might have been any of us.

"I don't know," Seliku said, and her voice held even more strain than Camy's. "But I think the station just blew up."

"The station?" Bej said. "The Mori station? *QUENTIAM's* station?" All the stations were, in one sense, QUENTIAM's. He created and maintained and ran them. "How could that be?"

"I don't know," Seliku said. "It can't be. Unless QUENTIAM did it."

"*Why?*"

"I said I don't know!"

"Sel," I said, "I saw something like that when we landed, just before I fell into that giant fern, only not as bright. A flash of light. Could that have been the shuttle blowing up, too? No, I know you don't *know*, but did you see a flash then as well?"

"No. But we all landed before you, and we were below the fronds—that first flash wasn't as bright as this?"

"No, not as bright. But I saw it."

Seliku said, with a reluctance I didn't understand, "If that big flash was the station, then I suppose what you saw could have been the shuttle. But there's no reason for QUENTIAM to blow up either of them."

"Maybe It didn't," Camy said.

We all looked at Haradil, still deeply sedated. If there were answers, they must come from her. But if the shuttle and station really had blown up—

"I think," Camy began, "that we better—" Men burst from the dense, pulpy foliage.

Twelve prisoners, all armed with longer, thicker, sharper versions of Camy's carved wood. *Spears*—my mouth tasted the archaic, slimy word. So the exiles had known all along where we were. They had experience in tracking, just as I had, and they'd stayed upwind of us.

I said quietly, "Draw your knives and make a circle facing outward around Haradil."

We did, four comparatively large women against a dozen frail pygmies. Only then did I see that the tip of the spear closest to me was sticky with something thick and green.

These people had had years of exile to learn about the flora here, as well as to develop warfare unrestrained by QUENTIAM's parameters. The spear could easily be tipped with some local poison. Our nanos could handle it, but while the nanos worked we would probably be automatically sedated, completely vulnerable.

A sense of unreality swept over me. I stood here—I, Jiuinip Akilo Self-Sister 7664-3, who had adjusted sentient seedings not dissimilar to these on scores of worlds—facing an enemy armed with spears, while I myself held only a ceramic knife. And the most unreal part was that these people, too, at least the ones not born here, had come from my same universe of nano, of abundance, of peace. Of QUENTIAM, who would never have permitted this.

Seliku said in a voice I didn't recognize, "Do . . . do any of you speak Standard?"

To my surprise, the closest prisoner answered, in a strange whining accent. "You do this! You and your magic! You destroy clouds and now we never have no rain!"

Magic. Five little girls, playing at "magic" and "death" and "nova," knowing, secure in QUENTIAM, that for us such things did not exist.

I said to the pygmy, who must be third- or fourth-generation to be so ignorant, "The clouds will return. But we did not destroy them. We are not destroyers."

He waved his spear at Haradil. "She is. She say it."

Oh, what had Haradil said? That she was a destroyer, perhaps that she wanted to die. She might have been trying to make them kill her. Suicide by fellow outcast.

Camy said, "But you did not kill her. You knew that if you killed her, all her bad magic would come to you."

I saw on his face, on all their diseased and debased faces, that it was true. They feared Haradil's powers of destruction too much to kill her. So what were they doing here now?

I said, "You want us to go far away."

"Yes! Go!"

That was why Haradil had lived apart from what could have been the comfort of shared misery. But, of course, she hadn't wanted comfort. She wanted death and suffering, as atonement for what she'd done.

Seliku said, "It could be a trick, to make us put down our knives."

I looked again at the pathetic creatures before us. Two, I saw now, had legs actually shivering with fear. I said quietly, "It's not a trick. Bej, carry Haradil. We'll move even farther inland. Move slowly but purposefully . . . now."

The prisoners watched us go. In just a few moments the sight of them was blocked by the everlasting spongy green.

*   *   *

So again we walked, all the rest of that day and the next, taking turns carrying Haradil. We saved the last of our concentrated nutrients for Haradil and ate only a safe kind of raw leaf snatched from plants as we marched. The leaf tasted vile. Nanomeds help with neither taste nor hunger; in any civilized place, both are enjoyable human sensations. I could feel my body shift into energy-conservation mode, which made it harder to keep going but easier to not think. That, now, was my hope. To not think.

Finally, as darkness fell, we made camp in another small clearing. A fire, the blankets from our belts, stars overhead but not, I saw with exhausted gratitude, the gas giant. And as we sat around the fire, too dispirited to talk, Haradil awoke.

"What—"

"You're with us. You've had nanomeds. Sit up," Camy ordered.

Haradil did. She looked around, and then at us. Maybe Camy and Bej, the artists, could have imagined such a tormented expression, but I could not have.

Seliku said, neither gently nor harshly, "Haradil, we've forced our way onto this planet, and now we—"

"QUENTIAM let you come? The Mori let you come?"

"No," Camy grated. "Sel just told you—we forced our way down. And now it looks as if our way home has just closed for good."

"What do you mean!" Haradil cried. At least she was talking.

I said, from sudden pity, "Camy, don't. QUENTIAM will rebuild the shuttle, you know that."

"We don't know anything!" Camy said.

Seliku said, still in that carefully neutral voice, as if she were addressing a skittish child, "Haradil, we'll talk about getting home in a moment. Right now, we're saying that we came all this way, with all this danger—we don't have implants now, you know, none of us—to find out what happened. Why you destroyed that inhabited star system."

Haradil looked at us hopelessly, her gaze moving from one face to another around the fire. In its flickering light, her gaunt face in its pygmy body looked older than QUENTIAM Itself.

Bej said, "Was it the Great Mission, Hari? Did you become an Arlbenist, and did that system include a planet with non-DNA life on it? There's documentation now, you know, the Arlbenists were wrong, the galaxy wasn't empty before humans began to fill it. If you became an Arlbenist—"

"I don't know whether any planet in the system had non-DNA life," Haradil said bleakly.

"So you—"

"I wasn't an Arlbenist."

Camy said, "Then *why?*" I saw her ferocity drive Haradil back into silence.

Seliku broke it. "And *how?* How could you turn an asteroid into a missile powerful enough to blow up a star? Even QUENTIAM said It didn't know how to do that!"

"It didn't," Haradil said.

I burst out, "Then what *happened?*"

"Light happened," Haradil said. "Pieces of light."

"Pieces of what?" Camy demanded angrily. "What are you talking about?"

"Photons," Seliku said. "Is that right, Haradil? You mean photons?"

"Yes." She looked down at her ugly hands, the digits so thick that even in her thinness, firelight did not shine through them. "I was transforming an asteroid, more of a planetoid, in orbit around the star. I was—"

"You couldn't have been," Seliku said. "I've seen the Morit data on the explosion. That asteroid was in a deeply eccentric orbit—it had been captured by the star's gravity only about a half million years ago and was spiraling in to the stellar disk. Just before the explosion, the asteroid was very close to the star, getting a slingshot gravity assist. There's no way even a machine body could have survived on it."

"I know," Haradil said. "I wasn't on the asteroid."

Seliku said, "Where were you?"

Instead of answering, Haradil said, "I was transforming the asteroid—trying to transform the asteroid—into a work of art. Light art. To be an artist like you, Bej. Like you, Camy. All four of you have . . . have things you do. I only had QUENTIAM."

Bej said, "That's where you were. Not on the star, but in upload with QUENTIAM. Directing the artwork through It. We've done that."

Haradil didn't look at Bej, and all at once I knew that she hadn't been in upload, either. Haradil said, "The art was merged photons. You know, to create increased energy."

"Yes," Seliku said, but she looked a little startled. The rest of us must have looked blank because she said, "It's how QUENTIAM operates, in part. It merges photons with atoms to create a temporary blend of matter and energy. It also forces shared photons between quantum states, to create entanglement. It's how QUENTIAM makes the t-holes, how It moves around information—how It exists, actually. The whole process is the basis for QUENTIAM's being woven into spacetime. That's just basic knowledge."

Not to me, it wasn't, and from Bej's and Camy's faces, not to them, either. But Haradil had apparently learned enough about it.

I said, trying to keep my voice soft enough not to push Haradil into more opposition, "Is that what happened, Hari? You were directing QUENTIAM to create this 'art' and somehow you massed enough photon energy or something to blow up the star?"

"QUENTIAM wouldn't permit that to happen," Seliku said. "Anyway, the energy you'd need would be huge, more than you'd get from any light sculpture."

Bej said, "Was it a sculpture, Hari?"

"No. It was . . . was going to be . . . what does it matter what I was making! I couldn't make it and I killed a star system!"

I said gently, "The sculpture doesn't matter if you don't think it does, my sister-self. What matters is how the system blew up. What happened?"

"I don't know!" Haradil cried. "I was there, working on the art, and all at once the asteroid slipped away from my control and sped toward the star, and I don't know how!"

"That doesn't make sense," Bej said. "If you were in upload with QUENTIAM and that happened, then It would tell you what happened the moment you asked."

Seliku said, "Did you ask?"

Haradil was silent. Camy rose to her feet and uncoiled her tentacles. Lit from the firelight below, she suddenly looked terrible, avenging. "Didn't you ask, Haradil? You blew up a star system and you *didn't ask what happened?*"

"Of course she did," Bej said. "Hari?"

"I asked later," Haradil said. I had seen that posture on primitive mammals on other worlds. Haradil cringed, from fear of her pack. It turned my stomach sick. "I asked later and QUENTIAM said . . . said It didn't know what I'd done."

"That's not possible!" Camy said angrily. "If you were in upload with QUENTIAM, It would know exactly what you'd done and so would you! You're lying!"

The two words hung in the firelit air. Insects whined, unseen, in the unfriendly dark. We never lied to each other. Sister-selves did not lie to each other. Your sister-selves were the only ones in the universe that you could say anything to, confess anything to, because the capacity for the same action lay in each of them. A sister-self always accepted everything about you, as no lover ever did, no friend, no one else but QUENTIAM.

"She's not lying," I said.

Camy turned on me. "But if she was in upload and did something to—"

"She wasn't in upload," I said slowly. "Were you, Haradil? You weren't in upload state, you were in merged state. You'd merged a second time with QUENTIAM."

Haradil turned her eyes to me, and in the relief mirrored in them, I knew that I'd been right. She was relieved that now we knew.

Bej burst out, "Oh, Hari! Why? The first time you did that you came back so . . . so . . . merging reduces people, destroys them! You left parts of yourself behind in QUENTIAM, or something—you know you were never the same after that!"

"I know," Hari said, so simply that my heart turned over. Haradil, knowing herself to be incomplete, fragmented, had gone back into merged state to find the lost pieces of herself. Or maybe just to redeem what she saw as a wasted life ("All four of you have . . . have things you do") by creating this one stupendous, innovative piece of art. Which of us hasn't dreamed of that kind of glory and fame for our work? Only Seliku had attained it.

It was Seliku who moved the discussion back from Haradil's state to what Seliku saw as the more important state: QUENTIAM's. She said quietly, "If Haradil is not lying, then QUENTIAM is."

We gaped at her. Seliku was a cosmologist; she knew QUENTIAM as well as any human could. She knew that QUENTIAM could not lie.

"That's impossible!" Bej said.

"Yes, it's impossible," Seliku agreed, and the four of us stared at each other across the low fire.

Haradil said despairingly, "Don't you see that it doesn't matter whether QUENTIAM's lying or not? It only matters that even if I don't know why, I destroyed *life*. A whole worldful of life. My art, my action. And nothing I can do—nothing anyone can do, not even QUENTIAM—can ever change even one tiny piece of that guilt and shame."

I think I knew then, in that moment, what would happen to Haradil. But my attention was on Seliku. She and I were the only scientists. I said to her, "If QUENTIAM can't lie, and if It *is* lying, what does that mean?"

She answered obliquely, her tentacles quiet in her lap, her voice just low enough to reach the four of us sealed in our circle of wavering firelight amid the dark. "I know none of you understand my work, the algorithms that won me the Zeotripab Prize. You'd have to understand how the universe itself works.

"Spacetime vibrates, you know, in its most minute particles. They vibrate through space. Gravitons—one of the particles, the ones that create the force of gravity—are the only particles that also oscillate minutely in time. That's what makes them the only particles—I don't know how to say this without the math—the only particles that 'leak' out of the universe, affecting its mass. That's why the universe keeps expanding. That loss of gravitons is what makes spacetime possible at all, which in turn makes everything else possible."

Bej said naively, "You proved all that?"

Seliku smiled. "No. Only a tiny part of it. It's old knowledge. QUENTIAM functions by manipulating those minute time oscillations, in even more minute ways. But it means that It cannot lie. It's bound by the physical constants of the universe. If It said that It doesn't know how Haradil blew up the star system, then It doesn't know."

"But," I said, "could It and Haradil together—they were merged, remember—have done it? Could It have used Haradil to do that? In fact, did anyone ask QUENTIAM if *It* had blown up the system?"

Camy gasped. "QUENTIAM?"

"It can't lie," I said, staring at Seliku, "but It can destroy, right? It destroyed the shuttle and the station. There might have been Mori on that station, we don't know. Within all those physical constants you mentioned, are there any that could absolutely keep QUENTIAM from destroying a star system with life on it?"

"Physical constants?" Seliku said. "No."

Bej said, "But there are QUENTIAM's own parameters! It preserves, not destroys! Everyone knows that! Everyone knows that!"

"Seliku," I said, "are QUENTIAM's moral parameters as woven into spacetime as Its inability to lie?"

"Yes. Its moral parameters are programming, but inviolable programming, core programming. Redundancy doesn't even begin to describe how deeply those parameters are a part of QUENTIAM. They can't be touched, not even by It."

"Nonetheless," I said, "if It can't lie, and if Haradil blew up the star system while she was merged with QUENTIAM, then It blew up the system. It destroyed life. Not you, Hari—" I turned to her, beseeching, "—*not you*. QUENTIAM."

"I don't believe it!" Camy said. "QUENTIAM can't do that! It can't destroy . . ." She fell silent, and I knew she remembered the shuttle, the station.

Haradil had not moved. She sat looking down at her tentacles in her lap, an unconscious mirror of Seliku's pose, although Hari's shoulders slumped forward.

"Haradil," I repeated, "you didn't do it. QUENTIAM did."

Finally she raised her eyes to mine. "It doesn't matter, Alo. There's no difference. I was in the merged state. At that time, I *was* QUENTIAM."

We all stared at her. None of us knew what to say to that. None of us but her had been there.

"I think," Bej finally said, "that it's time for us to go home."

We couldn't leave until morning. The engineered spores stored in our cloth belts, the same spores that had created the biological floaters that brought us downstairs, needed sunlight to feed on for both growth and inflation. We could only leave the surface on a clear, sunny day. We could only leave from a large, open space among the huge ferns.

And, of course, once we'd floated to the upper atmosphere, we could only survive if QUENTIAM had created another shuttle to pick us up.

Nobody mentioned this. We talked very little as we wrapped ourselves in blankets near the fire. I couldn't get to sleep, and I doubted the others could, either.

Seliku would be thinking about the paradox of QUENTIAM. It couldn't destroy, and It had destroyed. She would be going over the mathematics, the spacetime logic, trying to find a way out.

Bej and Camy would be wrestling with the moral problem. Haradil had been QUENTIAM; It had killed; had Haradil therefore really killed? Could you commit genocide without knowing it, and if you did, was it still genocide?

Haradil—I didn't know what Haradil was thinking. "I *was* QUENTIAM," she'd said. I didn't know, couldn't imagine, what that actually meant. But she was right, in one sense—she hadn't been Haradil for a long time now.

It seemed millennia before I fell asleep.

When I woke, as the first dismal light was filtering through the pulpy ferns, Haradil was gone.

✳   ✳   ✳

"Burn her in hell forever!" Camy cried. I didn't know what "hell" was; Camy liked to poke around in QUENTIAM's archaic deebees. Had liked to.

Seliku said, "Alo, can you track her?"

"Yes."

Hastily we packed. The morning was overcast and drizzly; we couldn't have left ^17843 that day even if Haradil hadn't run away. At first I scented her easily. After following for half the morning, I was sure. "She's heading back to the beach," I said. "To the settlements."

Bej, her dirty face set hard to avoid tears, said, "She wants them to kill her. She still thinks she was responsible for   for the genocide."

"Maybe she was," Camy said bitterly. I felt that bitterness echo in myself. Didn't Haradil realize we would follow her—and thereby risk our own lives? She knew we planned on leaving ^17843 today. She, one-fifth of a sister-self, was endangering the whole. At what point did moral atonement turn into selfishness?

And if our circumstances were reversed, would I have done the same thing?

I might have. The realization only worsened my bitterness.

We were taking a different, more direct route toward the coast than the one we'd arrived by. The ground sloped downward and became much more marshy. The flora changed, too. As the ground became wetter, the huge, looming ferns were replaced by smaller, sedge-like plants farther apart.

"Wait," Seliku called from the rear of our dismal procession. "Akilo, these plants here are the ones we've been eating and I don't see any ahead of us. I think we should stop and eat here, while we can."

"That's a good idea."

We stuffed handfuls of the vile things into our mouths and chewed. These small, light bodies packed very little extra fat; my tentacles had the thinned, bluish look of rapid weight loss. But at least the leaves temporarily stopped the ache in my stomach.

After eating, we slogged forward. In the marshland, walking was much harder. Each footstep made a quiet spurgling sound. The ground grew steadily wetter and muddier, broken by small hillocks that offered better footing but also swarmed with small, pale worms. The sun, behind thick, gray clouds, did little to warm my fur, and nothing could warm my heart.

"Alo . . . stop a minute . . ."

I turned in time to see Camy vomit. A moment later the cramps hit me. All the leaves I'd eaten came back up in a disgusting green mass. And then another. And then I felt it at the other end of my body.

When it was over, I moved away, toward a hillock of mossy sedge, and lay down. The nanomeds were efficient; I would feel better in just a few moments, and there would be no lingering toxins in my body. But that wasn't what bothered me.

"That takes care of lunch," Seliku said, flopping down beside me. Worms crawled toward her tail. "Oh, I hate this place."

Bej said passionately, "We weren't meant for this life. This is how animals live, not people!"

I took this as a moral statement, not a biological one. Anyway, I didn't have the heart to argue.

Camy, always the most fastidious of us, said, "There's sand over there. I'm going to scrub my disgusting ass."

Seliku rolled onto her side to face me. "Alo, those were the same leaves we've been eating all along. Exactly the same. You said so."

"Yes. The only thing I can figure out is that they were enantiomorphs."

Seliku said, "Mirror images."

"Yes. Some molecules, especially but not exclusively crystals, are right-handed and some are left-handed—they're called enantiomorphs of each other. Biologicals can usually digest only one or the other."

Bej said, "Mirror images of each other. Like us."

I smiled at her. "I sense an artwork coming on."

"Maybe." She smiled back, and I thought: *This is the only good moment we've had on this foul satellite.*

Camy screamed.

The three of us jumped up. Bej raced toward Camy and I yelled, "No, Bej! Stop!"

"She's sinking!"

"Stop! You'll go, too! I've seen this, I can help her! Camy, don't struggle! Arch backward and lie slowly—slowly—onto your back and spread your arms and legs as wide as you can. *Slowly.*"

She had only sunk into the quicksand a little above her ankles. She arched backward and spread her four tentacles. I could see them tremble. Her feet didn't come up from the sand but she sank no further, bent backward like a bow, her eyes and mouth just above the sand. "Please . . . oh, please . . ."

Arlbenists prayed. We did not. I yanked the rope from my belt and threw it toward Camy. It wasn't long enough and fell short. Before I could even ask, Bej had her rope out and was knotting the two together, her digits trembling. I talked to Camy, anything that came into my mind: "Camy it's going to be all right I've seen this on ^3982 and ^12983, it's just ordinary sand mixed with upswelling water and so it behaves like a liquid, it will buoy you up just like any water—" On ^3982 I had seen a small biological sucked down by quicksand in the time it took me to open my pack. "We'll get you out it's going to be fine, remember when we were children, we played at rescuing each other on quiet planets and—" What was I saying? This was no game. Fear makes idiots of us all.

The rope reached her on my second throw. Slowly, carefully, we pulled her out. The four of us collapsed in a heap on the dry hillock. No one spoke; we just clutched each other hard enough to bruise.

Nanomeds would fix the bruises.

It was Seliku who pulled away first. "Sister-selves—it's time to go home."

Bej said, shocked, "Without Haradil?"

"Without Haradil. Bejers, she'd dead. She wanted to die. This is the trail she was following. She came to this . . . this 'quicksand,' just as we did. And she wanted to die."

Bej's head whipped around to stare at the quicksand. I saw the moment she rejected Seliku's logic. "You don't know that!"

"But it's almost certainly true," I said. "Seliku's right. There's nothing more we can do here."

"We can find Haradil again!" Camy, surprising me. But I shouldn't have been surprised; she and Bej nearly always thought as one. "Akilo can go on tracking her!"

"No, I can't. Not through this."

"You mean you won't! How can you even think of leaving a sister-self? Especially *here*, in this place—"

Covered with wet sand, smelling of vomit and diarrhea, Camy took a step back from me. Bej went with her. Bej said, "We won't go back without Haradil. How can you even think about it? We came here to get her and to find out what happened and we haven't accomplished either one. Yet you want us to go back to Calyx, with everyone knowing that our sister-self, that we . . . that she destroyed a *planetful of sentients* and you just—"

"Which are you really terrified of, losing Haradil or your own shame?" I demanded, out of my own shame, my own loss. "Is Haradil the only one being selfish here?"

They flew at me, simultaneously, as if it were choreographed.

Bej's fist hit me in the mouth. Camy punched me in the stomach and I went down. I couldn't see, couldn't breathe. When I could, they had Seliku down, too. We would have been evenly matched, Seliku and I against the two of them, but they'd struck first. My nanomeds began working and I tried to get up, but my feet and tentacles were tangled in the long rope we had used to rescue Camy.

"I'm sorry, I'm sorry, it's Haradil," I heard Bej say. By the time Seliku and I had recovered our breath and untied the vine, Bej and Camy were running back the way we had come, toward the fern forest.

We could have followed them. Their fresh scent would have made it easy. But Seliku and I were equal in strength and stamina to them —*were* them. Sister-selves. They could probably stay as just ahead of us as they were now. And if we did catch them, then what? Another fight? Another unthinkable severing of self from self?

I had thought before that I knew what it was like to be alone. I had been wrong.

Seliku and I gazed at each other. Finally she nodded.

"Yes," I answered.

She gazed bleakly at the gray sky. "Not today, there's not enough sunlight. We'll need to spend the night here."

Silently we took out our blankets and spread them on the mossy hillock. It seemed to take forever for darkness to fall. Neither of us mentioned making a fire. It occurred to me then that Bej and Camy could have tied us up, cut off our cloth belts and taken not only our blankets but the spores of the floaters, thus ensuring that all four of us would stay here. Perhaps they hadn't had time, or hadn't thought of it. Perhaps it was something they wouldn't have done.

I no longer knew.

Toward morning the clouds blew over and the sky turned clear and starlit. The gas giant was just setting. I lay on my back, having slept not at all, and looked for a long time at the unfamiliar constellations. QUENTIAM was up there, among the cold stars.

"Seliku," I said softly, "are you awake?"

"Yes."

I groped for the way to phrase such an unfamiliar question. "When the gravitons you talked about 'leak' from the universe — where do they go?"

"The math says they go into other universes."

"Right beside ours?"

" 'Beside' isn't the right concept. Other universes co-exist with ours. It's called a multiverse."

"Do the other universes have their own spacetime?"

"Presumably."

"Is it like ours? Four-dimensional?"

"We don't know."

"Do these other universes—could they—have life?"

"Presumably," Seliku said. I heard her shift in the darkness.

"Could life there have created their own membranes, woven into the fabric of their spacetime?"

She said, "And could that universe be an enantiomorph of our own? Is that what you're asking?"

I raised myself on one elbow to gaze at her, but could only make out her blanketed profile. "You knew."

"No, of course not. But I guessed, after you described the enantiomorph flora. And right after that, Camy—"

"Yes. Sel, is another universe somehow contacting ours? Through QUENTIAM?"

" 'Contacting' may be the wrong word," Seliku said, and I recognized the scientist's caution. "It's more like . . . the two universes bump into each other. A lot of energy would be released from even a small bump. In fact, one theory about the origin of matter is that it resulted from a huge collision between universes. There's so much we don't know, Alo. Technology has gone so far ahead of basic theory. It couldn't always have been this way, or QUENTIAM wouldn't know as much as It does."

"But if two universes bump and energy is released, a lot of energy, wouldn't QUENTIAM absorb it?"

"As much as It could. Think of it this way: You drop a stone in a pond. It creates ripples. Then the pond settles back down. Drop a bigger stone, and you create bigger ripples. Afterward, the pond is subtly changed. The water level is a bit higher, the topography of the pond bottom a little different."

"Don't talk down to me, Sel."

"Sorry. I find it hard to talk to nonscientists about my field."

As did I. My irritation dissolved.

She continued, "To take the metaphor just a bit farther, hurl a big asteroid at a planet. Depending on where it hits, you get a huge crater, a tsunami, an axial wobble, climate changes, biological die-offs. Everything reconfigures. If QUENTIAM is getting hit with some sort of enantiomorph of energy or matter—maybe some version of gravitons—It's being forced to reconfigure spacetime.

That's been theoretically possible forever, in small dimensions: it's called a flop transition. We understand the mathematics. QUENTIAM might be doing that in our universal dimensions. And if parts of QUENTIAM Itself are being destroyed either by bumping the other universe or by the reconfiguration, It might not even know that was happening."

"Haradil—"

"She was merged with QUENTIAM. She wouldn't know, either. And a star system died."

All at once I remembered the machine body on the shuttle to Calyx. It had momentarily gone rigid, refused to function. I had said then, even knowing how ridiculous the statement was, that the machine body had "fainted." Machine states were intricately linked with QUENTIAM.

I said, with the numb calm of shock, "You have to tell QUENTIAM. Have to tell everybody. Maybe that's even why there was no record of the first seeding of that planet that Haradil destroyed . . . QUENTIAM's *records* . . . you have to tell—"

"Don't you think I know that?" Seliku's irritation was back. "That's why we're leaving our sister-selves here tomorrow."

Was that why? Or was it because we had finally come to some mental and moral place where our sisters were no longer ourselves? Or was it just because we could no longer stand this cursed moon one more minute?

I could no longer tell my reasons—our reasons—apart.

I could no longer be sure of anything.

Dawn came clear and warm. Seliku and I tore open our cloth belts and dumped the spores on the mossy ground. Carefully—so carefully—we sopped up a little water from the squishy edge of the quicksand and wrung it over them. In just a few minivals, the spores opened and the floaters began to form around us.

"Seliku, what if QUENTIAM hasn't recreated the shuttle or the station? What if It couldn't? If there's nothing there . . ." I had to ask, even though I already knew the answer.

"Then we die." A moment later she added, "I don't have enough information to do the math, Alo. I'm sorry."

All five of us take on more accountability than should properly be ours.

The floaters sealed and began to rise. I had engineered this group for a gravity greater than this one, and they would just rise until they ran out of air and died. Still, the trip upstairs, going against gravity, would be longer than the one going down. We drifted out over the quicksand, and I tried not to think of Haradil, possibly sunk somewhere beneath that gritty alien lake. The tough, thick membrane around me magnified the sunlight and I grew uncomfortably, but not dangerously, warm. I lay cradled in the sag of floater created by my weight. Maybe it was the warmth but, incredibly, I fell asleep. When I woke, the shuttle was in view, a dark speck growing larger against the pale-slug color of the gas giant.

We had no way to steer. I couldn't see Seliku's floater; winds had carried us apart. Already the membrane that was my floater had thinned, weakened by the less concentrated sunlight and fewer atmospheric molecules at this altitude.

QUENTIAM, come through for us . . .

The shuttle turned and started toward me.

I barely made it into the airlock, holding my breath and enduring the bodily shock while the airlock pressurized. The capillaries in my eyeballs popped and my eyes filled with blood. Then Seliku was pulling me into the shuttle and my nanomeds were going to work.

"Alo! Are you—"

"F-fine," I gasped.

"Rest here, sister." She stretched me out on the deck.

QUENTIAM said on the shuttle's system, "You two went downstairs to a quiet planet."

"It's been scolding me since I got aboard," Seliku said grimly.

"Going downstairs to a quiet planet is forbidden."

"S-Sel . . . did you . . ."

"I've been trying to tell It," she snapped. "QUENTIAM, *listen to me.* We found Haradil. When she destroyed that star system, she was merged with you, and it was *you* who destroyed it. One theory is—"

"I did not destroy the star system containing ^5387. I would remember."

"You don't remember because it wasn't a decision you actually made. Spacetime may have been reconfigured in a giant flop transition after another universe in the multiverse bumped into this universe—"

"I remember everything. I did not destroy the star system containing ^5387."

"—and huge amounts of energy were released. Haradil's art project with the asteroid must have been near the impact point. So—"

Lying on the floor, listening, an irrelevant part of my mind wondered at the ease with which Seliku spoke in whole universes.

"—your memory of the event was reconfigured when spacetime was. You lost a nanosecond of time. The energy—"

"I have lost no time. I cannot lose time. Oscillations of gravitons through time are part of my functioning."

"I'm not talking about gravitons, QUENTIAM. Listen—"

She launched into complicated explanations, with terms and principles I could not follow. What was clear to me was QUENTIAM's utter refusal of her reasoning. And in one sense Its refusal *was* more reasonable than her wild statements. QUENTIAM wanted proof, physical or experimental or mathematical. She had none.

My nanomeds repaired my body and I stood. The meal created by the food-synthesizer was the best I have ever tasted. I made Seliku eat. She didn't want to. She sat in the front seat of the shut-tle, no longer arguing with QUENTIAM, but instead asking for equations on the display, staring at them, asking QUENTIAM to perform various complex mathematical processes. I knew better than to interrupt for long. After she ate a few bites, I left them alone.

"The shuttle has reached the t-hole," QUENTIAM said to me. "Where do you wish to go?"

I hesitated, for more reasons than one.

"Seliku . . . Sel?"

I don't think she even heard me.

"Seliku!"

"What? I'm working!"

"We're at the t-hole. Where are we going? And is it safe to go through? If your parallel universe bumps while we're—"

"It's not 'my' parallel universe." Then her irritation vanished and she gave me her full attention. "I know what you're asking, Alo. It might not be safe. But if this goes on, if I'm right about the multiverse, and if this series of bumps and spacetime reconfigurations doesn't end soon, then nothing is going to be safe ever again."

"You are talking nonsense," QUENTIAM said.

I said, "Where do you need to go to make this . . . your theory known? To warn everyone?"

As soon as I said it, I knew how stupid it was. The way to warn everyone, the way to disseminate any kind of information throughout the galaxy, was through QUENTIAM. And QUENTIAM did not believe us.

I saw that Seliku was thinking the same thing. Slowly she said, "We should go back to Calyx, I guess. The Communion of Cosmology is there. It's something, anyway."

"QUENTIAM," I said, "We're going to Calyx."

The shuttle slipped through the t-hole. I would have held my breath, but of course I couldn't tell exactly when it happened until it was over and the stars changed configuration. Calyx rotated just below us. The city-continent came into view and the blue sea gave way to the riot of colors that was Bej and Camy's flower art. For the first time since Seliku had first told me about Haradil, my eyes filled with tears. We are not easy criers.

"I want a new body," Seliku said. "No matter what the risk. I won't stay in this one a minival longer than I have to. Not one minival."

Her tone was violent. I knew, without turning around, that she was crying, too.

The first thing I did on Calyx was get a new body from QUENTIAM. Burn the risk; I could not stay a minival longer in this ugly, ineffective shell whose every pore breathed ^17843.

"You know it's a risk," Seliku said. She had barely paused long enough to clean herself before hurrying off to the Communion of Cosmologists. "If QUENTIAM takes a bump near here while you're in the nanomachinery . . ."

"I'll take the chance," I said, and then added, "And so will you. You'll make your initial impact on all those unsuspecting cosmologists and then just work on in upload state while QUENTIAM makes you a body."

She did need to answer. "What body are you choosing?"

"The one we use in bond time."

She nodded sadly and left, dragging her body through the gravity it had not been designed for.

On my way to a vat room, I took the short walk to the sea. A fresh wind stirred up small waves and blew toward me the fragrance of blossoms. So much color: magenta and cerulean, scarlet and damson, rose and crimson and delphinium. I rolled the words in my mind. This, then, was how my remote ancestors had lived, wondering if each moment might be their last. They must have had unimaginable courage. Either that or they were all crazy all the time.

I went to the vat room, climbed into an available vat, and uploaded into QUENTIAM.

Are you sure, Akilo, that you don't want implants in the new body? It asked.

I'm sure. No implants.

Is this because of the nonsense Seliku has been saying?

No implants, QUENTIAM. That's my choice.

Yes, it is.

The human mind does not do well in upload without visual simulations. I considered my standard sim, a forested bedroom copied from ^894, and rejected it. Nor did I want our childhood home, or Calyx. Too many memories. Instead I created an austere room with a simple table, single chair, and display screen. An open window looked out on a bare, rocky plain. It was a room for thinking, for concentration.

Seliku would have known what to look for in QUENTIAM, what data or processes, to see if It was fundamentally different. I did not. Instead I asked questions, an endless stream of questions, about the multiverse and spacetime. Some of the answers I didn't understand. Some seemed contradictory. Since I didn't know whether this was inherent in the science or represented a flaw in QUENTIAM, I gave up on the whole thing, created a door in my room, and went for a walk on the soothingly blank plain. No pulpy green, no looming fronds, no treacherous sand. Firm ground underneath my "feet," and a horizon I could scan in all directions.

The Arlbenists are wrong to think that filling the universe is a divine mission. Sometimes the best healer is emptiness.

I was examining some old, round rocks of my own imagining when QUENTIAM suddenly said, *Akilo. Magnitude one news message.*

What?

The Mori Core has been destroyed.

Destroyed?

Yes. There was an explosion and the entire structure crumpled from within.

Do you . . . do you have visuals?

Yes.

And then I was back in my austere room, watching the huge Mori Core cease to exist. The visuals were from the outside and slightly above, perhaps from a very low orbital. The Core, a huge precise structure of concentric rings, covered half a subcontinent.

The Mori, in direct opposition to the Arlbenists, have over time made themselves more and more biologically similar, while the Arlbenists became more and more diverse in order to seed strange worlds. Mori favor substantial, heavily furred biologicals and cold worlds. The Core stood frosted with icicles, while the winter gardens between the concentric rings bloomed with low, lacy plants in alabaster, ivory, silver, very pale blue. People with white fur walked in the gardens.

The next moment the entire huge structure was gone and a blinding flash of light filled my screen.

★Was the First Mori in residence?★

★Yes.★

I tried to sort out my feelings. The Mori had claimed more and more worlds, had imposed their own ideas of order and justice on them, had sent Haradil to ^17843 for a monstrosity she did not commit. But the Mori were not fundamentally evil—and they were *people*.

★How many . . . how many sentients died?★

'19,805,012 humans, 15,090 androids, 598,654 enhanced dokins.★

I braced myself. ★What caused the explosion, QUENTIAM?★

★Quark release seems to best fit the data.★

★Who used a quark-release device?★

★Unknown.★

★QUENTIAM—★

★Akilo, I cannot monitor humans without implants if there are no sensors in their immediate indoor environments. You and your sister-selves demonstrated that already. I don't know what human had a quark-release device inside the Core, or why, or what motive existed for the sabotage. I have reported that to the new First Mori, on ^10236.★

★Are you sure the . . . the saboteur was human?★

★Androids are not created to cause any damage without direct human instruction, and dokins do not have the intellectual capacity to detonate, let alone create, a quark-release device. Therefore, by simple logic, the destroyer was human.★

In upload—but not in merger—my thoughts are a separate program, hidden from QUENTIAM unless I choose to address It.

★Is my new body almost done?★

★No.★

★Get me a link to Seliku.★

She looked at me from the display screen, still in her ^17843 body. She must have been standing in some great hall of the Communion of Cosmologists. Behind her rose tall pillars covered with flowers. "I heard, Akilo. And no, I can't tell one way or the other, not for certain. There are a lot of people who hate the Mori, for religious or personal reasons. It could have been a human or . . . or not."

"Your best guess."

"Not."

That is nonsense. QUENTIAM said. *Seliku, I wish you would stop disseminating this misinformation.*

In Seliku's eyes, an exact image of the real Seliku, I saw fear.

QUENTIAM's *parameters protect you from any retaliation by It*, I wanted to say to her. But she already knew that. And she knew, too, that Its parameters could be the next thing to change.

"Does the Communion have data on the explosion?" I asked her.

"Yes, we have all QUENTIAM's measurements. We're sorting the data now. Alo, come home."

She knew I couldn't hurry the creation of my body. Her plea had nothing to do with logic.

"I'm coming," I said, "as fast as I can."

Nothing else happened before my body was done, except for one thing: I dreamed.

This was the second time I had dreamed in upload, supposedly an impossibility. To shorten the unbearable time waiting for my biological, I had put myself in down-program mode within QUENTIAM. There should have been no thoughts, no sensation, no anything. But a sort of sudden current ran through me and then I had the dream, the same one as before: Something menacing and ill-defined chased me through a shifting landscape, something unknowably vast, coming closer and closer, its terrifying breath on my back, its—

Your body is ready.

I downloaded into the body, climbed from the vat, and looked in the mirror.

It was us, the body my sister-selves and I always used for bond time. A female all-human with pale brown skin, head hair in a dark green crest, black eyes. Four coiled tentacles, each a meter long, the digits slim and graceful—the body we would have grown up with had our creation occurred on a quiet planet. Nothing seemed amiss with the body. QUENTIAM had had the nanos make it perfectly.

I let out a long breath.

"I can still add an implant, you know. Not a full one, now that the brain is grown, but still very functional."

"No, thank you, QUENTIAM."

"It makes communication so much fuller."

"No, thank you."

"As you choose."

"Please tell Seliku that I'm done."

"She knows."

She came through the door a few minivals later, dragging her heavy, small body, looking as exhausted as she had on ^17843. I was over twice as tall as she, probably three times as strong. I picked her up and carried her, unprotesting, to the beach. We sat at the very edge of the land, our feet in the warm sea, away from any of QUENTIAM's sensors.

"Anything, Sel?"

"No. I can't even convince most of the Communion. They're good cosmologists, but they weren't there. They didn't see the shuttle go, the station go. They still think that Haradil destroyed that star system, and they probably think my demented theory is a mind-defense to keep from acknowledging that. The only thing I've got on my side is my reputation, and I'm straining that."

I nodded. "Sel, while I was in upload, I dreamed."

She didn't tell me that was impossible. She closed her eyes, as if absorbing a blow. I described the dream, adding, "I think it wasn't my dream. I think it was QUENTIAM's. Upload is supposed to be a separate subprogram within It, but I think I was—in some very tiny, tiny way—beyond upload into merged state. Sel, I don't think you should get another body."

Her eyes remained closed, and her face grimaced in pain.

"I'm not saying that nanomachinery and even t-holes aren't safe. Or if they're not, it will be one finite explosion, like Haradil's system or the Mori Core, and we'll be dead before we even realize it. But the upload state, even the machine state . . ." I remembered Haradil saying *I was QUENTIAM.*

"Yes," Seliku said. "You're right."

"Once before I dreamed in upload, the same dream. It was the day you first told me about Haradil. So even then . . . even then."

"Yes. You were just lucky about your body." She opened her eyes and looked at it longingly.

"I'm sorry," I said, inadequately.

"Not your fault. Will you carry me to the Communion hall? I'm very tired."

"Of course I will."

Tenderly I carried my sister-self back to her work. It was almost like cradling a child. I saw that there must come a new relationship between me and my one remaining sister-self, physically frail on this planet but mentally leading a crusade to convince the galaxy of cataclysmic danger. I would be her protector, caretaker, aide. The change between us was permanent. Nothing would ever be the same again.

I was wrong. Many things are the same.

Seliku has been unable to convince the galaxy of her theory. She has won a few adherents among cosmologists, but for most people, the idea that QUENTIAM might be decaying, might be unreliable, is impossible to even consider. It's like saying gravity is unreliable. Which, I suppose, might happen next. *That* would convince everybody, or at least everybody who survived it.

Meanwhile, some do not survive. There have been mistakes in vat nanos, creating bodies other than ordered, or killing the bodies before they were done. No one knows how many mistakes; I no longer trust QUENTIAM's records.

A new quasar has appeared in the sky, and six supernovas, all outside our galaxy. They filled the sky, night after night, with brilliant light. Seliku says that is too many supernovas to be statistically random, but not even her colleagues all believe her. She works night and day to find the evidence, physical or experimental or mathematical, that may convince them. Her big question is this: Is the unseen other universe just brushing ours in passing, creating supernovas and quasars and small reconfigurations of spacetime that also change and reconfigure QUENTIAM? Or are the two universes set for a full collision, from which neither will emerge without changes so fundamental that basic particles themselves are affected, and all life ceases?

The Arlbenists were wrong, in ways they could never have foreseen when Arlbeni created his Divine Mission over a hundred thousand years ago. We were never alone in the galaxy, and not only because spores have drifted in from beyond its edges and seeded non-DNA-based life here. Even without that panspermia, we were not alone. Humans were already everywhere because QUENTIAM, our collective and historical selves, filled spacetime. And we weren't alone in a much more profound sense.

I have suggested another question to Seliku, as well. Is it possible that the other universe, too, has a membrane like QUENTIAM, but more advanced? And that It knows what It's doing in probing ours? On ^17843, Seliku likened our brushes with the other universe to stones dropping in a pond. Dropped stones sometimes have droppers.

Seliku dismisses this question, not because it's completely stupid but because for that there really is no evidence. But I know she can imagine it. She is my sister-self, still, and sister-self to artists as well. She can imagine a Dropper of stones into the cosmic well between universes.

What is It, or Them, like? Do they guess what effects their experiments have on us?

None of this speculation reaches the Arlbenists, who still blithely seed worlds in the egocentric belief that only humans can create life. I, however, no longer correct and adjust Arlbenist seedings on other worlds. I won't risk the vat rooms necessary for that. And I have my own work here, now, both in aiding Seliku in her all-important fight and in caring for her. Her nanomeds keep her healthy, but her body is not meant for this planet and is not doing well here. It doesn't, surprisingly, bother me that I never leave Culyu. This is, finally, home, here with my new work and my sister-self. I am learning to grow a garden of edible plants, without nanos and without QUENTIAM, just in case. In a weird way, I'm not uncontent.

Not that Calyx looks the same, either. A new artist received the design privilege when Bej and Camy's franchise ended. His name is Kiibceroti, and he has made of Calyx a serene, spare city. Gone are the gorgeous, lush flowers, replaced by gentle curves of sand in soft pastels, with perhaps one dark rock placed precisely at the edge of the curve and a single tall fern. I don't much like the ferns, or the overall design. But I admit that it's beautiful in its own way. There is something melancholy about it, something of grief. Someone told me that Kiibceroti lost a brother-self in the Mori Core, but I don't know if that's true. I could ask QUENTIAM, but I ask QUENTIAM very little these days.

One good thing about Kiibceroti's city: All that low-key tranquility is good for dreaming. I dream now, nearly every night. Last night I dreamed of Bej and Camy.

I dreamed they had joined the settlement of prisoners on ^17843, somehow making peace with them, finding companionship and working together to create whatever good exists on that pulpy moon. Bej and Camy cut their arms and shared the nanomeds from their bodies, and the fungi disappeared from everyone's heads and feet. None of them would die.

Then I saw Bej and Camy walking on a seashore with their friends, all approaching some large object in the distance. In the dream, I walked with them. As we neared the object, I saw that it was a great boulder thrown up by the sea millennia ago. Camy and Bej had painstakingly chipped away at it over vast amounts of time, using other sharp stones and their own artistic talent. They had polished the stone with sand and the statue shone in the sunlight with bits of mica and quartz. It was Haradil, smiling and happy, solid by the blue sea for as long as the waves permitted the sculpture to last.

"Alo?" Seliku said sleepily beside me.

I laid my tentacles protectively across her body and moved slightly to nestle closer to her. "I'm here, sister-self. Go back to sleep. We're still here."

Afterword to "Mirror Image"

This is my favorite story in this collection, despite the fact that it got almost no attention from anybody else. I'm hard-pressed to say why it's my favorite. Akilo is not a particularly sympathetic main character. The story is very high-tech and far-future, almost demanding a background of reading much SF in order to be understood at all.

Perhaps it's my favorite because it allowed me to play with genuinely large ideas. After all, QUENTIAM spans the galaxy and monitors most of humanity. Haradil mistakenly destroys an entire star system. The climax involves other universes, or at least other theoretical, mysterious structures attributed to our own universe, such as branes. The first SF novel I ever read, Arthur C. Clarke's Childhood's End, *unfolded on a similarly vast canvas. Perhaps one can get imprinted, like a baby duck, on vastness.*

Much of the scientific background for "Mirror Image" was drawn from Brian Greene's wonderful and erudite book, The Fabric of the Cosmos. *Now there's a person who thinks large.*

My Mother, Dancing

FERMI'S PARADOX, CALIFORNIA, 1950: SINCE PLANET FORMAtion appears to be common, and since the processes that lead to the development of life are a continuation of those that develop planets, and since the development of life leads to intelligence and intelligence to technology—then why hasn't a single alien civilization contacted Earth?

Where is everybody?

They had agreed, laughing, on a form for the millennium contact, what Micah called "human standard," although Kabil had insisted on keeping hirs konfol and Deb had not dissolved hirs crest, which waved three inches above hirs and hummed. But, then, Deb! Ling had designed floating baktor for the entire ship, red and yellow mostly, that combined and recombined in kaleidoscopic loveliness only Ling could have programmed. The viewport was set to magnify, the air mixture just slightly intoxicating, the tinglies carefully balanced by Cal, that master. Ling had wanted "natural" sleep cycles, but Cal's argument had been more persuasive, and the tinglies massaged the limbic so pleasantly. Even the child had some. It was a party.

The ship slipped into orbit around the planet, a massive sub-Jovian far from its sun, streaked with muted color "Lovely," breathed Deb, who lived for beauty.

Cal, the biologist, was more practical: "I ran the equations; by now there should be around 200,000 of them in the rift, if the replication rate stayed constant."

"Why wouldn't it?" said Ling, the challenger, and the others laughed. The tinglies really were a good idea.

The child, Harrah, pressed hirs face to the window. "When can we land?"

The adults smiled at each other. They were so proud of Harrah, and so careful. Hirs was the first gene-donate for all of them except Micah, and probably the only one for the rest except Cal, who was a certified intellect donor. Kabil knelt beside Harrah, bringing hirs face to the child's height.

"Little love, we can't land. Not here. We must see the creations in holo."

"Oh," Harrah said, with the universal acceptance of childhood. It had not changed in five thousand years, Ling was fond of remarking, that child idea that whatever it lived was the norm. But, then . . . Ling.

"Access the data," Cal said, and Harrah obeyed, reciting it aloud as hirs parents had all taught hirs. Ling smiled to see that Harrah still closed hirs eyes to access, but opened them to recite.

"The creations were dropped on this planet 273 E-years ago. They were the one-hundred-fortieth drop in the Great Holy Mission that gives us our life. The creations were left in a closed-system rift . . . what does that mean?"

"The air in the creations' valley doesn't get out to the rest of the planet, because the valley is so deep and the gravity so great. They have their own air."

"Oh. The creations are cyborged replicators, programmed for self-awareness. They are also programmed to expect human contact at the millennium. They . . ."

"Enough," said Kabil, still kneeling beside Harrah. Hirs stroked hirs hair, black today. "The important thing, Harrah, is that you remember that these creations are beings, different from us but with the same life force, the only life force. They must be respected, just as people are, even if they look odd to you."

"Or if they don't know as much as you," said Cal. "They won't, you know."

"I know," Harrah said. They had made hirs an accommodater, with strong genes for bonding. They already had Ling for challenge. Harrah added, "Praise Fermi and Kwang and Arlbeni for the emptiness of the universe."

Ling frowned. Hirs had opposed teaching Harrah the simpler, older folklore of the Great Mission. Ling would have preferred that the child receive only truth, not religion. But Deb had insisted. Feed the imagination first, hirs had said, and later Harrah can separate science from prophecy. But the tinglies felt sweet, and the air mixture was set for a party, and hirs own baktors floated in such graceful pattern that Ling, not even Ling, could not quarrel.

"I wonder," Deb said dreamily, "what they have learned in 273 years."

"When will they holo?" Harrah said. "Are we there yet?"

Our mother is coming.

Two hours more and they will come, from beyond the top of the world. When they come, there will be much dancing. Much rejoicing. All of us will dance, even those who have detached and let the air carry them away. Those ones will receive our transmissions and dance with us.

Or maybe our mother will also transmit to where those of us now sit. Maybe they will transmit to all, even those colonies out of our own transmission range. Why not? Our mother, who made us, can do whatever is necessary.

First, the dancing. Then, the most necessary thing of all. Our mother will solve the program flaw. Completely, so that no more of us will die. Our mother doesn't die. We are not supposed to die, either. Our mother will transmit the program to correct this.

Then what dancing there will be!

Kwang's Resolution, Bohr Station, 2552: Since the development of the Quantum Transport, humanity has visited nearly a thousand planets in our galaxy and surveyed many more. Not one of them has developed any life of any kind, no matter how simple. Not one.

No aliens have contacted Earth because there is nobody else out there.

Harrah laughed in delight. Hirs long, black hair swung through a drift of yellow baktors. "The creations look like oysters!"

The holocube showed uneven, rocky ground through thick, murky air. A short distance away rose the abrupt, steep walls of the rift, thousands of feet high. Attached to the ground by thin, flexible, mineral-conducting tubes were hundreds of uniform, metal-alloy double shells. The shells held self-replicating nanomachinery, including the rudimentary AI, and living eukaryotes sealed into selectively permeable membranes. The machinery ran on the feeble sunlight and on energy produced by anaerobic bacteria, carefully engineered for the thick atmospheric stew of methane, hydrogen, helium, ammonia, and carbon dioxide.

The child knew none of this. Hirs saw the "oysters" jumping up in time on their filaments, jumping and falling, flapping their shells open and closed, twisting and flapping and bobbing. Dancing.

Kabil laughed, too. "Nowhere in the original programming! They learned it!"

"But what could the stimulus have been?" Ling said. "How lovely to find out!"

"Sssshhh, we're going to transmit," Micah said. Hirs eyes glowed. Micah was the oldest of them all; hirs had been on the original drop. "Seeding 140, are you there?"

"We are here! We are Seeding 140! Welcome, our mother!"

Harrah jabbed hirs finger at the holocube. "We're not your mother!"

Instantly Deb closed the transmission. Micah said harshly, "Harrah! Your manners!"

The child looked scared. Deb said, "Harrah, we talked about this. The creations are not like us, but their ideas are as true as ours, on their own world. Don't laugh at them."

From Kabil, "Don't you remember, Harrah? Access the learning session!"

"I . . . remember," Harrah faltered.

"Then show some respect!" Micah said. "This is the Great Mission!"

Harrah's eyes teared. Kabil, the tender-hearted, put hirs hand on Harrah's shoulder. "Small heart, the Great Mission gives meaning to our lives."

"I . . . know . . ."

Micah said, "You don't want to be like those people who just use up all their centuries in mere pleasure, with no structure to their wanderings across the galaxy, no purpose beyond seeing what the nanos can produce that they haven't produced before, no difference between today and tomorrow, no—"

"That's sufficient," Ling said. "Harrah understands, and regrets. Don't give an Arlbeni Day speech, Micah."

Micah said stiffly, "It matters, Ling."

"Of course it matters. But so do the creations, and they're waiting. Deb, open the transmission again. . . . Seeding 140, thank you for your welcome! We return!"

*   *   *

Arlbeni's Vision, Planet Cadrys, 2678: We have been fools.

Humanity is in despair. Nano has given us everything, and nothing. Endless pleasures empty of effort, endless tomorrows empty of purpose, endless experiences empty of meaning. From evolution to sentience, sentience to nano, nano to the decay of sentience.

But the fault is ours. We have overlooked the greatest gift ever given humanity: the illogical emptiness of the universe. It is against evolution, it is against known physical processes. Therefore, how can it exist? And why?

It can exist only by the intent of something greater than the physical processes of the universe. A conscious Intent.

The reason can only be to give humanity, the universe's sole inheritor, knowledge of this Intent. The emptiness of the universe— anomalous, unexplainable, impossible—has been left for us to discover, as the only convincing proof of God.

Our mother has come! We dance on the seabed. We transmit the news to the ones who have detached and floated away. We rejoice together, and consult the original program.

"You are above the planetary atmosphere," we say, new words until just this moment, but now understood. All will be understood now, all corrected. "You are in a ship, as we are in our shells."

"Yes," our mother says. "You know we cannot land."

"Yes," we say, and there is momentary dysfunction. How can they help us if they cannot land? But only momentary. This is our mother. And they landed us here once, didn't they? They can do whatever is necessary.

Our mother says, "How many are you now, Seeding 140?"

"We are 79,432," we say. Sadness comes. We endure it, as we must.

Our mother's voice changes in wavelength, in frequency. "Seventy-nine thousand? Are you . . . we had calculated more. Is this replication data right?"

A packet of data arrives. We scan it quickly; it matches our programming.

"The data is correct, our mother. That is the rate of replication. But . . ." We stop. It feels like another dying ceremony, suddenly, and it is not yet time for a dying ceremony. We will wait another few minutes; we will tell our mother in another few minutes. Instead, we ask, "What is your rate of replication, our mother?"

Another change in wavelength and frequency. We scan and

match data, and it is in our databanks: laughter, a form of rejoicing. Our mother rejoices.

"You aren't equipped for visuals, or I would show you our replicant," our mother says. "But the rate is much, much lower than yours. We have one new replicant with us on the ship."

"Welcome, new replicant!" we say, and there is more rejoicing. There, and here.

"I've restricted transmission . . . there's the t-field's visual," Micah said.

A hazy cloud appeared to one side of the holocube, large enough to hold two people comfortably, three close together. Only words spoken inside the field would now transmit. Raktors scuttled clear of the ionized haze. Deb stepped inside the field, with Harrah; Cal moved out of it. Hira frowned at Micah.

"They can't be only 79,000-plus if the rate of replication has held steady. Check the resource data, Micah."

"Scanning . . . No change in available raw materials . . . no change in sunlight per square unit."

"Scan their counting program."

"I already did. Fully functional."

"Then run a historical scan of replicants created."

"That will take time . . . there, it's started. What about attrition?"

Cal said, "Of course. I should have thought of that. Do a seismic survey and match it with the original data. A huge quake could easily have destroyed two-thirds of them, poor seedings . . ."

Ling said, "You could *ask* them."

Kabil said, "If it's not a cultural taboo. Remember, they have had time to evolve a culture, we left them that ability."

"Only in response to environmental stimuli. Would a quake or mudslide create enough stimulus pressure to evolve death taboos?"

They looked at each other. Something new in the universe, something humanity had not created . . . this was why they were here! Their eyes shone, their breaths came faster. Yet they were uncomfortable, too, at the mention of death. How long since any of them . . . oh, yes, Ling's clone, in that computer malfunction, but so many decades ago . . . Discomfort, excitement, compassion for Seeding 140, yes compassion most of all, how terrible if the poor creations had actually lost so many in a quake . . . All of them felt it, and meant it, the emotion was genuine. And in their minds the finger of God touched each for a moment, with the holiness of the tiny, human struggle against the emptiness of the universe.

"Praise Fermi and Kwang and Arlbeni . . ." one of them murmured, and no one was sure who, in the general embarrassment that took them a moment later. They were not children.

Micah said, "Match the seismic survey with the original data," and moved off to savor alone the residue of natural transcendence, rarest and strangest of the few things nano could not provide.

Inside the hazy field Harrah said, "Seeding! I am dancing just like you!" and moved hirs small body back and forth, up and down on the ship's deck.

Arlbeni's Vision, Planet Cadrys, 2678: In the proof of God lies its corollary. The Great Intent has left the universe empty, except for us. It is our mission to fill it.

Look around you, look at what we've become. At the pointless destruction, the aimless boredom, the spiritual despair. The human race cannot exist without purpose, without vision, without faith. Filling the emptiness of the universe will rescue us from our own.

Our mother says, "Do you play any games?"

We examine the data carefully. There is no match.

Our mother speaks again. "That was our new replicant speaking, Seeding 140. Hirs is only half-created as yet, and hirs program language is not fully functional. Hirs means, of the new programs you have created for yourselves since the original seeding, which ones are in response to the environment, are expressions of rejoicing? Like dancing?"

"Yes!" we say. "We dance in rejoicing. And we also throw pebbles in rejoicing and catch pebbles in rejoicing. But not for many years since."

"Do it now!" our mother says.

This is our mother. We are not rejoicing. But this is our mother. We pick up some pebbles.

"No," our mother says quickly, "you don't need to throw pebbles. That was the new replicant again. Hirs does not yet understand that seedings do what they wish, and only what they wish. Your . . . your mother does not command you. Anything you do, anything you have learned, is as necessary as what we do."

"I'm sorry again," our mother says, and there is physical movement registered in the field of transmission.

We do not understand. But our mother has spoken of new programs, of programs created since the seeding, in response to the environment. This we understand, and now is the time to tell our mother of our need. Our mother has asked. Sorrow floods us, rejoicing disappears, but now is the time to tell what is necessary.

Our mother will make all functional once more.

"Don't scold hirs like that, hirs is just a child," Kabil said. "Harrah, stop crying, we know you didn't mean to impute to them any inferiority."

Micah, hirs back turned to the tiny parental drama, said to Cal, "Seismic survey complete. No quakes, only the most minor geologic disturbances . . . really, the local history shows remarkable stability."

"Then what accounts for the difference between their count of themselves and the replication rate?"

"It can't be a real difference."

"But . . . oh!. Listen. Did they just say—"

Hirs turned slowly toward the holocube.

Harrah said at the same moment, through hirs tears, "They stopped dancing."

Cal said, "Repeat that," remembered hirself, and moved into the transmission field, replacing Harrah. "Repeat that, please, Seeding 140. Repeat your last transmission."

The motionless metal oysters said, "We have created a new program in response to the Others in the environment. The Others who destroy us."

Cal said, very pleasantly, " 'Others'? What Others?"

"The new ones. The mindless ones. The destroyers."

"There are no others in your environment," Micah said. "What are you trying to say?"

Ling, across the deck in a cloud of pink baktors, said, "Oh, oh . . . no . . . they must have divided into factions. Invented warfare among themselves! Oh . . ."

Harrah stopped sobbing and stood, wide-eyed, on hirs sturdy, short legs.

Cal said, still very pleasant, "Seeding 140, show us these Others. Transmit visuals."

"But if we get close enough to the Others to do that, we will be destroyed!"

Ling said sadly, "It *is* warfare."

Deb compressed hirs beautiful lips. Kabil turned away, to gaze out at the stars. Micah said, "Seeding . . . do you have any historical transmissions of the Others, in your databanks? Send those."

"Scanning . . . sending."

Ling said softly, "We always knew warfare was a possibility for any creations. After all, they have our unrefined DNA, and for millennia . . ." Hirs fell silent.

"The data is only partial," Seeding 140 said. "We were nearly destroyed when it was sent to us. But there is one data packet until the last few minutes of life."

The cheerful, dancing oysters had vanished from the holocube. In their place appeared the fronds of a tall, thin plant, waving slightly in the thick air. It was stark, unadorned, elemental. A multicellular organism rooted in the rocky ground, doing nothing.

No one on the ship spoke.

The holocube changed perspective, to a wide scan. Now there were whole stands of fronds, acres of them, filling huge sections of the rift. Plant after plant, drab olive green, blowing in the unseen wind.

After the long silence, Seeding 140 said, "Our mother? The Others were not there for ninety-two years. Then they came. They replicate much faster than we do, and we die. Our mother, can you do what is necessary?"

Still no one spoke, until Harrah, frightened, said, "What is it?"

Micah answered, hirs voice clipped and precise. "According to the data packet, it is an aerobic organism, using a process analogous to photosynthesis to create energy, giving off oxygen as a by-product. The data includes a specimen analysis, broken off very abruptly as if the AI failed. The specimen is non-carbon-based, non-DNA. The energy sources sealed in Seeding 140 are anaerobic."

Ling said sharply, "Present oxygen content of the rift atmosphere?"

Cal said, "Seven point six two percent." Hirs paused. "The oxygen created by these . . . these 'Others' is poisoning the seeding."

"But," Deb said, bewildered, "why did the original drop include such a thing?"

"It didn't," Micah said. "There is no match for this structure in the gene banks. It is not from Earth."

"Our mother?" Seeding 140 said, over the motionless fronds in the holocube. "Are you still there?"

Disciple Arlbeni, Grid 743.9, 2999: As we approach this millennium marker, rejoice that humanity has passed beyond both spiritual superstition and spiritual denial. We have a faith built on physical truth, on living genetics, on human need. We have, at long last, given our souls not to a formless Deity but to the science of life itself. We are safe, and we are blessed.

Micah said suddenly, "It's a trick."

The other adults stared at hirs. Harrah had been hastily reconfigured for sleep. Someone—Ling, most likely—had dissolved the floating baktors and blanked the wall displays, and only the empty transmission field added color to the room. That, and the cold stars beyond.

"Yes," Micah continued, "a trick. Not malicious, of course. But we programmed them to learn, and they did. They had some seismic event, or some interwarfare, and it made them wary of anything unusual. They learned that the unusual can be deadly. And the most unusual thing they know of is us, set to return at 3,000. So they created a transmission program designed to repel us. Xenophobia, in a stimulus-response learning program suited to this environment. You said it yourself, Ling, the learning components are built on human genes. And we have xenophobia as an evolved survival response!"

Cal jack-knifed across the room. Tension turned hirs ungraceful. "No. That sounds appealing, but nothing we gave Seeding 140 would let them evolve defenses that sophisticated. And there was no seismic event for the initial stimulus."

Micah said eagerly, "We're the stimulus! Our anticipated return! Don't you see . . . we're the 'Others'!"

Kabil said, "But they call us 'mother'. . . . They were thrilled to see us. They're not xenophobic to us."

Deb spoke so softly the others could barely hear. "Then it's a computer malfunction. Cosmic bombardment of their sensory equipment. Or at least, of the unit that was 'dying.' Malfunctioning before the end. All that sensory data about oxygen poisoning is compromised."

"Of course!" Ling said. But hirs was always honest. "At least . . . no, compromised data isn't that coherent, the pieces don't fit together so well biochemically . . ."

"And so non-terrestrially," Cal said, and at the jagged edge in hirs voice, Micah exploded.

"California, these are not native life! There is no native life in the galaxy except on Earth!"

"I know that, Micah," Cal said, with dignity. "But I also know this data does not match anything in the d-bees."

"Then the d-bees are incomplete!"

"Possibly."

Ling put hirs hands together. They were long, slender hands, with very long nails, created just yesterday. *I want to grab the new millennium with both hands,* Ling had laughed before the party, *and hold it firm.* "Spores. Panspermia."

"I won't listen to this!" Micah said.

"An old theory," Ling went on, gasping a little. "Seeding 140 said the Others weren't there for their first hundred years. But if spores blew in from space on the solar wind, and the environment was right for them to germinate—"

Deb said quickly, "Spores aren't really life. Wherever they came from, they're not alive."

"Yes, they are," Kabil said. "Don't quibble. They're alive."

Micah said loudly, "I've given my entire life to the Great Mission. I was on the original drop for this very planet."

"They're alive," Ling said, "and they're not ours."

"My entire life!" Micah said. Hirs looked at each of them in turn, hirs face stony, and something terrible glinted behind the beautiful, deep-green eyes.

Our mother does not answer. Has our mother gone away?

Our mother would not go away without helping us. It must be they are still dancing.

We can wait.

"The main thing is Harrah, after all," Kabil said. Hirs sat slumped on the floor. They had been talking so long.

"A child needs secure knowledge. Purpose. Faith," Cal said.

Ling said wearily, "A child needs truth."

"Harrah," Deb crooned softly. "Harrah, made of all of us, future of our genes, small heart Harrah . . ."

"Stop it, Debaron," Cal said. "Please."

Micah said, "Those things down there are not real. They are not. Test it, Micah. I've said so already. Test it. Send down a probe, and try to bring back samples. There's nothing there."

"You don't know that, Micah."

"I know," Micah said, and was subtly revitalized. Hirs sprang up. "Test it!"

Ling said, "A probe isn't necessary. We have the transmitted data and—"

"Not reliable!" Micah said.

"—and the rising oxygen content. Data from our own sensors."

"Outgassing!"

"Micah, that's ridiculous. And a probe—"

"A probe might come back contaminated," Cal said.

"Don't risk contamination," Kabil said suddenly, urgently. "Not with Harrah here."

"Harrah, made of us all . . ." Deb had turned hirs back on the rest now, and lay almost curled into a ball, lost in hirs powerful imagination. Deb!

Kabil said, almost pleadingly, to Ling, "Harrah's safety should come first."

"Harrah's safety lies in facing truth," Ling said. But hirs was not strong enough to sustain it alone. They were all so close, so knotted together, a family. Knotted by Harrah and by the Great Mission, to which Ling, no less than the others, had given hirs life.

"Harrah, small heart," sang Deb.

Kabil said, "It isn't as if we have proof about these 'Others.' Not real proof. We don't actually know."

"I know," Micah said.

Cal looked bleakly at Kabil. "No. And it is wrong to sacrifice a child to a supposition, to a packet of compromised data, to a . . . a superstition of creations so much less than we are. You know that's true, even though none of us never admit it. But I'm a biologist. The creations are limited DNA, with no ability to self-modify. Also strictly regulated nano, and AI only within careful parameters. Yes, of course they're life forms deserving respect on their own terms, of course of course I would never deny that—"

"None of us would," Kabil said.

"—but they're not us. Not ever us."

A long silence, broken only by Deb's singing.

"Leave orbit, Micah," Cal finally said, "before Harrah wakes up."

Disciple Arlbeni, Grid 743.9, 2999: We are not gods, never gods, no matter what the powers evolution and technology have given us, and we do not delude ourselves that we are gods, as other cultures have done at other millennia. We are human. Our salvation is that we know it, and do not pretend otherwise.

Our mother? Are you there? We need you to save us from the Others, to do what is necessary. Are you there?

Are you still dancing?

Afterword to "My Mother, Dancing"

Publishing is a convoluted place, and this story has had a very convoluted history. In 1999 Robert Silverberg contacted me about writing a story for a French anthology he was editing, Destination 3001. *This production, with an international cast, would be released in 2000 and feature stories all set in 3000. A year later an English edition would be brought out by Tor.*

I happily agreed and then immediately ran into a brick wall: Who has any idea what the year 3000 will look like? SF writers are supposed to find this very freeing, in that if anything goes, no one can say your particular anything is wrong. But in fact, it's hard to build a world from scratch, especially if you want it to be a high-tech world. So I made a list of areas I'd like to include: genetic engineering, galaxy-spanning space travel, aliens . . . Wait. Maybe it would be more interesting if there were no aliens, no life anywhere except Earth. How would far-future humanity react to that?

After I'd written the story, I waited impatiently for Flammarion to publish the French edition, since I can read French (sort of). To my future humans, gender is largely irrelevant, and so the all-purpose pronoun is "hirs." The French, however, are notoriously protective of their language, furiously resenting such constructions as "le weekend" and "le hotdog." Flammarion translated "hirs" with masculine singular pronouns.

Then I waited for the English edition, which surely would do better. The English edition collapsed into some kind of copyright hell from which it never emerged. Individual stories, however, staggered out of the flames, and Asimov's published "My Mother, Dancing" in 2004, making it eligible to be a Nebula nominee in 2005. I lost, but by that time I was simply glad to have the story published this side of the Atlantic.

Three thousand copies of this book have been printed by the Maple-Vail Book Manufacturing Group, Binghamton, NY, for Golden Gryphon Press, Urbana, IL. The typeset is Electra with Scriptek display, printed on 55# Sebago. Typesetting by The Composing Room, Inc., Kimberly, WI.